NO TIME OFF

THE LEXI CARMICHAEL MYSTERY SERIES

BOOK FIFTEEN

JULIE MOFFETT

NO TIME OFF is a work of fiction. Names, characters, places, and incidents are products of the author's imagination or are used fictitiously and are not to be construed as real. Any resemblance to actual locales, organizations, events, or persons, living or dead, is entirely coincidental.

NO AI TRAINING: Without in any way limiting the author's [and publisher's] exclusive rights under copyright, any use of this publication to "train" generative artificial intelligence (AI) technologies to generate text is expressly prohibited. The author reserves all rights to license uses of this work for generative AI training and development of machine learning language models.

NO TIME OFF

Copyright © 2025 by Julie Moffett

All rights reserved.

Published by True Airspeed Press

No part of this book may be used, scanned, uploaded, stored in a retrieval system, reproduced, distributed, or transmitted in any form whatsoever, except for brief quotations embodied in critical articles and reviews, without written permission from the publisher. For information contact True Airspeed Press, LLC, at PO Box 411046, Melbourne, FL 32941.

ISBN: 978-1-941787-41-0

Cover art by Earthly Charms

PRAISE FOR JULIE MOFFETT'S
LEXI CARMICHAEL MYSTERY SERIES

"The Lexi Carmichael mystery series runs a riveting gamut from hilarious to deadly, and the perfectly paced action in between will have you hanging onto Lexi's every word and breathless for her next geeked-out adventure." **~USA Today**

"I absolutely, positively loved this book... I found the humor terrific. I couldn't find a single thing I didn't like about this book except it ended." **~Night Owl Reviews**

"Wow, wow, and wow! I don't know how Julie Moffett does it, but every book is better than the last and all of them are awesome. I may have 6 authors in my top five now!" **~Goodreads Reader**

"Absolutely loved this book! I love the concept of a geek girl getting involved in all kinds of intrigue and, of course, all the men she gets to meet." **~Book Babe**

"This book can be described in one word. AMAZING! I was intrigued from the beginning to the end. There are so many twists and turns and unexpected agendas that you do not know who's on the good side or who's on the bad side." **~Once Upon a Twilight**

"Another amazing action-adventure novel with tons of laughs by one of my favorite authors, Julie Moffett. I started to say nonstop action, but thank goodness, Ms. Moffett shares

those moments that take this series above the action-adventure norm. ... The Lexi Carmichael Mystery series is like none other, and each book is worlds different from others in the series... A winner in all ways!" **~Goodreads**

"This series has been one of my happiest finds since I started blogging...It's going to be such a long wait until the next book." **~1 Girl 2 Many Books Blog**

"I've read each of the books as it came out and loved everyone one of them. You never know where a Lexi Carmichael book will take you. The romance is stunning, the mysteries complex, and the characters are so real you will want to hang with them. Humor and personal moments balance the intense suspense." **~Amazon Reader**

"To say I am fan of Julie is a small understatement. I adore her books with Lexi Carmichael, geek girl and sleuth. Lexi makes the mystery world a better place." **~Bibliophile Reviews**

"So awesome, so Lexi! Julie Moffett reinforces her position as one of my top 5 authors. One of the things that I love about the Lexi Carmichael series is that no two books are similar in plot and the characters, who provide the continuity, are amazing." **~Goodreads**

"Such a great book in one of my all-time favorite series ... I am not a computer geek nor can I write code, but these books are just so entertaining and Julie Moffett clearly does her research ...she is very smart & I suspect could give Lexi a run for her money." **~Amazon Reader**

PRAISE FOR JULIE MOFFETT'S
WHITE KNIGHTS YA MYSTERY/SPY SERIES

"This book is Hogwarts for geeks. It is the perfect blend of YA, computer geeks, and spies!... I am so thrilled to be sharing this book with you...because I loved it! Like—stop a stranger on the street and don't stop talking about this book until they run away screaming, thinking you've escaped from the psych ward! Crazy good!" **~Ginger Mom and the Kindle Quest Blog**

"Love this new YA spinoff series from the Lexi Carmichael series by Julie Moffett. Same great pace, excitement, mysteries to solve, hacks to make, character growth, and an ending that makes me excited for the next book! Geek girls rock!" **~Amazon Reader**

"I loved the whole entire concept of the book. This book had me guessing what was happening the entire time while not leaving me completely in the dark which was something that I personally LOVE. This book was completely intriguing, and it was just so AHHHHH, it was amazing. The book I believe targets all people of all ages. It has so many things that people who read Young Adult to New Adult to Adult books." **~The Hufflepuff Nerdette**

"Absolutely loved it—great first book in a new series. This YA series has already made my keeper list. Can't wait for the second book!" **~Amazon Reader**

"To say that I enjoyed this book would be an understatement. It was positively awesome and an epic read. I am not one that will usually get in a fan club moment on a YA novel, but this one does something for readers. It is smart, witty and just plain fun. Anyone between the ages 14 and oh heck 99 can enjoy this book. Trust me it is made for geeky readers, like me." **~Amazon Reader**

"What a great book for all ages! It shows how people with different personalities can come and work together and become friends. I love this series. I have only one problem, when can I read the next book?" **~Amazon Reader**

"Geek girls rule. I loved this. My daughter loved this. A fun story with teenagers using their brains and catching the bad guys." **~Goodreads**

"I love how I met the 3 teenagers in a Lexi book and they've moved into their own series within the Lexi universe. Julie's imagination and ability to bring her lovable geeks to life is amazing. While I wish she could write faster, I love the intelligence, detail, plotting, and the length of the book that results from making us wait. Time to read it again to see what I missed!" **~Goodreads**

"Just when I thought this series couldn't get any better, Julie Moffett outdoes herself! This book is considered YA fiction, but it is truly a book for any age. You can get so caught up in this book that you forget the main characters are kids ...Tension, humor & thoughtfulness are all present & accounted for." **~Amazon Reader**

BOOKS BY JULIE MOFFETT

The Lexi Carmichael Mystery Series

No One Lives Twice (Book 1)

No One to Trust (Book 2)

No Money Down (Book 2.5-novella)

No Place Like Rome (Book 3)

No Biz Like Showbiz (Book 4)

No Test for the Wicked (Book 5)

No Woman Left Behind (Book 6)

No Room for Error (Book 7)

No Strings Attached (Book 8)

No Living Soul (Book 9)

No Regrets (Book 10)

No Stone Unturned (Book 11)

No Questions Asked (Book 12)

No Escape (Book 13)

No Vow Broken (Book 14)

No Time Off (Book 15)

No Comment (*a free character interview with Lexi Carmichael*)

Lexi Carmichael Books 1-15 are available in print and audiobook (except for No Money Down). Several are MP3, or are on CDs.

White Knights Mystery/Spy Series (YA)

White Knights (Book 1)

Knight Moves (Book 2)

One-Knight Stand (Book 3)

The MacInness Legacy (Historical/Paranormal Romance)

The Fireweaver

The Seer (by Sandy Moffett)

The Healer

Time-Travel Romance

A Double-Edged Blade

Across a Moonswept Moor

Other Books (Historical Romance)

The Thorn & The Thistle

Her Kilt-Clad Rogue (novella)

A Touch of Fire

Fleeting Splendor

DEDICATION

This one's for you, Mom. Thank you for nurturing my love of reading and for giving me the freedom and confidence to the write the books in my head, starting with my very first one in the second grade (complete with illustrations). You have always championed me and read everything I've ever written (good or bad) from that book on.
Oh, how I love you!

ACKNOWLEDGMENTS

I love writing the Lexi Carmichael Mystery Series because it's like visiting friends every time I pop in to see what they are up to. And, as usual, they're up to a lot!

It doesn't matter how many books I write, the process is a predictable cycle of inspiration, sweat, butt in seat, doubt, despair, wrestling with my characters, elation that the story is finished, editing, more editing, depression, conviction this is the worst book I've ever written, more editing, eating a lot of unhealthy snacks, brain drain, sheer relief edits are done, sprinting toward the finish line, exhaustion, a last push, and finally a huge sigh of relief when I'm finished. But that's just writing the book. Then it's time for marketing, covers, book signings, social media, etc. Gah! It can feel like an author's work is never done.

The silver lining to all that is an author doesn't have to go it alone if she has a great team to help her. Luckily, I have the best team ever! First, I have to thank my brother, Brad, for pushing and guiding me to make this book a reality, and for all of his valuable research and insight. You're an amazing big brother, and I truly don't think the book would have been written without you! My brilliant sister-in-law, Beth, provided so many astute comments and valuable insights, I'm certain she could make a career of book reviewing and editing if she ever decided to leave retirement. My exceptional sister, Sandy—whose computer died right before she was to start formatting this book—scrambled quickly to get a new one and have it up in running so I could get the book to you on time. That's true dedication! She's so capable and excels at everything she does and tries, I don't know what I'd do without her.

I also have to thank my excellent cover artist, Su at Earthly Charms; my terrific copy editor, Sara Brady; Diane Rodes Garland for stepping out of her comfort zone and taking a stab at developmental edits; my assistant, Sandra Herndon Ross who keeps my fabulous Facebook Readers Group running smoothly; my kids, Alexander and Lucas, who hold my entire heart; my mom, Donna, for her unflagging support; and, of course, YOU my awesome readers. Thank you for all the notes, emails, reviews, and word-of-mouth encouragement about my books. Lexi and I thank you from the bottom of our hearts. You're the best! xoxoxx🤍

NO TIME OFF

ONE

Lexi Carmichael
Mid-May, three weeks after the wedding

We were being stalked...again.

Not by a serial killer, vicious animals, or high-paid assassins. No, it was even worse. We were being relentlessly pursued by groups of paparazzi that had followed our every move since our wedding.

It was *so* not cool.

My name is Lexi Carmichael, and if you ask me, I'm not worth following around for even one minute. I can't imagine a single sane person in this entire world who would care about what I'm wearing, where I'm going, or what I'm bringing home to eat. I'm just a girl in love with numbers, code, hacking, and my new husband, Slash. Being chased by grown men and women hiding in bushes or running down grocery store aisles trying to photograph us while screaming stupid questions is mindboggling. Why people care so much about a couple of geeks just trying to do their jobs is a complete mystery to me.

Sure, we have friends and family in powerful positions, but that's no reason to follow us around like a pack of hyenas. We're entitled to our privacy.

I glanced in the passenger's side mirror. The car tailing us since we'd left the house had edged closer as the traffic became heavier. Clearly, the dark-green Subaru following us was more concerned about losing us than being spotted. I glanced over at Slash. He drove as if he was unaware of the presence behind us, but I knew he knew the precise location of the car. He was calm, a pro at evasion. But for me, it was different. I'm an anxious introvert and loathe attention of any kind. This paparazzi thing is an introvert's nightmare, and it was far too common of late.

I hate it.

Slash must have sensed my distress, because he reached over to pat my hand. "Forget about it. We're going to have a lovely evening."

None of this was his fault, and I didn't blame him for it. He was as much a victim of the attention as I was. He couldn't help that the pope was a surrogate father to him, as much I couldn't help my friendship with the US president and his wife. We also couldn't help that the world had gone bonkers and warfare had moved largely into the shadows of cyberspace, where we happened to be experts in demand.

Anonymous experts.

At least, we were trying to keep it that way. We preferred a veil of secrecy to properly conduct our work, but a lot of crazy people were suddenly out to destroy that just because we had friends in high places. People wanted to know who we were and why such powerful people had attended our recent wedding. Many of our friends and family had been contacted or followed. They'd had to block numerous calls and ignore multiple cash-for-information requests. Fortunately for us, our friends were mostly amused, with a touch of annoyance, over the attention they were receiving.

So, I'd be damned if I let it ruin an important night in our lives.

Not tonight, you idiots.

Taking a deep breath, I smoothed my dress over my knees. I was in a dress...again, which was a bit of a shocker. These last two years I'd transformed from a complete loner who didn't know a thing about fashion, gamed incessantly, and ate Cheerios for dinner to a married woman with nice clothes who had lots of friends. Well, lots of friends by my standards. And to be perfectly clear, I hadn't given up either gaming or Cheerios, I'd just widened my horizons.

But right now, my emotions were a mixture of anticipation and weariness. I'd put on a cream-colored dress with a mint cardigan perfectly matching Slash's tie and pocket square, because tonight was an important evening for us. We were going to share a private and romantic dinner and decide where we were going for our honeymoon. We'd been doing research on potential locations independently. While I was confident in the quality of my recommendation, I could read Slash well enough now to know he'd come up with something special, too. This discussion was long overdue after the hurricane of our wedding and the media whirlwind ever since. But if we wanted a quiet dinner and a private discussion on this fine spring night, we had to take care of something else first.

Our tail.

Three of the four cars that had started tailing us from our house were lost long ago. Slash had detected several tracking tags hidden on our car, so he'd scooped them up and placed them on random cars in large, poorly lit parking lots with multiple exits as we drove around. He now seemed unconcerned about the remaining tail, who was clearly following us by sight and not electronics.

"Showtime," he said, skillfully swinging the car around to the front of a small French café in downtown Washington, DC, that we liked.

He gave me a smile, so I gave him one back. When we exited the car, I noticed the Subaru parked not far away. The driver was fussing with something in his lap.

Probably getting a camera ready.

Slash made a big deal of opening the car door on my side and made little effort to remain unobserved. I let my long hair fall across my face like a curtain. No need to provide a free shot. The restaurant, with large, glass front windows that reflected the lighted view of several historical statues in the park across the street, was a known location where we had shared a meal a few days after our wedding. We'd been filmed through the windows as we ate by almost a dozen paparazzi. It made me sick when I saw the pictures.

I hoped tonight's dinner would be a lot more private.

Slash handed the car keys off to the young man operating the valet parking and briefly spoke with him. After giving him a nice tip, Slash took my arm, steering me inside through the double doors.

The maître d' was waiting to greet us and nodded to his left. "Your table is waiting, as requested. I hope you'll find all the arrangements satisfactory."

"I'm sure we will," Slash replied. "We appreciate your assistance and discretion."

"Of course, sir. You're welcome here any time."

The small table was partially obscured from the front windows by a partition. Slash offered me the seat with the view out the windows, then took my cardigan and hung it over the back of the chair as he seated me. Slash took a seat out of sight of the windows and partially facing the dining room. We made small talk until the waiter brought water to our table. A brief nod of Slash's head as I sipped my water indicated it was, indeed, showtime.

"Ready?" Slash murmured to me.

"As much as I can be," I said. "Let's do this."

TWO

Mick Watson

Mick sat in his car and watched through the long lens of his expensive camera as his targets were ushered to a table in the back corner of the French café. Their table was partially hidden, and he could only see the woman. They appeared to be making small talk. He was pretty good at reading lips, but the angle was wrong, and she kept turning her head. It was okay, though—he could be patient.

Patience was an essential part of his job. He liked to compare himself to nature photographers, who would sit for weeks on end on some godforsaken mountainside trying to get a few seconds of snow leopards mating. It was the same principle, except the pay was exceptionally better and he got to sleep in his own bed most nights.

He'd been chasing celebrities and politicians for almost twenty years in this town, and he'd never had a case like this. Who were these people? He knew their names, sort of. The guy seemed to be operating under an alias. I mean, who chose Slash for a name other than the guitarist for Guns N' Roses? And Slash wasn't the guitarist's real name, either. His name was Saul Hudson. The Slash he was chasing had to have a real name somewhere, and it was just a matter of time before he found it.

His best guess was this Slash guy was some kind of spook, a spy. That fit with what his sources had come up with—Slash worked at the NSA in some capacity. That also fit with the man's demeanor—he seemed cool as a cucumber, and his evasion skills were impressive. None of that was unusually uncommon in this town, but Mick could smell a story, and this couple piqued his interest big-time. His senses were tingling, and he *always* trusted his senses.

The woman...her name seemed legit. Lexi Carmichael. Still, he could find very little on her, and he'd checked everywhere. No social media, no online presence. He knew she was a techie and worked for a cyberintelligence company called X-Corp located in Crystal City, Virginia near Washington DC. She'd attended Georgetown University and had once worked at the NSA. Maybe that's where she met this Slash guy. Taken as a whole, there was nothing special about her. There were a million techies in the DC metropolitan area who were either working or had worked for the government in one capacity or another.

The couple seemed downright ordinary. But the pope, the president of the United States, and the first lady didn't just show up to random weddings, did they? What did they have in common? It was driving his potential clients nuts, and they were committing significant resources to get answers. The guy who broke their *real* story and had a couple of pictures to go with it could auction off the information for well over seven figures.

That guy was going to be him.

Mick adjusted the lens, trying to bring the woman more into focus. It had been a stroke of luck for him that the feds and the DC government had cracked down on all drone flying in the city after the events of the couple's wedding two weeks prior. Several drones had blown up in what had appeared to be a potential attack on the first lady in a motorcade. Except it turned out the first lady hadn't been in the motorcade. But the couple he was following had, along with several of their friends and family. No other information about that attack had been released, and interest had died down.

But not his interest. This new generation of paparazzi were lazy. They relied too much on fancy tracking devices and drones instead of honing their basic investigative skills, instincts, and surveillance. Slash had easily dispatched the rest of his technology-dependent competition. But not Mick Watson. He was one of the few local paparazzi who knew this town like the back of his hand. He knew Slash had marked him—seen him following their car. That couldn't be helped. Unlike in the movies, properly tailing someone unobserved in a car typically took three or even four cars. It didn't matter. Mick was the only one left following them, so any photos tonight belonged to him. He'd earned it.

He didn't know what the couple was up to this evening. Maybe they were meeting someone important that would crack this mystery wide-open. Or maybe they were just out for a romantic dinner. All things considered, it was a win-win situation for him. Either way, he'd be the only one with pictures to sell tomorrow. Pictures equaled money no matter how you looked at it.

Mick lowered the lens and surveyed the area. The parking lot seemed quiet. No competition skulking around, and, in fact, no one had entered the restaurant since the couple had arrived.

He lifted the camera to observe the situation again. Inside, nothing exciting was happening. At least he had his snow leopards, but no mating yet. The waiter had visited their table, filled their water glasses, and appeared to take their drink order. It looked more like a romantic dinner given Lexi's posture and chair position.

At some point, she bent down and picked up her purse from where it hung on the back of the chair. Movement at last. She stood, looked around, and asked something of a passing waiter. The waiter pointed to the opposite end of the café, and Mick realized it was a false alarm.

Bathroom break.

Time to get a better angle. He set the camera aside and got out of the car. He pulled a tripod out of the back seat and slung his camera around his neck. Taking photos from a dark environment into a lighted window was tricky if you wanted to keep them from being oversaturated. He moved a few feet to his right to get a better angle on Lexi's seat and snapped a few trial pictures to make sure the settings were good. All was ready. It had the potential to be a profitable evening.

A glance at his watch showed she'd been in the restroom a long time. Typical woman...and she didn't even go in with a gaggle. A few more minutes passed, and suddenly alarm bells in his head started ringing. He swung the zoom lens toward the restroom area, hoping to capture some activity.

Nothing.

Out of the corner of his eye, he saw the maître d' walk over to the table and pick the woman's sweater off the chair.

"What the hell?" he uttered.

The maître d' was at his station near the door still

holding the sweater when Mick raced in through the front door. "Where is she?" he gasped.

"Where is who?" the maître d' asked in a stiff voice.

"The woman who owns that," Mick said impatiently, pointing at the sweater.

"Oh. She asked me to hold it for her until she comes back to pick it up. Apparently, they had to leave abruptly to meet with someone important. And, who, might I ask, are you?"

Mick frowned. "Screwed, I suspect."

Without asking for permission, he strode over to the table, ignoring the outraged protests from the maître d'. He peeked around the partition and saw the table was empty.

Damn!

Dreading, but almost certain what he'd find, Mick ran outside to the valet parking area. The car he'd so carefully followed was nowhere to be seen.

He'd been hoodwinked.

THREE

Slash

"You know, we didn't have to go to all that effort to lose the last of our tails," Lexi told me as we made the trip down the road to the Lapin Sauvage restaurant. It was one of my favorite haunts, although we hadn't dined there since long before the wedding. "Miguel could have provided us with a completely private table."

"I know," I agreed. "But the paparazzi have been making our life difficult, and I thought it was time to turn the tables for a change. Word will get out we were meeting someone important, and that will make them even more furious at having lost track of us."

"It did feel good," she said. "Maybe they'll get bored with us."

"If only. But, yes, it felt good to elude them. Really good."

"Regardless, I suspect there's another motive behind tonight's flashy escape. Am I right?"

I dipped my head at her. "Ah, *cara*, I can't ever get anything by you. It was practice, so to say. I've already begun planning for our honeymoon departure, and I want them to be jumpy and suspicious about being deceived. It will make them easier to fool when the time comes."

"I'm fine with that," she said. "The fooling them part. And speaking of our honeymoon, I'm really looking forward to getting away from this insane craziness and having a couple of quiet and uneventful weeks just to ourselves."

"I couldn't agree more," I said emphatically.

I pulled up to the street-side valet parking, tossed the attendant the keys, and helped Lexi out of the car. Her smile assured me she appreciated the effort to make tonight just our evening.

The woman at the door checked our reservation and gestured, "This way, Mr. and Mrs. Williamson."

Lexi glanced sideways at me with a raised eyebrow and a smile. "Williamson?" she mouthed.

I shrugged. "Can't take any chances."

We settled in at a secluded table in the back of the restaurant and ordered wine. We chatted about inconsequential matters, greatly enjoying our privacy until the waiter returned with our wine and a basket of warm rolls to take our order. I opted for the rack of lamb and Lexi, somewhat predictably, chose the *filet de bœuf avec sauce au poivre*. Once she found something she liked, *really* liked, it was hard to get her to try anything else.

"Seriously, these rolls are to die for," Lexi said as she bit into one and closed her eyes. "What do the French put in their bread?"

"I presume that's a rhetorical question," I said, amused.

"Unless you happen to know," she said, opening one eye hopefully.

I smiled. "I'm partial to Italian bread, but you already know that."

"Oh, trust me, she said, sighing happily. "Italian bread has its own virtues. Either way, I could die happy."

I winced even though I tried not to. "Let's not talk about dying, okay?"

She put the bread down and brushed off her hands on the napkin. "Fair point. I supposed it's time to get to the business of the evening anyway. Have you finished your research on the perfect honeymoon destination?"

"I have, and presume you have, too. Isn't that why we're here?"

"It is. I hope you like my honeymoon plan, Slash. It has spectacular scenery, romantic venues, and is very private."

"I greatly anticipate hearing the details, *cara*."

"And I can't wait to hear what you have in mind," she said. "By the way, did you factor in the possibility of an uninvited guest tagging along?"

I narrowed my eyes. "The paparazzi?"

"No. What *else* always follows us around?"

It took me a few seconds to get there. "Ah, your little black cloud?"

"Exactly," she said and then lowered her voice. "Contingency plans should be made."

I was way ahead of her. "Fair enough, and I do admit contingency planning is already a significant piece of my calculation. That's why my top priority for a honeymoon destination involves a remote location where nothing exciting ever happens. Like, ever. After what we've been through lately, peace and quiet is just what we need. I also sought a resort a long way from anyone who might know us. After all, we don't want a repeat of Xavier and Basia's honeymoon."

"You mean when I ran into them by accident at their not-so-secret honeymoon resort and got mistaken for the bride?" she asked.

"That's *exactly* what I mean."

"Well, then, why don't you go first with your selection? I'd love to hear about a place where my little black cloud can't get us into any trouble."

"No, you go first," I insisted. "Just be sure to outline your decision factors. It would help me clarify how strongly I feel about mine."

"All right." She opened her purse and pulled out her phone, swiping for a bit until she found what she wanted before setting it back down on the table. She grinned, her eyes alight with excitement. "I, too, was looking for a place far away from here where we could enjoy spectacular scenery, privacy, and a limited population. It was critical that any travel agency or resort we might choose must have an impeccable reputation for discretion."

"Sounds like an excellent criterion," I said, sipping my wine and greatly enjoying the conversation. "I presume your location is somewhere we haven't been before...and more importantly, it doesn't have spiders and snakes."

"If only," she said. "It pains me to admit there are indeed spiders and snakes at my destination, but my research indicates most of them are reclusive and uninterested in humans. As to your point, though, it's a location we haven't been to before."

I thought it over, decided to take a guess. "Australia? I hear there aren't a lot of people in the outback, only animals."

"True, but in Australia, spiders are the size of small dogs, and snakes are everywhere, and they're all venomous." She spoke a bit emphatically and then lowered her voice. "Well, maybe not *all*, but tons of them are. Regardless, I do want to visit Australia someday, if I have proper protection against said spiders and snakes. But Australia is not what I have in mind for our honeymoon."

I leaned forward in anticipation. "So, what do you have in mind? Pray tell."

Pausing, she spread out her hands. "Picture two glorious weeks alone among the greatest venues in Patagonia. We could visit some spectacular locales and stay at an exclusive resort on the shores of the Pacific Ocean, a luxurious boutique hotel near Tierra del Fuego and a private hunting lodge in the Andes."

Patagonia was an interesting and unexpected choice. I cocked my head, considering. "Argentina or Chile?"

"Chile," she said. "For fourteen glorious days, we hike the dramatic granite peaks of Torres del Paine, explore the waters of the Chilean Lake District, see the Tierra del Fuego, explore the fabulous wine region near Santiago, and then visit the mysterious and wonderful Atacama Desert."

I raised an eyebrow in surprise. "Did you say hike? That truly surprises me, because I thought you'd sworn off any such activity after being chased through the mountains of Papua New Guinea and across the Amazon rainforest in Brazil. Not at the same time of course."

She shuddered. "No, not those kinds of hikes. My idea of honeymoon hiking is being transported to the mountains in luxury vehicle with snacks, where we can stroll from amazing overlook to overlook at our own pace. Not the hauling-myself-through-rugged-terrain, or sweat-pouring-down-my-back, scared-out-of-my-mind, all-while-avoiding-someone-who-wants-to-kill-me hiking."

"Fair enough," I said with a chuckle. "I just wanted to

clear that up before I inadvertently suggested something inappropriate."

She gave me a smile that could still make my heart skip a beat. "So, what do you think so far, Slash?"

I had to give it to her—it was an excellent suggestion. "Honestly, it sounds amazing. How would we get around?"

She consulted the notes on her phone. "We could rent a car and drive ourselves, but if we want to make this as relaxing as possible, I think private drivers and guides would be the best approach. Amanda, our wedding planner, recommended a tour company that has a long-standing reputation for discretion. They select resorts and vendors who highly value their clients' privacy—not that anyone, hopefully, would recognize us outside Washington."

I loved the sound of that. "That seems like a wonderful adventure with a mix of activities that will keep us on our toes. I've always wanted to go to Chile and see the southern Andes. It's a great idea, *cara*."

"I have brochures of all the places we would stay and can send the rest via our personal, encrypted file-sharing app, but first I'd like to hear what you came up with." She set her phone down and put her elbows on the table before looking directly into my eyes. "Your turn."

I took another sip of my wine and leaned back in my chair. "I admit I took the opposite approach. Instead of choosing a so-called experience vacation, I opted for an ultra-private location where nothing ever happens and no one would know us. I just wanted to get away to somewhere we could relax, do nothing if we wanted, and spend a couple of *very* low-key weeks to be alone and reset. I imagined our focus to be on each other and not the craziness that seems to follow us around."

"Is there such a place on Earth?" Her eyes lit up with

interest. "A lovely, quiet retreat where nothing happens? Where no one knows us, and even if my little black cloud followed, it wouldn't matter?"

"I can't make promises about the little black cloud, but even if it does follow, I doubt there's much it could do in this place. That's how remote it is."

"And where exactly is this magical, secretive place?"

"Rarotonga, initially. It's the main island of the Cook Islands, and where the capital, Avarua, is located." I carefully watched her expression to gauge interest and saw she was definitely intrigued. "After a week there, we'd travel to another island nearby called Aitutaki, which is an even more secluded resort island—popular with honeymooners for exactly that reason."

Her brow wrinkled in a certain way which often happened when she recalled information. "The Cook Islands are in the southern Pacific Ocean, northeast of New Zealand and somewhere between American Samoa and French Polynesia. Right?"

"Yes. Your memory is infallible, as always."

She tilted her head and gave me a long look. "So, you want to have an island honeymoon? Beaches, sand, and sun? Again?"

"Hear me out," I said, lifting a hand. "The Cook Islands are an ideal location for our honeymoon for multiple reasons. The most important being they are exceptionally remote. There are fifteen islands with only fifteen thousand people total living on them. They are two thousand miles from any significant land mass and have great weather this time of year. There are only a handful of resorts on Rarotonga, and I'm willing to bet no resident there has ever read the *Washington Post*. In fact, the United States only just established diplomatic relations with them."

"I'm following, and I see the attractive logic in that approach," she said. "How big is Rarotonga?"

"Twenty-six square miles, with highlands and a couple of peaks in the middle, and a ring road around the island."

"What's there to do?"

"Not much," I admitted. "There are beaches, snorkeling, and boating, but the best part is the island has a reputation for being off-the-grid and *very* quiet. No major landmarks or museums, and few tourists flock there because there are no big cultural or scenic draws. It's basically a remote, little-known island in the middle of the ocean where no one will know or care who we are. We can do whatever we want, whenever we want, and only if we want to."

She sighed happily. "I wish I'd thought of that. It sounds perfect for us. Just the two of us with nothing to do but relax, engage in some romance, and simply be with each other. It's *exactly* what we need. You hit it out of the park, Slash. It's perfect."

"I think no matter what we choose, we're going to be happy. In fact, the more I think about it, the more I'm leaning toward Chile. Two weeks of doing nothing may be too much of a stretch for us."

"So, how do we decide which option is the best?" She lifted her hands. "We have Chile and the Cook Islands. Remote beaches versus the wilds of Patagonia. Multiple sights to see or no sights at all. Celebrity-level pampering or wine from a bottle on a beach."

"You choose. I'd be happy with either option, *cara*."

"Oh, no, you don't." She shook her head vigorously. "You're not putting this decision on me. We're married now, and the marriage code says we must share in all big decisions."

"Marriage code?" I repeated. I hadn't seen that one coming. "Hold on. What code are we talking about? Is there really such a thing as a marriage code?"

She looked surprised I wasn't aware of this. "Well, not exactly a code, but more like rules. There are thousands of guidelines and rules that, if you follow them, will supposedly lead you to a successful marriage."

I opened my mouth to say something and then shut it. After another few beats, I opened it again to ask a more specific question. "So, we're following marriage rules now?"

"Not rules. A code." The candle in the center of the table flickered, casting a slight shadow on her face. "I've been doing a lot of research on marriages around the world, determining how people from different backgrounds and cultures create successful and thriving marriages. It's fascinating, really. From Africa to Asia to South and North America to Europe—and honestly everywhere—I've discovered that marriage is basically a set of rules devised by couples and reinforced by society. Those rules are different depending on your cultural, religious, and personal preferences. But after researching all these different rules, I felt they weren't the right foundation for determining the success of a marriage, at least for us. After all, rules can be bent or broken—for good or bad, depending on the situation—so rules didn't seem an accurate way to determine, or even encourage, the stability and progress of a marriage. So, I've been writing a marriage code for us, instead. Consider it a blueprint of sorts, unique to us, with a specific set of directions and design to lead us to the optimum output which is, of course, marital bliss."

Her mind was truly a wondrous thing. I was riveted by this unexpected turn in the conversation. "A marriage code," I repeated slowly, leaning forward on the table. "I see. So, if we follow this marriage code that you're creating just for us, it will give us a perfect marriage?"

"No, not exactly, but it will help." She leaned back in the chair. "I'm picturing it like this—marriage is similar to a programming language. Everyone starts with the basics: functions, data types, variables, operators, control structures, and syntax. But that doesn't tell you *how* to write good code. Good programmers learn both from studying and experiencing their mistakes. Since we are distinctive in our values, personalities, and cultural and religious backgrounds, I'm factoring that in as I create a specific outcome unique to us, with as few mistakes as possible."

I stroked my chin, thinking. "Not a bad concept. So, you're programming our marriage?"

She picked up the napkin off her lap and began to wind it around her finger. "In a way, I suppose, but as we both know, we'll have to adapt to numerous unforeseen variables and inconsistencies in the code as we go along. Primarily, the code is supposed to be a general guide for us—a collection of keywords, actions, insights, and attitudes that determine how a couple's relationship works. From this, we can anticipate certain outcomes, expected results, and degrees of success, thereby adjusting our actions and behaviors accordingly."

God, I loved this woman with the very core of my being. "Have you started a spreadsheet yet?"

She gave me a look which meant I should already know the answer. And I did. I just wanted to hear her say it.

"Of course I have. And one of the most important elements of my code so far is shared decisions. So, we're making the important decision—the location of our honeymoon—jointly. A mutual decision, as supported by the marriage code, designed to strengthen our bond. So, keeping that in mind, what's your vote for our honeymoon location?"

I pretended to think for a moment, even though I'd already made up my mind. "I vote for your plan. Patagonia."

"And I choose your plan," she countered. "The Cook Islands. Which leaves us with no agreement."

I observed her for a moment. I knew she sincerely wanted us to make the right choice, even though both options were excellent. I abruptly leaned across the table and kissed her.

"What's that for?" she said, wrinkling her nose in puzzlement.

"I adore you. Absolutely, utterly adore you."

She looked at me suspiciously. "Are you trying to distract or sway me from my decision?"

I chuckled. "No, not at all. Just stating a fact. Now, since we both agree we have two outstanding options and cannot agree on which one is better, I propose we leave our honeymoon destination to chance, unless that's against the code."

"Ooh," she said. "Like the high card wins or a coin toss? Chance is not against the marriage code, by the way, so long as we both agree."

"Perfect." I spread my hands out on the table. "Then I propose using a random number derived from a calculation that neither of us could solve quickly in our head. We each choose a three-digit prime number. We multiply them together and divide the total by another two-digit prime number. That should give us a fraction to multiple decimal places. You pick a number, and we count that many places to the right of the decimal. If the number is zero to four, we're Patagonia bound. If it is five to nine, beaches ahoy. Sound fair?"

"Sounds fair. Phone calculator?"

"The phone calculator should suffice." I withdrew my phone from my pocket and set it on the table next to hers.

"Excellent." She reached in her purse and withdrew a folded receipt. She tore the paper in half and handed me a small piece along with a pen. "Write your number on this, and I'll write mine here. We're each picking a prime number, and I'll chose the two-digit divisor while you're picking the decimal place position."

"I'll say now that I select the seventh position to the right of the decimal place. Let's get started."

We wrote our choices, and I pulled out my phone and entered Lexi's first prime number, 313, and multiplied it by my choice, 593, and then divided it by the 71 Lexi gave me. As I was about to hit enter, Lexi stopped me.

"Wait. No matter where we choose, when we head out for our honeymoon, how are we going to shake the paparazzi to ensure no one follows us?"

"Don't worry," I said. "I already have a plan. Remember our little practice today? It should be a fun start to our honeymoon for everyone except the paparazzi. Trust me?"

"Unequivocally. In fact, during my research on marriages, I discovered that trust is the most popular tenet across all cultures, religions, and geographic locations. So, naturally, I made it number one in our marriage code because trust seemed the right place to start."

"I couldn't agree more," I said. I had to hold back a smile, so she didn't think I wasn't taking it seriously. Because while I *was* amused, I really did like this idea of keeping each other accountable and on the same page regarding our life goals and plans. She was right—a marriage code suited us.

"Okay, so what's number two in the marriage code?" I asked. "Mutual decision-making?"

She lifted her wineglass to me in a salute. "It is. Hey, if I didn't know any better, I'd think you know a thing or two about coding."

"Funny, *cara*. So, are you ready to know where we're going for our honeymoon?"

"I'm *so* ready...but wait." She leaned over and gave me a lingering kiss.

I raised an eyebrow when she pulled away. "What was that for?"

"I adore you," she said sweetly. "Absolutely, completely adore you."

My eyebrow inched higher. "Are you trying to distract me?"

She laughed. "Absolutely not. Let's do this."

Grinning, I hit enter, and *together* we slowly counted seven places to the right of the decimal point.

FOUR

Mick Watson

Mick was on edge. Something was about to happen. He was certain he'd read the signs correctly. The sun was still thirty minutes from officially rising, but the streetlights in the couple's Silver Spring residential neighborhood, and the pending dawn, cast enough light to observe the front of the white colonial. Inside, lights and activity behind drawn shades had been detectable for the last hour. This was decidedly unusual for this very early time of the morning. The weeks of staking out the couple had helped him to capture the rhythm of their daily activities, and this was definitely out of routine, confirming his suspicions from all the activity of the previous night.

Cars and people, most of them friends he recognized from prior encounters, had come and gone all evening, as if they were having a party, though strangely not all at the same time. His best guess was they were planning something. Perhaps they were expecting an important visitor, although he doubted it. He tended to agree with his competitors, who had been speculating for weeks the couple were intending to depart for a honeymoon soon. There was even a betting pool on where they would go. Most secretly hoped it would be an expensive, idyllic location where they would be assigned to follow the couple and capture revealing photos.

An all-expenses-paid vacation for most.

Whatever was going on, Mick knew he had to be alert. His quarry had already demonstrated their ability to elude tails, and he was determined not to be fooled again. The level of activity suggested that something important was going to happen, and their apparent lack of concern at hiding those preparations strongly suggested they expected to be followed if they left the house. Which, of course, they would be.

Two new cars stopped down the street near the position of several of his competitors. Men got out and shook hands with current monitoring crews. Obviously, others had noted the increased activity and elected to bring on additional resources in case the targets decided to run. They had clearly learned their lesson about overreliance on tracking devices. However, at this rate, it was going to look like a funeral procession when they left, and Mick didn't want to get stuck in the middle of a traffic jam.

If he assumed they knew that they'd be followed, he had to suspect they might be planning to elude everyone. He checked his notes. They could use a helicopter, but the nearest landing spot was at least a mile away. He didn't think they would try that. It would likely offer only a temporary reprieve. Even with three major airports within an hour, and several general aviation airports nearby where they could depart in a private plane, once he knew the direction taken, he was confident he could quickly track them. If they headed toward a major airport, it wouldn't be hard to pick up the trail. Alternatively, if they went to a private airport, he would use an internet site like Flight Radar to track the few filed flight departures from that field. Anonymous travel was difficult these days, and if you had dedicated trackers, they could easily narrow down your point of departure.

What concerned him most was government transportation. They certainly had the connections and the resources to use that, and it would definitely complicate his situation. However, it would only add to the mystery of this power couple. Based on what he had seen of them from afar, his gut told him they didn't want that kind of additional attention. So, what was their game going to be?

The front door suddenly opened, and a man peeked out briefly. Along the street, there was a flurry of activity as everyone prepared to move. Just then a set of headlights slowly moved down the street as if searching for an address. It was a limousine. The limo pulled into the driveway, and two men in attendant uniforms hopped out, approached the house, and went in. Mick angled to the side to get a picture of the license plate just in case.

Just then another car arrived and parked besides the limousine, followed by a second limo that parked on the street.

Mick's heart began to beat hard. He suddenly had a hunch what the plan was, and he didn't like it one bit.

Not one single bit.

FIVE

Lexi

It was Operation Honeymoon Go time.

Our family and friends assembled in our dimly lit dining room at this godforsaken hour of the morning to see us off on our honeymoon in the most unusual and craziest way ever. Everyone agreed that this adventure was "so us," whatever that meant.

Everyone was dressed in black and wore dark hats or scarves to make it difficult to distinguish features. Currently present were my best friend, Basia, her husband, Xavier, his twin, Elvis, and Elvis's fiancée, Gwen. My mom and dad were also here, as were our close friends, Hands, and his girlfriend, Gray. My brothers, Rock and Beau, and Beau's girlfriend, Bonnie, also stood ready to assist. Finally, my boss, Finn, and two of my interns, Wally and Angel (who was also Gwen's younger sister), were partaking in the shenanigans. It truly took a village just to get us to the airport for our honeymoon.

Finn leaned against the door frame, sipping coffee from

a travel mug and making jokes in a heavy Irish brogue to keep things light. Angel and Wally stood nearby, laughing at every bad joke he made.

"Don't encourage him," I warned them. "He'll never stop."

Finn, his eyes twinkling, lifted his coffee mug at me in a mock toast. "Ye dare challenge an Irishman telling a joke?" he asked, laying the accent on thick. "Angel, lass, have you heard this one? Why don't ye ever iron a four-leaf clover?"

Angel thought for a moment and then shook her head. "I don't know. Why?"

"Because ye don't want to press your luck."

She and Wally broke out in peals of laughter. I rolled my eyes at Finn, who grinned and gave me a thumbs-up before I headed upstairs to one of our guest bedrooms. Slash and I had set aside two rooms for changing into the disguises we'd need to pull this operation off, mostly suits, hats, and wigs for the so-called limo drivers and porters. There were multiple decoys for me and for Slash. The rest would be chauffeurs or porters, all to keep things moving along smoothly.

All the decoys were dressed in black. Black pants, black shirts, and even black shoes. Dark shades, ball caps or beanies, and scarves wound up to the nose completed the look. We wanted the decoys as indistinguishable as possible.

Basia had ordered special shoes and long brown wigs for my decoys. She managed some fabulous and creative silhouetting to make the women look remarkably similar to my height and shape. It had only taken one fitting before she turned them each into me.

For Slash's decoys, Basia worked her magic adding stuffing, belting, padding, and foam to create silhouettes that were comparable to Slash. She also had also bought a few toupees to match Slash's dark hair. We all got a good laugh seeing how the toupees looked on the decoys, especially on Hands. Gray could barely breathe, she was laughing so hard.

Finally, it was time to put the last touches on my outfit. Basia led me to one of the bedrooms to finalize the look.

"Do you really think this will work?" she asked while fussing with my hair, pinning it in a million places to get it to stay put under the porter's hat.

"Slash is thorough in his planning," I responded. "I wouldn't bet against him."

"I wouldn't, either. You deserve the time away and the honeymoon you want without having to dodge those piranhas all the time. It stinks that you have to go to all this trouble just to get away. But my sixth sense tells me that this honeymoon is destined to be special."

"I couldn't agree more. It seems like we've all been under the microscope for months, even though it's only been a matter of weeks."

She finished pinning my hair just as Gray opened the door and strolled inside. She did a twirl with her hands held out. "So, do I look sufficiently Lexi-like?"

"Actually, you need to walk a bit more awkwardly," I advised. "I only wish I walked like you."

Gray laughed, fluffing her brown wig. "Don't be ridiculous, Lexi. But I'll tell you one thing, this wig is incredibly hot."

"I bought the cheap versions, okay?" Basia said, with bobby pins still clenched in her teeth. "You only have to wear it for a short time."

"Not complaining," Gray said. "I'm just glad it's not a permanent thing. Hands said the same thing about his fake hair."

Elvis peeked his head in the door, dressed sharply as a chauffeur. "Are you wizards ready yet? Dumbledore wants to know."

He referred to Slash, I presumed. Elvis had started calling our plan the Mad-Eye Moody Escape. It was funny because Slash had no idea what he was talking about, as he'd not yet had the time to read the Harry Potter books or see the movies. But I'd done both, and I knew the principle of decoy was sound: Deploy one more Lexi and Slash pairs than the paparazzi had the resources to follow. Then Slash had added one more twist, and another.

Mom swept into the bedroom, squeezing past Elvis in the doorway. She looked like a dead ringer for me now that her blond hair was covered by a brown wig. "Another day and another adventure with my quiet, unassuming daughter. Oh, wait, that's not you anymore. You're always off saving the world. Did you know your father is wearing his bulletproof vest today, just in case."

I sighed. "Jeez, Mom. No one is going to be shooting anything at us except a camera. I don't want anyone to get hurt today. It's not worth it. We've already been over this a hundred times. It's just a honeymoon. No heroics, no crazy driving. If we get found out or followed by the paparazzi, so be it. I don't want anyone to get hurt on our behalf."

Gray put a hand on my shoulder. "Relax, we've got this, Lexi. It's going to work. Slash isn't stupid, and neither are we. None of us will do anything to get hurt."

My mom kissed my cheek. "She's right. I'm just teasing you, darling. You're going to have a wonderful, tranquil honeymoon with your fabulous husband and come home rested, bored, and rejuvenated. It sounds heavenly."

Basia suddenly threw her arms around me, nearly knocking me over. Now that she was pregnant, her emotions were all over the place, and I wasn't always sure how to react. "Your mom is right, Lexi. It's going to be an epic, relaxing honeymoon. Just what the doctor ordered for you two." She started sniffling and I patted her awkwardly on the back.

"Thanks, Basia. I appreciate all the hard work you did to get this off the ground."

"You could have let me be one of the decoys," she said with a little pout.

"The pregnant lady stays home," I said firmly. "That's nonnegotiable."

Elvis joined the hug, squishing me between him and Basia. "I hope it goes flawlessly, Lexi. But what I really wish is for you to have a safe and relaxing honeymoon without that little black cloud of yours."

"Oh, please, someone, make it happen," I said, and everyone laughed. "I think we're ready. Let's get out of here. It's time to put Operation Honeymoon Go into action."

SIX

Mick Watson

There were now four cars in front of the house, two in the driveway and two parked on the street. Mick had counted at least fifteen people who'd entered so far. If Lexi and Slash were in the house, that would make seventeen. This was a massive undertaking.

They were all dressed similarly in dark clothes and had hurried inside, hunched to hide their appearance as much as possible. There appeared to be more men than women, not counting the two from the first limousine. There was no way to be sure. Regardless, he could see their plan developing and expected to have to make some snap decisions soon.

They weren't going to make this easy.

Abruptly the porch light at the front of house went out, plunging the driveway into semidarkness. That was followed seconds later by all the streetlights going dark. Mick looked up in astonishment. How had they pulled that off?

He didn't have time to worry about that before four couples and several people he presumed were drivers suddenly emerged from the house, all dragging suitcases and heading for separate vehicles. There were differences among the couples in how they moved, but their outfits were dark, and in the shadows, with their faces obscured, it was impossible to identify the real couple. Several camera flashes from the street lit up the scene as his competition tried furiously to sniff out the real pair.

One couple immediately got into the white limousine and waited while the driver and a porter loaded their luggage. They were the first ones finished and quickly headed off. Scant seconds later, the SUV in the driveway departed, making a U-turn before heading in the opposite direction. The third car to move was one of the paparazzi as they raced off after the white limousine. A second photographer's car followed the SUV. The second limousine parked on the street pulled out in the same direction as the white limo, though Mick was certain it would be headed to a different destination.

There was some confusion and shouting among the paparazzi on the curb before one of them ran down the street, jumped in his car, and peeled out after the second limo. The fourth car, a black sedan parked on the street, just sat there with its engine running. The last remaining paparazzo, a guy in a hooded gray sweatshirt, tried to approach the car, but as he got closer, the car slowly drove away from him, and stopped a little farther down the street. Taunting him, the clever bastards.

Cat and mouse.

Mick was torn as to whether to follow this last car. It was almost as if the car was giving him time to make up his mind. Finally, the car started moving in earnest, and he saw the last paparazzi car pull out after them with the man in the gray hoodie driving.

The house was now quiet, and Mick was alone. He pulled around the corner and got out of the car, walking back to observe the house on foot. He wasn't sure why he was waiting, but his instincts told him the couple was far too clever to assume their brazen decoy maneuver would shake all their tails.

He knew he was taking a big risk in waiting, but he needed to be patient.

Sure enough, about thirty minutes after the departure of the last car from the house, the garage door opened, and a dark SUV slowly backed out of the driveway and headed down the street. Mick sprinted back to his car, wishing he had parked a little closer. They were out of sight by the time he got started, but there were only a few ways out of the neighborhood, and he guessed the right one.

The black SUV drove nonchalantly, heading north toward the Beltway.

Mick stayed back, hoping that they hadn't seen him. After a few minutes, they turned onto the Beltway, following the interstate west. Traffic was still light but would grow quickly as rush hour approached. Mick decided to follow them from ahead. He moved over a couple of lanes and pulled ahead by several cars. He was confident he could make any exit if they decided to get off.

After ten minutes, they turned farther north on I-270 toward Germantown. Mick started racking his brains trying to figure out what airport was in this part of Maryland. He wanted to check his phone, but it wasn't possible to drive in the heavy traffic, stay abreast of them, and search for airports on his phone.

He used the traffic to hide his presence by dropping

back and speeding ahead of them between exits. Thankfully, they seemed oblivious to his presence and were driving at a very conservative speed. They almost fooled him when they suddenly changed lanes and exited onto a county road with little warning.

"Sly little devil," Mick muttered to himself as he managed to cross multiple lanes and exit as well. He slowed and let them get well ahead of him, since the traffic was much lighter now.

When they stopped at a light, he pulled out his phone and searched for nearby airfields. Just as he'd suspected, Montgomery County Airpark was only a few miles away. His quarry seemed to be carefully checking for tails now as they turned away, instead of toward the airport. They were probably doing a final check for tails by driving around on empty country roads before heading to the airport.

Gambling he was right, Mick turned in the opposite direction and drove to the airfield ahead of them. He parked his car in a location where he could surveil both the parking lot and the airfield.

It wasn't long before his intuition was rewarded. The SUV pulled in and parked next to the small terminal. The couple unloaded their suitcases and went inside.

"Bingo," he murmured.

He wondered which plane on the airfield was theirs. He saw several executive jets parked on the ramp, but none looked like they'd be leaving anytime soon. He waited five minutes, then he grabbed his camera and strolled into the terminal.

He found them sitting in the small restaurant staring out the window at the runway with their backs to him. They were sipping coffee and chatting as if they didn't have a care in the world. The woman was still wearing a scarf, but he could see her trademark brown hair underneath.

Success. They were clever. Very clever, but they weren't fooling him twice. No one fooled Mick Watson twice.

He picked a seat at a table near the door and ordered himself a cup of coffee. While he waited for his coffee, he fiddled with his camera, getting it ready for when they stood up and saw him.

But strangely, they just sat there. Fifteen minutes passed, then twenty, and finally they asked for the check. They rose slowly and turned.

Mick's mouth dropped open. The woman wasn't the right one. She had the same build as Lexi, but she was at least twenty years older. The tall young man with her was also the wrong man. He pulled the suitcases that had been by their chairs.

The woman must have noticed the look on Mick's face, because she stopped at his table and offered a sympathetic smile.

"It was a lovely morning for a drive, don't you think so?" she said in a light voice. "We'll be heading back now if you'd like to follow us. If not, I have some parting words for you: Leave my daughter the hell alone."

She strode off, and the young man shrugged at Mick. "I'd listen to her if I were you. Nothing good ever comes from pissing her off." He easily hefted the suitcases in one hand. "Empty, of course, but quite effective. Have a good day. Not."

As they walked out of the terminal, Mick could hear their laughter trailing behind them. He finally snapped his mouth shut, put his head in his hands, and swore like he hadn't sworn for a very long time.

SEVEN

Lexi

The drive to Dulles was mostly uneventful. Slash adeptly steered the limousine as if he had been driving it his entire life. In the back, Hands and Gray were sipping champagne from the limo's minifridge and keeping Slash and me abreast of our tails. It appeared only one car had left the house with us, but Gray was convinced a second car had joined while we were en route.

"They're such amateurs," Hands said. "You're really enjoying this, aren't you, Slash?"

Slash didn't respond, but I saw the small smile on his face.

"How can you be sure we have two tails?" I asked Gray. I didn't see it and didn't dare turn around to check from the front passenger seat, but she seemed confident, and Slash wasn't contradicting her. Of course, as a CIA agent, she had a lot more experience and training in this area than I did.

"That gray Toyota has been staying just behind us since we got onto the freeway," she said. "He's totally the pap."

"I believe you, babe," Hands said and then gave her a kiss. "Let's play up our part. If anyone is checking us out, they will see the happy couple starting off their honeymoon in the back seat of a limo drinking champagne and making out."

Gray smacked his arm. "Knock it off, Hands. We're on a mission. Stay focused."

"I *am* focused," Hands said, and we all laughed.

At one point, our main tail attempted to pull their car alongside ours to look inside. Hands and Gray ducked down, and Slash kept changing speeds and maneuvering around other cars to make it difficult for them. Finally, they gave up and settled in behind us for the rest of the trip to the airport.

When we arrived at Dulles, Slash guided the limousine into a small slot near the international departures doors. Our main tail and the gray Toyota pulled in behind us. Gray had been right—we did have two tails.

"Have a good trip, you two," Gray murmured as Slash opened her door. "Safe travels."

"Thanks for everything," I said as she slipped out, followed quickly by Hands.

They kept their heads down, their faces still hidden as much as possible. Slash handed them the luggage from the back like a good driver, and they hurried into the terminal. The paparazzi hung back slightly, but one person from each car followed them into the terminal as Slash and I drove off.

We left the terminal area and headed toward the business aviation hangars and warehouses. One of the paparazzi followed us, but we pulled up to a gate and spoke to the guard. We waited while she made a call on her phone.

Soon afterward, the gate swung open, and we pulled into a secure parking area inside a large, mostly empty hangar. The paparazzo, unable to follow, peeled away, headed in a different direction.

Slash and I exchanged a smile.

We retrieved our luggage from the back of limo that we'd placed there the day before and entered a small office area. We went into the restrooms and changed into our traveling clothes: I removed my hat and porter outfit and put on a pair of soft traveling pants, a white shirt, and a long tan sweater. Disguise or not, I was going to be comfortable on the plane.

I finished off my new look with a blond wig in a blunt cut and some badly applied makeup. We are who we are.

I met Slash outside. He looked ravishing in slacks, a polo, a jaunty sailor's hat, and a neatly trimmed mustache. Slash had determined there should be no issues with our passport photos since women dye and cut their hair all the time, and Slash could certainly grow a mustache. Nonetheless, the overall effect, according to Slash's trained eye, was we now appeared to be two completely different people.

My phone vibrated as we caught the parking bus back to the airport terminal. It was Gray. I swiped my phone on and pressed it to my ear.

"Hello," I said.

"How's it going?" Gray asked. "All's well?"

"All's well," I confirmed. "We lost them. How about you?"

"We got busted in line at the ticket counter. It was hilarious. I'll never forget it for as long as I live. The paparazzi were livid, especially when I told them they'd got the wrong airport...suckers."

I stifled a laugh. "Good for you."

"Trust me, I've never seen faces so mad. They might

have even gotten violent if Hands wasn't there looking so menacing in his long, dark toupee."

"I bet." Now a laugh escaped, and Slash looked at me questioningly. He'd only heard my side of the conversation, so I'd have to fill him in later.

As we got off the bus at the terminal, I could see one of the paparazzi cars returning to pick up the two men. They never even glanced our way.

I nodded in their direction to Slash. "I think they'd be quite disappointed to know how close they really were to getting us."

He chuckled. "Au contraire, *cara*. They were never really close at all."

EIGHT

Slash

The bag drop for our domestic flight to Hawaii was at the opposite end of the terminal from most international airlines. I kept a steady scan of the crowd, searching for anyone who might be paying unusual attention to us. Nothing stood out, and we dropped our bags and headed to security.

"Do you think we'll have any problem getting through TSA?" Lexi asked me anxiously, even though we'd already discussed it a dozen times.

"I'd be surprised if we did. We still look like our passport photos, and we aren't using a false identity. It not against the law to change your hair color, wear a wig, or don a fake mustache. Plus, they don't give more than passing attention to the pictures. We'll be fine."

"I know." She blew out a breath. "But I had a nightmare last night that everything went perfectly with our plan, but then we were arrested because I had too much liquid in my backpack. Not surprisingly, I've checked it three times already."

"Just relax," I assured her. "It's time for us to wind down and start enjoying our honeymoon."

"Easy for you to say, you don't mind flying."

Her voice sounded irritable, but I knew it was prompted by a genuine dislike for airplanes. None of which I could blame her for, because crazy things had happened when she was in the air, including an actual crash that she had miraculously survived.

"I'm right here with you," I said taking her hand. "We've got this."

Despite her nervousness, she smiled, and we passed through security uneventfully. We headed to the transportation that took us to our gate area.

Lexi's stomach growled. "Can we get some breakfast first? With all the excitement, we didn't eat anything."

"Sure. Remember, the flight is supposed to serve us breakfast in first class, too. But let's get something to tide us over until then, including coffee. I could definitely use some of that."

We each grabbed a bagel and coffee and a fruit cup to share and then headed to the gate to eat.

We found several seats with our backs to the windows. Sitting across from us were two older women. One of them was wearing a calf-length, flowered dress and staring at me. When my gaze met hers, she smiled, and I smiled back. She whispered something to her friend, and they started giggling. I wasn't sure what that was all about, but it seemed harmless.

Lexi and I ate our bagels and drank bad airport coffee as I continued to survey the gate area for unwanted attention.

I threw our trash away, and when I returned to my seat,

Lexi whispered in my ear, "Slash, check out the paper she's reading."

The woman on the left had opened a gossip tabloid called the *Global Enquirer*. On the front page were multiple images of us. One of the photos showed us racing from the church at our wedding. Another showed Lexi at the grocery store buying a box of Cheerios. The last picture was a more recent closeup of both of us getting into our car in front of our house.

"Stay calm," I murmured quietly. "They're not going to recognize us in our disguises." Yet, despite my reassurances, I had real doubts, as our faces occupied more than half of the front page of the tabloid.

Finished, the woman handed the paper to her friend in the flowered dress. "Look at these two on the cover," she said, tapping her finger directly on my photo. "He kind of looks like a movie star. James Bond, maybe, but his hair is longer and darker, and he's a lot sexier than that stuffy British guy. Maybe he's Spanish. The girl, however, doesn't look like any Bond girl I remember."

"Well, Maybelle, you don't remember like you used to," her friend cackled.

Maybelle chuffed. "Ha. The paper claims they work for the government, but no one knows who they are. They're probably secret agents like Bond. That girl, though—who eats Cheerios anymore?"

I felt Lexi stiffen beside me as I tried not to laugh.

"Don't be ridiculous, Maybelle. I just had Cheerios for breakfast before I came to the airport," the woman in the dress said. "But you're not even close to knowing what's going on. I know who they really are."

Maybelle glanced at her with wide eyes. "You do? Are you going to tell me?"

"Of course I am. They're part of the X-Files."

"The X-Files?"

"You know, aliens. They're among us. That's why they're hiding their identities." She tapped her finger on my photo again. "No one is this good-looking. He must be some artificial intelligence robot or an alien who they trapped using a fake wedding to lure him out."

Maybelle looked at her in disbelief. "Why would a wedding attract an alien?"

"How would I know the motivations of an alien?"

Lexi and I exchanged incredulous glances, and I could tell she was struggling to keep a straight face. I hoped my expression didn't betray my thoughts, which were decidedly mixed at the moment.

"Aliens blend in so well, they could be anywhere," the woman in the flowered dress continued, lowering her voice. "They could be *right in front of us* and we'd never know it."

I suddenly had an idea, so I leaned forward to engage them. "Excuse me, ladies, would you mind if we borrowed your paper when you're finished with it? My wife left her reading material at home."

Lexi cast me a surprised glance but went along with it. "Yeah, I...ah, love reading the *Global Enquirer*."

"Of course," Maybelle said, promptly handing me the paper. "We're done with it. Just be warned, young man, there's not much substance in these papers. Only fools believe everything they read. When I want the truth, I go to the internet."

"Is that so?" I said politely, accepting the paper. "Thank you for sharing."

"Our pleasure," she said.

The two women went back to chatting, so I handed

Lexi the paper, lowering my voice. "Hey, Scully, check out the article and see what it says about us."

"Very funny," she hissed back.

I chuckled. "Just keep our photos out of sight, and hopefully no one else will see them."

"Sure, Mulder. Your wish is my command."

She pretended to read the paper with the front page deftly folded inside until it was time to board. When they called for first class to board, we stood along with the ladies. They boarded ahead of us and took the two seats directly across the aisle from us.

"This could be interesting," Lexi murmured.

"Or a long flight," I replied.

We stowed our carry-ons and sat down in the seats, stretching out our legs. The flight attendant brought us champagne, orange juice, and small canapés for a snack before we took off. Lexi disappeared to the bathroom, still nervous, so I took a couple of sips of the champagne and leaned back in my seat, closing my eyes.

It had been an eventful morning.

After a few minutes, I started to get a funny feeling I was being watched, so I cracked open an eye. The woman in the flowered dress had turned around in her seat and was staring me.

"You know, young man, you look familiar. Do I know you?"

Inwardly, I tensed, but I kept a pleasant expression on my face. "I can't recall that we've ever met, ma'am, other than at the gate a few minutes ago. Perhaps you're thinking of someone else?"

Her forehead wrinkled, and she stroked her chin. "Maybelle, how do I know this young man?" she asked her friend, who leaned forward in her seat and began staring at me, too.

"I don't know, but you're right. There *is* something familiar about him."

The first woman continued to stare at me with fierce intensity, as if the answer would materialize based on sheer will alone. "Oh, *that's* how I know you," she suddenly exclaimed. "I never forget a face."

Lexi returned to her seat at that moment, looking between me and the women in alarm. I gave her a reassuring smile as she sat down and fastened her seat belt. She picked up her champagne and took a sip.

"And how is it you know me?" I asked calmly.

"You're the Tampon Hero," she said.

Lexi spewed her champagne, and I blinked in a mix of shock and surprise. Of all the things she could have said, I hadn't seen that one coming.

"Am I right, Maybelle? That's him, isn't it?"

The older woman nodded. "You're right. He's the guy. That's him. You're the guy who stopped the robbery at that gas station mart where you'd gone to buy some tampons for your girlfriend. You have a mustache now, but I'd recognize those eyes anywhere." She pointed to Lexi. "Are you his girl?"

Lexi grinned, patting her mouth with a napkin. "I am. I'm that girl who needed the tampons."

A small choking noise came from my throat, and I coughed once to clear it.

"Oh my goodness," the woman gushed. "Your man singlehandedly saved everyone's lives that day and trussed up the robber like a cooked goose before bringing home your goodies. I read the entire story in the *Global Enquirer* right after it happened."

"That story was...in the *Global Enquirer*?" I choked again and this time took a large swig of champagne.

"It was. There were photos of you standing with the policeman in front of the mart and you were holding the tampon boxes. There were interviews with the cashier, the owner, and the police, who said you took down the robber all by yourself. There was shattered glass and bullet holes and Cheetos and potato chips scattered across the floor where you'd fought for your life and the lives of everyone in that mart. It was an amazing story. I *knew* you were famous."

I glanced at Lexi, who had pressed her lips together to keep from laughing. I certainly wasn't getting any help there. Better to nip this in the bud and hopefully they'd leave us alone.

I gave her a sheepish smile. "Ah, I'm afraid you have me, madam. But as that was months ago, and it really wasn't that big of a deal, we'd appreciate it if you kept our little secret."

The woman looked at me with widened eyes. "It certainly was a big deal, young man. You're a real-life hero, putting your life on the line for the safety of others. Your humility is admirable, but for heaven's sake, take credit where credit is due."

Lexi smacked me on the arm, smiling widely. "Yeah, take credit where credit is due."

I lifted an eyebrow, promising retribution later, as Maybelle lowered her voice. "Listen, I understand you're embarrassed by the attention. The sign of a true hero. If you don't want us to say anything, we won't. Our lips are sealed."

"Sealed," the other lady agreed, nodding conspiratorially.

"I appreciate that," I said.

Lexi was still chuckling as we took off, having forgotten, or at least ignoring, her fear of flying.

I took her hand, squeezing it lightly. "I'm never going to live that down, am I?" I asked her softly.

"Nope," she replied, shaking her head. "And you shouldn't. You're a hero to many, Slash. But more importantly, you're *my* hero."

Her words touched me because I knew she meant them. She was the most genuine person I'd ever met. As an adult, I'd been trained to lie, deceive, and even hurt people in the name of national security until I believed it was the only way to right a wrong or stop an evil. I thought all people acted deceitfully in one way or another. No, I *expected* it. That distrustful, dark part of me still existed, but I'd changed after I met her. Not everyone was like that. What you saw with Lexi was what you got. She was blessedly authentic, intelligent, and loving. No games, no lies, no ulterior motives. Deceit simply wasn't in her. It still surprised me that despite knowing the real me—darkness and all—she still loved me. She was unquestionably the best part of my life, and I couldn't imagine living it without her.

The rest of the flight was blessedly quiet. We sat holding hands, watching movies, and napping. Slowly, the constant presence of coiled tension in my gut began to lessen, and I relaxed.

"Happy honeymoon," I whispered to Lexi in the dim cabin as she began to drift off to sleep.

"Happy honeymoon, Slash," she whispered, smiling drowsily. "May it be our best time together yet."

We fell asleep still holding hands. The entire flight, we never even pulled out our laptops once.

NINE

Lexi

The first thing that came to my mind when we walked out of the airport in Hawaii was that the sun was so bright neither of us could see. I shielded my eyes with my hand, squinting. When that didn't work, we paused a moment to slip on our sunglasses as the warmth from the sun instantly heated our heads and shoulders.

"Wow, it's hot." I fanned myself with my fingers. "And this wig isn't helping matters."

"It's more humid than hot," Slash replied, the sun glinting off his dark sunglasses. "That's Hawaii for you. I'm worried my mustache will slide off. We just have to wear our disguises until we get to the hotel."

"It won't be soon enough," I groused.

He pointed in the distance over a raised highway toward lush, green mountains, their peaks hidden by a soft, rolling mist. "Look at that gorgeous view. We can't quite see it from here, but that's Pearl Harbor at the base of those peaks."

"Cool. Are any of those mountains volcanoes? If so, I bet it would be fun to get a closer look at them."

"I'm pretty sure there are no active volcanoes on Oahu. The active ones are primarily on the big island of Hawaii. Anyway, I don't think a volcano visit is a good plan, given your history of calamities. Does your spreadsheet have a column for volcano eruptions?"

"In fact, it does not. But I get your point. We opted for the quiet, nothing happens honeymoon, so let's not tempt fate." I sniffed the air. "What smells so good? Is that perfume?"

"Plumerias." Slash gestured to his left, where a riot of purple and white flowers burst from several small trees, apparently part of the airport's immaculate tropical landscape. "It reminds me of Sicily. We have white plumerias there. They look and smell slightly different from these, but similar enough. We call them *frangipani* or *pomelia*."

"It's really pleasant, and I typically don't like strong smells."

"I'm with you there. But this is a soft fragrance. Very nice. Apparently, we're going to have a lot to see in our short time here."

Slash steered me toward the car, where our driver stood waiting for us, the trunk open for our luggage. We piled in and admired the landscape as we drove toward our beachside resort.

Slash stared out the window. "Exotic and stunning beauty. I can already tell we should have planned for more than a day in Hawaii. That's on me."

"We wanted remote for our honeymoon," I reminded

him. "As far away from prying eyes and paparazzi as possible. Hawaii doesn't really give us that option."

He sighed. "I know."

"But I'm glad we decided to risk a one-day layover here. It's always been a dream of mine to see Hawaii."

"Mine, too."

"Then we made the right choice." I leaned my head against his shoulder. "It doesn't mean we can't come back someday for a longer stay when all the craziness at home dies down. If it ever does."

"It will." He took my hand and lifted it to his lips. "We'll make it happen."

I liked his confidence. "I hope you're right."

We enjoyed the view as we passed giant ferns, lush bushes, and colorful and vibrant flowers. We climbed through the mountains that divided the island, and as we descended toward the coast, we caught glimpses of turquoise waters dotted with small boats and sparkling white beaches.

Finally, we pulled up at our beachside resort and headed inside to check in. Once we got to our bungalow, the first thing I did was open the French doors onto the balcony.

"Wow, Slash, look at this!" I said, stepping out onto a private veranda framed by coconut palms and lovely flowering bushes. An empty beach stretched out in front of us, a beautiful expanse of soft, white sand glimmering under the midday sun.

Slash slipped up behind me, wrapping his arms around my waist and resting his chin on my shoulder. I could feel his body relax into mine. Relaxing, rejuvenating, and revitalizing. Things we both needed badly.

The ocean was a mesmerizing mesh of turquoise and

dark blue. "This view is stunning," he said. "I keep saying that, don't I?"

"You do, but you're right. The waves are surprisingly calm. I hope that is a metaphor for our honeymoon." I turned around, still in his embrace. "So, what's the plan for the first official night? I remember you saying something about a luau."

"Yes, but the natives call it *'aha'aina*. It literally means 'a meal gathering.' But it's a luau of sorts. I've booked us a tour and dinner, or luau, if you will, at a nearby Polynesian village for the evening."

"That sounds incredibly interesting and fun."

"Don't forget romantic," he added. "At least, that's the plan."

"I'm so glad you said that, as romance and intimacy is another important piece of the marriage code," I said. "It's number three, by the way."

"Is it now?" he said, sounding amused. "So, we have trust as the number one piece of the code, followed by mutual decision making. Now we have an intimacy element. This code keeps getting better and better. You can rest assured I'm fully on board for this code. In fact, I'm willing to help make it even more robust, if you'd agree. Do I get to see the code when you're finished programming it?"

"Absolutely. Your input will be vital, as the outcome is a shared achievement."

"Excellent." Grinning, he headed back into the room, pulling off his fake mustache with a grimace. "Oh, it feels good to have that *bruco* off my face."

"What's a *bruco*?" I asked, pulling the pins out and removing my wig with a grateful sigh. I tossed it on the bed, unpinned my hair, and massaged my scalp.

"A caterpillar," he said.

I laughed. "It did kind of look like an insect."

He gave a mock sigh. "So, not sexy at all?" He removed his sports coat and shirt and hung them on the back of a chair.

"Ha. Only you could make a caterpillar mustache look sexy." He chuckled as I walked over to my suitcase, flipped it on its side, and rolled the small combination lock to open it. "Do we have time to shower before the luau?"

A slow smile crossed his face. "We have plenty of time for that...and maybe a bit more."

I glanced at him over my shoulder. "A bit more what? Don't tell me you're referring to gaming."

He rolled his eyes. "I'm not referring to gaming."

I straightened, pretending to ignore the eyeroll. "So, what did you have in mind? Are you saying I'm going to get lei'ed?"

He winced. "Ouch. You did not just say that."

"I did." I laughed happily, kissing him on the chin. "I thought you'd be proud of me for recognizing a sexual innuendo at first blush. You didn't like my pun?"

"I did not. But we *are* in Hawaii, so I *am* hoping the lei'ed part is on the agenda."

"Well, hope no more." I pulled him toward the bed, and we fell on it together. "I think it's a perfect activity for the first day of our honeymoon, and, well, with you, anytime, actually."

He grinned, rolling us over until he was on top. "You were kidding about the gaming, right?"

"Of course I was kidding. Now that I fully understand my options, if you're among the choices, nothing else is ever going to win. That includes gaming. You've ruined me for life, you know." It was the absolute truth.

He tucked a stray hair behind my ear. "Good. Because

until I met you, nothing would have kept me away from the keyboard for twenty-four hours, either. And now look at us."

"Yes. Look at us." I touched his unshaven cheek with my fingertips, marveling that this man was my husband. "Happily married...twice...and finally on our honeymoon. And the funny thing is, Slash, when I'm with you, I don't even miss the gaming."

A smile lit his face. "Me, neither. But it doesn't mean we can't do it from time to time or even often, on occasion."

I paused for a moment, hoping he meant what I thought he meant. "I'm really glad you said that."

He laughed. "I know you are, *cara*. That's why I said it." He nuzzled my neck with his lips. "Now, where were we?"

I tugged his mouth toward my lips. "About to officially start our epic and über-relaxing honeymoon."

"It's about time," he said.

TEN

Lexi

It was late afternoon when the hotel arranged a car to pick us up in front of the resort to take us on our tour and special ʻahaʻaina at the Polynesian village.

We were fully dressed for the occasion. Slash wore black slacks and a light-blue Hawaiian shirt decorated with dark-blue palm trees. He looked more like an Italian model, with his hair slicked back behind his ears and dark sunglasses, than an American tourist, but we are who we are. I wore a dark-blue Hawaiian wrap dress with white flowers that went down to just above my ankles, a gauzy white shawl, sandals, and a white flower in my hair that Slash helped me pin behind my ear. I added dark sunglasses, as well.

Somehow, we complemented each other, with both of us embracing the Hawaiian theme. That, of course, meant none of the fashion choices were mine. Basia had literally designed my entire honeymoon wardrobe, roping in Slash for a consult when it required him to wear a complementary outfit, which, apparently, tonight it did. The whole fashion thing added more than I expected to the overall ambience and expectations for a wonderful and romantic evening.

Slash asked the driver to take a picture of us since we were all dressed up and had a lovely backdrop with flowering bushes underneath a large ficus tree with low-hanging branches. He agreed, and after a few snaps we climbed into the car, ready for our first out-of-the-room honeymoon activity.

Our car wound lazily along roads flanked by dense foliage, eucalyptus trees, and a variety of palms swaying in the breeze. The car windows were open, so we enjoyed the warmth and fragrance of the tropical air. It carried the intoxicating scent of flowers—including what I now recognized as plumeria—the ocean's salty tang, and a hint of the rich, musky volcanic soil.

The sun had just begun its descent by the time we arrived at the Polynesian village. Slash checked us in, and we were immediately given lovely blue-and-white leis that matched our outfits (they had an assortment of colored leis to choose from) and introduced us to our personal guide, Kai.

Kai was a young guy, maybe twenty or twenty-one, who was shirtless and wore a bold black-and-white-patterned sarong. He had several fascinating tattoos on his extremely buff torso, including one that look like a decorated mask, surrounded by an intricate pattern of swirls and lines.

He caught me staring and smiled broadly, flashing the whitest teeth I'd ever seen. "Aloha, *e komo mai*. That means hello and welcome. I see you're interested in my tattoo."

My cheeks heated. "I couldn't help but be fascinated. It's beautiful."

"*Mahalo*." He bowed his head slightly. "It was done by

kākau, the ancient Hawaiian art of tattooing. This tattoo is a generational representation of me, my family, and my ancestors, a visual reminder of my responsibility to my family, community, and heritage. We don't use needles to piece the skin—instead we use bone, usually from the Hawaiian albatross, because it is so hard. The designs are native and ancestral. I do not choose my design. Instead, the master tattooist chooses a unique design for me based on my personality and my genealogy. It is genuinely a part of me."

"That's really cool." I glanced down at my wrist, where I had a semi-tattoo of my own. A ring, my *engagement* ring, had been burned into my wrist as part of our native marriage ceremony in Brazil. Slash had the same mark on his wrist. He caught my glance and turned his arm slightly toward mine, indicating he was thinking the same thing. Like Kai, our tattoos were a part of the history of us.

Again, Kai gifted us with his wide smile. "We're happy to have you visit our village and learn about our heritage. Is this your first time here?"

"Yes, it is." We both nodded.

"How do you like Hawaii so far?"

"It's stunning," Slash said. "In many ways, but especially in terms of landscape, flora, and geological features. We're only here for a short visit this time, but I assure you, it didn't take us long to decide we intend to return for a much longer stay."

"I'm happy to hear that. I do hope you enjoy yourselves this evening."

"We already are," Slash said, meeting my eyes before taking my hand and giving it a gentle squeeze.

The village bustled with activity, a nice blend of the past and present. Polynesian villagers, clad in vibrant attire, moved among us, their smiles warm and welcoming. We strolled hand in hand through the village as Kai pointed out the historical and cultural aspects of life for native Hawaiians. Ancient Polynesian villages were typically centered around a wooden thatched gathering house and a stone temple, while smaller huts were built on platforms with a framework of wooden poles lashed together with a coarse twine. They thatched the roofs with pandanus, sugarcane leaves, and swatches of pili grass.

"When were the Hawaiian Islands originally settled?" I asked Kai.

"Our traditions and archaeologists place the arrival of the first Polynesians around 900 AD," Kai answered. "The Polynesian people arrived as far west as Fiji, Samoa, and Tonga over a thousand years before that, but oddly, eastern expansion stopped for almost a millennium."

"So, Hawaii was settled from the south?" Slash asked. "I've always assumed it was from the west."

"That's a common misconception largely due to a misunderstanding of the prevailing winds in the Pacific," Kai said. "Unlike North America, where the prevailing winds move west to east, in the central Pacific, the winds move east to west. The prevailing wind in Hawaii is from the northeast to the southwest. Thus, the original Polynesian explorers were sailing into the wind searching for land."

"Into the wind?" I shuddered. "On primitive boats with no life vests or Dramamine? That's crazy. It scares me just thinking about it."

"Our ancestors were certainly brave and amazing people," Kai said proudly. "To think they were able to return to their islands and bring back their families to settle is an amazing feat."

"It is, indeed," Slash said.

Kai seemed genuinely delighted we were so interested in learning about his heritage and culture. "Here's another interesting fact about my Polynesians ancestors," he said as we walked along. "See if you can answer this question. What was the last landmass in the world to be inhabited by people, apart from Antarctica and the Arctic?"

"Easter Island?" Slash guessed.

Kai shook his head and glanced at me. "Want to give it a try?"

"How about the Pitcairn Islands?"

Slash looked at me and raised an eyebrow. "The... what?"

I laughed. "I may have done some research on our trip, too. The Pitcairn Islands are a group of four islands in the Pacific Ocean, not too far from Easter Island, actually. They're also believed to be settled by the ancient Polynesians."

Kai clapped his hands in delight. "What excellent guesses, you two. But you're both wrong. You may be quite surprised by the answer. It's New Zealand. New Zealand was settled about a hundred years after Easter Island, around 1200 AD, by Polynesians who eventually became the Māori."

"Wow, that *is* a fascinating fact," I said, and Slash nodded in agreement.

Kai continued his history lesson as we toured the village. We stopped at a fenced area where they kept the village animals. Inside, a couple of goats, two donkeys, and some sheep looked bored with the tourists hanging over the fence snapping photos of them. Adjacent to the animal pen was the pigpen, presumably the source of the main course for the luau. I was confident that the smell hanging over the pigpen kept anyone from lingering too long near their wallow.

"Pigs are not native to Hawaii," Kai explained as we approached the pigpen. "They were introduced by European settlers in the late 1700s. Yet they've thrived on our islands."

I leaned over and took a closer look at the pigpen. There were two large sows trailed by tiny cohorts of piglets. The half dozen male pigs were smaller than the sows. I suspect they were the optimum luau size, big enough to feed about a crowd of seventy. Their pink snouts twitched as they rooted in the dirt and mud. One of them, with beady eyes and a white splotch on his forehead, was watching me with an intensity akin to a lion stalking an antelope. The pig started slowly advancing toward me, and I involuntarily stepped back, bumping into a goat that was reaching over the adjacent fence to nibble on my sleeve. Both of us bleated simultaneously, and I would have fallen if Slash hadn't caught me. When I recovered, the pig was at the fence pawing the ground as if he was trying to get to me.

"Looks like you have a new friend, or maybe I should say friends," Kai said, chuckling, as the pig madly pawed at the ground, trying to get near me and the goat stuck its head back over the fence, trying to eat my hair.

Slash grinned. "What is it with you and animals?" I could tell he was trying not to laugh, but he was wise enough not to give in to temptation.

I rolled my eyes as the pig snuffled in frustration and banged his head on the fence. I wagged a warning finger at him. "Thanks, bud, but I don't need any more friends."

We thankfully left the animal area and Kai showed us the rest of the village and a couple of demonstrations, including a villager with a machete practically running up a tall palm tree to lop off a coconut. At some point, the villagers brought us tropical drinks, which I drank out of the coconut using a straw. Sunset deepened and the sky turned into a canvas of vibrant colors—shades of pink, orange, and yellow. The warmth of the day still lingered in the air.

As the evening shadows lengthened, a festive atmosphere came over the village. Drums began to beat, calling everyone to gather for what Kai told us would be the royal court procession. We were seated with the other tourists at a long wooden table with a stage to the right of us. The procession, a living tableau of ancient traditions, danced in from the left. I snapped several photos with my phone as men and women adorned in feathered cloaks and gleaming ornaments swayed, their movements perfectly synchronized to the rhythm of the chanting and drumming. Two of the men carried flaming, whirling torches. It was both fascinating and mesmerizing.

Once the procession concluded, the villagers ceremoniously unearthed the cooked pig from the *imu*, an underground oven covered with sand where they'd roasted the pig for the evening's feast. Its succulent aroma elicited murmurs of anticipation from the crowd, me included. Plates of traditional food soon followed, laden with lomilomi salmon, poi, and sweet coconut pudding. We ate slowly, sampling the fare and savoring each bite on our tongues while watching an amazing show of hula and flame juggling.

At some point, I excused myself to use the restroom. One of the villagers pointed me toward a thatched building adjacent to the animal pens. Logically, the location made sense since all the so-called aromatic areas would be in the same location.

I was almost to the bathroom when a sudden commotion erupted behind me near the pigpen. I turned and saw a young boy straining to hold a pig on a leash. It appeared that he was trying to lead the pig from the enclosure, but the swine had other ideas. The pig dragged him unwillingly along as he tried to hang on. With horror I realized they were headed right at me. I had just enough time to recognize the pig had a white patch on its head before I turned to run.

Gah!

I dashed toward the bathroom hut but adjusted my route when I realized the hut had no main door. Instead, I looped around the hut with the pig and his handler hot on my tail. The boy shouted, but apparently it wasn't having any effect. I considered myself lucky the kid still had something of a grip on the pig, as that slowed them down just enough for me to stay ahead of them.

It may not have been my finest moment, but I shrieked bloody murder as I dashed back toward the tables. I ran as fast as I could on a full stomach, as I'd just eaten an enormous meal that had likely included one of his former pen mates. I'd also consumed at least two coconut-hosted drinks filled with alcohol and had to pee badly. Still, I impressed myself with my ability to run like an Olympic wannabe while screeching like a maniac.

As I approached the tables, tourists leapt from their seats in terror and began to shout and run about, unsure what was happening. I tried to find Slash, but everyone was dressed in Hawaiian outfits, and in the dim light, with people running around, I couldn't see him.

"Slash!" I shouted, but he didn't respond in the chaos.

The fire jugglers on the stage caught my eye. I raced past the tables where people were either abandoning their seats or standing on them. I remembered reading somewhere that pigs are afraid of fire, so that was my destination.

It wasn't the soundest strategy I'd ever had, but it was the best I could come up with under immediate distress. I swerved toward the guys with the flaming torches and hurled myself onto the stage.

In retrospect, it would have been an excellent plan if I hadn't inadvertently kicked one of the jugglers, causing him to drop one of his torches into the pile of grass skirts in the corner they kept for later in the show. The skirts went up in a magnificent swoosh of fire, keeping the pig, and everyone else, away from the stage.

I bolted across the stage, glancing to my left. Kai and another guy were attempting to corral the wayward porker. Somehow, the pig had lost the boy, although he was still trailing the leash around his neck.

The swine deftly continued to elude capture, sliding through the hands of everyone who tried to grab it. The phrase *slippery as a pig* gained absolute clarity for me in that moment.

Sensing his moments of freedom might be fleeting, the boar zigzagged through the area, squealing and grunting, causing a ruckus at every turn. He barreled beneath a table, knocking over benches, chairs, and several tiki torches planted in the sand.

I found a temporary haven at the side of the stage opposite the fire, where I stood panting. A middle-aged man with a beard who wore a red Hawaiian shirt too tight around the middle and a funky straw hat stood next to me, sweating profusely while filming with a fancy camera.

"Have you ever seen anything like this?" He spoke with such enthusiasm and excitement I wanted to deck him. "Here we are, in Hawaii at a luau, being treated to the Great Pig Chase. Hee-haw!"

He laughed, snorting so loudly it caught the attention of

the pig. The angry mammal glanced over at him, but immediately locked eyes with me, again.

Oh, crap.

The man in the Hawaiian shirt suddenly stopped laughing as the pig made deep, guttural sounds from his belly. I realized at that moment pigs do *not* make a benign oinking noise. Nope, this pig was not oinking. He was grunting something far more threatening...at me.

The pig lowered his head, a fierce glare in his eyes. Before I could even process what was happening, he churned madly on his piggy hooves and came straight at me. The man in the red Hawaiian shirt dropped his camera and screamed so loudly, it temporarily deafened me.

OMG!

The pig was coming for me.

ELEVEN

Lexi

Yelping, I leaped up the stage steps to get away. A scream caught in my throat as the pig adeptly followed me up.

How had I not known pigs could climb stairs?

I shrieked and rolled off the stage a mere second before the pig headbutted me. I landed on the ground with a jarring thump, scrambling to my knees as the pig assessed the drop and backed up to jump.

I was rooted to the spot in a weird terror when I saw Slash. He was on the stage behind the pig, creeping up on it. Before he could reach it, the pig lunged at me, lifting his body off the stage like Jennifer Grey leaping into the arms of Patrick Swayze in the movie, *Dirty Dancing*.

We were milliseconds from porcine impact, proving that pigs could indeed fly, when the pig jerked sideways on his leash and fell squealing back into the front of the stage. Slash held the other end of the leash, his feet splayed to absorb the shock. He held steady as Kai and another villager nabbed it. It squealed in loud protest, but the villagers held firmly.

Assured the pig was finally secure, I sighed in relief, sinking back to the ground. Slash released the leash and jumped from the stage to land beside me.

"Are you okay, *cara*?" he asked, holding out a hand to help me up.

"Do I look okay?" I snapped. "I was just chased by a pig who wanted to kill me."

His lips twitched. "Okay, let me rephrase that. Are you hurt?"

Slightly mollified, I checked myself over. "I don't think so, but it was a close call. I lost the flower in my hair, darn it."

He kissed my cheek. "Pig magnet or not, you still look beautiful to me."

Kai and two villagers, in a well-coordinated effort, lifted and carried the uncooperative pig back to the pen. The crowd erupted into applause and cheers. Meanwhile, others were extinguishing the fire on the other side of the stage.

A young woman rushed up to us with her phone out. "Can I get a closeup picture of you two? I got it all on video. It's amazing. I'll bet I'll get two million views on Instagram."

"Sure, we'll pose for a photo," Slash said, causing me to look at him in surprise. "But you have to let us watch the video afterwards."

"Of course," she said, beaming.

Puzzled, I stood next to Slash and smiled while she snapped the photo and then handed her phone to Slash. Slash started watching the video when the villagers started using a fire extinguisher on the corner of the stage where the grass skirts went up in flames. We watched in awe as steam and smoke swirled about the stage and the fire was finally put out.

Everyone cheered again.

"That was an amazing video," Slash said, handing the woman back her phone. "Thank you for sharing."

I was still in a bit of shock as we started walking back to our table. "So much for a quiet, romantic evening," I groused. "And I still have to go to the bathroom. Will you walk me there?"

"Why? In case the goat gets loose?"

"Very funny." I pursed my lips at him. "But maybe."

He chuckled and kissed the top of my head. "Sorry, couldn't help myself. Okay, *cara*. I've got your back while you're in the bathroom."

I was finally able to safely use the restroom, and Slash spent some time washing his hands and face in the men's room before the excitement finally settled down.

Once we got back to our table, the man with the red Hawaiian shirt barged up to us. "Wow, lady!" he shouted, causing me to wince. "This is the most exciting luau I've ever been to. I've never been attacked by my dinner before. That pig really had it in for you. What in the blazes did you do to it?"

"I didn't do anything," I said. "Animals just hate me. I was headed to the bathroom, and it got away from the boy and started chasing me."

"Well, it was lucky that guy saved you," he said, pointing at Slash.

"That *guy* is my husband," I said.

"Well, he was certainly in the right place at the right time."

"He usually is." I glanced over at Slash and saw his lips twitch into a smile.

"You know, young man, I can't tell you how amazing that rescue was." He snatched Slash's hand off the table and enthusiastically pumped it. "You came out of nowhere to stop that pig. You're a true, blue, pig-wrangling Hawaiian hero. Can I take a selfie with you two?"

"I'd rather no—" Slash started, but the man had already snapped two or three photos of them together and then rushed back to a group that was waving excitedly at him.

I sighed. "So much for a quiet evening. Looks like our honeymoon is ruined. We're probably already social media celebrities."

Slash took my hand and raised it to his lips. "Au contraire. We're good. Nothing, *especially* our honeymoon, is ruined."

"How can you say that? That woman has probably already uploaded her video to every known social media platform in the universe, and he will probably post those awful selfies all over the place." I let my gaze drift to where the man was talking to his family and friends.

Slash brushed a fingertip across my cheek. "Trust me. At this point, the woman is probably wondering what she screwed up, since she can't find her video or the picture of us. And that man will be terribly disappointed with his photo."

I narrowed my eyes. "You deleted their photos and video?"

"The woman's, *si*. Why do you think I let her take a picture of us in exchange for getting her phone to see the video?"

"Oh, Slash, that's brilliant. What about the guy who just took those selfies?"

"He forgot to switch around his camera. He got a great

shot of the rest of the luau." He cupped my cheeks in his hand. "So, now, dear wife, what do I get for saving your bacon?"

"Oh, no." I smacked him on the arm. "You did *not* just say that."

"Ah, but I did." He grinned, looking way too pleased with himself. "I think I'm really getting the hang of American colloquial phrases, as odd as they may be."

We both laughed as the music resumed and free drinks were handed out. After the villagers reset the venue and reorganized what was left of the stage, the evening returned to its regularly scheduled program, minus the hula performances.

After dinner and a few Polynesian dance numbers, I began to relax. It may have been the alcohol or the different kind of beauty nighttime in Hawaii provided. The air cooled slightly, carrying the fresh, clean scent of the ocean and the subtle fragrance of night-blooming flowers. The current dancers swayed and wove gracefully across the stage under the flickering tiki lights, spinning tales of ancient history, conflict, and love. They twirled, tossed torches, and waved spears while the Hawaiian drums and music offered a crescendo of excitement. I glanced up, amazed at how a clear sea of stars sparkled brightly, free from the interference of city lights here on the east coast of Oahu.

Eventually, we were all invited to dance with the villagers. The setting was so enchanting that I took Slash's hand without hesitation when he offered it, even though I didn't really like dancing. We found a spot on the beach where we kicked off our sandals and swayed barefoot, our toes gripping the sand. Under a canopy of diamond stars, we danced until we were breathless as the drums, chanting, and laughter blended into the night.

It was the first and best night of our honeymoon.

TWELVE

Slash

Our plane landed smoothly on the tarmac of Rarotonga International Airport after a six-and-a-half-hour flight, bringing us to our final honeymoon destination, the Cook Islands. The airport was a long concrete strip running parallel to the water.

Lexi and I stepped out into the humid air, holding our carry-ons and looking around. The airport was quaint, almost charming, with vibrant floral decorations and welcoming smiles from the locals. The airport consisted of two main buildings, a control tower with an operations center and a passenger terminal. A quick view of the landscape showed green turtleback mountains rising two thousand feet above the airport against the backdrop of a deep blue sky.

Our exclusive resort was on the opposite side of the island from the airport, though that was only about a twenty-minute drive. Truthfully, everything was within a short drive, as the island was only twenty-six miles around.

On the map, Rarotonga was shaped like a kidney—about eight miles at its widest. A reef surrounded the island with the water inside the coral a gorgeous turquoise blue.

We passed east, clockwise, through Avarua, the capital, on the island's primary road called Ara Tapu, or "sacred path" in Māori. The two-lane road completely encircled the island, and almost all other roads connected to it. Avarua was more of a town than a city, with a population of only five thousand people. It was easy to see why nothing happened here. It seemed Avarua was the capital mainly because of the airport, which was critical to the economic viability of the island.

As our taxi wound around the narrow, hedge-lined streets, our driver, Jared, pointed and commented on sites as we drove along. "That's Avatiu Harbour out there to the left. That pier area is the Cook Islands' only real port."

"With all the islands in the country, why is this is the only port?" Lexi asked.

"Our islands are either extinct volcanoes surrounded by coral reefs or atolls," Jared explained. "Either way, the reefs make shallow lagoons around the islands that are great for beaches, but lousy for shipping. In the 1980s, we started dredging a channel through the reef to create a port here. Took us years to dredge and build the infrastructure. But now, larger ships can dock. It's been a real boost to the economy."

To our right, we glimpsed mountain slopes smothered in dense jungle vegetation that included towering coconut palms and banana trees.

"The tallest peak there is called Te Manga," Jared said. "It's the highest point in the country—a little over six hundred meters high. The other peak nearby is Te Rua Manga. There's a tall rock on the peak called the Needle. If you're up for a hike, the view is impressive from either peak. If you're lazy, you can buy some great pictures in the gift shops."

Given Lexi's earlier clarification on what constituted hiking, it was safe to say we'd never see those views except on a postcard. Lexi leaned forward in her seat, staring out the window. "Jared, what's that building on the right?"

I followed Lexi's gaze to a two-story modern building with lots of gleaming aluminum siding and large glass doors. It was entirely out of place among the rest of the single-story cinder block or concrete structures, most of which had flat or corrugated metal roofs.

"Oh, that's our new police station," Jared said. "It was just completed a year ago. It was funded with a boatload of Chinese money and is quite controversial around here."

"Why is it controversial?" Lexi asked.

"Well, the Chinese have been giving the police department special training and lots of new equipment, including boats they can use to patrol the islands, bulletproof vests, radios, and, of course, the new police station. Some people are accusing them of trying to buy influence."

"Why would the Chinese want to buy influence here?" Lexi asked. "Do they want to turn it into a special tourist destination? Or do you have valuable minerals they want?"

Jared shrugged. "Everyone is asking questions like that, and no one really knows the answers. We do have some minerals in the ocean around our islands, but they're not especially rare and are hard to mine. Our biggest exports are pearls, pineapples, and bananas, and most of those go to New Zealand. It's hard to see where China benefits from that."

"Do you have any other industry?" I asked.

"In recent years, we have gotten into offshore banking. I

don't know much about it, but some nations are accusing us of being a tax haven for rich people. I'm not sure how that works, but apparently, it's been bringing in good money for the country. But combined with the Chinese helping to support our police force, it's making some people uncomfortable and wondering if what we're doing is above board."

We didn't have anything to say to that, and there weren't a lot more sights to see along the road, so we drove the rest of the way in silence with the windows down. Our resort was in the Muri Beach area on the southeast side of the island. We planned to stay here for a week and then take an hour's flight north in a small plane to the island of Aitutaki, or what was known as the romantic island, for our second week.

Jared dropped us off at the resort check-in, and after we checked in, a bellman led us to a luxurious bungalow perched on the edge of a private beach. The second we walked in the door; I knew this was going to be the perfect spot for a quiet and relaxing honeymoon.

Light streamed in through the open windows and French doors, and gauzy white curtains fluttered in the breeze. Lexi immediately walked across the room to fling open the doors to a private veranda. The aquamarine water sparkled in the sun as the waves crested against the surrounding reef. The sand on the beach looked pristine. But it was the large, freestanding hot tub, set on the veranda and overlooking the ocean, that made me smile.

"Wow, this is spectacular," Lexi said as I came up behind her, wrapping her in my arms.

"Better than even I expected," I agreed.

"I'm guessing we're going to get a lot of use from that hot tub."

"I'm guessing you're right," I said.

She smiled, and I left her still admiring the view to check out the rest of our room. My gaze drifted to the expansive bed—a king-size masterpiece draped in airy white linens, the canopy above billowing like clouds. The steady easterly winds eliminated the need for air-conditioning, although the bungalow apparently had ceiling fans for the hottest days. The floor was made of a dark, rich wood, probably native to the island, and the lavish bathroom just off the main area was spacious. It had a roomy and sleek design, and the polished marble counters gleamed in the light. The double rain shower configuration and large glassed-in area with a bench promised relaxation and comfort.

A cozy sitting area was tucked into one side of the room. The space was intimate, with a sleek, modern television mounted on the wall. The room was clearly designed to feel like an extension of the outdoors, with a white sofa and teal pillows, inviting us to sink into their comfort. Local art adorned the walls, each piece telling the story of the island. A silver bucket with a bright teal bow—presumably to match the sofa pillows—and a bottle of champagne sat on the coffee table, along with a platter of local fruits, wrapped cheese, and crackers.

Lexi came in from the veranda and sat down on a corner of the bed. Her cheeks were pink from our excursions in Hawaii, her eyes aglow, her hair up in a messy ponytail. My heart stumbled in my chest. She was my everything. I'd never expected this level of happiness, and I still wasn't convinced I deserved it.

"I need a nap," she declared, sitting on the side of the bed and taking off her shoes. "That was a long flight from Hawaii."

"It was shorter than the flight from Dulles," I pointed out.

"It felt longer for some reason. Probably because we were so relaxed last night."

"True." I joined her on the bed and removed my shoes as well. "But it was a tiring flight. Nap and then dinner at the resort?"

"Nap, dinner at the resort, and then a long soak in the hot tub in the moonlight," she suggested. "Alone. No paparazzi, no runaway pigs, no guys in tight red Hawaiian shirts trying to take our picture. Just you and me."

"I can't think of anything more perfect," I said, meaning it with every fiber of my being. I tucked her body against mine as we set our heads on the pillow and closed our eyes. The breeze drifted over us, its softness carrying the smells of the ocean and beach. It reminded me of home in Italy, and I began to silently congratulate myself on finding this remote paradise.

As if she read my mind, she spoke. "Great choice on location, Slash. I think I'm really going to like it here."

"Me, too," I murmured. "We may have finally found the most isolated yet beautiful spot on Earth."

"And no sight of my black cloud," she said. "Except for the pig incident, and I'm not sure we can blame that on the cloud."

"I'm not blaming the cloud for that," I agreed. "And to think I was worried about a volcano. But if a runaway pig is the worst that happens on our honeymoon, I'll be satisfied."

"Yeah, me, too."

She was quiet and I could hear her breathing slow and deepen. I was just nodding off to sleep when I heard her murmur, "I love you, Slash. Thank you for being you."

"*Ti amo, cara,*" I whispered.

In that moment, I felt a surge of gratitude so deep, it almost hurt. How could I ever repay her for bringing light into my darkness? Before I met her, I had made peace with my loneliness, my past, my emotional solitude. I had neither expected nor believed I had earned the right to live a long life given my chosen career. But she was the first person who made me look inside myself and consider I might be worthy of happiness. And for that, I owed her everything.

I slipped a hand beneath my shirt, pulling out my father's cross, the one I always wore. I pressed my lips to it, thanking him and others in my life who seemed to be looking out for me, even if they weren't physically here. I believed they'd led me to Lexi. Because somehow, she was the only one who could fully love and accept the real me, all the good and the bad.

And for me...that would always be enough.

THIRTEEN

Slash

The next morning, we decided to explore the island by returning to the town center of Avarua. We asked the concierge at the resort how to summon a taxi, but she advised us to take the bus instead. Apparently, the buses were quite comfortable and circled the island on a regular schedule—one clockwise and one counterclockwise.

Taking the bus seemed like an adventure, so we waited out in front of the resort on a bench in the shade until the bus arrived. We'd exchanged enough American dollars for New Zealand dollars when we were at the airport, so we'd have plenty of local cash on hand for two weeks.

We hopped on the bus and paid our fare, while Lexi snapped a photo of our resort from the window. There were just a few other people on the bus; most looked like locals, not tourists.

Fantastic.

The bus made a couple more stops when a lady with

two chickens in an open crate got on and sat directly across from us. Lexi drew in a sharp breath, her body tensing.

I sat in the aisle between Lexi and the chickens. I lowered my voice. "Don't make eye contact with the chickens."

"Very funny," she whispered. "If those chickens get out, I can't be responsible for what I might do."

I pressed my lips together so I didn't laugh. "I will protect you with my life," I said as solemnly as possible.

She narrowed her eyes at me. "You'd better. It's in the marriage code, number…thirteen."

"You made that up," I said.

"How do you know?" she challenged me. "You haven't seen the code yet."

I crossed my arms against my chest. "Because you paused before you picked a random number. So you made it up."

"Well, maybe," she confessed with a smile that warranted a kiss. "But I think I may add it. It fits us."

That made me laugh, and I gave her the kiss I'd been thinking about. Thankfully, the chickens remained safely in their crate until we exited the bus near a busy shopping area.

"That was a close call," she said, wiping her brow, and I laughed again.

Hand in hand, we walked along the side streets observing several newer government buildings and offices.

"That's the administrative center for the country," Lexi said, pointing at a nearby sign. "Looks like it was just built."

"Looks like it," I agreed.

There were several nearby markets and a few local food trucks. Most sold seafood with various types of breads and sodas. I needed coffee and some water, so when I spotted a small café, I suggested to Lexi we sit outside, relax, and sample some of the offerings while people watching.

We stood in line, and I ordered a coffee—long, black, and in the local parlance, while Lexi got a latte. I also bought a serving of poke, a traditional Cook Islands recipe of cooked bananas, milk, arrowroot, and baked sugar, served in a thick coconut cream.

We found a seat outside, and while we shared the poke, I studied the gleaming modern structure diagonally from the café. It looked oddly out of place amid the backdrop of island architecture. To the right of the door were some Chinese characters, probably identifying the purpose of the place.

"Well, that's an eyesore," Lexi observed, following my gaze. "What is it?"

"I think it's a police station." I carved out a piece of poke, sliding it onto my spoon. "I've observed several uniformed officers going in and out."

"I thought we already saw the new police station back toward the airport," she said. "How many police stations do they need to keep the peace in paradise?"

"That's not a Cook Islands police station," I said. "It's a Chinese one. Their flag is flying out front."

"A Chinese police station?" She stared in puzzlement at the flag. "I thought the Cook Islands was self-governing and in some association with New Zealand."

"They are."

"So, why is there a Chinese police station here? What jurisdiction would they have?"

"All really great questions." I sat back, sipping my coffee and eyeing the building. "If I had to guess, I'd presume it was built as an initial gesture of Chinese goodwill. Some kind of international collaboration to bolster the islands' law enforcement capabilities or something like that. It probably also involved the Chinese providing equipment, training, and weapons the Cook Islands couldn't afford to purchase on their own. A totally friendly gesture from a friendly nearby country."

Lexi lowered her shades to look at me. "China? Except we know better."

"We know better," I agreed. "I suspect the Chinese have an entirely different agenda."

"Which is?"

"It's no secret Chinese influence in Southeast Asia has been growing steadily over the past decade. Beijing has invested heavily in infrastructure in the region, which, on the surface, seems beneficial. But there's a darker side to it." I set my cup down, thinking. "I'd bet another plateful of that delicious dessert that station operates with a special degree of autonomy."

"What kind of autonomy?"

"Autonomy similar to an embassy in a foreign country, including control over any Chinese citizens in the area."

Lexi paused, the fork inches from her mouth. "That's crazy. Why would the local government allow that?"

"Hard to say. There could be many reasons. It wouldn't be a stretch for the Chinese to argue it's for the safety and security of any Chinese nationals on the islands. However, it might also be to oversee Chinese businessmen trying to park their assets offshore and away from Mother China's reach. Either way, an agreement like that severely undermines the Cook Islands' sovereignty. If my guess is correct, that would mean the Chinese police station operates independently of local law enforcement agencies."

Lexi let her fork clatter to the plate. "I don't understand

how that would work. How would local police fit into that arrangement?"

I shrugged. "My best guess, a quid pro quo of some kind that bolsters their influence while making the local police force dependent on them."

"Wow. That's sincerely shocking."

"I agree. The newly elected prime minister is in a tough spot. From what I've read, she's lukewarm about the Chinese presence. Educated in the UK and US, she understands the Western perspective and the risk of foreign influence. But she's also aware of the immediate benefits and the pressure from certain factions within her government that are quite supportive of the Chinese."

"You've been reading up on the Cook Islands?" She looked at me suspiciously.

I gave her an easy smile. "Do you know me or not? Any place I go with you, I'm reading, thinking, and planning ahead. Just in case."

She thought about it, conceded my point. "Fair enough, since I did my own research after we agreed to come here. But even given this, you still believe this is one of the safest and most remote and beautiful spots in the world?"

"I do, and that's with all the intelligence at my fingertips. Let the Chinese have their police station. We're on a remote, sleepy little island with exquisite lagoons, volcanic peaks, and dazzling palm-fringed beaches where nothing ever happens. Let's enjoy the peace and quiet."

She reached across the table and took my hand. "Just two geeky castaways on their honeymoon."

A smile touched my lips. "Exactly."

"It's perfect, Slash. I appreciate you doing all the legwork to find this hidden gem. The trip has been flawless so far, other than a runaway pig. So, what's on the honeymoon agenda for tomorrow? A trek to the volcanic mountain top? Snorkeling? A dip in the fancy resort pool?"

I leaned back in my chair, steepling my fingers together. "Jet-skiing."

"Jet-skiing? Why am I not surprised? Of course you'd choose a high-speed activity."

I laughed. "Not just jet-skiing. We'll ski out to an even more remote island, where we'll drink wine, walk the beach, and experience the wonders of a crystal-clear lagoon in utter and complete privacy. We can even go au naturel if you so desire, though I can't guarantee some kayakers won't crash our party."

She snorted. "Au naturel with my pasty white skin? I think I'll pass. However, if we pack lots of suntan lotion, a life vest, my beach hat, and beach shoes, I'm in. And you're driving the Jet Ski."

"Deal." Still smiling, I rose from my chair, holding out a hand to help her up. "And for tonight, I think we'll ask the resort concierge for a recommendation for a nice restaurant in town for dinner and the location of a shop where we can buy some local wine for our excursion tomorrow."

"Perfect. And after dinner?"

"Perhaps a stroll along a moonlit beach or sampling some of the wine while enjoying the view of the ocean from our hot tub. Or both. It's totally up to us, since neither of us has a care in the world, which is exactly the way we wanted it. Just rest and relaxation."

She linked hands with me. "You know, Slash, this is turning out to be the most spectacular honeymoon ever."

"That's the idea."

As we left the café, a couple of women approached the police station waving signs and yelling. Two police officers emerged from inside and yelled at them before grabbing their signs and destroying them.

"Holy crap," Lexi said. "Did you see that?"

"I did." The aggressiveness of the police surprised me. The Chinese were foreigners on the island, and their own police station notwithstanding, they shouldn't have been permitted to assault local citizens. Frowning, I scanned the street but saw no other local police coming to the women's rescue.

People along the street had stopped to watch, as we had. The protesters left without their signs, but still shouting and gesturing at the Chinese police. It appeared many locals sympathized with the women, as they also began yelling and waving their fists. My professional curiosity was piqued by the scene, but we continued with our walk.

Lexi was silent until we reached the next corner. "What do you think that was all about?"

"I'm not sure," I said. "But it looks like all might not be perfect in paradise." I didn't like the fact that my senses were tingling, and my mind had moved from a relaxed state to heightened awareness. I wanted to keep a relaxed appearance for Lexi's sake, but I was already having trouble viewing the situation as a tourist and not a trained professional.

Maybe I was just overreacting and I'd needed this honeymoon more than I thought.

Or maybe...it was something else.

FOURTEEN

Lexi

After strolling around the town for a while, we rode the bus back to the resort. Fortunately, there were no chickens on the bus to give me the willies this time. We lounged around and I spent an entire hour on the beach under a large umbrella in a lounge chair watching the waves and the seabirds. Slash did a lot of swimming and I read a bit, but nothing that involved computers. Instead, the book was a historical thriller set in Egypt. It reminded me of our trip to Egypt and a runaway camel named Arnold, but I quickly shoved that memory out of my mind.

I was on vacation, after all.

There might have been a stretch of time when I napped, but I wasn't sure. It was really nice just to relax. Eventually Slash got out of the ocean and shook droplets of cool water on me as he leaned over to kiss me.

"It's time to get ready for dinner," he said, stretching out a hand. "Unless you want to order room service."

I stood up, shaking the sand off my feet before I slipped

them into my flip-flops. "I'd prefer to go out. I think I've relaxed enough for one day. In fact, if I relax anymore, I'll begin to seep into the webbing of this beach chair."

"That's exactly the idea," he said, grabbing a towel and drying off. "Minus the seeping."

We returned to the room, showered, and opted for a fancy dinner at an upscale seafood restaurant recommended by the concierge. I decided to change into clothing a little nicer to match the occasion. I wore one of the three sundresses Basia picked out for me. This one was white and had a square neck with fancy yellow swirls on it. The dress fell to just below my knees, which I preferred, and I especially liked it because I could wear my favorite white sandals with it. A cropped yellow sweater and yellow earrings in the shape of small flowers were the only extra accessories I agreed to. The dress had a pocket, so I was able to slip my phone into it and leave my purse in the room. After brushing my hair and swiping on some lip gloss, I was ready to go.

Slash shaved and put on a short-sleeved burgundy button-down shirt with black slacks. He looked effortlessly perfect and smelled heavenly with a hint of my favorite cologne. Slash had arranged with the concierge to hire a taxi to take us back into Avarua, so the driver was waiting for us when we got to the front of the resort.

After the short trip back to town, we asked the driver to drop us a few blocks from the restaurant. We wanted to enjoy the evening atmosphere. Hand in hand, we strolled the side streets along the Ara Tapu. The sea breeze rustling the palm trees and the sound of the waves crashing against the beach was the perfect accompaniment to our evening.

As we approached the government center of town,

which we had visited earlier, our peaceful walk was suddenly interrupted by a low, rhythmic chant.

"What's that noise?" I asked, looking at Slash.

He shrugged. "No idea. Maybe some kind of performance?"

Curious, we quickened our pace. The parking lot, which had been busy in the afternoon, was now packed and alive with the buzz of an impassioned crowd. We moved closer to get a better look.

As we approached, I noticed two uniformed Chinese police officers eyeing us carefully from the other side of the street. I nudged Slash, but I could feel him tense, which indicated he was already aware of their presence. I found their presence odd and, for reasons I couldn't explain, unsettling. They weren't directing traffic or working crowd control or anything. Why they were standing there staring just didn't feel right. As we passed them, I noted that most of the locals gave them a wide berth as well.

A makeshift stage had been erected in the center of the parking area. A woman stood on it, her presence commanding the attention of everyone around her. She held a wireless microphone, and there were portable speakers arranged around her. She spoke about social reform for the islands, her words striking a chord with many in the gathered mass. Her strong voice, amplified by the microphone, cut through the air.

"Fellow citizens," she declared in English with a clipped Kiwi accent. "I know I'm new in my post, but I have been appointed to bring change. We must not allow our islands to be swallowed by foreign interests. We should preserve our heritage, our way of life, and our sovereignty."

A roar of support went up from the crowd.

"Gee, I wonder which foreign interest she's referring to," I said to Slash.

He lifted an eyebrow. "I think that police station and those thugs back there speak for themselves."

"No kidding."

"You're wrong," a person yelled from the crowd. "They've helped both the economy and our defense. You don't understand."

Boos went up from several in the crowd, and a small scuffle started in the vicinity of the person who'd expressed an opposing view.

The woman on the platform tried to regain order. "Please, this is a safe space where we can honestly and transparently discuss our issues."

"Then do something about the damn Chinese or get out of our way," another voice yelled from the crowd.

I turned worriedly to Slash. "That doesn't sound good."

He nodded grimly. "Apparently, it's become more of a problem than I expected. Luckily, it's not ours. Let's go." He kept us moving around the periphery of the crowd as the atmosphere grew more tense.

A group of men in sunglasses and uniforms, different from the Chinese, standing at the edge of the crowd, caught my attention. They were watching the woman on the podium intently, their expressions unreadable.

I nudged Slash. "Look over there. You think it's her security?"

"Probably the local police. They're here to make sure this doesn't turn into a disturbance."

"I wonder who the woman is?"

"A politician, most likely."

Slash stopped abruptly, and I bumped into the back of him. "What's wrong?"

I followed his gaze and noticed a man moving through the crowd toward the stage with deliberate intent. He had dark hair tied back in a knot and a large, spiked fish tattooed on his neck. His hand was stuffed in the pocket of his billowy shirt, and when it shifted it a bit, I glimpsed the outline of a gun.

I opened my mouth to say something when Slash released my hand. "Stay here."

He immediately started pushing through the crowd. I watched as he closed in on the jacketed man, who was now only a few feet from the stage.

The man withdrew his hand from beneath his jacket. He had the gun, and as he began to lift it, his gaze fixed firmly on the woman.

"Gun!" I shouted.

Slash was way ahead of me. He lunged at the last second, grabbing the man's wrist and twisting it sharply just as the gun went off, the bullet hitting a corner of the stage. The gun fell to the ground with a thud as screams rose from the crowd and people scattered in panic. Almost simultaneously, the police I'd noticed earlier moved in, tackling Slash and the would-be assailant.

I lost sight of Slash as I tried to avoid being trampled. In the melee, I glanced up at the stage. The woman was clearly shaken and was flanked by a man in a dark suit and a policeman, who was speaking into a radio. Her eyes were wide with shock. The rest of the police swiftly secured the area, and the crowd began to disperse, murmuring anxiously. After a minute, I started making my way to where I'd last seen Slash.

I spotted his dark hair and saw that he was talking to a couple of police officers. The would-be assassin with the fish tattoo had been cuffed and was being dragged away by the local police. Several Chinese police officers had now joined the fray and were clearing the square. I had to avoid two of them as I ran toward Slash.

"Slash," I called out when I got closer. "Are you okay?"

"I'm fine," Slash said as I ran up beside him. "They're just asking me some questions."

"Why are you cuffed?" I asked in outrage. "What's going on?"

"They're just sorting things out."

A burly man with an earpiece and his pistol out stepped between us. "Who are you?"

"I'm Lexi Carmichael. That's my husband, and he just saved that woman up there." I pointed to the stage. "Why is he in cuffs?"

Before he could answer, the woman from the stage and her two guardians approached. Her face was pale, but she seemed steadier on her feet than she had minutes before.

"Thank you," she said to Slash, her voice calm despite the slight tremor of her hands. "You saved my life."

Slash dipped his head slightly. "I'm just glad I was here."

She turned to the burly man with a mustache who stood next to her. "Captain Enoka, please remove the handcuffs from this man. I saw what happened."

"Ma'am, I'm not sure that's a good idea. We have yet to fully interview him."

"There is no need for an interview," she said. "He saved my life, Captain. He took down that man with the gun. If not for him, I wouldn't be standing here. There's no uncertainty about that."

An awkward silence fell over our group. There was obviously some history between the politician and the captain. Nevertheless, though she hadn't said it aloud, the message was clear: Slash had stopped what the captain's men hadn't.

Color crept into his face as the captain nodded at the man standing next to Slash. In seconds, the cuffs were removed from Slash's wrists. Slash came to stand beside me, putting a hand at the small of my back.

The woman extended her hand toward Slash. "I'm sorry for all of this. I'm Petra Askari, the prime minister of the Cook Islands. It's a pleasure to meet you."

Slash took her hand and shook it. "I'm Slash, and this is my wife, Lexi."

"Slash? That is a most interesting name. I'm sure there is quite a story behind it, especially considering the way you dispatched my assailant. Anyway, I'm exceedingly glad to meet you. What brings you to our island?"

"We're presently on our honeymoon," Slash responded. "Quite frankly, we picked your island because we hoped it would be quiet and out of the way. And we needed some time away from any...uh...excitement."

"Well, then, I must apologize for letting you down, but I'm personally grateful you're here. We're also honored you chose our island for such a special occasion. Where are you from?"

"Maryland," he responded. "Not too far from Washington, DC."

"Americans. How delightful. I'm quite familiar with that area, as I attended Georgetown University for one of my doctorates."

"I attended Georgetown University, too." It slipped out before I could stop myself.

"Well, we must compare stories." She turned to Slash. "Are you in security?"

"Computer security," Slash responded and left it at

that. There was no way he would admit he worked for the NSA.

"And you, Lexi?" She looked at me. "What do you do?"

"I'm also in computer security," I said. "Just a couple of geeks looking to get away from it all and spend some quiet time on the beach."

"Brilliant," she said smiling.

The prime minister seemed way more composed than I would have been mere minutes after an assassination attempt. Maybe it was a politician thing, or maybe she was used to getting shot at. How would I know?

She didn't say anything else as she looked us up and down. Her gaze drifted thoughtfully back toward Slash. It didn't take a genius to see she was curious how a computer nerd had skillfully taken down the gunman.

"Well, we really must talk more," she finally said. "As a token of my gratitude, I'd like to invite you both to join me and my family for dinner tomorrow night at my house."

Slash and I looked at each other in surprise. "While that's really kind of you, that won't be necessary," he said.

"Oh, it would be such an honor for me if you would agree," she insisted. "I really would like to thank you, and it's been so long since I've talked to anyone from the Georgetown area. I promise it's the one and only time I'll bother you on your honeymoon. Besides, I can tell you all the best things to do on the island from the vantage point of someone who grew up here. And I assure you, I have the best chef on the island. You'd get a truly authentic Cook Islands meal. It really would mean a lot to me."

I wasn't sure what to say, so I glanced at Slash. He looked conflicted but finally nodded. "Of course, we'd be honored to come to dinner. What time would you like us to arrive?"

"I'll have a driver pick you up wherever you are staying at seven. Would that suit you?"

We agreed and then hammered out the details before the prime minister was whisked away in her car. As the car disappeared, we stood in the now mostly deserted parking lot looking at each other.

"What the heck just happened?" I finally asked.

"There was an assassination attempt on the prime minister."

"And you stopped it."

"And I stopped it," he confirmed. "Just in the nick of time, it seems."

I reached out and lightly touched his shirt near his waist. "Your shirt got ripped. You could have been shot, Slash." My stomach turned at the thought of it. "That police security detail was either wholly inadequate or poorly trained."

"Both, in my opinion."

"Is it normal for the prime minister to gather people in a parking lot to discuss political issues? Couldn't they just use Zoom?"

He shrugged. "This is a small island, or islands, to be exact. Maybe it's a thing. If I remember, her office is only a couple of blocks that way." He pointed in the direction her car had gone.

"Maybe. But she seemed incredibly poised for a woman who was almost assassinated."

"Politicians have tough skins," he said. "Part of the job description these days, I suppose. But I wouldn't recommend she hold another town meeting until she gets her security beefed up or better prepared."

"No kidding. She said she'd been appointed to protect the nation's sovereignty. You think she's anti-Chinese?"

"I certainly got that vibe. I suppose we can ask her tomorrow. But as an aside, I heard one of the officers say the shooter was local. For all we know, he could just have a beef with the government or her in particular."

"True, I guess." But somehow, it didn't feel right. Maybe hanging around Slash for so long, I'd started to get a nose for those things.

I turned to look at the Chinese police station. There were several officers milling around out front of the building, but no one was really doing anything.

"Do you think they'll get any information from the shooter?" I asked. "Like why he targeted her?"

"Hard to say." He slipped an arm around my waist. "But there's one thing I'm sure of. Whatever just happened is *not* going to stop us from having a nice, quiet honeymoon dinner tonight. Let's consider that a one-off, an anomaly, a freak moment in time. At least no one was trying to kill *us*."

He took me by the arm and steered me toward a store. "So, first, we buy a bottle or two of the local wine, as planned. Then, after a fabulous dinner with delicious delicacies, we'll have a lovely barefoot walk on the beach and then drink some delightful wine on our balcony while listening to the sound of the ocean either in or out of the hot tub."

"It sounds really nice, Slash." I leaned my head against his shoulder. "Honestly, that was enough excitement for our entire honeymoon. So, let's keep it quiet and simple from here on out, okay?"

"Fine with me, *cara*."

I lifted my head to look at him. "I just thought of one good thing that did come from this evening—besides no one getting hurt, of course."

"What's that?"

"I don't have to add a new column to my personal black cloud spreadsheet. I already have one for assassination attempts, so there's that."

"Thank God. After adding the pig incident, that spreadsheet is getting out of control."

"You think?" I kicked at a stone. "We really need the universe to stop throwing weird stuff our way."

"We do, indeed. Maybe I need to have a talk with someone about that."

"Maybe you do. Who'd you have in mind?"

He pointed upward with a smile. "Not certain it will do any good, but it's worth a try."

"It's *always* worth a try," I said as we walked into the wine shop hand in hand. "And if anyone has some goodwill there, it'd be you."

"I'm not sure about that, but prayers won't hurt."

"They won't, indeed," I agreed.

FIFTEEN

Lexi

After a quiet and relaxing evening drinking wine in our private hot tub, we got up bright and early to get a start on our day. We picked up the Jet Ski near the pier at our resort in Miri, ready for adventure. North of us, along the east side of the island, were several small islets inside the reef. The young local who rented and checked us out on the Jet Ski recommended we head for the second island, Koromiri, for privacy and a lovely beach.

My first time on a Jet Ski was both terrifying and exhilarating. I sat behind Slash, clutching him so tightly around the middle I wasn't sure he could breathe. Throwing caution to the wind, Slash opened the Jet Ski full throttle, whooping with wild abandon. He reached speeds that would have been illegal if speed limits on a Jet Ski were a thing in the Cook Islands. My hair whipped around and the sea sprayed my face.

I just closed my eyes and held on.

At some point he insisted I drive, so I did. But I kept

taking my hands off the gas when I felt we were going too fast, so there was more whiplash than I would have liked. Still, Slash remained patient and encouraged me to keep trying, cheering when I reached what he considered an acceptable speed. Fortunately, the waves of the lagoon were diminished by the surrounding reef. The ride was smooth, and the water shallow and clear. It was easy to see the bottom as we sped along.

It was about a twenty-minute ride before we reached Koromiri. It was bigger than I expected, with small trees and shrubs and lovely, white sandy beaches. Still, it was more like a sandbar on top of a reef. I didn't mind, because it was completely deserted.

We parked the Jet Ski in a tiny cove on the ocean side and opened our backpacks. Slash pulled out a large beach towel, water, and a bottle of wine, while I got my hat, our lunch, and more suntan lotion out of my bag.

We made ourselves a small picnic, munching on cheese, crackers, salami, and pineapple chunks while drinking one of the most delicious wines I'd ever had.

"Oh my gosh," I said after taking another sip. "I taste banana. In red wine. That's crazy, and yet it's so freaking good."

Slash sipped and considered. "Definitely fruity, but you're right. It's quite tasty and is both light and crisp. This bottle is from the famous Koteka Winery, one of the most well-known wineries in the Cook Islands. They create their wines using bananas, along with grapes, and sometimes whatever fresh fruits are on hand, like mango, pawpaw, yellow-tinged oranges, and the *venevene* fruit."

"What's a *venevene* fruit?"

"They're small dark-purple berries that grow wild on the island, at least according to the store owner last night.

Vene means sweet. So, perhaps, *venevene* means extra sweet?"

I took another sip. "I don't know, and I don't care. I love it so much. I don't know what kind of genius thought bananas would work well in wine, but it's shockingly delicious. I think I've found my new favorite wine. We must buy extra bottles to send to Basia, Elvis, and everyone back home so they can taste this. It's amazing."

"I think we can arrange that," Slash said, smiling and running his hand down my hair. "In fact, the winery is only a few blocks from our resort, according to the store owner. He would, of course, love to sell us more. The winery owner is a relative, and I'm sure he'd show us around the place if we ask."

"That is an excellent plan."

"I'm glad you approve." He brushed some sand off my leg and murmured, "I love to see you relaxed, happy, and even a little tipsy."

I grinned. "Same for you. You seemed to be having a good time on that Jet Ski."

"The best." He leaned over, tipping my chin up so he could see my face clearly under the hat. "Look at us. Both finding happiness and fulfillment, and we're nowhere near computers."

"Imagine that."

He cocked his head. "Hmm...do you hear that?"

I paused and listened. "I don't hear anything."

"Exactly." He smiled, reaching over to rub my nose, probably because I still had a blob of suntan lotion on it. "It's the sound of blessed silence. No one is following us. No one is trying to take our picture. No one is trying to kill us. And no one, including a runaway pig, is ruining our honeymoon. It's just you and me. I'm going to cherish every moment."

"Me, too." I held up my cup, thinking Slash was right—I *was* feeling tipsy. "To us, this island, sweet privacy, and this absolutely stellar wine."

He tapped his plastic cup to mine. "To us and a fabulous, not to mention well-deserved, honeymoon."

"I'll drink even more to that."

We drank the rest of the bottle, then took a tour of our little Pacific hideaway, looking for shells. I found a large and intact sand dollar, which I rinsed off and kept as a souvenir. We spotted dozens of crabs, clams, fish, and especially coral beneath the crystal-clear water. I was struck that I didn't notice the heavy scent of saltwater that I expected from the ocean. Perhaps it was that the next piece of land to our east was over five thousand miles away, or maybe the small amount of seaweed moderated the smell.

As we walked, I reflected on how many of the important moments of my life occurred on or near the beach, starting with meeting the Zimmerman twins. For someone who wasn't a big fan of the water, I was loving every minute. The sun and the sand were hot, but with my beach shoes and floppy hat protecting me, I didn't mind that much.

Eventually we packed up and climbed on the Jet Ski to head back to the resort. I felt reluctant to leave our private oasis, which would be a first for me and the beach.

"Dang it, you're making me like the beach," I said to Slash as I climbed on the Jet Ski behind him. "I feel like ever since I've known you, little by little, you're bringing me into communion with the sand, ocean, and waves."

He laughed. "Ah, *cara*, it's a part of me I want to share with you."

"Well, it's working. I had the best time today."

"Good to know."

We jetted back to the resort and turned in the Jet Ski, deciding we might yet do it again another day.

We had just enough time to shower, change, and head downstairs before the prime minister's car arrived to meet us. Slash had changed into a crisp white shirt and his black slacks, and I wore my favorite sky-blue dress and white sandals. My face was pink from the sun despite having glopped on loads of suntan lotion, and my muscles felt warm and relaxed from a day spent in the fresh air, water, and sunshine.

I pulled my damp hair back into a sleek ponytail at the nape of my neck and added a pair of blue stud earrings instead of my favorite diamond set that Slash had given me over a year ago. I could embrace fashion if I had to.

"It's a good thing Basia picked out my honeymoon wardrobe," I said, checking in the mirror and smoothing down the material of my dress. "She packed three dresses I wouldn't have thought I needed."

"Basia is a gem. Though I suspect she could not have anticipated you'd be having a private meeting with the head of a foreign government. If so, she would have packed more formal wear, or perhaps even a bulletproof vest?"

I rolled my eyes. "Ha-ha. Point made. Regardless, I sure lucked out in the friend department." I glanced down at my engagement ring and wedding band. The blue stone in my ring matched the dress exactly, and somehow that felt right. "And the husband one, too. Still, after wearing this dress, any other fancy events will require recycling one of the three dresses."

"I'm fine with you in no clothes," he said, amused, lifting a dark eyebrow.

"Likewise," I said without hesitation, and we both laughed.

SIXTEEN

Lexi

The sun had already begun to set, casting a golden glow over the island, when our driver, a quiet man in a gray suit, arrived in a dark sedan. He ushered us into the car, and we headed out for the prime minister's house. Her home was on the same side of the island as our resort, so it was less than a ten-minute drive. We tried to engage the driver in conversation, but all we got out of him was one-word answers.

Ara Tapu on this part of the island was regularly lined with green hedges, limiting the view of the houses beyond. As the car slowed to turn off onto a side road, my nerves began to get to me. I'm an introvert by nature, so the thought of meeting with people I didn't know, not to mention a prime minister, was more than a bit daunting. I had hoped that over time, meeting important people would get easier, given my close association with the president of the United States and the pope. But it never did.

Slash, understanding my anxiety, gently squeezed my

hand, reassuring me in a way only he could. Trying to relax, I turned my attention to the view. We passed through several blocks of single-story, concrete houses. At the end of the road, a crushed-shell driveway led off to the left, lined with overhanging trees that hid both the path ahead and the house. The tires crunched on the driveway as we slowly approached the house, emerging back into the waning sunlight onto a circular drive that fronted a two-story, plantation-style house.

The white house with its brown roof had a veranda that ran the entire front. The house was adorned with large windows and a double front door. The bushes around the house were carefully trimmed and reflected a gardener's care and an owner's attention to detail. Behind the house and on the left side were fields of what looked like pineapple. On the other side, the land rose sharply to the green slopes of Te Manga.

The driver pulled up in front of the house and stepped out of the car to open our door. He offered a hand, and I climbed out. Slash followed.

"Welcome," a booming voice said from the house's entrance. A man with rich brown skin and a closely cropped haircut walked over to meet us. He was impeccably dressed in a dark suit and an ocean blue tie.

"I'm Rangi Taufua, personal assistant to Prime Minister Askari," he said, stretching out a hand to us. "It is a pleasure to have you at the house. You honor us tonight by being here. The entire nation is grateful for your actions yesterday, which saved the life of our prime minister."

Slash tried to keep it light. "I'm just happy to have been in the right place at the right time."

"It's no coincidence," Rangi said in a somber tone, shaking Slash's hand and then mine. "It was destiny, I'm sure of it. Now, please, follow me. The prime minister and her family await you."

Slash and I exchanged a glance as we entered the house. I stopped at the threshold, admiring the simple beauty of the interior.

While the house wasn't palatial, it reflected a blend of elegance and cultural richness. Rangi gave us a quick tour as we walked along.

"This house was originally built by a wealthy British businessman and farmer who relocated from New Zealand in the early 1900s. This area had some of the best arable land on the island, and he used it to grow and ship fruits that weren't viable in the colder New Zealand climate. He was successful enough to be appointed the king's representative for the Cook Islands, which were still a part of New Zealand.

"The house turned over several times since then, before Ms. Askari and her family acquired it. They have worked to keep up its heritage on the island."

Polynesian art and sculptures were tastefully displayed, each piece telling a story of the islands' rich heritage. When we reached the dining room, we found the prime minister standing, waiting with her family. A tall man with dark hair and graying sideburns stood beside her, as well as a teenage girl and a young boy. The kids watched us with curious eyes.

"Lexi, Slash, it's so nice to see you again. Thank you for coming." The prime minister stepped forward and greeted us warmly, her smile genuine.

"It's our pleasure, Prime Minister," Slash said. "We hope you didn't go to too much trouble on our behalf."

"Please call me Petra. And this is hardly repayment for saving my life, but I'd like you to meet my husband, Henry, and my children, Leilani, or Lani for short, and Noa, my son."

I had several burning questions on the tip of my tongue. I wanted to ask her about the assassination attempt, including how she was feeling, whether they'd gotten any useful information from the assassin, and if the attempt was related to the Chinese. But I didn't ask because of the kids. I didn't know how much they knew, and discussing the attempted murder of their mother didn't seem appropriate dinner conversation. A glance at Slash and a tiny shake of his head confirmed he, too, had decided now was not the time to bring up the topic. Hopefully there would be an opportunity to discuss later.

"That's a beautiful pin on your lapel," Slash said to Petra, and I followed his gaze to a large, sparkling red, yellow, blue, and white pin. "What does it symbolize?"

She smiled proudly. "It's the coat of arms of the Cook Islands. The blue shield and circle of stars are a part of our flag, with the fifteen stars representing the number of islands we have. The fish to the left of the shield is our famous *maroro*, a flying fish, and it's supporting the *momore taringavaru*, which was a club used by orators during traditional island debates."

She then pointed at what looked like a yellow bird with wings outstretched. "This is the *kakaia*, a small seabird that represents Christianity and is shouldering a red cross. As you can see, the fish and the bird are holding up a yellow banner that reads 'Cook Islands.'"

"What's the fuzzy red ball above the shield?" I asked.

"It's the *pare kura* helmet," she answered. "It's a traditional headdress made of red feathers, and it symbolizes the rank system our island had for many years. It's long been tradition for this pin to be presented to each prime minister of the Cook Islands in a special ceremony and passed down. It is my honor and privilege to wear it."

"It's stunning," I said, and Slash agreed.

We strolled around the room, admiring the paintings on the walls and making some small talk. The decor was lovely and tasteful. A long table was set with exquisite plates and crystal glasses—the centerpiece a vibrant display of tropical flowers. The dinner aroma was intoxicating, a tantalizing mix of local delicacies and fresh island fruits. My stomach growled loudly, and I flushed, making my cheeks even more noticeably red given the sun I'd had today.

Rangi disappeared, and we finally took our seats, me next to Slash, thankfully. My earlier nerves melted a bit in the face of the Askaris' genuine hospitality. As the first course was served, a salad and a lovely white wine, Petra raised her glass in a toast, the flickering candlelight casting a warm glow over the table.

"To new friends," she said.

"To new friends," we echoed, lifting our glasses. The kids lifted their water goblets and the young boy, Noa, gave me a shy smile.

Lani, with her long, dark hair neatly braided and her eyes sparkling with intelligence, leaned forward slightly. "So, what is it like living in the United States?" she asked Slash, her voice a mix of excitement and formality. "Is it as big and busy as it looks on television? Do you get to see celebrities all the time?"

I guessed she was somewhere between twelve and fourteen years of age, and apparently not immune to Slash's charm, because she blushed as she asked the question. Henry, Petra's husband, opened his mouth to say something and then closed it, letting Slash take the reins.

Slash smiled. "It can be very busy, especially in the big

cities like New York or Los Angeles. But there are also many beautiful places that are quiet and peaceful, like our national parks and countryside. But you rarely, if ever, see a Hollywood or music celebrity unless you go to a concert or a Broadway show."

I heard pride in his voice, and it occurred to me he loved his adopted homeland as much as it loved him.

"Really?" She seemed disappointed. "But you have so many magazines about famous people—I was sure that they must be everywhere in the big cities."

"Do you have lots of superheroes?" Noa piped up eagerly. "You know, like in the movies?"

"Not exactly, but we do have a lot of people who do amazing things," Slash responded, clearly amused. "Scientists, doctors, and teachers. They might not wear capes, but they're heroes in their own way."

Lani jumped back in. "Do you have big celebrations like we do here? With lots of food and dancing?"

"We do, especially during holidays like Thanksgiving, Christmas, and the Fourth of July," he said. "There's a lot of food, parades, and sometimes fireworks. But I suspect your celebrations are just as colorful and lively."

Lani smiled, her gaze drifting to the long table filled with local delicacies, from fresh seafood to the famous coconut pie. "We do love our celebrations. And our food."

The conversation remained light, and the meal was every bit as delicious as Petra promised. We ate an island specialty called *ika mata*, which Petra explained was fresh-caught fish marinated in lemon juice and smothered in coconut cream, onions, and chilis. Slash loved the grilled *maroro*, and I particularly enjoyed the steamed taro leaves called *rukau*.

After finishing off the meal with coffee and coconut pie,

the kids were released and ran off to do whatever kids on the Cook Islands did. Curious, I asked Henry, and he told me they were off to play on their cell phones or video games. I guess life with teens and preteens in the Cook Islands was about the same as in the US.

"I'd like to invite you to adjourn to our library for what I promise is an excellent brandy and a few more minutes of engaging conversation," Petra said. "Oh, and I apologize for Lani carrying on about celebrities. She is, as are many young teens, a tabloid and movie fanatic. She's convinced she's destined to meet a famous person and get her picture taken with them—that if she can get a unique photo of a true celebrity and post it on Instagram, it'll go viral and all her dreams will come true."

"But you're the prime minister of a country," I pointed out. "Isn't that famous enough for her?"

"Oh, heavens no," Petra answered. "I'm just her mom, who embarrasses her way too often."

We all laughed and followed her out of the dining room. Once we reached the library, Henry opened the door for us. Just then, the house phone rang, and Henry went to answer it. We used the time to examine the numerous shelves of books. Petra had an extensive collection of history, political science, fiction, and biology titles.

"Are all of these yours?" I asked Petra.

"The biology books, yes. Oh, and the fiction books as well. I love a good mystery. The others belong to my husband. He was a professor in international relations at Oxford before joining me here."

"How interesting," I said. "Is he still teaching?"

Petra laughed. "Unfortunately, no. He's a farmer at heart and will be the first to tell you he likes plants a lot more than students."

We laughed and sank into lovely, overstuffed chairs just as Henry returned.

"The dinner was delicious," Slash said as Henry sat in a chair near his wife. "Thank you for inviting us. I hope you'll share our appreciation with the chef."

"I certainly will," Henry responded. "But I can't help but feel it's a small gesture in comparison for saving my wife's life."

"A life in politics is not for the fainthearted," Slash commented. "I commend you for your service, Prime Minister. How long do you serve before you are up for reelection?"

"Thankfully, I don't have to run for election," she responded. "I'm appointed. I don't know how much you know about our government here, but our constitution is quite different from yours. Our constitution reflects our historical connection as a territory of New Zealand, which was itself a colony of England. When we negotiated our independence from New Zealand in 1965, we retained many close ties to them that are embedded in our constitution. Technically, we're a self-governing country in free association with New Zealand. We're fully responsible for our internal affairs, while New Zealand retains responsibility for external affairs and defense—in consultation with us, of course."

"Fascinating," Slash said, steepling his fingers together. "And quite unique."

"Yes," Petra said. "*Unique* is a good word for it. You might be surprised to know our constitution declares our head of state is the king of New Zealand who, by New Zealand law, is the reigning king or queen of England."

She must have seen the surprised look on my face,

because she nodded. "Yes. Technically, our head of state lives ten thousand miles away."

"How easy is it to get things done with that situation?" I asked, genuinely curious.

"Well, the king appoints the king's representative for the Cook Islands to oversee our government on behalf of the king. Technically, the king's representative is the de facto head of state, though he or she does no actual governing. They just appoint people, like me, the prime minister, to run the executive branch for a five-year term or until the Parliament loses confidence in the government."

"That is an unusual arrangement," Slash said. "How are you accountable to the people?"

"There are two ways. First, I can be removed by the king's representative if he or she decides I'm not looking out for the people's best interests. Second, the prime minister must be an elected member of Parliament to be eligible to be selected prime minister. So, if I'm not reelected to Parliament, or I resign from Parliament, I'm out."

Slash and I sat digesting that information for a bit before I spoke.

"It's hard to get my head around all the restrictions and ramifications of your government," I said. "Given all that, why someone would want to assassinate you?"

Henry leaned forward and spoke quietly. "You must understand that my wife has ruffled a few important feathers. In recent years, a small group of wealthy men have basically traded the key government positions in the Cook Islands of king's representative, prime minister, and deputy prime minister amongst themselves. They would work with their contacts in far-off England to have one of them appointed as the king's representative, who would then appoint the others. When the king's representative's term was up, they'd get one of the others appointed in his place. However, things recently changed, when the new king appointed a woman as the king's representative, and she appointed my wife. That has upset some very entrenched interests, as you may imagine, especially when she selected a new slate of ministers, who have been questioning some prior government commitments."

"Chinese influence," Slash immediately said.

"Yes, that's certainly an important one," Petra responded. "But I also want to know where all the money we're making from the offshore banking is going."

"Don't you have a government finance minister or something like that?" I asked.

"Yes, but it's taking time," Petra responded. "Previous administrations have been quite lax about ensuring our share of the transactions is actually remitted to the government. Trust me, this is a system ripe for corruption, and I'm not going to stand for it."

"Somebody is clearly unhappy with your efforts," Slash commented. "So, what's next?"

"I'm not sure, but let's turn the discussion to more pleasant matters."

We spoke for a few more minutes about inconsequential matters until Henry left, saying he had a few personal matters to which he needed to attend. The prime minister closed the door after him and proceeded to pour us all snifters of brandy.

After she'd given us ours, she took her glass and sat in a chair opposite us. She took a sip and then set her glass down on a coaster. "May I be honest with you? Both of you?" she asked rather abruptly.

I glanced at Slash and saw his left eyebrow raise slightly. "Of course," he said.

"I asked you to come to the library because this room and my office are the only two spots in the islands that I'm certain are bug-free. And I'd like to speak frankly with you."

The fact that she openly suspected her home was being bugged surprised me. But it wasn't my place to ask about it, so I didn't. Instead, I asked, "What would you want to discuss with us?"

She sighed. "I hope you forgive me, but I admit to having a friend, a former intelligence officer in New Zealand, run a check on both of you before dinner tonight, and I can't say I'm surprised at what I found."

SEVENTEEN

Slash

I glanced at Lexi and saw the startled look on her face. I wasn't overly surprised. I'd expected no less, although the prime minister's candid admission indicated a certain level of concern.

"We didn't get very far in our research on you." She dipped her head at me, smiling ruefully. "Which probably means you're just a bit more than just a computer guy. Finding you featured in the *Global Enquirer*, though, is certainly something I didn't expect when we got started."

My surprised expression must have shown, because she chuckled. "Taking down an armed thief solo in a petrol market is quite impressive, although I can't say I'm surprised, since I personally watched you dispatch my potential assassin with minimal effort. There's an Italian connection, however, which is quite intriguing given your high placement in the US government. Overall, what little we did find in our brief search suggests you are a federal employee, most likely with an intelligence agency. But where, and at what level, wasn't readily available. Clearly, your skill at quickly identifying and then taking down the assassin suggests that you are, or have been, in military or intelligence operations at some point. And I'm certain there is much more to you."

She then turned her attention to Lexi. "And you used to work at the National Security Agency, although it looks like you're now with the private sector. More money, I presume. Good for you. Regardless, the fact that the president of the United States and the pope both attended your wedding... well, that speaks for itself."

We said nothing, neither confirming nor denying her presumption.

She sighed. "Look. I apologize for my forwardness, especially after you saved my life, but I'm not going to let this opportunity go to waste. I can't."

"What opportunity?" Lexi finally asked.

The prime minister threaded her fingers together in her lap. "Aside from the fact that I'm unequivocally grateful you were in the right place at the right time for me yesterday, it's not often we have such important American officials on the island." She quickly held up a hand as if to stave off our protest. "Although I genuinely believe you're on your honeymoon and not here in any official capacity. Still, I wouldn't object to you sharing any parts of our conversation this evening with someone in the government you trust. If you felt comfortable doing that."

Lexi glanced at me, letting me take the lead. I wasn't exactly sure where the prime minister was going with this, but I could listen and pass on anything of value to my colleagues in the State Department or CIA.

"We're legitimately here on our honeymoon," I finally confirmed. "We just wanted to get away for a while. Far, far away. That being said, we can listen to whatever you need to say. But first, tell us how you're really doing after yesterday evening's attempt on your life."

She exhaled a deep brief, pressing a hand against her chest. "As best as can be expected, I suppose. I could have died if not for you. My children would be motherless and my husband a widower. It affected me deeply, of course, although I pretend it doesn't for the sake of my family and my people."

"That's completely understandable," I said gently. "But you had no intelligence, no hint, that something like this might happen? Is there an opposition group that opposes you?"

"No opposition group that I know of, and no intelligence something like this was coming, which in itself is worrisome." She closed her eyes for a moment as if recalling the scene. "As a political figure, I recognize citizen dissatisfaction and discontent is part of the job, although we on the Cook Islands are largely peaceful. We don't have a military or internal defense structure, relying only on our local police force for protection and maintaining law and order. But things have been changing in our quiet part of the world for some time now. The government of the Cook Islands, headed by me, has some serious concerns about the Chinese presence on our island. The arrival of the Chinese police here to the Cook Islands a few years ago brought with it more than just training manuals and uniforms to help modernize our own island force, which was the initial agreement signed by my predecessor."

"Isn't New Zealand supposed to perform that role?" I asked.

"Yes, but quite frankly, we're about their lowest funding priority. That means, unfortunately, we get very little of what we need. When we complain, they argue we don't really have any actual external threats and don't require the funding. They often commit to more, but deliver less, year after year. So, when the Chinese came offering to solve our problems, and not asking much, my predecessors jumped at the opportunity."

"What kind of problems?" Lexi asked.

"The Chinese wanted the ability to establish a police station on our island to help protect their citizens who might be visiting the islands."

I let that sink in for a moment. "Protect, in what way? Were they being threatened?"

Petra shook her head. "No, and that's what's strange. We get very few Chinese tourists here. Those we do get are largely businessmen setting up international bank accounts. They also wanted the ability to investigate Chinese citizens who they suspected were breaking the law. I was in Parliament at the time and wasn't enthusiastic about the agreement, but it seemed so little for what they were willing to invest."

"So, what's changed?"

"A lot. They've built themselves a big compound on the south side of the island and have erected a police station of their own in Avarua. You've probably already seen it."

"We have," Lexi confirmed. "But why would they need their own police station?"

"Great question," Petra responded. "They don't. But now, we've discovered some Chinese police officers are arresting Chinese nationals directly within the Cook Islands, bypassing our local jurisdiction entirely. Trust me, that's *not* part of the agreement. Also, their influence seems to be growing, especially over our police force, as they are training our officers, supplying them, and even rewarding them when they assist in their investigations. I feel like our police force now answers to them as much as to us."

"A direct affront to the island's autonomy," I murmured.

"Indeed, it is," Petra said, nodding. "Furthermore, the Chinese appear to be planning to significantly expand transiting goods through the Cook Islands to whitewash their products and get around international tariffs and sanctions. It has been going on for years, but at such a low level it wasn't worth stopping, and it did provide a few extra dollars to the economy. However, the increase has been dramatic, and the money they are tossing around to ensure a permissive business environment here is starting to corrupt our government."

"And such investigations are difficult if your police might be compromised," Slash said.

"Not might be but *are* compromised. It's just a matter of how much. And right now, given the opposition of my predecessors to my investigations, there are very few people in my government I trust fully."

I lifted an eyebrow. "There are vocal supporters of the Chinese on your staff or in Parliament?"

"There are. Definitely in Parliament. I suspect the Chinese are providing campaign funds for some members under the table, and offering key government employees economic benefits, jobs, and bonuses. They do not see, or are paid not to see, what's really happening."

"Bribes," Lexi said.

"In a word, yes. I have evidence of some of it. And it is not just the Chinese. I'm convinced our bankers have long used their money to shield their business practices. Perhaps access to those funds or the ability to move and hide international transactions is of interest to the Chinese as well. It's hard to say right now. But I'm biding my time, being careful, and gathering as much information as possible. I understand the importance of building a case."

She was smart and cautious, and I liked that. "So, in your opinion, what's the Chinese long game?"

"My opinion?" Petra picked up her brandy and took a sip, taking a minute to formulate her answer. "Besides the obvious international trade shenanigans, I think the Chinese are buying support in the United Nations on the cheap. One country, one vote. Islands like ours would be important to them there, especially in the Indonesia/India region. If they got enough government proxies, they could block almost any action against them."

The room fell silent until Lexi spoke up. "Excuse me for asking what may be considered an indelicate question, but since you are in a free association with New Zealand, have you expressed your concerns to them?"

"Of course we have. But we are fifteen very small islands with little influence on the world stage. As it is, I'm walking an exceedingly dangerous path, trying to keep in check a superpower that has already demonstrated its willingness to exert control far beyond its borders. But with a growing divide between those supporting the Chinese, especially among the wealthy, and an active and growing resistance against the Chinese on the rise among many of my poorest people, who see them buying up our land and our heritage, things are getting worrisome. And truthfully, the Chinese and their supporters are beginning to realize I'm not going to be as pliable as my predecessor."

I could well imagine how things were going for her. China had long been trying to strengthen its foothold in the Pacific, and it wouldn't easily abandon its hold on the Cook Islands. Growing local resistance, or a new prime minister sympathetic to the concerns of her people, could jeopardize the country's broader strategic objectives.

"How are you managing it so far?" I asked, truly curious.

She took another sip of her brandy. "As I said, we've been gathering evidence, documenting instances where local law enforcement has been sidelined, and compiling testimonies from those who have experienced the heavy hand of the Chinese officers. My legal team and I are revisiting the agreement, and we are preparing a move to negate the Chinese presence on the island. We've been doing this as discreetly as possible, but I'm concerned the Chinese may be on to us...or particularly me."

I considered a moment. "You think they may be responsible for the attack on you yesterday?"

"Maybe." She shrugged. "It's a hefty accusation, and one I can't make public yet, for obvious reasons. We've been interrogating the gunman, but he hasn't said a word. Literally, he's not talking at all. He's a resident of ours, and he's been in trouble with the law before—disorderly conduct, public drunkenness, petty theft...mostly misdemeanors. It wouldn't be a stretch to imagine he'd been paid or somehow convinced shooting me would be the right thing to do. That's all I've been told...so far."

I heard something in her voice. "So, you suspect the police aren't sharing everything with you?"

"It's just a feeling," she said. "I don't have proof, but my gut is telling me there is more to this than is readily evident."

This had gone farther and deeper than I had expected, and it wasn't in my expertise nor purview, so I finished my brandy and stood, holding out a hand to Lexi to signal the end of the conversation. "Thank you for sharing your concerns with us, Prime Minister, and for a delicious dinner. I honestly don't know if there's anything we can do, and I don't envy your situation, but Lexi and I certainly wish you the best of luck."

Petra stood and held out a hand. "I understand. I'm not sure New Zealand has fully shared our situation and challenges with other countries that have a vested interest in limiting China's influence in the Pacific. I feel it's important for the US to know, especially since we're expecting a consular official to be stationed here soon and things are... well, dynamic. But enough business. I appreciate you listening and understanding my concerns. Please enjoy the rest of your honeymoon, and congratulations on your wedding. I'll have Rangi call your driver to take you back to the resort. If you need anything while you're here, give Rangi a call. He's my right-hand man, and you can trust him with anything."

We shook hands cordially before Rangi appeared. We exchanged contact information at Petra's request, and he led us back to the car.

Lexi glanced at me questioningly as we got into the vehicle, but I shook my head slightly at her, so we rode back to the resort in silence. After thanking our driver, we exited the vehicle at the front of the resort. Lexi headed to the entrance, but I took her hand, pulling her to my side.

"Let's take a moonlit walk on the beach," I said, squeezing her hand.

"Sure," she said.

I didn't speak again until we had removed our shoes and started our stroll down the beach.

"You want to tell me what that was all about?" Lexi said.

"The prime minister is in trouble."

"No kidding. My question is, what exactly are the Chinese doing?"

I looked out over the moonlight reflecting on the dark water. "Expanding their sphere of influence, and not so subtly. The prime minister is right. By providing aid and investments to other small island nations and developing countries, they're securing votes and alliances within the region and the country. The Cook Islands are not the first country in this area where this is happening. It's a strategic move to bolster Chinese claims and presence in the Pacific region. The Cook Islands are just a part of a larger puzzle."

"That's comforting—not. Apparently, however, not everyone on the island is a fan of the Chinese strategic moves. From the protest we saw, the Chinese are facing at least some grassroots resistance from the local communities, as well as the prime minister herself."

I nodded. "Clearly. But opinions seem mixed. Most likely there are some communities that see the immediate benefits of Chinese support. Better infrastructure, job opportunities, and safety. But others, including the prime minister, are rightfully wary of losing their autonomy and becoming too dependent on a foreign power."

"It's a delicate balance."

"It is."

"So, what are we supposed to do?" Lexi asked, stopping to admire the moonlight reflecting off the water. "I guess we're out here talking about it because the Chinese are now most likely monitoring us and might have our hotel room bugged."

I nodded. "Probably not yet, but I expect we will be soon. After I stopped the assassination, followed by our subsequent visit to the prime minister's home, we should assume they'll be quite curious about us. I doubt they are so efficient as to have already bugged our room, but better safe than sorry. I'll do a sweep when we get back. I just wanted you to be careful with what you say."

"Great." She heaved a big sigh. "Do we *ever* get time off?"

I patted her shoulder. "Oh, I assure you, we're *going* to enjoy our honeymoon, *cara*. There's nothing else we can do here—this is a deeply complex and strategic issue that does not fall within our expertise. This kind of issue is left to State Department diplomats, CIA analysts, and long-term strategic planners. Obviously, I can, and will, report what the prime minister told us and, honestly, I think that's all she wanted. But otherwise, this situation is not ours to worry about, for a change."

She looked up at me. "Promise?"

"Promise." I cupped her chin with my hand and kissed her softly on the mouth. "Now, let's finish our moonlit walk and banish any thought of politics and the Chinese from our minds. From here on out, it's all about us and relaxation."

"That works for me," she said, slipping her hand into mine.

In that moment, as we strolled down the beach with the warm water lapping our feet and the stars glistening in the sky, I truly believed what I'd said.

Unfortunately, the universe had other plans for us.

EIGHTEEN

Lexi

The next morning dawned with the promise of another perfect beach day. Sunlight streamed in through the balcony doors as we finally got out of bed.

My mood had significantly improved last night after Slash had conducted a sweep of our hotel room, meticulously checking every corner, lamp, light, and surface for bugs or listening devices. Even though we'd spotted two Chinese police officers in the lobby, they hadn't bothered us, and Slash's trained eye hadn't spotted anything suspicious.

"No bugs, but we have to remain cautious," he'd murmured, pulling me into a hug. "At least while we're in here."

He'd then pulled out his laptop and sent an encrypted message to one of his coworkers telling him what the prime minister had told us. Closing his laptop, he considered our work done, and I felt like I could finally breathe easy. The rest was up to the State Department or the CIA. We could go back to enjoying our honeymoon.

It hadn't exactly set the mood for a romantic evening, but we were exhausted from our busy day anyway, so we quickly fell asleep nestled in each other's arms.

Today was a new day, a restart of what had started out as a magnificent honeymoon. I stretched and walked over to the doors, opening them to the salty, tropical air. I stepped out on the balcony, still in my pajamas, and let the sun warm my cheeks and hair.

A few early beachgoers were already camped out on the sand. But when I looked away from the beach toward the resort, the scene was not as normal. I could see several members of the resort staff and a few guests running around looking panicked. One couple threw their suitcases quickly into the trunk of a car and raced out of the parking lot. Someone ran after them shouting.

That was weird for a place where nothing ever happens.

While Slash was shaving in the bathroom, I picked up my phone to check the weather. Instead, I froze as I saw the news alerts. I tossed my phone on the bed and ran to the television, clicking it on. On the screen, instead of the cheerful weather forecast I expected, I saw scenes of chaos. The television showed several small groups of two to three men herding people off the streets near the government buildings where we'd just been yesterday. A few people were screaming and running in fear while others chanted protests. Oddly, in the middle of it all stood a single policeman, who appeared to be just watching, not interfering in any way.

But what I saw next chilled me to the bone. A man with long, dark hair in a knot at the back of his head and a large fish tattoo with spines stood next to the cop, arms crossed against his chest, a smile on his face as he chatted with the policeman.

Abruptly, the camera pivoted toward the floor, and the broadcast went dead.

"Slash, you'd better get in here quick," I called out.

Slash hurried out of the bathroom with a towel around his waist and patting his cheeks with another just as the television feed resumed. "What's wrong?"

"Something's going on. I just saw the guy who tried to assassinate the prime minister on television. He's not in jail and was talking to a policeman. People are running around in total chaos."

Slash perched on the edge of the bed just as the television feed came back up and the camera zoomed in on a female news anchor, visibly shaken, who looked over her shoulder several times before reading from a script in her hand.

"Ah, we are receiving reports that...um, Prime Minister Petra Askari has resigned," she said. "We urge everyone to remain calm until a new prime minister is installed." She looked as shocked and dazed as we felt.

I ran to the bed and grabbed my phone, checking social media and then the Cook Islands government webpage. "This can't be right," I exclaimed. "The government webpage is down, but the social media posts are offering a confused and conflicting perspective. There's no way she resigned after what she told us last night."

"She didn't," Slash said. "This is a coup."

"A coup?" I repeated. "You've got to be kidding me." I stared at him in shock. "How did we end up in the middle of a freaking coup on our honeymoon?"

"Ask your little black cloud later. We need to get out of here now." He tossed his towel on the bed and pulled on underwear and pants before grabbing his laptop bag and yanking out his computer. He opened it and started tapping on the keyboard.

"What are you doing?" I asked.

"Looking for the next flight out. At the least the internet is still up. Get us packed."

I quickly got dressed and had just started throwing stuff into our suitcases when Slash spoke. "The airport is closed. Temporarily, supposedly, but we're not going anywhere soon."

"So, what are we going to do?" I asked.

A knock at the door jolted us both. Slash and I froze, our eyes locking in a silent, tense exchange. After a long moment, Slash strode to the door, still shirtless, peering through the peephole. He glanced back at me over his shoulder, his expression worried. Without saying a word, he opened the door.

Rangi slipped inside. Slash glanced out, ensuring no one else was around, before closing the door behind him.

"We've got a problem," Rangi said, his voice low and urgent.

"No kidding," I said. "I just saw the prime minister's would-be assassin on television, talking to a policeman. He's not even locked up anymore. What's going on?"

"We're in an extremely dangerous situation," Rangi replied.

"Where's the prime minister?" Slash asked, his tone steady but eyes sharp.

"Safe...for now. The police aren't stopping the armed men in the street who appear to be celebrating the resignation of the prime minister and threatening anyone who isn't agreeing with them. Fortunately, there don't appear to be many of them, but they have guns when very few of the populace do. It's suspicious, to say the least."

"So, the prime minister resigned?" Slash asked.

"Of course not," Rangi said. "They have forcefully taken over the government and the prime minister has gone into hiding."

"Who is *they*, and why aren't the police protecting the prime minister?" I asked, incredulous. In a country without a military, the police were the last line of defense.

"We're not sure who they are yet, and the police is not protecting her at the moment," Rangi said. "Not en masse, anyway. She does have a few trusted police officers, and they're her security...for now. For how long remains to be seen."

I looked at Slash, whose expression seemed inscrutable, although I noticed the tightening of his jaw.

"The rebels have hacked into the media and now control the television, radio, and even several official government social media accounts. I fear her house is next. In fact, I'm surprised they haven't approached her residence yet. They've already arrested some of her allies and are rounding up anyone who is protesting her resignation."

"She shouldn't stay at her home," Slash said. "They know where she is, and if her security isn't sufficient, the rebels will break through in no time."

"She's no longer there," Rangi repeated. "She's safe, but she needs your help. Desperately."

Slash stepped over to the bed, pulling on a shirt and buttoning it up. "That's not possible. We're just tourists here, Rangi. We have no diplomatic immunity, no official capacity, and no way to help you or your country. I'm not sure we'd be allowed to assist even if we *were* here in some official capacity. I'm sorry, but this is a sovereign matter. The US typically doesn't get involved in coups, especially ones where their international security is assured by one of our allies."

"The prime minister is officially requesting aid from the US," Rangi pressed on. "Her communications, personal and official, have been cut off, with the rest of us in the government. But yours hasn't...yet."

"If they control the media, why haven't they taken down the internet yet?" I asked. "Slash was just trying to get us a flight out, and that's how we saw the airport was closed. So, we know it's still working."

"This is just my personal speculation, but I believe they want to project an image of normalcy. My sources tell me Liko Maivia, currently the commissioner of police, is somehow involved. I suspect whoever planned this didn't expect the prime minister to survive or be in any condition to resist after the assassination attempt. They had to quickly move to plan B, and it wasn't very well thought out. I am sure they didn't want to project the image of thugs running around with guns and instead, envisioned a quiet takeover of key locations and a calming message of peaceful change. But they had to act quickly. They might have felt taking down the internet would signify something more than just a peaceful exchange of power. Besides, they need the internet to get their false narrative out to the populace that the prime minister has resigned and they are merely stepping forward to ensure continuity of government."

"Why now?" Slash asked. "Why initiate the coup right now, so soon after the assassination attempt? It seems sloppy."

"I think you interrupted their plan," Rangi replied. "If the prime minister had been assassinated or even incapacitated, these coup plotters would have slid in a new and supposedly 'approved' interim prime minister, and no outcry would have happened."

"You messed up their timetable," I said to Slash. "They had to pivot to stick to their plan. But that doesn't answer why."

"I don't know why," Rangi said, lifting his hands. "Not yet anyway."

"This has the Chinese written all over it," Slash said grimly. "What's the prime minister doing right now and why is she coming to us? Hasn't she contacted officials in New Zealand?"

"She has, not directly, but through intermediaries. The problem is her official email account has been used to falsely notify the New Zealand authorities she has resigned and turned the government over to representatives who will be contacting Wellington shortly. When she gets word to those same officials through unofficial channels that she hasn't resigned, it will put them in a tough spot. For now, they're just waiting to see how this plays out."

"So, right now, the internet staying up seems to be the only thing going for you," Slash said.

"Well, that and you. Again, she's formally asking for you to make the request to the US on her behalf and relay our side of the story."

Slash frowned, running his fingers through his damp hair. His frustration was evident. "I already told them what we talked about last night. This coup, Rangi, is something entirely different. It's way over our heads. Seriously."

"I understand, and in normal circumstances, I would respect that. But at this time, you're the only option she's got. We're just asking you to reach out to your country and let them know she's officially requested assistance. Most importantly, she needs the US to confirm the existence of a coup to the Kiwis."

Slash paused. "Fine. The best I can do is alert the State Department and let them handle it. But as I've already said, they're unlikely to interfere. And even if they wanted to, we don't have any resources on the ground to help. I'm sure the plotters have taken control of the airports on the islands to prevent outside interference."

Rangi exhaled a deep breath. "Would it change things for your State Department if I told you the prime minister has hard evidence that China is behind the coup?"

Slash stopped and then sighed. "It might," he admitted.

"Then—" His sentence was interrupted by loud shouts coming from outside, toward the front of the resort. Rangi cautiously opened the door to the bungalow, leaned out, and swore under his breath. "We must leave. Right now."

"Why, what's happening?" I asked in alarm.

"A car with several armed men just pulled up in front of the hotel and ran inside. I recognized one of them—Moe Tataroa, Maivia's right-hand man. He's little more than a trained thug."

I peeked out the window and saw a bald, burly man in a policeman's uniform standing by the car.

"They're coming for you," Rangi said. "There's no other reason they'd be here right now. You two were seen with the prime minister in the parking lot, and others probably heard her invite you to her house. They've probably already searched the immigration records and know you're Americans. That likely puts you at the top of their friends-of-the-prime-minister list. They'll want to know what she said to you and might even take extra steps to find out...if you know what I mean."

We both knew perfectly well what that meant.

"Right now, they're not sure who you are, or in which bungalow you're staying, so they're likely checking with the hotel staff," Rangi continued. "I'm friends with the resort manager. That's how I got your bungalow number. He'll delay them as much as he can. But I suggest you come with me for your own safety. Immediately."

Alarmed, I looked at Slash. "Should we?"

"It's not like we have much of a choice," Slash replied, his expression grim.

Rangi nodded. "Good. I'll get you out of here safely. Grab your stuff, essentials only, and let's move out."

"What's essential other than the laptop bags?" I asked Slash, grabbing my pajamas and stuffing them into the bag.

"A change of clothes and our toilet kits. Throw them into one of the duffel bags. We'll leave the rest behind for the time being."

"I guess this means I'm not taking any of my fancy dresses, right?"

"No fancy anything," Slash said. "We're in survival mode now."

I walked over to the closet, lightly touching one of the dresses hanging there. "Jeez. If I lose those dresses, Basia is going to kill me."

He shoved his feet into his shoes. "Right now, that's the least of our problems."

"I know," I sighed. "Somehow, it always is."

NINETEEN

Lexi

Rangi led us away from the bungalow, avoiding the main resort building. We walked as nonchalantly as possible, each of us carrying a laptop bag and Slash holding the stuffed duffel as well. We didn't want to run or draw attention to ourselves in any way, so a stroll it was, even as two other couples ran past us looking worried.

It felt like this peaceful, beautiful island was now shrouded with danger.

"Stay calm," Rangi urged us. "We only have one hundred police officers total for all the islands. Even with Chinese help, most of them are surely guarding the airport and the news media at the moment. The rest are scattered, looking for the prime minister. They clearly have hired muscle, but not many, I suspect. Other than the few we just saw out front of the resort building, there shouldn't be any others out here walking the perimeter. They were counting on the element of surprise—not brute force—to capture you."

Slash suddenly stopped. "Wait, that gives me an idea."

"What kind of idea?" Rangi and I asked at the same time.

"Lexi, give me one of your earrings," he said to me, holding out a hand. "Quickly."

I stared at him, dumbfounded. "You want one of my earrings?"

He nodded impatiently. "Yes. I want to track this Moe Tataroa. It may help us determine where he is at any given time, and that could lead us to others."

"Oh, okay," I said, reaching behind my ear to tug one of them off. "I get it. You need a tracking device."

"Exactly."

Rangi stared at us in disbelief during this exchange. "What's going on? I'm not sure what to be in shock about first—that you want to track Moe, or that she's wearing trackable earrings. Who *are* you people?"

"Just two geeks on a honeymoon," Slash said, taking the earring I gave him and dropping his bags at my feet. "Given our current situation, the best defense might just be a good offense. Both of you, stay here. I'll be right back."

He disappeared before Rangi could protest. We moved closer to the shadows of the trees, but I could feel Rangi staring at me.

"Look, it's not what you think," I finally said, lifting my hands. "I have this habit of getting into trouble, and it helps when Slash can track me quickly and efficiently. Think of it as a kind of Find My Phone app, but without the phone part. You know, like Find My Lexi?"

He didn't laugh or comment. Thankfully, Slash returned quickly, relieving the awkward silence.

"I wasn't seen. I put the earring under the mat of the passenger seat of Moe's vehicle," Slash said, retrieving the duffel and his laptop bag. "It may be a long shot, but worth taking if it leads us to where the so-called coup team may be setting up."

Rangi nodded. "Hate to say it, but that was smart, if not dangerous. You could have been caught."

"And yet here I am," Slash said. "Safe and sound."

We picked up the pace and ducked down a path that led to the pool and then swerved onto a sandy path that led away from the hotel and back toward the center of the island. Rangi took the lead, I followed, and Slash brought up the rear.

"How much farther is the car?" I asked.

"It's parked a few more blocks away," Rangi said, glancing over his shoulder.

We crossed a small side road and Rangi quickly ushered us into the shadows until a police car and an open truck with some armed men in the back drove past.

"More thugs," Rangi said in disgust and then motioned for us to continue. "We don't have much time. They'll be back around."

We crossed a few more side streets before arriving at a dark sedan. Rangi opened the door for us, and we climbed in. Slash sat in the passenger seat, and I got into the back.

"Where are we going?" I asked, fastening my seat belt.

"To the prime minister, but not by a direct route, just in case," Rangi answered.

He pulled away from the curb and we headed in the opposite direction of the resort, the prime minister's house, and the capital.

"Hoping to avoid a roadblock?" Slash asked.

"I am," Rangi said. "Not sure how lucky we'll get.

There's essentially one major road on the island, and there are places where there are no side streets; everything just funnels to the Ara Tapu. Those are the logical spots for the roadblocks. I just hope they haven't had time to set up everywhere yet."

We drove slowly for about five minutes before Rangi swore and pulled off to the side of the road. "Roadblock ahead and no way around it."

It was possible to see in the distance the unmistakable flashing of police lights. The sight sent a spike of adrenaline through my veins.

"What are we going to do?" I asked.

"You're going to get in the trunk," Rangi said.

"What?" I exclaimed from the back seat. "The trunk?"

"They could be looking for you, as well as the prime minister," Rangi said. "It's safer that way."

"What about you?" I asked. "Won't they recognize you?"

"You overestimate my popularity," he said. "They won't be looking for me."

Slash had already unbuckled his seat belt. "He's right, *cara*. We can't risk it. Time to play sardines."

I got out of the car just as Rangi swung open the trunk. As I joined the men, I saw it contained a folded umbrella, some empty canvas bags, and the faint aroma of food. Likely Rangi kept his groceries in here while transporting them from the store to home.

"I'm not thrilled about this," I said, but climbed in and made myself as small as possible to make room for Slash. It wasn't easy, because at five foot eleven, I'm far from petite.

Slash got in next, contorting himself tightly into the cramped space. He had to fold himself uncomfortably, his body jammed against mine, his face resting against my cheek. We'd already started to sweat.

"It's a good thing we're married," I joked. "Our positioning is leaving nothing to the imagination."

"I think this brings the phrase *our love is tight* to a new level," he agreed. "Is there anything in the marriage code about trunk intimacy?"

"I'd roll it into the third one—romance and intimacy."

Before Slash could speak, Rangi spoke. "Okay, kids, looks like you're in all the way. With a little luck, we'll get through quickly." He closed the trunk, and we were immediately plunged into a humid darkness.

A minute later, we felt Rangi pull back onto the road and move forward. Soon, we came to a stop but didn't hear Rangi talking to anyone.

"There's probably a queue," Slash murmured against my cheek.

"Probably," I whispered, moisture sliding down my temples.

The car inched forward on and off for a few more minutes. Finally, we heard Rangi call out in a relaxed, conversational tone. "Afternoon, Officer. Enjoying the fine weather?" His voice was light, most likely designed to put the cop at ease.

"Yes, sir. I sure am. Just doing my duty." The officer sounded young, which could work in our favor, unless he was a stickler for the job and checked the trunk. But Rangi was keeping his focus on him.

"What duty is that, Officer?"

"Well, the prime minister has resigned, but she's missing," the officer replied. "We're stopping cars, looking for her. I'm supposed to bring her in if I find her."

"Is that so?" Rangi said, feigning surprise. "So, that's

what this roadblock is for. Hey, I don't know if it means anything, but I just heard on the radio a caravan was spotted on the road not too far behind me. That might be her. In fact, she could be on her way to you right now. Wouldn't that make you the hero of the day if you were the one to find her?"

"Yes, sir. It would."

"Well, good luck to you. I sure hope it's you who finds her. May I proceed? I don't want to be late to work."

There was a pause, and then the officer spoke. "Of course. You're good to go, sir. Keep your eyes peeled, though. If you see or hear anything about the prime minister, you call it in, okay?"

"Will do. Thank you."

We drove for a while longer before Rangi turned off the main road and then pulled over and popped the trunk. "It's safe to come out now."

Slash climbed out and held out a hand to help get me out. I noticed he had a black smudge on his left cheek. I reached to rub it off, but he was already moving, checking out our situation. The car was hidden from the main road by one of the numerous gardenia hedges that lined the streets. We both stretched for a minute, and I got him to hold still long enough to rub the grime off his cheek.

"You look much better now," I said. "Suitably presentable to meet the leader, or perhaps ex-leader, of a foreign country."

"Even if I'm sweating like a pig watching the start of a luau fire?" he quipped.

"Ha. Even then," I assured him.

Rangi drove cautiously for about another quarter mile, eventually pulling off onto a road that turned out to be a really long driveway to a secluded white farmhouse nestled among the trees. The ground crunched loudly beneath us as we drove, the driveway made of sand and shells.

As we got closer to the farmhouse, we could see several outbuildings behind the house and distantly in the fields. There were no visible cars, and the house looked deserted. Rangi pulled up close to the house and stopped the car.

We piled out, and Rangi strode to the front door. He completed a series of knocks on the door until it finally swung open.

A man stood in the doorway holding a rifle pointed at the ground. Rangi waved us forward, and we followed him into the house and past the man with the rifle. The man closed the door behind us, then stayed by the door.

Petra stepped out from the shadows of a small side room, her face a mix of relief and exhaustion. She and Rangi exchanged glances, and then Rangi walked on toward the back of the house.

"You made it," Petra said quietly, coming forward to greet us. "You're safe, thank goodness."

"For now," Slash said. He put an arm around my waist, pulling me close. "Looks like you've got a serious problem on your hands, Prime Minister."

"I do, indeed. More than one, it seems, and I could use your help."

"We'll do what we can," Slash said.

"Thank you. Please, let's head to the kitchen and sit down. Slash, can I get you something to drink? I see you're sweating."

Slash shot me a married look that said, *I told you so*, even as he accepted her offer.

As we followed Petra to the kitchen, I glanced around the house. There weren't many people, and those I could see were talking in hushed voices, some hunched over their cell phones, probably trying to keep track of what was going on. I didn't see her family, but I guessed they were upstairs. I wasn't sure how safe this house was or for how long the prime minister could stay here undetected. The island wasn't that big. It was only a matter of time of time until a house-to-house search would reach this location. And who knew what that would mean for Slash and me.

Right now, the only thing I knew was that our honeymoon had gone from bliss to crisis.

TWENTY

Lexi

We walked into the kitchen, which was quite homey despite our rather dire situation. Cabinets hewn from what was certainly a local wood lined two walls, accentuated by a soft blue-green backsplash made of sea glass. Billowy green curtains hung from the windows, and an enormous wooden table was positioned in the middle of the room. A blue teapot with ocean waves sat on a lazy Susan in the middle of the large wooden table. We sat down at the table, and Petra took a few mugs out of the cabinet and handed them to us just as Rangi walked in.

"I'm just so grateful you're okay," she said. "I can't tell you how reassuring it is that you agreed to come with Rangi."

"It wasn't like we had much of a choice," Slash said.

I could hear the coolness and tightness in his voice. He wasn't happy about this situation, and I didn't blame him. Instead of lounging around on a remote island, we'd been dragged into a coup and led to a safe house where we were now co-conspirators with the fallen prime minister.

How was any of this relaxing? I could just imagine what my friends and family would be thinking when they heard about this. Probably ribbing Slash because he hadn't had the foresight to write an extensive emergency plan for a coup.

"I got there just before the police," Rangi told her. "Tom gave me their bungalow number and I got them out in time. I'm sure he bought us some time with the police, so it all worked out well." He paused for a moment. "As we were leaving, Slash decided it would be useful to track Moe to give us some intel on where the leaders might be assembling. He planted a device right under the mat under the front passenger seat of their vehicle while they were inside the resort lobby. A risky but well-executed and potentially valuable move by just an ordinary IT guy," he stated while giving Slash a long look.

Petra glanced at Slash in surprise. "You had a tracking device on you?"

"It's a long story, but yes." He didn't offer any more information, and Petra didn't ask.

As Rangi filled her in on the rest of our escape, including the roadblock, I poured myself some tea and added three cubes of sugar, stirring vigorously. I offered Slash a cup, but he declined. I passed the pot over to Rangi, who poured himself a cup and took several big sips right away.

"What happened to you, Prime Minister?" Slash asked. "How did this so-called coup go down? How did you manage to get away before you were arrested or captured?"

Petra cupped her hands around the mug. "Well, I was lucky. I got a call late last night from one of my friends who's a policeman. He told me something significant was being planned for this morning. He didn't know the details, but the assassination attempt made us consider the worst possibilities, so we decided to relocate temporarily. Henry, the kids, and I—along with a handful of my security staff—left out the back by way of an old farm road used to haul pineapple to market. It joins some other farm roads south of here. We turned off our phones, went dark, and headed here—a farmhouse that belongs to a good friend of my family's. The family no longer lives on the island full-time but keeps it as a summer home. I check in on it from time to time and knew I'd be safe here, at least temporarily."

She'd been smart to trust the tip about something happening. Now the coup leaders' work would be significantly harder the longer she could stay hidden. But only if she could effectively marshal her forces.

"When did you hear about the coup?" I asked her.

"Early this morning, just before everything broke loose. It all began to make sense. I think they tried to assassinate me to get me out of the way, so they could take over. My police friend contacted me through Rangi to say the police were on their way to my house to arrest me. He was worried and confused. The police were told I had committed a serious crime and, when confronted, I acknowledged said crimes and resigned to the commissioner of police, Liko Maivia. While they were arranging to book me, I somehow managed to escape. He knew it was all untrue, but he wanted to hear it from me directly. Rangi assured him I'd not committed any crimes nor resigned, and that these people were trying to take over the government. My friend told Rangi we had to be careful, as I'm now a wanted person, as are any staff who showed me loyalty."

"You're right about the assassination attempt and the

coup being linked," I said. "I saw the guy who tried to assassinate you on television. He's not in jail—he's roaming free."

She nodded grimly. "I wish I could say I'm surprised."

"Are you still in touch with your police friend?" Slash asked her. "Can he help us?"

"I am, but I doubt he can be of much help other than keeping us informed. I already mentioned, we've turned off all our personal and governmental phones and are working with borrowed phones so we can't be tracked. Fortunately, there are only a few cell towers on the island, so it's hard to directly triangulate a position. Still, better safe than sorry. We wouldn't put it past them to try and ping our phones to reveal our location."

"What's the latest you've heard?" I asked.

Petra paused a moment to take a breath. "Supposedly Parliament has appointed Liko Maivia the interim prime minister. It's ostensibly to maintain order, though neither I, nor any member of Parliament I know, has taken any such vote. But it allows the plotters to claim anyone working against Maivia and the so-called new, legitimate government are really the enemy. The police are supposedly working to restore order against those who are trying to instigate an uprising against Maivia. All untrue and ironic, certainly, since they are the ones instigating a coup."

"This sounds like it was well planned, and not just a spontaneous response to something you said or did," Slash commented.

"I agree completely. Despite the images of a few well-known thugs running loose in the streets, they moved quickly. If we hadn't been warned, I'd have been arrested and my family held hostage to ensure my cooperation. My house manager sent word that the police arrived shortly after dawn and were quite upset neither me nor my family was there. They threatened him, but he stuck to his story that I'd left early to attend some meetings and my family was off visiting friends. They were furious with him and thoroughly searched my home. Eventually, they left, but someone stayed behind to watch my residence."

"And now they've set up roadblocks to find you," I said.

"Apparently. My escape has caused quite a problem for them. Once I realized I was cut off from my official accounts and any means of officially contacting our allies for assistance, I sent Rangi to get you. My security detail also cautiously reached out to some police friends who might still support my government. As we suspected, not everyone likes what's happening, and for most of them, their loyalty must have been suspected, as they were unaware of the plot. They hadn't been assigned any duties and so, with some risk, we asked them to join us here. They've brought their police radios, a few weapons and equipment, so we have at least some idea of what's transpiring. Before I left my house, I reached a few of my associates in the government to warn them, but many didn't answer. I fear some may have already been arrested, including Iona Engu, the king's representative to the Cook Islands. I suspect she'll likely be coerced to support the coup. She has a husband and three teenage children."

We fell silent for a moment, digesting that uncomfortable information.

After a moment, the prime minister continued. "I've been completely cut off from all official and personal channels. Silenced." Her voice was taut with anger. "They're telling people I'm resting and in seclusion while they install their puppet prime minister. But that's *not* what's happening, as you can see."

Slash stroked his chin, thinking. "You've upset their

plans, first by not dying in the assassination attempt and then by eluding arrest. They didn't expect that, either. Now, they must deal with the fact that you're still alive, and they can't coerce you, and you obviously don't intend to be silenced. What about this temporary prime minister they've installed, Liko Maivia? What else can you tell us about him?"

Petra's eyes burned with frustration. "As I mentioned, Maivia is the commissioner of police and a longtime opponent of mine who has been beholden to the old boys' network that has run the island for many years. They kept him around and promoted him because he was easy to manipulate and would look the other way when told. Honestly, he's a fool—the man couldn't organize a village meeting, let alone a coup. He's a pawn—motivated by money, power, and adulation. I suspect the Chinese are pulling the strings."

"Do you have a picture of him?" I asked.

Rangi pulled out a phone from his pocket and typed some commands. He turned his phone around to show us Liko Maivia. He was short, broad-shouldered man with cropped gray hair, round cheeks, caramel-colored skin, and a weak chin. He was dressed in a police uniform, a formal one apparently, because he wore a hat and gloves. It looked like he'd tried to appear fierce in the photo, but his mouth was twisted more in a grimace instead.

After looking at the photo, Slash leaned back in his chair, regarding the prime minister. "If you have proof of Chinese involvement, it could change things on an international scale. What exactly are you referring to in terms of evidence?"

Petra's eyes met his, fierce and unwavering. "There's a compound on this side of the island. We're a small island, only eight miles wide, so it's not that far away. The compound sits on its own, fairly isolated. Two years ago, a company called Signet Investments, purportedly out of Singapore, purchased the compound. It used to be a small luxury resort on the beach. They've been building and fortifying it ever since. Ostensibly, the Chinese police stationed here have leased the compound and added a new building to house them when they're not on duty. The compound is protected by a fence and is presumed to be well guarded. We've done some initial research into Signet Investments, and we're pretty sure it's a front for a Chinese intelligence operation."

"Pretty sure?" I asked, lifting an eyebrow.

"Pretty sure," she repeated. "Unfortunately, we're quite limited in our technical capability, so obtaining the proof against the Chinese is not as easy for us as it may be for you."

Slash glanced at me, and without him saying a word, I knew what he was thinking. I wasn't sure I liked it, but I'd save my argument for a later, more private discussion.

"One of my most trusted men has been surveilling the compound for months," Petra continued. "His name is Manny, and he's a former New Zealand counterintelligence officer who retired here. He does some work for me in his spare time. Apparently, Maivia has been in and out of the compound a half dozen times in the past three weeks. That's not a coincidence. An operation of this scope requires organization, planning, and money. I know we could find the evidence if we could just get into that compound. But even if I get the evidence, I'm still going to need help to get our country back. The Chinese have money and influence, and it's hard to compete with that on our own."

"Even then, it's not that simple," Slash warned.

"I know," Petra said dryly. "Believe me, of all people, I understand the nuances and nature of politics. But the Chinese engineered this to control a sovereign island in a geopolitical struggle with a sphere of influence at stake. If I don't act, they'll destroy everything we've built in the Cook Islands, starting with our independence. They've already tried to silence me—and if we hadn't been warned, they might have already killed me and my family. But they can't stop the truth from coming out—*if* I can get to it."

Her words were resolute and chilling. The safe house suddenly felt stifling, as if the jungle outside was too close, too quiet.

"I'm not sure it makes any difference, but I believe you," Slash said quietly. "I'll contact the State Department and let them know what's going on so they can reach out to your contacts in New Zealand. But it's going to take time, and there are no guarantees. You're dealing with more than just a local uprising. If what you're saying is true, you're essentially declaring war on the Chinese presence here."

"Oh, I'm clear on that part." Petra straightened her shoulders, her expression grim but determined. "But time is the one thing I don't have. They're coming for me. If they silence me, they'll solidify their control over the islands, and eventually the people will believe their lies. I must act now."

We all stared at her, but no one challenged her assertion. She wasn't wrong, and all of us knew it. Outside a strong gust of wind rattled the trees and broke the silence.

"The clock is ticking," she said quietly. "So, let me be clear. I'm not going down without a fight. Unfortunately, that means I cannot guarantee your safety, whether you support me or not. Intellectually, I'm not sure there's a lot you can do to help. We are hunted, have few resources, and limited time. The situation looks hopeless. Still, my instincts tell me you can make a difference. And I *always* trust my instincts."

I exchanged a glance with Slash again, but we said nothing.

Petra leaned forward, her expression grim. "I'm sorry you've been dragged into this of no volition of your own, and on your honeymoon. I understand I have no right to ask this, but I also have no choice. The Cook Islands would be honored if you'd fight with us."

TWENTY-ONE

Slash

A long minute ticked past before I spoke. I didn't see any other options for Lexi and me at this point, which meant if we were going to help the prime minister, we needed to go all in.

"We'll help you," I said. "But we need a place to set up. We have minimal equipment, but we also need a quiet place to think and make some calls I don't want overheard."

Relief spread across her face. "Thank you. I deeply appreciate it. It's pretty rustic here, but we'll find you what you need." She exchanged a glance with Rangi. "Get them a couple of chairs and a table in the back office. Run everyone out of there, if necessary. Can you check and see if Liam has been able to get the hotspot and Wi-Fi equipment we brought set up yet? Make sure you let everyone know we need to give them their privacy, okay? Oh, and see if you can find Manny and get him here. We're going to need him."

"Yes, ma'am." Rangi stood up from the table and motioned to us. "Come with me, please."

Lexi and I followed Rangi to the back of the house to a small home office. There was a desk in one corner with a computer that looked like it was from the 1990s.

"Will this do?" Rangi asked, spreading out his arm.

"If I can unplug that computer and put it elsewhere," I said.

"Of course. Do what you need to do. Is there anything else I can get you? I'll go check on our hotspot status."

"Thanks, that's it for the moment. We'd like the hotspot info and password as soon as you have it. I'll let you know if we need anything else."

Rangi nodded and left the room, closing the door behind him. Before I could unzip my computer bag, Lexi put a hand on my arm.

"Slash, are you sure about this?"

"Not really, but at the moment, it's the only way I have to protect you...us. As soon as I have the information at hand, I'm going to talk to Candace." Candace Kim was the new director of the NSA and my direct boss. She was also a trusted friend. She'd know how to go up the chain so the right people got the information they needed.

"So, we're getting involved," Lexi said.

"We're *already* involved. And at this point, time is of the essence. We're on an island approximately eight miles wide. How long do you think it will take until the Chinese and their police stooges find her...find us? A day or two at the most, even if we move locations, which is something I'd advise the prime minister to do again by this evening. We've been backed into a proverbial corner. It is hard to mount a defense or an offense until we know what we are up against. We need information that leads to action."

I paused, caught the disappointed look on her face, and suddenly knew I was in trouble. My mind quickly searched through reasons for her disapproval, and it didn't take long for me to find it.

Exhaling a deep breath, I shoved a hand through my hair. "I'm sorry. I made a mistake. I should have asked if you agreed with this. I've already violated number two in the marriage code—mutual decision-making."

"Yes, you did," she confirmed. "A decision that involves both of our lives should be made together. But lucky for you, I'm not opposed. I just want to understand your logic and have you talk to me about it before rushing in with a plan."

She was right, so I had to own it. "I don't have any excuse other than I'm not used to mutual decision-making when it comes to fieldwork."

Her expression softened. "I know, and I guess this marriage thing is still new for both of us. But two minds, one decision. That's the way it must be. Compromise is fine, but after a discussion. Having said that, I don't see any other options here, either. And since I trust you implicitly—that's number one in the marriage code—how can I help make the plan work?"

God, I loved her. Really loved her. She could keep me accountable while logically evaluating the information at hand, much like I did. Two like minds. Unless I gave her reason to object—and there were plenty of times I did—she trusted me. I felt the same way about her, which made us perfect for each other. I just needed to work on the *us* part of deciding, even if my decisions were always focused on keeping her safe.

That meant, given her little black cloud's proclivity for getting her into trouble, I'd prepared an emergency disaster plan for our honeymoon...just in case. She hadn't asked, so I hadn't told her about it. However, my plans were based on contingencies for just the two of us and our planned activities. Now here we were surrounded by loads of people who had no idea how hazardous Lexi could be to herself or others. I didn't have time for a full plan rewrite, so I'd have to improvise on ways to keep her safe within my initial disaster plan while including her in key decisions. Marriage was turning out to be a lot harder than I expected, even while it was worth every minute.

I reached up and cupped her cheek. "I love you, *cara*. So very much."

"I love you, too. And the odds are in our favor we'll find something if we can stay ahead of those hunting us. And my gut is telling me—like it's telling you—the Chinese are involved. So, what's our first step?"

"After I talk to Candace, I think we follow the money trail. You agree?"

"I do. But are you sure Candace will support this?"

"Not officially and not yet. She'll need proof, just like everyone else. So, we find the evidence. After that, depending on what we find, it could be a whole different story."

"So, you think this is about the money?"

"No, not just money. A coup seems like an awful bold play. If they were to screw this up, it would have big repercussions on other Chinese ventures in the region. There must be something else driving the timing. Why now?" I paused for a moment, thinking. "Let me call Candace and see what she thinks."

While Lexi continued to set up our computers using our special adapters, I calculated the time zone difference between here and Washington, DC. It was six hours, so it would be midafternoon for Candace. I used a VPN on my phone to call her direct line.

"Candace, it's me," I said as soon as I heard her voice. "We have a situation."

"So, I've heard," she replied, not wasting a beat. "Aren't you supposed to be on your honeymoon?"

So, someone had already appraised her of my earlier call after the dinner with Petra. No surprise there. "Yeah, about that honeymoon..." I let the sentence trail off.

"There's never any time off for you two, is there?" She paused. "How secure is this line?"

"Not much. But it is what is."

"Understood. So, what can I do for you?"

I considered the best way to say it and decided direct was the simplest and most powerful. "Things have progressed dramatically since last night. There's been an uprising that has overthrown the government, and the prime minister reached out to me for help. She's safe for the moment, but she's asking for US assistance. She suspects the coup has foreign support, and I agree with her."

There was a long pause, and I knew I'd caught her off guard. I could imagine the expression on her face and a dark eyebrow lifting just a fraction.

"That's extremely unfortunate. Interesting timing, too, considering we're only just laying the groundwork for a consulate there."

"It's not coincidental," I said.

"No, it's not. Which may account for the accelerated timeline on behalf of our...friends."

"Maybe, but my gut tells me there's something else, too," I said. "So, we're on the same page as to whom we suspect is behind this?"

"We are," she confirmed. "But you know as well as I do,

the State Department's hands are tied without actual evidence."

"Understood. But what if I could get it? The prime minister has been gathering some, and we could possibly help her get more."

"Then you'd have to bring us that evidence," Candace said firmly. "Her word alone isn't enough to swing any real action. However, if you *were* able to find anything that tied this back to our...friends...well, direct intervention in the sovereignty of a state isn't unheard-of, but it's definitely frowned upon internationally, especially when it's a big country versus a small country. The look wouldn't be good internationally, and the State Department would have no choice but to step up. Even if was only in a 'supportive' capacity."

I hadn't expected more than this, but even a 'supportive' capacity would be a significant win for the prime minister. "So, you're saying a little creative digging might make all the difference?"

"It might. Just don't expect any official help while digging. You'll be on your own. If anything goes south, this conversation never happened."

"Understood."

Her voice softened. "Are you sure you want to do this?"

"Right now, I'm up to my neck in this, as unfortunate as that might be. I don't have a choice."

"Then get me the proof, and I'll make sure whoever needs to get it, gets it. Just be careful, okay? You're having one hell of a honeymoon. Hope it isn't as bad as your wedding. That was legendary. Still sorry I missed that."

"Saved yourself some trouble there," I said. "I hope to save you some trouble this time around as well."

"I appreciate you're always looking out for your boss," she joked.

"I like my job and the people I work with. I'd just like a break occasionally when I'm on vacation."

"Trouble does follow you. Be safe, my friend. I mean it."

"I'm on it," I said and hung up with an increased sense of urgency.

TWENTY-TWO

Lexi

I watched as Slash slipped his phone in his pocket and leaned back in his chair with a deep exhale.

"How did it go?" I asked even though I already had a pretty good idea from the side of the conversation I'd heard.

A single lamp illuminated the room, casting shadows across his face. "They need the evidence—no surprise there—so we're going to get it for them."

"Of course we are," I replied. "Starting with me trying to hack into Signet Investments with limited equipment and even more limited bandwidth. It won't be easy."

"It never is, which means we might need a little help from our friends."

"Already ahead of you," I said, straightening in the chair, my fingers already itching for the keyboard. "Just wanted your agreement."

"You have it. The goal is to find out who's pulling the strings and, more importantly, who's funding this effort."

He kept his voice soft, even though the room was empty except for us.

I didn't need him to explain further. I knew if we could determine who was lurking behind the company's glossy facade, we could find our investors. I hadn't tapped even one stroke on the keyboard, and I was already pretty sure that Signet Investments was nothing more than a shell used by the Chinese government to funnel money, people, and equipment into strategic locations. In this case, it was the Cook Islands. That compound had all the makings of a command center.

"And the newly hatched prime minister, Maivia?" I asked, already starting to plan the hack in my head. "You think he's working directly for Beijing?"

"That's what we need to find out," Slash replied. "If we can trace the money back to him, prove this was financed by China, that gives the State Department something they can't ignore. We would need dates, amounts…hell, anything that shows how long this has been in motion and that would give us a chance."

My mind raced. "Okay, so, we go after Signet's finances and Maivia's accounts. Cross-reference the two, find out how deep this goes. If we're lucky, we might get names, timelines, and contacts. I'm assuming that we also ought to try and see if we can access Maivia's email, both official and personal. Ideally, if he's as unsophisticated as Petra said, he might not be too careful or cautious."

"Exactly," he replied, nodding in approval. "But watch your back. If we're right about who's behind this, they'll have eyes everywhere. If they're using their better professionals, we may not be able to get in and may encounter traps if we do. If they can track the inquiries back to this island, it won't take them too long to figure out who we are or why we are looking, and they'll take extra precautions if they discover we're sniffing around their business."

"So why don't we have our team back home go after Signet while I see what I can find locally on Maivia and the compound? That way, if they hit a roadblock, they have more bandwidth and resources. Plus, if they're discovered, it wouldn't be tracked back to the island."

"Sounds like a good strategy."

"All right, I'll contact Elvis and Xavier immediately and let you know when we have anything solid," I said. "But while we're doing that, what's your play?"

Slash stood, running his fingers through his hair. "The compound. The prime minister said she has a guy who ran surveillance on it, Manny. I want him to take me out to see it."

I blinked in surprise. "What for?"

"If we can plant some listening devices in or near the compound, we may be able to get useful information that will either incriminate them or point us in the right direction."

"What? The prime minister said the compound was well guarded, and apparently, aside from the prime minister, right now we're Public Enemy Number One. How wise would it be to literally walk into the lion's den?"

"Her definition of well guarded and mine may be different. I need a firsthand look at that compound, *cara*. Just a look...for now."

I sighed. He was digging in, and I didn't see a win in sight for me. "Is it too much to ask you not to get shot or hurt on our honeymoon? That's not officially in the marriage code, but it should be."

He kissed me on the top of the head. "I won't get shot. I promise."

"When are you planning this surveillance trip?"

"No time like the present. You okay to take things from here?"

"Of course. I'm asking for help from our friends right now." I pushed send on my email request to Elvis and Xavier and leaned back in the uncomfortable chair. "Clearly, we'll need all hands on deck for this one."

Lifting one of my hands from the keyboard, he brought it to his lips. "Your hands are the ones most precious to me." He pressed his mouth to the small scar on the inside of my wrist, letting it linger for an extra beat. Gently, he touched the back of my wedding ring with his thumb. "My wife. *Ti amo.*"

I stood and wrapped my arms around him. "I love you, too, Slash. Be careful. I mean it."

"I will. I fully intend to get back to our honeymoon as soon as possible."

"Ha! And I thought you were the realist and I was the optimist," I said.

He squeezed me for a moment longer. "Guess that means you're rubbing off on me."

TWENTY-THREE

Slash

"Manny," the prime minister began, her voice steady but edged with authority, "I'd like you to meet Slash. His wife, Lexi, is in the back office. They're both helping us, and I want you to assist them however you can, okay?" When he nodded, the prime minister excused herself, leaving us to talk alone.

Manny held out a hand, and I shook it. His grip was firm and his gaze straightforward. He had short hair, cropped military-style and a beard that was peppered with gray. The lines around his blue eyes were deeply carved, and he had a scar above his right eye. I put him at about fifty-seven to sixty years old. He wasn't shy about sizing me up, and for good reason: He knew the prime minister expected help from me, but he had to wonder exactly what that might be. He trusted her, but he didn't trust or even know me.

Yet, when he spoke, I heard no wariness, only curiosity.

"It's always nice to put a face to a man on whom I've done a background investigation."

I raised an eyebrow at his candid admission. "So, you're the former intelligence officer from New Zealand who checked up on us for the prime minister."

"Officially retired," Manny said cheerfully. "I help Petra when I can and when the fishing isn't going as well as expected. You know, there wasn't a lot of information out there on either you or your wife. Only what I could find in open sources and, of course, the *Global Enquirer*, which all good intelligence agencies use to get information on their targets."

I winced at that one, and he responded with a hearty laugh. "Just kidding. So, Tampon Hero, how can I help you help Petra?"

I ignored the dig and got straight to the point. "There's a compound on the island belonging to what you suspect is a Chinese shell company. You've been surveilling it."

Manny didn't flinch at my candor, and in fact, I got a feeling he appreciated it. "I have. In fact, I've had eyes on and off it for months. They've made several modifications and even added what looks like a dormitory, presumably to host their police force. The place is secured with cameras, intermittent patrols, and even an armed guard at the gate. A little peculiar, if you ask me."

"Agreed. The prime minister said she has reason to suspect the Chinese are behind this coup. Since this compound appears to be the focus of their activity, I'd like to see this place for myself. Can you take me?"

Surprise flickered in his eyes. "Now? Travel is likely to be risky."

"I know, but we don't have a lot of time. The prime minister needs hard evidence, and the odds are best we can get it there. I'd like to see the layout and get a sense of the security for myself."

"So, a surveillance mission," Manny mused. "And after that?"

"After that, we discuss my plan to penetrate the compound."

I'd surprised him again. I could see it in his eyes. Manny remained quiet for a moment, clearly weighing my request. He was a careful, thoughtful man, and I liked that.

"Let me make sure I understand this," Manny said. "You want to break into a guarded compound owned by the Chinese?"

"First, I want to surveil it. But breaking in is the direction I'm leaning, yes."

Many narrowed his eyes. "I assume that this falls under skills you just happen to possess from your...ah, cybersecurity training. You do realize if you're caught, I won't be able to help you, and neither will the prime minister."

I met his gaze evenly. "I possess the necessary skills, and I also understand the consequences if I'm caught."

He regarded me for a long moment, presumably to determine if I was completely out of my mind, before he decided. "Okay, but I don't have much equipment to offer you for this excursion."

I appreciated I didn't have to argue further with him. "Show me what you've got, and I'll make the plan work around it."

He'd agreed to help, but I could still see the doubt in his eyes. I needed him to be on my side, so I decided to be direct with him. "Look, Manny, I can't say I'm enthusiastic about the idea of breaking in and maybe I won't have to, but I don't see any alternatives to help the prime minister end this coup in the limited time we have. I also expect to have some assistance in dealing with the cameras and alarms, so I'm not going in blind. But I'm open to any better recommendations."

Manny sighed. "Breaking into that compound is bloody mental, but at this point, I don't see how we can stay on the sidelines any longer. They've played their hand, so we need to play ours. I've got nothing better to suggest." He jerked his thumb toward the door. "You ready to check out my equipment?"

"I am," I replied. "Any schematics or drawings you could provide of the compound would also be helpful."

"I've got some of those, too. I'm also in possession of a nice set of lockpicks. Just to be clear, I acquired them legally, with the only requirement being I use them for legal purposes only. Might we be using these for legal purposes?"

"Very legal," I responded. "Authorized by the prime minister herself."

"Excellent. I'm glad we're clear on that. Will you be requiring any training on their use?"

"Probably not, but a little refresher wouldn't hurt. Let's get to it, then."

Manny nodded. "Hell, yes. We're running out of time."

LEXI

I SAT HUNCHED over my laptop in the dimly lit room, worried about Slash, worried about the prime minister and her family, and worried if we'd be able to amass enough proof to get the US government to help. It was a stretch, and both Slash and I knew it. I glanced at the fading wallpaper, feeling like the walls were closing in around me.

I pushed my concerns aside, typed some commands, and sat back in my chair. Elvis had seen my encrypted message and request, and I was just awaiting his reply.

Finally, a message came through.

"A COUP? You're kidding me. Ha, ha. Good one, Lexi."

I sighed as I typed my response.

"I wish I were kidding. Somehow, we're up to our necks in an extremely tense situation. Slash unexpectedly prevented an assassination attempt on the legit prime minister and now the coup leaders think we're on her side. So, by default, we are."

A full two minutes passed before I got a response. *"THIS HAPPENED ON YOUR HONEYMOON? Seriously? The odds of this are…crazy astronomical. You know that, right?*

The fact that Elvis was expressing his feelings in capital letters—which he never did—indicated he was completely freaking out. Plus, he was talking about the odds, and that exercise seemed counterproductive to my current situation. Now my anxiety was going through the roof when I needed to be calm and focused.

"You don't have to quote the odds to me," I typed. *"I'm fully aware of them. Is Xavier there with you?"*

"He's looking over my shoulder. Sorry, I got off track there. It's just a bit of a shock if you know what I mean. A coup on a remote island where you just happen to be honeymooning. That's just kismet to the extreme. But enough on that. What can we do to help?"

Wasn't that the question of the hour? His response pulled me back from the edge. I took a minute to gather my thoughts about how to best outline the plan of action so they could adequately support us. But first I had to give them the overview.

"Here's the situation. We're in the Cook Islands, on the run from the coup leaders, and holed up with the prime minister. The leader of the coup is the commissioner of police for the islands, a Liko Maivia. It's doubtful the US government or New Zealand will intercede in any way if it's just a local change of power. However, the prime minister believes the coup is being sponsored and supported by China, using Maivia as a manipulated front man. We're seeking evidence to prove that and encourage support to the ousted government, thereby thwarting the Chinese. We need proof that Maivia is on the Chinese payroll or emails that confirm financial or other kinds of agreements between them."

There was a long pause between the time I sent the message and I responded. I wasn't sure if it was due to bandwidth issues or Elvis and Xavier needed time to process what I'd just unloaded on them. Probably both. Finally, Elvis responded.

"The Cook Islands? Guess you guys really did go remote. Unfortunately, it looks like you didn't get two tickets to paradise. Sigh. So, China is up to something again? Why am I not surprised? Let us know the plan—we're ready."

A wave of relief swept over me. I hadn't doubted they would help—it was just a comfort to know they had our backs. There was no one in the world I trusted more to do what Slash and I needed them to do. I exhaled a deep breath and outlined the initial plan.

"I need you two to follow the money. The Chinese have a compound on Rarotonga that houses the Chinese police and officials stationed here. The compound was purchased by a

company that we believe is a front for the Chinese, called Signet Investments. We think it's the command center for orchestrating the coup. I'm sending now what information I've found so far on the compound. We need to go as deep as we can on this."

I attached the file containing the information I'd compiled so far and sent it to them. It would likely take several minutes to arrive, so I continued the discussion.

"While you do that, I'm going after Maivia's social media, email accounts, and whatever I can find. Hopefully, between all of us, we can find the connection that shows their hand in the coup. I have limited bandwidth and am reluctant to tackle the higher-end security at the Chinese front company. If you can get in, you'll need someone who can read and write Mandarin. I believe Angel's friend Frankie is fluent, so you might reach out to her. Please be careful, we don't want the Chinese to know we're on to them and trace the probes back to us."

"Got it," Elvis responded. *"We'll reach out to Angel and Frankie. And we'll cover our tracks. We know how to handle the Chinese.*

"You certainly do," I typed. *"I almost envy you the hack. But we are pressed for time. Slash and I are being actively hunted by coup forces. The island is small, and we can't hide for long, so we need everything you can get us as quickly as you can."*

"Understood. What's Slash doing?"

"Surveilling the compound and seeing what he can do from that end." I glanced again at the stained wallpaper, worrying about Slash. I hated when we had to work apart.

Rough activity for a honeymoon," Elvis replied. *"Anything else?*

My fingers hovered over the keyboard as I went through the steps in my head one more time to make sure I hadn't forgotten anything.

"Nothing else, just that the situation is very dynamic. Please have someone always monitoring communications. I have no idea what other help we may need, but when we do, we'll need it immediately. I'm sorry to put such demands on you all."

It took a bit longer before Elvis answered, so I stood up and paced the room while I waited. Finally, I heard the incoming chime of his response. *"Don't be sorry for even a second. We haven't had this much fun since your wedding. A whole three weeks of a boring, quiet existence. We should have known."*

I wasn't sure if I should roll my eyes or laugh. I laughed because it was better than crying.

"Thanks, guys. If you find anything relevant, also take it to NSA as soon as possible. I'll give you an email where you can send the stuff. An accumulation of materials is key. The government needs proof, so we are going to give it to them. We will expose this."

"Damn right, we will," Elvis replied. *"Just check in when you can. And, Lexi, stay safe, okay?"*

Like he had to tell me that. Of course staying safe was paramount at the moment, it just wasn't going to be as easy as it sounded. Still, I wanted to sound confident. *"Trust me, guys, that's the plan. No worries on that front.*

"ALL the worries on that front. We know you."

He had a point, but no sense in getting everyone any more worried or riled up than they already were. After a moment, I typed back.

"I'll be extra careful. Talk to you soon."

I logged off and sat for a moment in the stillness of the room. I could make all the promises I wanted, but there was no way I could predict what would happen next. The clock was ticking toward midnight, and Slash and I were betting our lives we could live to fight another day.

TWENTY-FOUR

Slash

The air buzzed with the chatter of insects, and the occasional screech of a bird cut through the humidity. We were close enough to the sea to smell the salt in the air and hear the crash of the waves on the beach.

I adjusted the high-powered binoculars and focused on the compound. It had taken us about forty-five minutes to get into position, including a stroll down the southern beach of the island leading to the compound. We were finally in a safe spot on a small rise to the east, partially sheltered by trees where we could look down into the compound.

The Pacific sun burned against the nondescript gray walls—hurricane-proof, as noted on Manny's drawings. I spotted one man wandering lazily from the gate area, his path predictable and shoulders slouched. He was likely the guard stationed at the gate. I didn't see a sophisticated comm unit on him, just a walkie-talkie on a belt. There were no other patrols. The roofline was empty, and I didn't see evidence of dogs. Whoever was in that compound didn't appear to be expecting company. All of which worked in our favor.

"One guard," Manny muttered, also looking through binoculars and shaking his head. "He's barely paying attention. You'd think he were guarding a luxury spa, not...whatever this is."

"That's the point," I replied, not looking away from the compound. "They're banking on appearances. They are trying to find the right balance between fortress and private residence. They obviously don't want to advertise that they're an armed compound, but clearly, they're protecting something inside."

Manny nodded, glancing back at the rise. "In the past, they've had three, even four sentries, though I can't imagine why. Maybe they had a high-level visitor. Way too many armed guards for just a private residence, which is how it drew our attention in the first place. But apparently they're stretched thin supporting the coup, maintaining civil order, and searching for the prime minister. My guess is they're mostly out securing the airfield, television stations, and other high-value sites like the power plant and telecommunications switching center. By the way, Liko Maivia—the new coup leader—has been here before."

I lowered the binoculars. "You've actually seen him here yourself?"

"I have. Three times in the past two weeks and eleven times total since I started surveilling six months ago," Manny said. "He's probably been here a lot more than that. Since the prime minister doesn't have a counterintelligence office—it's essentially just me doing some work for her—I couldn't blanket this place 24-7. I can give you the video and the list of times and corresponding dates I saw him here, along with everyone else I recorded going in and out of the compound over the past six months. Maivia always came after dark and left before dawn. He thinks he's being discreet, but he's as dumb as a sack of pineapples. It's no wonder the Chinese picked him as the so-called face of the rebellion. He's about as pliable as you can get."

It was encouraging that Manny had useful intel. "Do you have summaries of the important names who have visited and your analysis?"

"Sure. I provided weekly summaries to the prime minister. I don't have printed copies, but I can bring up or send you what I have."

"That would be useful. How accurate are the locations and purposes of rooms inside?" I asked.

Manny shrugged. "Pretty good. They've been verified by my cousin, who makes weekly deliveries to the kitchen and has been around most of the first floor. The second-floor rooms are also likely to be fairly accurate in layout—I got the blueprints from the contractor who filed them when he modified the compound three years ago, so I'm reasonably confident in the floor plan. The upper rooms on the east side near us must be rarely used, as I hardly ever see any lights there."

I nodded, thinking. "Changing subjects, when would you say is potentially the best time to break into this place?"

Manny considered for a moment. "Probably before the shift change, which occurs at eight o'clock in the morning. So, somewhere between six and seven would be best. It's mostly quiet and there aren't a lot of people up and about yet. The outgoing shift will be tired and possibly inattentive. You'd have the best chance of slipping in and out at that point."

I nodded. It made sense. "What else have you seen that raised any questions in your mind?"

"Not a lot," Manny said. "Just a gut feeling and the fact that a lot of Chinese caravans and cars we've traced back to the police go in and out of this place on a regular basis."

"Ah, that reminds me." I pulled out my phone, called up an app, and waited for it to load. "Well, look at that." I angled my phone toward Manny. "Our friend Moe, who is supposedly Maivia's right-hand man, is currently parked at the compound." I glanced back at the compound through the binoculars. "I don't see the truck, but it could be parked in the back."

"Yeah, Rangi told me you planted a tracker on his car. Bloody ballsy, that was. It's something a good counterintelligence officer might do."

I shrugged. "Or just a regular guy with a good idea. It made sense at the time."

"I bet it did."

I took my phone and snapped several photos of the compound. No one had entered or left since we'd been here. "Have you ever seen them together—Maivia and the Chinese?"

"Sure. I've got several long-lens photos taken through a window."

"This keeps getting better. Which window?"

Manny took the binoculars and trained them on a window and then handed the binoculars to me. "That one. According to my cousin, it's a conference room of some kind."

I adjusted the view to the bottom floor, left side of the house, second window from the back. I studied the window but couldn't see inside. Instead, I zoomed in on one of the security cameras situated on top of the wall at the nearest corner. I could see an orange logo of some sort on the side of the camera.

"I'm going to need to get closer to the compound so I can get a better look at that camera on the wall," I said. "I think if I can get into position by those bushes over there, I should be close enough. What is the best way to get there?"

"No need to risk it. I can tell you whatever you need to know. I recognize the camera from here."

"Great. Who's the manufacturer?"

"It a company called Supra Vision Technology, LLC. It's a pretty popular brand here on the island. Chinese-made...like everything else. Not the highest end, but reliable. We use them on most of our government buildings."

"Good to know. Stand by for a minute." I pressed Lexi's number on my phone, and after two rings, she picked up.

"Hi. How's it going?"

"Fine. I need you to stop what you're doing and pull up everything you can find on a Chinese security camera company called Supra Vision Technology, LLC, and their products. The compound is using them as their security camera of choice. It would be a big help if we could take them down at the right time."

"Ok. Any indication if they are wired or Wi-Fi?"

"Can't tell from this distance, but I'm hoping your research will let us know. Probably wireless."

"Definitely wireless," Manny interjected. "Sorry to eavesdrop, but while the cameras are powered by cords, the communications are wireless."

"That checks with what their product catalog shows," Lexi added. "I just pulled them up. Almost all their models are Wi-Fi enabled, though a few of the high-end models can be configured wired or wireless."

"That helps, thanks. I just need to know if we can

detect their network from outside the fence. Lexi, I'm going to get closer to the compound and see if I can detect their network. If so, I'm going to connect you to my laptop so you can see what the system looks like."

"Remind me again why you need the cameras down?" she asked.

"I'd like to get inside the compound to plant some recording devices."

She was silent for a moment. "Inside the grounds or inside the compound?" Her voice was cautious.

"Potentially both. We can discuss in greater detail when I get back, okay?"

She was silent, which meant she wasn't necessarily in agreement, but she hadn't said no, either. I wasn't sure if that was progress or not in terms of shared operational and marital decision-making. For now, she said, "We'll discuss. Ping me when you're ready to network." She clicked off.

I slipped my phone in my pocket and looked up to see Manny staring at me. "What?" I asked.

"So, what did you do?"

I was baffled by his question. "What do you mean?"

"Her voice was tight. That's the tone my missus used when I was in trouble."

"I'm not in trouble," I said. At least, I hoped I wasn't.

"If you say so," Manny replied. "But I'd be prepared if I were you."

"Prepared for what?"

"The talk."

I lifted an eyebrow, feeling slightly attacked. "You said your missus *used* that tone on you," I said. "So, she doesn't use it anymore?"

"No, she doesn't." Manny looked down at the ground,

scuffed his foot a bit. "She, ah, passed seven years ago. Cancer."

It hit me like a fist in the gut, making me feel like an idiot. "I'm sorry to hear that, Manny."

"It's okay. She went out on her own terms. But here's some unsolicited advice from an old married guy: Don't ignore or wish that tone away. Face it like a man. You didn't tell her you'd decided to break into the compound itself, did you?"

I had to give it to him, he got straight to the point. I wavered between telling him to mind his own business and listening to him, and finally decided on the latter. "Not exactly...I needed to surveil the outside first," I admitted. "But I appreciate the advice. This married thing is new for me...for us."

He clapped a hand on my shoulder. "There's no actual playbook, son. It's a dance for the rest of your life. But your particular situation takes the relationship to another level. It must be tough working in the field with someone you love."

"We're not working in the field," I said and then amended. "Well, maybe in this case...we are."

"You are." Manny stared at me thoughtfully. "And you might do it again in the future. So, work it out now. Are you guys really hackers? I thought it was a cover story and you're just CIA."

"We're computer security experts," I confirmed.

"For the CIA."

"Not for the CIA, Manny."

He held up his hands. "Okay, fine. It's your story, so whatever. Just explain to me how you're going to connect your laptop to her computer without a cell connection."

"My laptop has some special features built into it, including a high-end cellular capability."

"Sweet," he said. "Where did you get it? I wouldn't mind having a laptop like that."

"It was provided to me with certain modifications I personally requested," I said. "I doubt you could buy it at a store."

"Aha. That's because it's super-secret CIA spy equipment."

"It's not spy equipment," I said because it was the truth. This was my personal computer, not my work one, and I'd paid for everything I'd done to it. But he wasn't far off in terms of being similar to one that might be designed for an in-the-field operative. Still, he'd broken the tension—maybe that was his goal all along—and I chuckled as he gave me a lopsided grin and motioned for me to follow him.

We started moving down from the rise on the far side to prevent being seen by anyone from the compound. We headed to the beach and then back up toward the compound behind a screen of thick bushes and trees.

"We'll be exposed if a camera is mounted on one of those trees looking our way," I said.

"I don't think there's anything there," Manny responded. "I've been down here many times, and there's never been a response from their security."

"That's good news."

Once we reached the bushes with the palm trees looming over our heads, we found a tiny clearing in the foliage and crouched down. I pulled out my laptop and called Lexi. She instinctively knew to use text instead of voice as I shared my screen and typed a message.

"I'm approximately 50 feet from the camera and am picking up three Wi-Fi networks."

There was a long pause before she responded. *"Okay, I see them. One is much weaker, so I'm suspecting another source, perhaps a router from the police dormitory on the far side of the main building."*

"Agreed."

"It could be either of the remaining two," she typed. *"We must know for sure, however, as I won't have time to waste hacking the wrong network."*

"Stand by."

I opened my network-scanning tools. I could detect the presence of multiple transmitting devices nearby. I wasn't sure which one was the camera near us, or which network it was on.

"Manny, I need you to creep up closer to the camera and toss something into its field of view on my signal and then come back here. Make sure you aren't seen."

"Easy for you to say. How big an item do you need me to throw, and how close to the camera do I have to be?"

I considered. "Toss a rock or shell over the fence about ten feet or so in front of the camera."

"You're going to have to speak to me in meters, mate," Manny said.

"Oh, sorry, force of habit," I replied. "Three meters."

Manny nodded and moved into position, picking up a rock on the way. He gave me a thumbs-up and tossed the rock.

It bounced off the top of the fence and into the compound. Simultaneously, I could see one of the signals I was monitoring jump.

Perfect.

Seconds later, Manny was back at my side. "Did it work?"

I nodded, watching the network signals, when one of the networks flashed additional traffic. Through the leaves I could make out the camera slowly searching for the source of the disturbance.

"Freeze," I breathed.

While Manny and I froze, I could see a text ping in from Lexi.

"Got it. Network #2. If you can wait a few minutes longer, it will help me get a head start on hacking in tomorrow."

I didn't respond for several minutes until the camera swiveled back to its original position and the operator determined it was a false alarm.

"You can move now," I said to Manny, and he breathed a sigh of relief.

"That was way too bloody close," he said.

I texted Lexi to see if she'd gotten what she needed. When she answered in the affirmative, I closed my laptop and stuffed it into my backpack.

"Let's go," I said to Manny.

We carefully made our way back to the beach and headed toward the farmhouse. Manny, who had been relatively quiet since we left the compound, finally spoke up.

"So, what's the plan for tomorrow?"

"If Lexi agrees—and apparently it's critical I get her input—we head back to the farmhouse and get some food, sleep, and the recording devices," I replied. "We return with everything before dawn. After that, it's simple: Lexi hacks the network and takes the security cameras down. Once she does that, I'll go in and plant those recording devices and get out."

"How long will it take her to hack into the network?"

"We'll get here early so she has at least an hour before the preferred time to enter, but I doubt it will take her that long."

"She can do that all that in such a short time?" Manny said, looking stunned.

"She can."

"Damn, that's bloody impressive."

"She's very, very good at her work," I said.

"Apparently. Let's just hope she agrees with your plan. It's a whole different world today than when I was in the New Zealand intelligence service. The technology is crazy." He shook his head in disbelief. "Okay, then, where do you intend to place the recorders once your brilliant wife helps you get into the compound by compromising the security cameras?"

"Right now, I'm leaning toward putting one in the conference room where you saw Maivia speaking with some Chinese officials. Where do you think the other one should go?"

Manny thought it over. "I'd say the chief of staff's office. Locally, he's the top Chinese guy. His boss is here occasionally, but not often, as he comes and goes as he pleases. Everything runs through the chief of staff, so that seems like the best spot to get our evidence. Speaking of the boss, given what's going on, my bet is we'll see him soon, too, if he's not already here."

"You don't know if he's here or not?" I asked, puzzled.

"I don't," Manny said. "The Chinese police handle all his travels, not the local island custom officers."

I stopped in my tracks, staring at him in surprise. "Are you kidding me? Is that true of all Chinese nationals or just him?"

"All Chinese nationals," he confirmed. "And yeah, the Chinese could, and probably have, set up quite a smuggling operation through our islands to avoid sanctions and scrutiny. That's initially what the prime minister wanted me to investigate when I started my surveillance here six months ago. Obviously, it's now a lot more than that."

That was a pretty big chunk of information, so I took a moment to digest it.

"Slash, you understand this operation is not going to be easy," Manny said. "These recording devices are old and aren't like the fancy bugs you are probably used to working with. They're just mini recording devices with no transmission capability. That means not only will you have to break in to plant them, but you'll also have to break in a second time to retrieve them. And, by the way, those devices are Chinese-made, too."

"Well, that's about as far from an ideal situation as we can get," I admitted. "But you intended at some point to plant those recorders yourself, didn't you? What was your plan?"

"My cousin Ari," Manny said. "He owns the grocery store that delivers food to the compound every Tuesday and Friday," he said. "At some point I was going to go along on a delivery and see what I could get planted. We could have potentially used that to get you into the compound, but tomorrow is Monday, and I have a feeling we don't have a full day to wait."

"We don't," I agreed. "But we could use the delivery option to retrieve the devices. Either way, we'll have to work with what we've got and keep things as simple as possible."

"Simple?" Manny echoed. "There's nothing simple about any of this. This isn't some locked office door in New York City. Breaking into the compound is just the first step. Then you need to avoid detection while you find your way to the locations where you want to plant the recorders. Doors may be locked, and while the guards might be sloppy, they do have guns. Furthermore, it would only take one bit of bad luck, a person in the wrong spot at the wrong time, and you're caught."

"They won't be expecting anyone to try to break in," I countered calmly. "That's their weakness. They're complacent. Even if their security team was half-competent—which I don't think they are—they'd have a plan to sweep for bugs regularly. At least these mini recorders won't set off the equipment, so that's a plus for us."

Manny folded his arms, studying me. "You've got confidence, I'll give you that. But if they catch you, there's no embassy here to bail you out."

"Good thing they won't catch me, then."

Manny snorted and shook his head. "Who exactly are you again?"

"Just a guy on his honeymoon in an unfortunate situation."

Manny sighed. "Fine. Don't tell me. But if this goes south, I'm not writing your eulogy. I'm terrible with words."

"Deal," I said, putting the binoculars to my eyes again. "I hate funerals anyway."

TWENTY-FIVE

Lexi

I felt relieved knowing that Slash was on his way back from the compound. It would be interesting to hear his overall assessment of the compound's security, although from our brief conversation it was clear he'd already made up his mind to break into it. I intended to challenge him on that decision, so we'd see where that went.

While Slash was gone, I'd been busy looking into Maivia's online presence. Frankly, it wasn't much. He had a couple of social media accounts, but they were largely dormant, except for some postings by citizens over the past few hours who were not thrilled with their new interim prime minister. Clearly, he had made some enemies in the past. I prowled professional associations, police and government websites, and even neighborhood pages looking for an email associated with him, all to no avail. As my frustrations were growing, Petra stepped in.

"Sorry to interrupt, Lexi, but would you like some tea or coffee?"

"I'd love some coffee, and maybe a bottle of water," I said.

"Sure," Petra said. "I'll bring them to you right away. How are things going?"

"Slowly, I'm afraid. I'm trying to track down more information on Maivia, but it appears as if he's a technology caveman."

She chuckled. "Actually, he's a caveman in most aspects. What are you looking to find?"

"I was hoping to find an email address so I can see if I can hack in and confirm a direct relationship with the Chinese and the coup. However, I can't find anything. Even his official email doesn't follow your government's standard formatting."

She nodded. "Oh, that's a huge inside joke. When his email was first set up, the IT technician misspelled his name as 'Maiva,' without the second *i*. Get this—he didn't notice it for weeks until someone pointed it out to him. Then he was too embarrassed to have it changed."

I sat back in my chair looking at her in surprise. "I wish I'd thought to come ask you first. It would have saved me some time. Thanks, that was super helpful."

"I'm happy I could help."

Petra left, and I found Maivia's government account easily. I quickly set up a malicious link, but now I needed an enticing email in which to embed the link. I checked my watch and did a quick calculation. It would be just before midnight back in DC. Hopefully the help I needed was still awake.

I texted through my VPN, frustrated that the sluggish internet connection was too slow for voice at the moment.

"Away team calling Starfleet HQ."

Within a couple of minutes, I received an answer. As anticipated, the twins were on high alert.

"Kirk here, with Spock and three junior ensigns in red shirts standing by online."

Since that sounded like Elvis's humor, I assumed Spock must be Xavier, and the three ensigns standing by on their computers were Angel, Frankie, and Wally. Just the team I needed. Angel's and Wally's exceptional hacking skills and Frankie's fluency in Mandarin would be critical for my plan. I quickly typed a message and sat in to wait as our exchange wasn't as instantaneous as I was used to.

"Can you provide an update on what you've found so far on Signet Investments and the other tasks," I typed. *"But first I have need for specialized assistance from Frankie if she's there."*

A bit later his response came through. *"Frankie's here and says she's up for whatever you need."*

"Great," I responded. *"I'm trying to hack into Liko Maivia's official email using a phishing attack. He isn't very technology savvy, but as a result he may not open his emails very often unless it's from someone he knows. I'll send a malicious link I've created and want it embedded in an email he's likely to open. Ideally, it would come from a source he perceives as Chinese."*

"Clever."

"I hope so. See if you can combine what you know about Signet Investments' emails and Frankie sprinkling a few Chinese words in the title to produce an email he can't resist. Once he clicks the link, we'll have access to his account."

Elvis responded with several clapping emojis. *"You've just made some kids here very happy."*

"I bet," I typed, smiling. *"Just didn't want them to get bored without me."*

"Ha, not anymore. BTW, the additional ensigns working on the holodeck are having some success and estimate they'll have full control by early tomorrow."

He referred to Piper and Brandon, my other two interns, who were working with Wally on breaching the Cook Islands' official government website and social media accounts so we could take them back from the plotters. Once they broke in, they would await my command to execute the next steps of our plan at a moment's notice. While I was digesting that, Elvis sent another message.

"Spock and I have been researching Signet," he continued. *"Quite frankly, it's been easier than we expected. There's more information on them publicly available than you might imagine, and their systems show only ordinary commercial security, and not the signs of a state-sponsored intelligence front. Our assessment is their connection to the Cook Islands is first and foremost commercial. They invest in import/export business that transits to China. My guess is they are more of a front for businesses smuggling or white-washing commercial products from China to avoid tariffs or sanctions. That doesn't mean that they aren't being used to support Chinese foreign policy in the region, but only that they started out as a commercial enterprise whose interests and resources have been co-opted."*

This was interesting information, but it didn't necessarily connect Maivia or the coup to China.

"Have you been able to get into their system?" I asked.

"Not yet. Their security may be commercial, but it's good. We're avoiding any sort of brute-force attacks, as that would be impossible to hide. I'm convinced we can get in, but not on your timeline. We think you'll have better luck trying to track the money and the connection directly through Maivia and the local Chinese officials. Sorry."

It was disappointing news, but not a deal breaker. It also helped me focus on what might now be a better plan of attack.

"It's okay. Thanks for the update. Let me talk to Slash and we'll let you know whether to investigate further. Meanwhile, I'm going to need your and Frankie's help tomorrow. We have about an hour starting at 0600 local time to crack a secure Wi-Fi network and take control of their security system. When I send the malicious link for the email, I'll also send you the information on the wireless router and what I observed today. Use the time to research known vulnerabilities and plan attack options, and I'll do the same here. We'll connect 30 minutes prior to discuss strategy."

"How will we connect to attack the system?" Elvis asked when his text finally came through.

"Slash will use his laptop to remote network with me so I can get access to their Wi-Fi and start the penetration. Between us, I propose we use high-side screen sharing so that you can see my screen. NinjaGhost is the only program I have on my laptop here. I didn't come fully prepared, obviously. We'll connect first and then I'll sync to hubby's laptop at the compound. Once we're in, we'll need Frankie to help us navigate the network to the cameras, as everything will undoubtedly be in Chinese."

There was a pause, probably the twins discussing the plan with Angel, Wally, and Frankie and figuring out exactly what they needed for the plan to work. After another several minutes, Elvis responded.

"Gotcha. We'll solidify our plan of attack. The kids are onboard—they've already been excused from school tomorrow. Everyone will be ready to go at 0530 your time. That will be before lunchtime here, so we should have plenty of time to do our research and be ready."

"Thanks, team. Appreciate the assist."

"Live long and prosper. Literally and figuratively."

Smiling, I closed the VPN and my laptop. I was confident we could hack into the cameras within an hour if Slash decided there was no other option than to break in to plant the recording devices. But was that good enough? What if I failed and he was hurt, captured, or killed? Could I live with that? Did he really need to do this...alone?

I'd just stood to get some water and stretch when Slash entered the room. He quickly crossed to meet me and pulled me into his arms.

"How's my girl?" he asked. His presence was a comforting anchor amid the intense stress of the afternoon.

"Worried," I said. "And not fully onboard with you breaking into the compound."

"So I was told," he said, and then sighed. "Manny could hear it in your voice that you were upset with me. I'm sorry. I have a feeling I'm going to be saying that a lot until I figure out how this marriage thing works. I do want to make important life decisions with you. But it's hard, because many of my decisions revolve around keeping you safe, and that skews my outlook and prevents me from either hearing you or taking your input into account if I think it runs counter to that outcome."

"You do realize I have exactly the same problem, right?" I asked.

He rubbed the back of his neck. "I do, but the truth is I feel like your life is more important than mine."

I looked straight into his serious eyes. "You couldn't be more wrong, Slash. This is an equal partnership with equal importance, and we must work *together* to protect ourselves in unison. It will likely be a bit more intense for us than other couples simply because of the nature of our work. It's not going to be an easy adjustment for either of us. But we *can* do this if we talk things out and respect each other's perspectives."

"You're right. It won't be easy to change my mindset, but I'm willing to try."

"Good," I said. "Because that's where we need to start. Now, let's talk over this breaking and entering plan of yours." I took a step back and blew out a breath. "I know why you think you should do it, and I'm not against it... completely. I just need to know why you feel risking your life is the only option in this case. What's your logic? For example, what if I'm able to get the evidence we need by hacking into Maivia's email? Do you still feel it's necessary to break into the compound?"

He nodded. "I really do. What if we find nothing incriminating in Maivia's email? What if Elvis and Xavier's hack into Signet comes up empty? We don't have time to try all avenues in sequence. We're going to have to run some in parallel, and that includes planting some recording devices in the hopes of picking up some critical information."

I considered. "Okay, but once I'm able to access those security cameras, why do you still have to go in? We could just use the cameras to collect all the evidence we need without the risk being caught."

"Two reasons. Manny reports that his cousin—who has been inside the compound on the bottom floor—has not seen any internal cameras. So, the only cameras we know of are the external ones, which won't provide us with the evidence we need. Second, even if they had cameras in the halls, they'd be unlikely to pick up the very specific and private conversations we need to hear unless we were to get exceptionally lucky. It's rudimentary, old-fashioned, and dangerous to physically plant recording devices, but it's what we have to work with here."

I closed my eyes. "I don't like it."

"I agree, it's not ideal. But our options are severely limited. It would be golden to catch them discussing their plans and the coup. Manny already has some solid intel on the connection between Maivia and the Chinese—he's got photos and videos he took during his own personal surveillance of the compound. I'm going to send all that to Candace tonight. We're collecting the other evidence we need, but we still need a smoking gun, a solid tie between this coup planning and execution and the Chinese."

"So why doesn't Manny break in?" I asked. "Why does it have to be you?"

"You know why. He's nearly thirty years older than me." Slash scrubbed his face with his hands. "While he's sharp and certainly capable, I'm not convinced he could stealthily climb the fence and get out of the compound undetected. Look, the one guard I saw at the gate was barely engaged. They're stretched thin in terms of manpower. They'll be relying heavily on the security cameras, so if we can bring those down or use them to our advantage, it should be easy for me to stroll in and plant the recorders. In and out within ten minutes."

I took a deep breath to steady my nerves. "Okay, I'm in. I don't like you putting yourself in harm's way, but I understand the reasoning and the urgency. I bring down the cameras, you plant the devices and get out. Then what?"

"As soon as Manny and I return to the farmhouse, we get the prime minister out of here. She's been in this spot too long and is in imminent danger of discovery."

"It hasn't even been twenty-four hours," I exclaimed.

"This is a small island, and the longer the prime

minister remains out of their grasp, the more dangerous she is to their plans. They will, or already are, ramping up search efforts to find her. We must keep her out of their hands and get her the resources and information to fight back. While we need to worry about everyone's safety, those are our priorities."

I sighed. "Well, *my* priority is finishing our honeymoon with lots of relaxation, but that doesn't appear to be in the cards."

Slash stopped and took my hands. "I promise you, *cara*, we'll have our honeymoon. But now we need to stay focused on the endgame to make sure we get out of this situation alive."

"I know, I'm just frustrated." I squeezed his hand. "But this situation did precipitate a new addition to the marriage code, number four. We give each other grace when we're irritable or scared in high-stress situations."

"Grace under pressure," he said. "I like it. Number four is a must for us, given our line of work and that little black cloud of ours."

I stared at him for a moment not sure I heard what I thought I heard. "Wait a minute, you said *our* black cloud. Are you implying you want to share ownership of my diabolical puffball?"

He raised a dark eyebrow. "Your puffball is my puffball. If it affects you, it affects me. Together we'll weather any storm our little black cloud decides to unleash on us."

My heart stumbled in my chest. "Oh, Slash, that's the nicest thing you've ever said to me besides our marriage vows...twice." My thumb touched the back of my engagement and wedding rings. "Thank you."

He smiled and cupped my cheeks. "You can't even fathom how you've saved me, *cara*. I can't live this life without you, which is why I'd do anything to protect you, even against that infernal cloud. *Te adoro. Il cuore mio.* I adore you, my heart."

He kissed me, and I wrapped my arms around his waist. We stood like that for a long time. Then I reluctantly pulled back, knowing we had to keep working.

"So, now what?" I asked.

Slash shoved his fingers through his hair. "I gather the intel and photos Manny has collected and send them to Candace as soon as possible. Then Manny and I will try to convince the prime minister and her team to move as soon as we've returned from the compound in the morning. How about you?"

"Things are progressing, but it's going a lot slower than I'd like. The bandwidth is killing me. However, Elvis and Xavier—who are not hampered by said bandwidth—have made good progress on getting the information we need on Signet and the compound. They haven't penetrated their networks, though, and doubt they can do so, unobserved, to meet our timelines. They recommend we pursue the Maivia angle. I've made good progress on that front and hope to have control of his government account shortly."

"Good work all around. Time is not our friend."

"It's not. Also, Xavier reports that Wally, Piper, and Brandon are close to hacking into the government's social media accounts and webpages. I expect they'll be ready when the time comes."

"They will." He gave me a quick kiss. "I'll be back shortly."

I nodded, and he left the room. After drinking some more water and another stretch or two, I got back to work on my laptop researching the cameras Wi-Fi router's possible vulnerabilities.

Slash returned a bit later, letting me know the prime minister had agreed to move to a different location in the morning and already had a safe place secured.

"There's a yacht anchored just offshore that has already been searched," Slash explained. "It belongs to a close friend of hers. It will be stocked before she gets there, and gassed up, in case she needs to make a quick exit."

"Smart to choose a place already cleared," I said. "Although, as you know, I'm not much into boats."

"Hopefully it won't have to set sail," he said, patting my shoulder.

We decided to work for a bit longer, so Slash set up his computer next to mine, and hours blurred into night as we worked in tandem on penetration options. At some point, Rangi brought us food and drink, but otherwise, no one bothered us. At some point, I had a sudden thought and went and found Rangi.

"Rangi, we're going to be heavy users of the local Wi-Fi bandwidth tomorrow. It likely will be critical to our success or failure. I will need every byte that your system can manage. Could you arrange to have everyone log off the network before going to bed tonight and not log back on until I give the all-clear signal tomorrow?"

"Certainly. I'll let everyone know your request right now."

I returned to the office. The air hummed with the sound of our fingers tapping on the keyboards. It mingled with our sighs of frustration and fatigue, but also with an unspoken trust, familiarity, and self-assurance that kept us working perfectly in sync.

It was after midnight when Slash insisted we shut down for the night.

I didn't argue and quickly logged off. My eyesight was

starting to blur. "I do have a question for you," I said to Slash as I closed my laptop. "How do you want to play the camera angle tomorrow? Disable the cameras or freeze the picture?"

Slash stood, stretching his arms above his head. "Disabling would be the easiest choice, but it may prompt the guards to initiate a patrol if they were to notice. Freezing the image would be better, but it can't be maintained for more than a few minutes without being detected. And once it's discovered, it would be far more worrisome than if the cameras just went down."

"Which option gives you the best protection?" I asked.

He considered for a moment. "Freezing. But only until I'm inside. Then, when it's time to come out, refreeze again until I'm in the clear. In the unlikely event I'm caught, they won't know their network has been compromised and we can still use it to gather information."

"I can do that, but you'd better not get caught. I mean it."

"I won't. I've been in far more precarious situations."

"I know, but I don't want to have to say, 'I told you so.' In fact, I feel so strongly about this phrase, I'm making the I Told You So piece number five in our marriage code."

"You won't have to say it." He took my hand, helping me from the chair. "I'll be in and out in under ten minutes. Piece of cake—or cupcake—or whatever you want to eat. Come on, it's time for us to get some rest, too. Manny and I are heading out at about 0500. I could use a few hours to refuel, and you look exhausted. I need you at your best tomorrow."

He led me to a worn couch in the corner of the room that reminded me a bit of a couch we had shared at his grandmother's house in Italy. "I'm feeling déjà vu," I said as we kicked off our shoes and turned off the lights. "The last time we shared at a couch was at Nonna's house in Sperlonga. Remember?"

We settled in close, our bodies tired but hearts happy to be together, hopefully not for the last time.

"I remember," he said, and I could hear the smile in his voice.

"You kissed me, and I was so surprised, I hit your head with mine by accident. We rolled off the couch and Nonna thought something completely inappropriate was going on."

He chuckled. "She already knew how I felt about you, even if I was still working it out."

I smiled at the thought of it. "That was such a memorable time. Sperlonga is so beautiful. Promise me we'll get through this and go back, Slash."

He kissed me on the forehead. "We'll get through this," he said, tightening his arms around me. "I promise. Nonna would kill me if anything happened to you. I think she loves you more than me."

"That's *so* untrue," I said, but I smiled as I touched my engagement ring with my thumb. Slash's grandmother had given him her beautiful antique ring to give me upon our engagement, and it had made me feel special and wholly welcomed into his tight-knit family.

I could feel Slash relax against me. I thought I'd be so wound up, it would take me forever to fall asleep. But the warmth of Slash's body and the happy memory of our time at Nonna's caused me to easily drift off to sleep.

The last thing I remember was Slash murmuring something to me in Italian as I sank into the warmth of his embrace.

TWENTY-SIX

Slash

I woke when my phone vibrated nearby. I rose quietly from the couch, retrieving my phone, laptop, the compound diagram, and the two small recording devices, placing them into my backpack. I glanced out the window, confirming it was still dark. I slipped out of the room and saw Manny near the bottom of the stairs, putting on his shoes.

"Morning," I said softly.

"Morning," Manny responded. "You two get any sleep?"

"Some. Lexi is still asleep. I need to wake her and have her set up before we go. I just wanted to check that you're ready."

"I'm ready," he said, tying the last shoe. "Coffee or water?"

"Coffee, black." I needed to be fully alert this morning.

I returned to the office to wake Lexi. She stirred and finally opened her eyes, sitting up on the couch, her hair tousled, her eyes fogged with a hacker blur I knew so well. She looked beautiful.

"Good morning," I said, kissing her on the cheek. "How'd you sleep?"

"Not enough," she said, rolling her neck. "Is it time?"

"It's time," I confirmed.

"So, what's the plan?" She stretched and then walked over to her laptop. "What do you need me to do?"

"Just like yesterday, I'll set up my laptop so you can connect through it to the Wi-Fi. I'll give you that hour I promised to get in. Once you're in, let me know."

"One hour?"

"One hour," I confirmed. "Our communications will be phones only, since that's what we have at hand except for texting via the laptop. Though once I head into the compound, the laptop stays with Manny. I'll call Manny on my phone, and Manny will loop you in, muting his end unless one of you needs to talk to me. That way any noise from your end won't inadvertently reveal my presence. You'll take down the cameras on my signal, and I'll let you know to put them back up once I'm in. I'll plant the devices and let you know when I'm ready to exit. You take everything down again until I'm in the clear. Straightforward and simple. No fancy moves."

"Do you know where you're going to plant the devices?" she asked. "How many do you have?"

"Two devices, and, yes, I know where I'm going to plant them. One will be in the chief of staff's office and the other in a conference room where Manny took photos of Maivia speaking to various Chinese officials. Unfortunately, the devices are not the bugs like you might expect. Manny doesn't have any actual bugs in his arsenal. They're just mini recorders. Which means I'll have to go back in again and retrieve them."

"You have to break in twice?" she asked in disbelief.

"Yes, but Manny has a plan for that," I assured her. "We may not even have to be involved in the recovery. That is yet to be determined."

She didn't look convinced, but there was no further time for discussion.

"Why can't it ever be the easy button for us?" she asked with a sigh.

"It's not a difficult assignment, *cara*," I assured her. "With you handling the cameras, it *will* be easy."

"Sure, and this is supposed to be a remote island where nothing exciting ever happens."

Ouch. "Point taken. Let's just consider this a small blip on the honeymoon radar. We'll get through it. We always do."

She nodded. "We always do."

I gently cupped the sides of her face with my hands. "One hour for that hack, ten minutes to plant the devices, and another hour before I'm back. We've got this."

"We better." She wrapped her arms around my neck. "Be careful with my husband, okay?"

"Only if you keep my wife safe."

"Deal," she murmured against my lips as she gave me a kiss.

TWENTY-SEVEN

Slash

Manny and I were in position at the compound. We'd moved quickly in the dark under a waxing moon that provided excellent visibility. Once we'd arrived in the bushes near where we had hidden yesterday, I set up my laptop, giving Lexi access to the Wi-Fi network where she was currently hacking away. I sipped coffee from a thermos Manny had provided while mentally walking through the steps of the operation. I didn't look at the time. I knew I didn't need to.

Fifty-two minutes after I set up the laptop, my phone vibrated. "Yes?" I answered.

"I'm in," Lexi said.

I felt a surge of pride and relief. "Good work, *cara*. You did it."

"*We* did it," she said. "I got critical help from Wally, Frankie, and Angel. They are unbelievably talented. Well, Xavier and Elvis helped, too, but you knew that."

"I knew that." I smiled.

"By the way, there are a couple of things you should be aware of," Lexi said. "The compound has its door alarms tied into the network. I've got control of those, too."

She never failed to amaze me. "That's excellent news, *cara*. Maybe we did get to press that easy button just once."

"Maybe just this once. Good luck, Slash. I've got your back."

"You always do." I hung up and pocketed my phone, turning to Manny.

"Did she break into the network controlling the security cameras?" he asked.

"She did and also got control of the door alarms while she was at it."

"Damn," Manny said, shaking his head in disbelief. "Is there any information that's sacred or secure these days? Or does the CIA have access to everything?"

"We're not the CIA," I said.

"Of course you're not. Are you ready to go?"

I looked around. "No better time than the present."

I took out my phone and called him. Once our connection was secure, he looped in Lexi. I left Manny perched behind a large bush with binoculars and a clear view of the front of the compound and the guard by the gate. My open and running laptop sat next to him.

While it was still dark outside, the sky had begun to lighten as dawn approached, helping me see without having to use a flashlight. The lights from the compound gave me a clear view of where I was going, but also meant I'd be visible to anyone who happened to look out a window once I scaled the fence.

"No sentries or patrols noted," Manny whispered through the phone. "The one sentry we saw earlier is nowhere in sight. You can climb that fence anytime."

"Roger that," I said. "Lexi, bring down the cameras and alarms."

"On it," she responded.

I waited a couple of minutes to give Lexi time to do her magic before I headed for the fence. I double-checked to ensure it wasn't an electric one—even though I hadn't seen any evidence it was—and scaled it with ease. I passed directly in front of the security camera mounted nearby. I felt my pulse quicken as I jumped to the ground and slipped into the shadows.

No alarm had been raised.

"Phone silence from here on," I whispered into my cell. "I'll provide two clicks once I'm inside so you can put the cameras and alarms back on, and three clicks when I'm ready to exit again."

"Got it," Manny murmured. "Good luck."

I didn't respond, but I already knew what he was thinking: If my plan failed, we didn't have many other options.

I surveyed the compound from my shadowed position against the building, pressing my body close to the wall. I was exposed here and needed to move, and fast.

I hugged the building until I got to the front right corner. A quick glance around the corner showed the area to the gate was empty and no one was around. The grass felt spongy beneath my feet, damp from the tropical humidity. I ducked around the corner underneath a security camera mounted under the eaves that I sincerely hoped had its image currently frozen. I did another check of the environment over my shoulder before slipping around the corner and testing the door.

It was locked. I dipped my hand into my pocket, where I had put the small lockpicking kit Manny had given me, when the door suddenly popped open.

Startled, I took a step back before realizing Lexi must have opened the door for me. I cautiously opened the door wider and peered in. The dim hallway was empty.

Mentally thanking my wife, I slipped inside, closing the door quietly behind me. I paused, hearing no noise aside from a low hum, which was probably the air conditioner.

I pictured the compound's layout as Manny had described it to me. The closed door immediately to my right should be the chief of staff's office, and next to that on the same side was a recreation room. To the left of me would be a gym—which I confirmed, since the door had a glass window through which I could see the darkened outlines of exercise equipment. Beyond the exercise room was a storage closet and, finally, the kitchen manager's office. Straight ahead would be the large kitchen. The conference room, where I needed to plant the other device, would be on the same floor, but on the other side of the compound. I'd have to pass the kitchen, dining room, stairway, and other offices to get there. I would be the most exposed at that time, so I needed to hurry and get the devices planted and get out before the next staff change occurred.

I'd just put my hand on the chief of staff's door when I heard a clunking noise coming from the kitchen area. I quickly ducked into the office, grateful the door wasn't locked. It was another sign of lax security. To my relief, no one was inside.

I closed the door behind me and began to hunt for the best place to plant the recording device. I didn't dare turn on the light, so I looked around using the dim light from my phone. I noted a metal statue on the desk with several holes in it, which seemed like a good fit. I quickly took the recording device out of my bag, turned it on, and slid it into the statue, where it was perfectly hidden.

The entire action took under a minute. Time to move on.

I had just reached for the door handle when I heard a sound in the hall outside, then silence. After a few seconds, I heard the unmistakable sound of a door closing.

I opened the office door slightly to exit and listened. It had started to rain, and I could hear the water pelting the window. The noise would cover any small sounds I might make, but it would also mask the approaching presence of others. I noticed that the light was now on in the gym across the hall. Someone was working out early.

I left the office, ducked down below the window in the gym door and headed down the hallway, my ears straining for footsteps, noise, or conversation.

I carefully approached the kitchen. I pressed myself flat against the wall when I heard people speaking softly in a language I presumed was Mandarin. Most likely someone was preparing breakfast. I needed to move quickly to plant the next bug. The longer I lingered, the more I increased my odds of discovery.

I timed my movement with the sounds I heard coming from the kitchen as I slipped past the entrance. There appeared to be a staff dining room on the left next to a staircase. Ahead, I saw an open door leading into a formal dining room. Since there seemed to be more activity happening in the house than expected, I made the executive decision to plant the second bug there instead of the conference room.

I dashed across the hall and into the dining room. The room contained a long, polished table with high-backed chairs, a giant map of the Cook Islands in a gilded frame, and a large red roaring lion statue near the window. I took the second mini recorder out of my bag, turned it on, and stuck it in the back of the lion's mouth. That should do it. It was time to get out.

I glanced out of the door of the dining room and saw the hallway was empty. I reached into my pocket, clicking three times to indicate I was ready to exit so Lexi would take down the cameras and door alarms. The area remained quiet, so I dashed into the hallway, past the kitchen, and turned onto the hallway with the office where I'd planted the first recorder.

I'd just passed the gym door and was nearly to the exit when I heard the gym door start to open. I'd never make it out the exterior door in time without being seen, so I ducked back into the chief of staff's office where I'd planted the first recorder to wait it out.

I stood motionless, but didn't hear anyone challenging me or calling for help. The rain had picked up, and I hoped Manny had the foresight to protect my laptop. At least I hadn't been spotted, though I'd had several close calls. I blew out a breath of relief and was just trying to decide if I should alert Lexi that I wasn't out yet when a jarring squawk behind me gashed the silence.

I jolted backward, my heart hammering. Framed against the lightening sky near the window sat a bright-green bird. It was on a cageless perch. The bird had a blue head and a red beak—a parrot of some kind—tilting its head and studying me with round, beady eyes.

"Che cavolo," I murmured in Italian—"What the hell?" That I spoke in Italian and not English indicated the unexpected noise had startled me deeply.

"Where did you come from?" I murmured to the parrot. I hadn't heard or noticed the bird the first time around, although the room had brightened considerably in the past minutes alone. Who the hell kept a cageless bird in an office as a pet?

The parrot suddenly screeched loudly and launched itself at me, claws out, shaking its wings. I tried to grab it, but it flew too high, clearly intending to frighten rather than attack me. It continued to squawk loudly, flying like a maniac around the room.

"Shh," I ordered, but it was too late. I heard another door open down the hall and footsteps approaching.

Cursing under my breath, I forced myself to think. I quickly locked the office door from the inside, buying myself a little more time and hoping that anyone who investigated would just shrug it off as a bothersome parrot. Someone tried the door and then went silent, surely listening. I hoped for a moment they might just leave. Then the phone in my pocket vibrated and the parrot went completely berserk, shrieking and flapping its wings. The sound was piercing, echoing off the walls.

That was the tipping point for the man at the door. He started yelling in Chinese, probably asking someone to bring a key. He either suspected someone was inside or was afraid of the mess the parrot might be making. I checked the window, but it wouldn't budge, somehow sealed in place. There was no way I could avoid being caught. I could hear more voices coming down the hall. I had just seconds before I was discovered. I pulled out my phone and spoke in a low voice.

"I've been discovered," I said, hoping Manny and Lexi could hear me over the parrot shrieking. "The two devices are planted but my position was compromised by an unexpected parrot in the office. I'm going to leave my phone on and hide it in this room so you can hear what's going on. Don't hang up. Take my laptop and get the hell out of here.

They'll likely do a sweep of the area as soon as they discover me."

There was no time to say anything else. I slid my phone into an opening under the floor trim of the desk. It was impossible to see unless someone started looking on the floor with a flashlight.

I stood up, moved away from the desk, and put my hands on my head. Moments later, there was silence outside, and then I heard a key in the lock and the door swung open. The light in the room came on, and one of the guards pointed at me in shock. It didn't take them long to respond before I was promptly staring down the muzzle of a gun.

A man growled something at me in Chinese. I didn't need a translator to know he'd told me if I moved, I died.

My mind raced, trying to figure a way out. The mission was complete, but I was captured, stuck in an enemy stronghold with a loaded gun aimed at my skull. I wasn't sure what would happen next.

Damn that parrot. Lexi was going to kill me if I ever got out of this alive.

TWENTY-EIGHT

Lexi

It had started to rain, and the droplets pelted the corrugated-metal roof of the farmhouse with a steady pinging, obscuring most other sounds except for the weird squawking coming from my phone and Slash cursing and saying something about a parrot. A parrot?

My fingers froze over the keyboard. I'd just taken the security cameras and the door alarms down for his exit, but something had happened.

But what? I strained to hear above the pounding of the rain. Had he escaped? Should I turn the security systems back on? I waffled, then set them to come back on in thirty seconds using a timer. Just as I finished, I abruptly lost access to the network. I didn't even have time to troubleshoot it when my phone pinged. I opened my messages and saw Manny had texted me.

"Slash captured. I'm on the run. Don't hang up, he left his phone on so we could monitor."

I was about to respond when the door to the office flew

open and Rangi ran in without bothering to knock. He was out of breath, his eyes wide with urgency.

"Lexi, shut everything down," he hissed, running a hand through his wet hair. I had no idea where he'd been other than somewhere out in the rain. "Government forces are headed this way. They're searching all the homes nearby and will be here very soon. We must get the prime minister out—now!"

"But Slash—"

I started to protest when Rangi grabbed my arm. "Now, Lexi. There's no time."

My heart skipped a couple of beats as I stuck my phone in my pocket without hanging up. I unplugged my laptop and shoved it in its bag. I swept the computer, cords, peripherals, and notes into the bag as well.

"How close are they?" I asked.

"Five minutes out at most. Come on. Hurry."

There was no time to get anything else. My passport was in my laptop bag, as was some money and additional IDs. I passed our small duffel bag as I was leaving the room and grabbed that, too. It would have to do.

"I'm ready," I said. "Let's go."

Rangi led me into the dark hallway where two of the prime minister's security men were scrambling. They were coordinating using hand signals with other police officers out the front and back doors. The prime minister stood nearby, speaking softly with her husband and children. She looked composed but anxious. Out the back door, I could see one of the police officers shrugging into a bulletproof vest.

Things were getting serious.

Petra glanced over at me, and I could see the worry in her eyes. There was certainly concern for her country, but I knew the look of a worried mother when I saw one. I couldn't imagine what she was going through right now. I gave her a quick nod of encouragement, and she smiled slightly.

"Let's go, Prime Minister," Rangi said grimly, and she gave him a brief nod. We quietly followed him toward the back of the house. Two armed guards fell into line behind us.

Rangi led us out the large wooden door at the back of the farmhouse toward a small shed where four off-road motorcycles, caked in mud, stood ready. The rain had blessedly softened to a light drizzle, but I had to blink to keep the water out of my eyes. I instinctively moved my backpack to my chest to protect the computer from the rain. The duffel hung on my shoulder, resting on my back. Two security personnel—men with rifles strapped across their chests—were already securing the camouflage tarps they'd used to hide the motorbikes and now rolling them into the woods behind the shed. The other pair of guards were barely visible in front of the house, wearing police uniform pants, but their upper bodies were masked by fatigue jackets. They were hidden in the foliage facing the darkened road that led to the house.

Rangi saw where I was looking. "They're monitoring the searchers' progress," he said. "It is only a few men in a couple of cars and a motorcycle. They don't know we're here yet. We could stop them, especially with surprise, but if we attacked them, they would call for assistance and the entire area would be cordoned off, trapping us. If we can leave before they find us, then they may know we were here, but not how long ago."

A motorbike roared to life, and I looked up to see Petra and her son sitting behind a policeman. They started off down a puddled path into the fields. I stared at Rangi. "Oh, please don't tell me we're escaping on motorcycles?"

"Yes," he replied. "The road we came in on, it's the only one passable by car. It is now blocked by the searchers coming for us. We are going to use farm paths to loop around them and get to the beach. They won't be able to follow us."

As he spoke, the next two bikes left with Petra's husband and daughter as passengers, each behind a policeman. Finally, it was my turn and I carefully climbed onto the bike, behind the man who would be my driver.

"You're staying behind?" I asked Rangi, panic creeping into my voice.

"I am. We're out of bikes, but don't worry about us. We're not going to get in a shootout with them unless we must. You'll be safe with the prime minister. But as soon as you're able, let Slash and Manny know it's not safe to return here, okay? Now get going."

I didn't even have a chance to say goodbye or tell him about Slash's possible capture before our bike jumped and I almost tumbled off the back. I grabbed onto the driver's waist in panic.

"Hold tight," the driver warned me in what sounded like an Aussie accent. "No matter what happens, don't let go of me."

We shot out of the clearing, leaving the farmhouse behind. We were moving much faster than my paved-road comfort level as we raced along a muddy, single-track path tracing the edge of a pineapple field. I struggled to adjust my packs without falling off as the bike lurched and bumped. I was sure if my mother could see me now, I'd receive a healthy scolding for not wearing a helmet, though that was the least of my concerns.

"Use your legs," my driver yelled at me. "Try and keep your butt off the seat and use your legs to absorb the shock like you're riding a horse. It will make the bike steadier for both of us."

I considered mentioning to him that I had no intention of climbing on a horse or camel ever again, but that mental debate was ended when the bike hit a hole that momentarily tried to reposition my anus to my collar.

As I recovered and tried to follow the driver's instructions, I dared a glance over my shoulder. We made a sharp turn and I saw we were being chased by the one motorcycle that had apparently been part of the search group. The rider was wearing dark clothes and a black helmet with the visor down. Since his bike was carrying only one rider, he was closing on us, about fifty yards behind.

"We've got company," I shouted to the driver.

We hit another bump, and my driver took a big, skidding turn, forcing me to concentrate on staying aboard the bike instead of tracking our pursuer's progress. On a smoother stretch, I momentarily hazarded another peek and saw our pursuer was much closer. So close that I could see he held a gun in his hand.

"Gun!" I screamed.

While I watched in horror, our pursuer raised his arm and aimed at us. My driver abruptly swerved to avoid a huge puddle just as the gun fired, missing us. The gunman, however, failed to miss the puddle, and fountains of water and mud sprayed into the air and on him as he followed.

I fervently hoped the puddle would make him crash, but he emerged from the other side still on the bike. On the upside, he had significantly slowed and was covered in mud spray. Once he got his bearings and wiped his visor, however, he began rapidly accelerating after us again.

"He's still following," I shouted at the driver.

"Don't worry," my driver yelled back. "It's hard to hit a moving target."

I wasn't as confident as he was, but for the moment, I just held on for dear life. Thankfully, the foliage thickened as we left the fields, and the tropical jungle closed around us. Thick vines and massive ferns whipped at our shoulders as my driver maneuvered down narrow and overgrown paths. Rainwater pooled in hidden depressions, spraying muddy arcs high into the air as we sped through them. The trail occasionally forked and rejoined as generations of people and animals sought the easiest path.

We wound back and forth beneath the canopy and ferns. I'd lost sight of our pursuer as I gritted my teeth and pressed my face against the driver's back after being whacked by a branch several times. I was starting to get the hang of anticipating the bumps and leaning in concert with the driver. My eyes narrowed into slits against the mud sprays, and my hair was snagged with leaves and twigs.

The faint sound of our pursuer echoed behind us until finally I couldn't hear him anymore. I let myself relax slightly, praying we'd finally lost him.

Suddenly, a gunshot snapped through the undergrowth, the hum slicing the air inches from me. I gasped as wood chips exploded off a nearby tree trunk. I spotted the dark silhouette of a motorbike on a parallel path to the left of us, still weaving in pursuit.

"I thought you said he'd never hit anything," I shrieked at the driver.

"He didn't hit anything," the driver shouted back. "Why are you screaming? He just got lucky that once. Trust me, it won't happen again."

The bike's left-side mirror exploded, hurling glass fragments all over the driver.

"Okay, maybe it will happen again," the driver conceded. "Just keep your head down. I'm going to try and go a little faster."

A little faster? Was he insane? We were already careening through the jungle at suicidal speeds, like a cheetah on a coffee high.

Another shot came perilously close, but my driver appeared to be quite experienced and maneuvered expertly, making us a difficult target. I kept an eye on our pursuer the best I could, but I expected a bullet through my back at any moment.

At some point, the paths merged again, and once again the shooter was behind us. Thankfully, he had stopped shooting...at least for the moment. He was either having trouble keeping up with the increased pace we had set, or he needed to reload his gun and couldn't do that while driving so fast. Nevertheless, I tried to squeeze myself into the tiniest target I could while I held on tightly.

"Hold on!" my driver yelled, as if I wasn't already squeezing my arms around his waist with all my might. Then, without warning, he slowed and suddenly swung the motorcycle around in a 180, facing the gunman and returning fire in short bursts. It forced our pursuer to throttle back and guide his bike into the jungle for cover.

"What the heck?" I shrieked as he wheeled us back around and throttled forward again, putting some important distance between us. "How about a warning next time?"

"I did warn you," he yelled.

"Not that you had a gun and were going to shoot him."

He didn't answer and pushed onward for what seemed like forever but was probably only another mile. As best I could tell, we had swung away from the mountains and were headed back toward the beach. Our pursuer had dropped farther back, and I couldn't hear him anymore over the roar of our bike and the jungle's natural soundtrack—chirping insects and shrieking birds.

Just as I thought we might have shaken our pursuer, an unexpected slope flung us down a small ravine. The path curved to the left, and the driver angled our bike sharply to avoid slamming into a boulder. I clung to him with the last of my strength. Finally, we came to an abrupt stop.

The driver twisted around on the seat. "Are you okay?" he asked me.

I considered. "I don't know. I might not be breathing at the moment."

He grinned. "You're doing good, and we're getting closer to our destination. We either need to lose our friend for good or we'll have to lead him away from the prime minister. This part is going to be tricky, so just stay with me, okay?"

I nodded. "Okay."

"Hold tight." I gripped him around the waist as he maneuvered the bike slowly around the boulder and drove slowly and carefully down the rest of the ravine.

Even going slowly, it was challenging, with the tires skidding on the wet and slimy rocks and the driver fighting to keep our bike upright. My heart was pounding. Miraculously, he somehow kept control of the bike until we finally exited the ravine.

Just as we reached the rise on the far side, we pulled to a stop and saw the dark rider come into view. He had obviously been pushing high speeds to catch up with us. Carrying the extra speed, he couldn't control his bike, and he and his bike slid down the ravine, heading directly for the boulder we'd barely avoided. When impact was imminent, he threw himself off the bike just as it hit the boulder with a grinding crunch, parts of the bike scattering around the ravine.

I gasped, covering my mouth. I couldn't see the driver at first and wondered if he was dead. But after a minute, I saw him stagger into view. His clothes on his right side were shredded and bloody from the gravel where he slid with the bike. His visor was up and cracked, and he was limping badly, holding his right arm. He was alive, but it would be a while until he could get back to civilization, and he would have no idea in which direction we were headed.

Our pursuit ended, we sped away, following the path at a sedate pace until we soon came out of the dense foliage and onto a crushed-shell road. Shortly we could see a paved road ahead. The rain had stopped altogether now, though there were puddles remaining everywhere, but not for long, based on my experience with sandy soils. My driver pulled off to the side and waited and watched cautiously, scanning for trouble.

"We're close," my driver said, his eyes continuously searching the road ahead. "We just have to follow that road for a short distance, cross over towards the beach, and we're there."

"So, why are we stopping here?"

"Just being extra careful. It would be most unfortunate to get caught now. What's your name?"

"Lexi," I said.

"Ah, so you're Lexi. I'm Paul. Well, Lexi, you held it together quite well. Good on ya, sheila. I'm impressed."

I wasn't sure why he called me Sheila and what was so impressive about my hanging onto him for dear life, but maybe he was just thankful I hadn't barfed down the back of his jacket...yet.

"Thanks," I said, my voice sounding wispy and strained, probably on account of all the hyperventilating I did for most of the ride.

Finally, satisfied no one was around, Paul pulled out on the pavement, drove a bit down the road, and stopped near the beach.

Waves crashed against the surrounding reef, the pink sunrise illuminating the ocean's expanse. A few boats dotted the water. Behind a dune and a copse of palm trees that hid us from the main road, he slid our bike to a stop alongside the others, putting his legs down to steady us. He turned off the bike, and the engine ticked as it cooled.

"What happened to you?" asked Petra, spotting us and coming forward. "We were worried when you took so long."

"We had to do evasion, prime minister," Paul explained, scraping the mud off his jacket. "Had one bloke following us on a bike with a gun. It was touch-and-go, but we lost him. The only thing he'll be searching for in the immediate future is a hospital bed. Our escape is secure."

"Thank God. Are you okay, Lexi?" she asked me.

I'm sure I'd looked better, but I wasn't too worried about that at the moment. "I'm alive, thanks to Paul. What about the others and Rangi? Did they get away?"

Petra answered, "I don't know, but I hope so. We haven't heard anything from them yet. Rangi is a very resourceful man."

I thought she sounded more hopeful than sure.

"Hurry now, Prime Minister, we need to get you off the beach where you are exposed," the officer who had been Petra's driver said to her.

As they hurried off, I took a better look around and

saw we'd disembarked on the edge of a sand dune. One of the security guys mounted a bike and drove it off up toward the road, only to return several minutes later and pick up another bike. I noticed that none of the bikes had license plates. I wondered if that wasn't a requirement in the Cook Islands or if they'd been taken off deliberately so they couldn't be traced. Either way, they wouldn't be easily linked to us if they were found—aside from the one with the bullet hole in the mirror.

Suddenly, I remembered about Slash. Panicked, I grabbed my phone, thankful to see I was still connected. I listened but couldn't hear anything. My alarm rose with every passing minute, as I sent a quick text to Manny.

"Do not return to farmhouse. It's compromised. I'm with the PM at the new location. Text me ASAP regarding your situation and what happened."

"Let's go," Paul said, motioning for me to put my phone away and follow the others down a narrow pathway through some dune shrubs to the shore.

Petra walked ahead, holding her son Noa's hand, while her husband had his arm protectively around their daughter, Lani. I hadn't heard a peep from either of the kids and was impressed they had seemingly held up better than me. My ego hoped it was because their ride was a lot less scary than mine.

We quickly reached the shoreline, where there was a small skiff capable of seating five. One of the police officers hopped in and motioned for the PM and her family. They climbed into the boat, and the others pushed it out into the water, where the helmsman started a small trolling motor. The skiff headed out to a distant boat, moored just inside the reef. It was a large boat compared to the others I could see, but it appeared unoccupied, as I could see no lights or movement.

I sat down on the sand and set the bags next to me while we waited for the boat to return. I kept my phone nearby, listening, but still nothing. My stomach twisted into knots, worrying about Slash.

I wrapped my arms around my knees and looked out at the boat. The skiff was pulling alongside. The policeman guiding the boat tied it quickly to the larger boat and then leaped onboard. He was gone for a minute and then came back and began helping the others onboard. He must have been checking the yacht before letting them aboard.

The skiff departed the yacht after about ten minutes. Oddly, it didn't return directly to our position but headed the opposite way along the beach.

"Where's he going?" I asked Paul, who had sat down not far from me.

"He's just being cautious in case someone is watching. If he headed directly toward us, someone who was observing him could get here before he could. Also, he's trying to avoid attracting attention from a casual watcher who might wonder about successive loads of people being transported to the yacht. He'll come back parallel to the beach at some point, so no one knows where he's going. When he gets close, we head to the water and hop on."

I was really beginning to appreciate the talents of the men who were protecting the prime minister. For a small island, they knew their job well.

Five minutes later I saw the skiff make a slow turn toward shore and then begin to head back to us.

"Get ready, Lexi," Paul said. "Walk slowly and try not to attract any attention."

Easy for them to say. "Am I going by myself?"

"No, I'll go with you," one of the other policemen replied.

"What about everyone else?" I asked.

"We'll be watching from the shore," Paul said. "That way, we can monitor any approaching threats and also be available to pick up people or supplies, as needed."

I stood and casually sauntered toward the water. The skiff hovered closer. The small waves slapped the skiff broadside, causing it to rock a lot more than I was comfortable with.

"Go on, Lexi, off with you now," Paul said. "And try not to trip and fall. Your husband warned us about you."

My mouth dropped open. "My husband did what?"

"He urged us to keep a close eye on you because sometimes unexpected things happen around you."

"Wait. He told that to how many people?"

Paul considered. "Everyone, I think. I'm sure he was just trying to look out for you, love. Well, and maybe for us, too. I think he used the word *accident-prone*, and we all got the message." He chuckled, and the other policeman also wore a broad smile.

I narrowed my eyes. I was definitely going to have to talk with Slash when I saw him again. For now, I tried to balance the bags evenly over each of my shoulders. The skiff pulled up close to the beach, but the water was so shallow I was going to have to wade a couple of steps to the boat. While I paused to consider this challenge, Paul swooped in and picked me up from behind. Before I had time to do more than squawk, he took two quick steps into the water and set me down in the boat.

"Hey, I could have done that on my own," I complained. "I'm not afraid of getting my feet wet."

"Wasn't as worried about you, Lexi, but I intended to keep those bags of yours safe, just in case you took a spill."

Oh, yes. Slash and I were going to talk.

When we finally got to the yacht and I climbed aboard, they led me into the small main cabin. Though compact, the yacht was polished and luxurious: warm wood paneling, plush seating, and a table that could seat four comfortably. Stairs led down in the back of the cabin to what I suspected was a galley stocked with supplies. The curtains were drawn tight, and there were only a couple of small lights turned on. I could hear a thrumming sound coming from below.

The prime minister and her husband, Henry, were sitting on a bench seat under the curtained window with their kids on either side. Henry rose in concern when he saw me.

"We're so sorry for dragging you into this nightmare, Lexi," he said. "I understand you were shot at. Are you okay? Do you need to clean up?"

I wasn't remotely okay, but I couldn't blame him or the prime minister. All of this was out of their control, obviously.

I reached up to touch my hair and realized my hands and arms were covered with mud. There were sticks and leaves in my hair, and it felt like I'd blow-dried it straight up and sprayed it with glue. My shirt, jeans, and shoes were covered in mud spatter. I had no idea how my face looked, but from the way people were staring at me, it wasn't good. I probably smelled, too.

Petra handed me a towel. "The bathroom is that way."

"Thanks." Resigned, I put my bags on a chair, took the towel, and went to clean up in the tiny bathroom. A glance in the mirror indicated I looked remarkably similar to a cartoon cat who had just climbed out of a pigsty and saw a ghost. My hair stuck out in several places. Mud and grime streaked across my cheeks and forehead. There were strange dirt balls in my hair, and a piece of a vine hung off my left ear. My eyes were like two white pinballs in a face that was hardly recognizable, even to myself.

I turned on the water and washed and scrubbed at my face, arms, and hands until the brown water finally turned clear and my face was pink from all the scrubbing. The towel was a complete loss, so I tossed it in the bottom of the shower stall so as not to track any more dirt around. I did my best to remove the sticks and leaves and wound my hair back into a ponytail. There wasn't much more I could do short of a full shower, and there was no time for that now.

I returned to the main room, where everyone was waiting.

The prime minister sat calmly, but I could see how deeply the morning's ordeal had shaken her.

Henry reached into a small mini fridge, pulling out bottles of water and handing them to us. I screwed off the top and took a long drink.

"How are you guys holding up?" I asked them.

Petra glanced worriedly at the kids. "We're...ah, holding up. Where's Slash and Manny?"

My stomach twisted again, but I didn't want to worry anyone regarding what was going on with them yet. I decided to keep it simple until the children weren't present and I could talk to Manny to get the full story.

"They went to the compound this morning to plant the recording devices. I texted Manny that the farmhouse was compromised. Hopefully, he'll text me when he's able."

Thankfully, no more questions came my way. I felt nauseous, so I took another long drink of water before setting the bottle aside. I dragged my laptop bag onto the table and pulled out my laptop and cord, looking for a place to plug it in. When I found one, I was grateful the outlet on the yacht worked. The thrumming must be the generator.

I needed to plan my next move. If Slash had been captured, I had to figure out what to do about that. But I needed more information from Manny, and he was likely on the run and not able to respond to my texts. I put my phone on the table and plugged it in, too, listening to the open phone line with Slash. Still nothing. Wherever Slash had planted his phone, he wasn't with it now.

There was nothing I could do on that front for the moment, so I needed to check in with Xavier and Elvis to let them know I was okay after we'd terminated contact so abruptly. They were likely going crazy.

"Is there any chance this boat has Wi-Fi?" I asked. "I can't use my phone as a hotspot because I'm monitoring communications with Slash and Manny." I avoided mentioning my phone was my last link to Slash.

"I think I saw a small sign with a password by the TV in the big bedroom," Lani said. "Let me go see." She darted down the stairs and came back seconds later with the paper in hand.

Indeed, it had the Wi-Fi and password listed. I just hoped it ran when the generator was operating. It didn't take long to confirm it was indeed operational.

I reached out, my hands flying across the keyboard, to connect with Elvis and Xavier. I sent a quick encrypted text explaining the situation. When I looked up, I saw Noa had come to stand behind me. He looked remarkably calm, considering what we'd just been through.

"What are you doing?" he asked me.

"Not gaming, unfortunately," I said, trying to keep it light. "Just trying to get us out of this mess."

"Can you?" he asked. "Get us out this mess?"

"I'm sure going to try."

He shrugged and returned to his seat. My gaze met Petra's across the table, and she gave me a slight nod.

I returned to the matter at hand, realizing time was ticking. I didn't know what was happening to Slash in that compound or where Manny had gone. I had no idea what was going on back at the farmhouse since we'd left, and I didn't have a clue how long it would be until the bad guys came back to recheck this boat. But there was one thing I did know: Slash needed my help, and he was going to get it. It was just a matter of time until I figured out how.

Outside, the ocean lapped softly against the hull, while inside the cabin walls, Slash's predicament weighed heavy on my mind. I needed to lock in and focus on what I could control, not what I couldn't.

It's what Slash always said to me: Stay with the mission. Worrying doesn't solve anything. Planning does.

It was clear I had a lot of work to do if I wanted to save my husband, the Cook Islands, and my honeymoon, and in that order.

TWENTY-NINE

Slash

I felt every muscle in my body as I sat on the floor of the dark, empty room.

Calling it a room was generous. It was more like a narrow closet that was positioned across from the conference room and adjacent to the office with the parrot where I'd been caught. Manny's schematics of the compound had listed it as a storage room, but it was a closet. No windows, no ventilation system, and no light. I could stand in the middle and touch the side walls with both hands. I'd noted the cypher lock on the door when they brought me down and threw me inside after they had spent some time roughing me up a bit. They likely secured valuables of some kind in here.

It was barely big enough to fit a man, but here I was.

Not surprisingly, my captors hadn't bought my story about getting lost and wandering into the compound by accident. I didn't have anything on me other than the small lockpick kit and the small knife I always carried in my boot.

The lockpicks hadn't helped my story. They had immediately divested me of those and pulled off my shirt, which was a bit odd, but it was what it was. Probably they wanted to scare me or to make me think torture was imminent.

It had been an extremely fortunate stroke of luck they decided to question me right in the office where they'd captured me—where I'd planted both my phone and one of the recording devices. If Manny had escaped and Lexi was still listening, they would at least have an idea of what was happening with me inside the compound. Once Lexi got the recording off to Frankie to translate, of course. The language barrier slowed everyone down. Eventually, I hoped they'd be able to get the information we needed to tie the coup to the Chinese.

For my initial interrogation, I'd been tossed in a chair with my hands tied behind my back. For at least an hour, they asked me questions in heavily accented English. I consistently stuck to my story of being lost and not knowing where I was. It cost me several blows to the face, jaw, and abdomen, but all in all, I'd had worse. These guys were mostly muscle, not particularly inventive or trained in how to really cause pain. As they weren't sure who I was or what I was doing here, they seemed conflicted on how much harm they could actually cause me. I used that to my advantage.

My captors hadn't called the Cook Islands police when they found me—no surprise or need, I presumed—and instead had thrown me into the storage closet and left. They hadn't figured out who I was yet, but it wouldn't be long until that changed. A lot of people had seen me save the prime minister from the assassination attempt, so I had to assume it was only a matter of time.

I rolled my neck and shoulders, trying to prevent them

from knotting up. My muscles ached from the interrogation and the way my arms had been twisted and tied behind the chair. My jaw throbbed where a guard's fist had made contact a time or two. Thankfully and unexpectedly, they had untied me when they placed me here, so that gave my arms and shoulders a slight physical break. I had a hunch it was to see what I might do. I was confident that there was a guard stationed right outside my door. Even so, he was being very quiet. I repeatedly listened but heard nothing. My mouth was swollen, but nothing was broken, and the pain would lessen with time. I'd just have to ask Lexi to be careful the next time she kissed me.

I had tried the door, but it was locked, of course, and explored every inch of the tiny closet. I'd found exactly nothing. So, I sat on the floor, meditated, and rested my body for whatever was to come next.

LEXI

I HUNCHED over my laptop at the round dining room table in the yacht's main area off the galley. I'd exchanged numerous emails with Candace, Elvis, Xavier, and Angel, updating everyone on what had happened, or at least what little I knew regarding Slash.

The prime minister's kids had disappeared into one of the yacht's two bedrooms to watch television—I could hear the laugh track of the cartoons—and the prime minister and her husband were talking in a nearby room. One of her security personnel sat in a chair near the stairs that led up to the deck, keeping a discreet eye on us. I wasn't too worried about our immediate safety, as I could hear the footsteps of the other guard above and the soft murmur of their voices.

But time was stealing away, and I knew it.

I heard the motor of the skiff as it came alongside and then the security guys helping someone aboard. We all turned to look at the cabin entryway. A moment later, Manny appeared and clambered down the stairs.

"Manny," I exclaimed, jumping up from the table. "Are you okay?" His cotton shirt was wet from the passing storm. His hair was tousled, and he wore a grim look on his face.

"I'm fine," he said, pushing his dark hair back from his face. "I'm just wet and concerned. Here's Slash's laptop. I tried to keep it as dry as possible. I hope it still works."

"Thanks, Manny," I said, ushering him toward the table, where he sat down. "What happened? I couldn't hear clearly. There was yelling and screeching, and something about a parrot before the network suddenly went down. You said Slash was captured." I hoped with all my heart he'd say it had all been a mistake.

But Manny nodded. "I'm sorry, Lexi. Apparently, he stumbled across a parrot in the chief of staff's office. He startled it, and it gave him away. He managed to say he was hiding his phone in the room and to keep the line open. Then he told me to take his laptop and run. Is your phone line still open?"

"Yes." I walked over and held up my phone. "And I'm still on mute, but I haven't heard anything. But there was a stretch when we were on the run that I wouldn't have heard anything even if they'd been shouting."

"Mine is still open, too. I did hear voices while I was running, probably him being captured, but didn't have time to listen carefully. But I did think to record it."

I looked at him in surprise. "You recorded it?" When he

nodded, I gave him a hug. "Manny, that's brilliant. I need that recording now."

He pulled his phone from his pocket. "Take it. I have no idea how to give it to you. I did stop recording when it had been silent for a while. But you'd better hurry. My phone's running out of juice."

"No worries. I'll take it from here." I took his phone to my computer and plugged it in.

Manny grabbed a towel from the bathroom to dry his hair and face. He then got a bottle of water from the fridge and sat down across from me.

I started the download of the audio file and worried because it was big, it would take a long time to complete. I decided the best way was to break the file up during compression. That way I could send the initial part to Elvis and Frankie so that they could start translating.

"If the voices are in Chinese, how will the recording help if we don't know what they're saying?" Manny asked me and took a big swig of water.

"I've got people who can translate," I said. "All I need is to get the audio file to them to start working on whatever is being said inside that compound."

Manny perked up. "It's that easy?"

"I didn't say it was easy, but it can be done. You didn't hear Slash speaking at all?"

"I heard something while I was running. I just can't confirm it was him. We'll have to listen to it to find out for sure."

I blew out a breath. It wasn't the confirmation I wanted that Slash was still alive, but I had to be patient. He could take care of himself, and I needed to keep my focus to help him.

Just then Petra and Henry came into the room and saw

Manny. Petra rushed to hug him, and he quickly filled her and Henry in on what had happened at the compound. I kept focused on uploading the audio file.

The prime minister looked horrified when he finished his story. "I'll turn myself in if they release Slash."

"That's not a viable solution, Petra," I said without removing my gaze from my screen. "We can't take the Chinese by their word. I don't think they'll hurt Slash...yet... because they want to use him as leverage. But if you turn yourself in, they'd have no use for him. And my guess is they'd force you to resign and then you might just... disappear."

She paled, but she sat, her chin steady. "What do you mean, disappear?"

I sighed, finally lifting my gaze to hers. "Clearly, you'll not be resigning of your own free will. Keeping you around afterward would leave a dangerous loose end for them."

"You're saying they'd kill me? My family?"

"They've already tried to assassinate you, Petra," Manny said gently. "The bottom line is, there is a good chance none of us will survive if they capture you now."

She closed her eyes, pressing the back of her hand against her mouth. "My children? Henry?" She looked up at her husband, a stricken expression on her face.

"I don't know." I put a gentle hand on her arm. "I don't want to alarm you. This is all just speculation at this point. But we do need to come up with a way to get Slash out of there as soon as possible."

"Will the recording devices he planted there help us?" she asked.

"Not unless we can retrieve them. Unfortunately, the Chinese will likely be on high alert now. We do have Slash's phone transmitting what is happening near him. Manny was able to use the open line to record what happened during his capture. Right now, I'm downloading that audio file to send to my translator. It's a big file, so it's taking some time."

"Are you going to tell your government the Chinese have kidnapped him?" she asked me.

"I already have," I said. "But there's nothing they can do at this point. The Chinese could simply insist they don't know who we're talking about. They've never seen him, heard of him, etc. We can't prove they have him...yet. So that's not a good option, either. On a more positive note, they are reaching out to contacts in New Zealand and the UK to let them know what's going on and solicit their assistance. But beyond that, we're basically on our own."

Petra got up and walked over to the coffee maker, pouring a cup and handing it to me. "I'm so sorry, Lexi. I never meant to put you two in such danger. You're exhausted. Is there anything I can do to help?"

"I wish there were, Prime Minister," I said. "As soon as this file uploads and sends, I'll breathe easier knowing it's being worked on. And then hopefully we can listen to it ourselves."

I took the mug and added some milk from a small carton that was sitting on the table. I'd just taken a sip of the coffee when we heard a noise on my and Manny's phones. We all froze.

There was some shuffling, muttering, and then, as clear as day, I heard some loud squawking noises.

"I told you there was a parrot," Manny whispered.

"Shh," the prime minister and I said at the same time as we all huddled around the table. I held out my hand for Manny to give me my phone, and he quickly turned it over. I pressed the record button just as we heard people start speaking Chinese. I could make out at least three different voices, but it was frustrating that we had no idea what they were saying.

Then suddenly that changed when we heard the bang of a door and voice speaking in English. "What's going on here? What happened?"

"That's Maivia," Henry hissed. "I recognize his voice. That son of a gun is in the compound."

"We had an intruder at the compound," someone responded in accented English. "But it's under control."

"What kind of intruder?" Maivia asked. "What was he doing here?"

"We're not sure. He was caught in here, looking around the office. We ran a sweep for bugs in this room and on the entire first floor but found nothing. Nothing appears to be missing, either. We don't know what he was after, and he's not talking."

"Who is he?"

"That's what we're trying to find out. He didn't have any identification on him. He speaks English and says he wandered into the compound by accident, but he's lying, and he won't give us a name. It's hard to tell if English is his native language. We're not sure what's he's doing here, whether he's working for the prime minister or someone else. He's locked up for now until we determine our next steps."

"This is intolerable," Maivia fumed. "I don't like this. Not one bloody bit." We could hear the clomp of his footsteps as he presumably paced the office. "I'm worried. We need to get the boss here immediately. Where is he? I was assured he'd be here today in case there were any problems. And we have problems. What do I do now? The prime minister is still missing and now this. What if we can't find her? She shouldn't even be alive, and now we have this incident."

"Please calm down, my friend," a voice said soothingly. "He's already on the way, and he's been briefed on the situation. He should be here within the hour. His personal plane lands from Kiribati in about half an hour. Trust me, things are going as planned. In China we say, 'All things are difficult before they are easy.' So, just be patient and keep your activity focused on finding the prime minister. She hasn't left and the island is small. It is just a matter of time before you capture her."

We could hear Maivia's heavy sigh. "I'm just worried things are not going as planned."

"Of course, we understand your concern. We'll let you know when the boss has arrived."

"What about the intruder?"

"We'll take care of him. You have enough to deal with, so go find the prime minister and any who still support her."

There was a pause before a door slammed, followed by a murmur of voices in Chinese. After another minute, the door squeaked open and then shut.

The room went silent.

THIRTY

Lexi

I let out a breath of relief so sharp, it almost caused me to double over. Calming myself, I hit the stop button on the recording function. While the conversation was alarming, it had also just confirmed Slash was still alive. If he was alive, I could function. I could figure out how to save him.

"Maivia *is* working with the Chinese," Petra said in outrage, jumping to her feet. "I knew it. He just said so himself."

"He said something *like* that," I warned. "That conversation could be twisted or rephrased to mean anything. It's not enough to directly link him to Chinese in this coup. It's a start, but we need more."

Petra scowled, clearly furious. "He'll pay for this. That traitorous bastard."

I didn't respond, because my first audio file was finally ready, so I queued it up and sent it off to Angel and Frankie, asking them to prioritize the translation and telling them another, shorter audio file would follow shortly.

"Well, the good news is they apparently didn't find the recording devices," Manny said. "Slash was right. It was safer to use the recorders than it would have been to use the bugs."

"Well, it's not like you had any choice," I responded. "That was all you had, but it was a lucky break, and we've had far too few of those lately."

"But you said Slash hid his phone in the office where he was captured," Henry pointed out. "Why didn't they find it? Doesn't a bug sweeper look for transmissions? A phone would emit that, right?"

"Everyone has a phone," I explained. "They would have just assumed the sweeper was picking up the transmissions from the phones in their pockets. Obviously, they didn't find the recording device in the office or his phone."

"Right. Thank God for that," Henry said.

I looked over at Manny. "Maivia said he wanted the boss to come. Any idea who this is?"

Manny glanced at Petra. "I don't. You got any thoughts as to who this boss might be, Prime Minister?"

She thought for a moment. "I'm not sure. There's a higher-level Chinese official that circulates around the islands occasionally. I've never met him, and I don't know his name. It could be him. I've seen a private plane at the airport occasionally. I think it might be his. We don't run Chinese nationals through our customs system, so it's hard for me to say for sure."

I stared at her in astonishment. "What? You don't check Chinese nationals through some kind of customs when they come into the Cook Islands?"

"We do not," the prime minister confirmed. "They have

their own system here for that. It was part of the agreement for the police training and equipment. It's crazy, I know. I was working to change that. It's an inconceivable situation, but here we are."

"Slash was surprised to hear that, too," Manny commented. "It's just another way for the Chinese to circumvent the authority of the Cook Islands."

That this agreement had been signed in the first place was truly shocking to me, but I had bigger concerns on my plate at the moment. "I wonder what Maivia expects this Chinese boss guy to do?" I speculated aloud.

"I suspect that since things aren't going exactly as planned, Maivia wants to know what to do next," Henry guessed. "He sounded worried and clearly needs guidance."

"Because he can't think for himself," Petra added contemptuously, "I'm sure he's mainly concerned for himself. He's also likely worried the Chinese might be upset with him because things have gone awry. If I show up alive and protesting the coup, there are people who will be upset with him because he lied."

"Well, I guess we'll find out who this Chinese boss is and what his role is in all this, because he's supposed to arrive within the hour," Manny said.

I paled. My relief that Slash was still alive had been quickly replaced by a wave of dread. Slash was trapped in a compound run by the Chinese who had just orchestrated a successful coup and were using the Cook Islands as a pawn on their strategic geopolitical chessboard. All while we were on our freaking honeymoon on a remote island where nothing ever, ever happens.

I blew out a breath, trying to think clearly. I had a feeling Slash would not be treated kindly by whoever this Chinese boss turned out to be. And if they ever found out who he *really* was…well, that would be worse than disastrous. I had to rescue him, and fast.

I downloaded the second audio file and sent it to Angel and Frankie, requesting the translation as soon as possible. Then I turned to Manny.

"We need to get Slash out of there as soon as possible."

Manny nodded. "I agree, and it just so happens I have a plan. It's the same plan Slash and I came up with to get the recording devices out once we had planted them. The compound gets food deliveries Tuesday and Friday mornings. Tomorrow is Tuesday. It could be our best chance of getting inside undetected."

"I'm in," I said. "What do we do?"

Manny grabbed his bag and pulled out the drawing he had shared with Slash of the compound, then used a napkin and a pen from the table to quickly draw a crude map of the island, marking the compound's location. After he was done, he traced a finger along the narrow road that led to the compound. "The compound is just off the Ara Tapu, with a short driveway to the guarded gate. If my plan works, we should be able to coast right in. Lucky for us, the store owner who supplies the compound groceries and supplies is my first cousin Ari. We can use that to our advantage."

"What's your plan?" I asked.

"We go in as food delivery workers," Manny's said. His voice was calm, though I sensed the tension underlying each word. "We'll sit in the back of the truck among the crates and produce as the hired help. I'll speak to Ari, but I know he'll be willing to do it. Even though the Chinese are his best customers, he loathes them. He evens charges them what he calls his *ka peke koe* surcharge."

Petra laughed, and Henry joined her.

I looked between the two of them. "What's so funny? What does that mean?"

"It is like a middle finger surcharge, only more explicit," Henry answered.

"Ah, okay, I get it. We can trust Ari. So, once we're in, how do we figure out where Slash is and release him?"

"Well, that's the trickier part," Manny said. "I have an outline of the compound and can make an educated guess as to where they might be keeping him. I've talked to Ari and his assistant several times to get as clear a picture as possible. There are two potential places: There is the main guard room, which is on the first floor in the corridor across from where he was captured. But that's not a large room, and it might be awkward to hold him there while they are working. The only other place I could think of is an odd storage-type room across from the chief of staff's office, where Slash planted one of the recording devices. The room has an electronic keypad lock on it. I'd start there."

"What if it's just for equipment or drugs, and he's not in there?"

Manny lifted his hands. "Then we improvise."

That was something I was usually pretty good at...when it came to hacking. But breaking into an armed compound and rescuing someone...well, I wasn't as confident about my abilities on that front.

"What about weapons?" I asked. "Do you have one?"

"I have a gun, but if we use it, we bring the entire guard force down on us and no one escapes." He took another swig of water. "We have to be smart about this."

"What else do you have?" I asked. "I don't do guns well, anyway. Slash once accused me of holding a gun like a television show cop."

Manny spewed his water and then reached for a napkin. "He said *what?*"

"In my defense, he was in pain and wasn't thinking clearly at the time when he said it. It's a long story, but there was a bad guy, and he was trying to hurt Slash, so I shot him."

Petra, Henry, and Manny stared at me, transfixed. "Did you kill him?" Petra finally asked.

"No. I might have if I'd hit the torso—which is where I was aiming—but I hit him in the leg instead. Still, it brought him down and I rescued Slash, so I don't know why he was complaining about my stance. I haven't had a lot of time to practice at the range."

"You two have a most unusual relationship," Manny said. "How about a Taser? Have you ever used one?"

I thought back to the time I was in Hollywood working on a dating show for nerds. I'd sort of tased one of the contestants, but it hadn't been my fault. We'd been struggling for the Taser, and it went off...on him. Still, he'd been down for the count, so I guess I had to answer in the affirmative.

"Yes," I said. "Will it work without making too much noise?"

"Trust me, someone who gets hit with one of these is in so much pain they can barely mew like a kitten. I'll get one for both of us. Our security folks should have several that aren't being used right now."

He walked over to the policeman sitting near the stairs and talked quietly with him. The man immediately reached into his belt and handed him something. Manny then climbed the stairs to the upper deck, presumably looking for the other policeman.

Petra sighed, and Henry put an arm around her. "I feel

so helpless right now. Are you sure you want to do this, Lexi?" she asked. "Do you think it's a good idea?"

I put my fingers on the keyboard just as an email from Angel pinged in my inbox. "Right now, Prime Minister, there's no other options. We're running out of time."

"I seem to recall hearing Slash saying something similar," she replied. "I don't want to lose you, too."

Before I could respond, I jumped as sounds came from mine and Manny's phones again. We all instantly fell quiet. We heard a door open, and people started talking softly in Chinese.

"They're back," I whispered.

THIRTY-ONE

Slash

I must have dozed off, because I snapped awake when I heard someone at the door. I stood, bracing myself against one of the walls, blinking as a guard yanked open the door and hauled me out by the arm. Another guard stood nearby, holding an automatic weapon.

I stumbled over the closet threshold, squinting at the light as I was shoved down the hall and back into the office where I'd hid the recorder and my phone. Another stroke of luck for me, although I couldn't confirm whether they'd found them.

My eyes watered slightly, still adjusting from the cramped darkness of the closet. The parrot sat on its perch, and when it saw me, it flapped its wings and squawked as if offended by my presence.

I gave it a dirty look, but it just kept squawking until one of the guards snapped something to it in Chinese and it shut up.

They forced me into the same chair where I'd sat before, retied my hands behind my back, and waited. For what, I wasn't sure. There were three people in the office now. My gaze flicked around, noting the positions of guards. The two that had yanked me from the closet were sporting tactical vests with Chinese characters embroidered on patches and wore the insignia of the local police. The other was dressed in a similar uniform, but without the vest. A supervisor, I suspected. All were armed. My gaze swept over the statue where I'd hid the recorder, but I did not linger on it. It appeared untouched since I'd hidden it, so that was encouraging. However, I knew better than to get my hopes up.

Two of the Chinese guys said something to each other and then looked at me, smirking. I kept my expression neutral. No need to antagonize them at this point.

Finally, I heard some noise in the hallway, and two men entered. Both were dressed in suits. I didn't recognize the first man. He was tall and heavyset, probably the chief of staff, whose office we were in. When he moved aside, a Chinese man, impeccably dressed in a gray suit and tie that looked alien in the tropical humidity, walked into the office. Our eyes met, and a jolt of shock ran through both of us at the exact same moment.

To say I was surprised to see him would be an understatement, and clearly, he had the same reaction upon seeing me.

His eyes widened and time seemed to slow before he let out a low, disbelieving whistle. "Slash?" My name rolled off his lips in sheer incredulity. "Am I dreaming? What are you doing here? You're the last person I expected to see in this godforsaken place."

"Jiang Shi," I murmured.

The Chinese hacker and I had a history. A *long* history. Shi had once run the Chinese government's cybersecurity division until he went rogue, almost causing World War III with a computer virus. I'd tracked down Shi's brother and gained valuable intel for the US government before he landed in a US prison, where he still sat today.

Shi had come after me for that, and several other things, but I'd caught on to his planning and had personally placed him in the crosshairs of both the Chinese and American governments. We had all worked together to bring him down. As far as I'd known, Shi had lost everything: his job, his credibility, and, eventually, his freedom. I'd presumed Shi was rotting away in a Beijing prison. So, to now find Shi at the edge of the Pacific Ocean, orchestrating a coup in the Cook Islands at the very location Lexi and I had chosen to celebrate our honeymoon, was more than just a surprise. It was mind-blowing. That little black cloud had now topped all its previous achievements.

Without taking his gaze off my face, Shi reached into the pocket of his suit and pulled out a small silver coin and started twirling it between his fingers. I recognized the twirling as an old habit from our past encounters, a tic that revealed how Shi channeled his psychotic mind and restless focus. I had seen him spin a coin in endless loops on screens, cameras, and in person. I took note of the deep lines on his face and the subtle bitterness etched into them. That bitterness had grown even deeper since the last time I'd seen him—no surprise.

The tension in the room tightened as the silence stretched on. Everyone seemed to sense it. I was acutely aware of the shifting stances of the guards flanking me, their weapons poised but not exactly aimed, waiting for a command from Shi.

It finally came.

"Get out," he growled at the guards and then repeated it in Chinese when no one moved. "Now!" The guards, looking slightly bewildered, snapped to attention and then left the room. The chief of staff lingered, clearly wondering if the order applied to him as well. The look Shi gave him provided him all the clarity he needed, and he exited quickly, pulling the door shut behind him.

Once they were gone, Shi rubbed the coin between his palms and let it spin between his fingers again. "I can't believe you're actually here," he said, his voice quiet but laced with undisguised hatred. "I've dreamed of facing you again a million times. Followed your every move. But having you show up in the Cook Islands at the very moment of my comeback?" He paused with exaggerated drama. "It's almost poetic. No, it's fate."

"There's nothing poetic about it all, Shi," I replied, my tone measured. "It's just me being a step ahead of you once again."

That hit a nerve. Shi bobbled the coin and then squeezed it tight in his fist. But I could see the worry and alarm on his face even as he tried to play it off. "There is no way you knew about this in advance," he insisted. "This is coincidence. Fate."

True, but better to keep him second-guessing. I needed him to believe we knew everything in advance and this was all part of the plan.

"Sure," I said lightly. "You believe in whatever you want. I'm happy to lend an ear. Got anything you want to confess?"

"Confess?" Shi flashed a thin, joyless smile. "Oh, you'd like that, wouldn't you? Proof that somehow China engineered this coup. A reason for the US to step in, all noble and righteous. But you see, I know how you Americans do things. If your government has plausible deniability, they'll turn a blind eye. Weak." Shi paused, then added, "But if they had hard proof...that would be an entirely different story, wouldn't it?"

"What proof do I need?" I asked calmly. "China's actions already speak for themselves. No customs clearance and full authority on the island regarding your so-called law enforcement activities and the movement of Chinese citizens. The amount of money laundering, illegal weapons, drug trading, and intelligence activity flowing through the islands is certainly impressive."

Shi laughed. "It bothers you, doesn't it? That you prostrate yourself for meager pay in service to a government that doesn't appreciate or see the value in your work. While here I am, effortlessly advancing China's geopolitical influence and domination of the area, and I barely lift a finger. These poor, fourth-rate countries are so desperate, they beg us for money and recognition and, in turn, are willing to sell their sovereignty for a dime. Pathetic."

"Oh, I'm sure the lucrative cut you're getting makes things all better."

That amused him. "Jealous, I see. You know nothing of what I get. I'm the richest I've ever been. I make money three ways, only one of which the Chinese government is aware of."

I goaded him further. "Let me guess, you charge Chinese businessmen who want to move money or goods a particular fee for permitting them to do business on—or should I say, through—the islands."

"You underestimate me," Shi said. "Not only do I require an operating fee, but I get a percentage of the profits. Tariffs are a real thing these days, and my services helping them get around those sanctions and tariffs are invaluable. Furthermore, it's not just moving money. I have many, shall we say, clients, who wish to have a secure location to place funds where they are free from the eyes of prying governments. I have a special arrangement with some bankers here, and I connect them with customers and money and charge them both a fee for my services and, of course, my discretion."

There was a disturbance in the hall—two men arguing. The door suddenly opened and in strolled Liko Maivia. I recognized him from the photo Manny had showed us earlier. He was wearing a crisp suit and pressed a handkerchief to his sweating brow. But my eyes were immediately drawn to the sparkling coat of arms pin he wore on his lapel. The same pin Petra had showed us the night of the dinner, which was passed on by tradition, from prime minister to prime minister. Maivia had already co-opted it. The audacity of the man should have surprised me, but it didn't.

Maivia looked at me in shock, his eyes widening, before he sidled up to Jiang Shi.

Shi was visibly annoyed but plastered a fake smile on his face as he greeted Maivia. "Greetings, Prime Minister. What brings you here?"

Maivia didn't answer. "You know who this is, right?" he fumed, pointing at me. "He's the guy who stopped the assassination attempt on Askari. He must be working with her. He's an American and he's trouble. Everything is going wrong, and that's why I called you here."

The prime minister and Manny had been right about Maivia. He was a simpering man put in power by Chinese influence—egotistical and easy to manipulate. He was nothing more than a veneer to maintain the illusion of a local, organic power grab, while in reality, Beijing was tightening its grip on the islands.

Maivia caught my eye, and I glared at him, wondering if he were susceptible to intimidation. I shouldn't have wondered. He immediately lowered his gaze, revealing a trace of fear. He fiddled nervously with his handkerchief, staying well out of my range despite the fact I was tied to a chair.

But his revelation had shocked Shi. "*This* is the man that stopped the assassination?" Shi asked, as if he hadn't heard him right. "Him?" He pointed at me, apparently to ensure they were on the same page.

"Yes, him," Maivia said irritably. "I told you we had trouble and—"

"Shut up," Shi said, abruptly standing up and pressing his hands to the sides of his head. "Why wasn't I notified of this at once? I need to think."

Maivia obliged, shifting his weight from one foot to the other anxiously, his gaze flickering between me and Shi. "I did notify you right away," he said defensively.

Shi ignored him, lost in thought. Finally, he spoke. "What was he doing in the compound? Where was he caught?"

"The guards say they caught him here, right in this office. The parrot gave him up. They swept for bugs and searched the entire first floor but didn't find anything or catch anyone else."

"He had nothing on him?"

Maivia shrugged. "Just a knife and a lockpicking kit. Maybe he was looking for documents or something. You don't have any incriminating documents about me...do you?" He suddenly looked worried.

Shi again ignored him and examined me thoughtfully.

"Was there anyone else with him? Not here at the compound, but on the island. A friend, a group?"

Maivia shrugged. "Just a woman."

My stomach tightened, but I kept my expression blank as Shi turned toward me, his dark eyes narrowing. "A woman, you say?"

"Yes, a woman," Maivia repeated annoyed. "A girlfriend, wife, mistress. I don't know or care. What are we going to do about him and how are we going to find the prime minister? She's still missing. He probably knows where she is. We should torture him to find out."

A smug grin curled on Shi's lips as he stared at me. "Oh, don't worry, I have plans for him. Specific plans. Plans I will enjoy implementing."

"But what about the prime minister?" Maivia asked, his voice turning into a whine. "We need to find her. I want her gone. We can't have the old government regrouping. We need to get rid of her once and for all."

Shi tore his gaze away from mine to address Maivia. I could see him visibly struggle to keep his temper from flaring. "Relax. The real prime minister has no power here anymore. We have taken care of that. But if you're wondering, we'll find her. It's just a matter of time." He glanced back at me, his eyes cold. "And while we're at it, we'll find anyone who is helping him."

The threat was implicit in his gaze, and I had to relax my fingers to keep them from tightening into fists behind my back.

"Tell the guards to spread their search for the prime minister to the outer islands. She may have avoided our searches by relocating there. Use your loyalists there to search every possible hiding spot. No one leaves or enters the islands without our permission. If found, bring the prime minister to me—alive. The same goes for the woman who was with him." He pointed at me. "Get information on her from the customs office and plaster her face on posters everywhere. Say she's a terrorist wanted for questioning about the assassination attempt on the former prime minister. Anyone who turns her in gets a reward. Add a photo of him, too. Maybe we can get some useful information as to who else might be here with him and what they are doing. Make sure the public knows they are terrorists—the both of them."

Maivia seemed confused by the request. "This will help us find the prime minister?"

"It will. Everyone else can be collateral damage, for all I care." He let his gaze linger on me a moment longer before he turned to Maivia and flashed a feral smile. "See? We have everything in hand."

Maivia swallowed nervously, nodding his head. "Well, what about him? We can't just let him sit here and not help us find her."

"He's mine," Shi snapped with such ferocity that Maivia stepped backward, looking stunned. Then, realizing how badly he'd lost his composure, Shi tried to speak more calmly.

"What I mean is, don't worry about him. I intend to extract him personally from the Cook Islands tomorrow afternoon, and you won't have to worry about him any longer. I'll take him to China—to an undisclosed location. One of our more discreet facilities. He'll be...cooperative, given enough time. I'd like to have the woman, too, but he leaves with me tomorrow. I can come back for her, as needed."

I knew exactly what Beijing would do if given an asset as valuable as me—a man with a deep well of intelligence connections and top knowledge of US cyberwarfare. I'd be tortured until I gave them everything. That was unlikely to happen, though, as the little chip in my body would be activated to prevent just that. By that point, I was certain I'd welcome it.

But I had no intention of letting that happen.

Shi turned his attention back to me, thinking. He spun the coin faster, a metallic blur between his fingers. "Anything you'd like to say to me? Because once we're on that plane, you won't have another chance. I might even cripple those hands you rely on so much for hacking."

Maivia blanched and dropped his gaze, clearly uncomfortable at the sudden turn in the conversation. He spoke a good game about torture, but clearly, he didn't have the stomach for it.

Shi, too, seemed to sense Maivia's uneasiness, so he waved a hand at the man. "Leave us. He and I have unfinished business to discuss. Ask Chen, my chief of staff, to get my plane ready to leave tomorrow afternoon. Then find the prime minister you're still so worried about for some reason. If you can't or won't do that, then perhaps I'll find a new prime minister who can. I want the woman who was with him." He pointed at Slash. "I'm delaying my flight a few hours, until tomorrow afternoon, so you have time to find and bring her to me."

"But he can tell us where the prime minister is right now," Maivia whined.

"She'll be ours if you do your job and find her," Shi snapped. "In fact, it would best for you to have forgotten you've ever seen this man. Do I make myself clear? For now, do as I say."

Maivia clamped his mouth shut and then nodded. "Fine." He turned and left the room, closing the door behind him, clearly unhappy his concerns had not been taken more seriously.

If it wasn't clear who was running this show before, it certainly was now. Every word, every piece of evidence was ammunition in our arsenal. If Lexi and Manny could hear this, it would make a strong case Beijing was behind this entire operation, justifying international intervention.

But I still needed more.

I forced a grin. "You haven't changed at all, Shi. Corruption. Threats. Torture. Revenge. It's all so pedestrian. Still bitter over what happened to your brother?"

Shi whirled around, anger flashing. "My brother? You think this is about my brother? He's a traitor. He gave up information instead of taking an honorable death. Oh, I'm bitter, all right, but I assure you, that only scratches the surface. You ruined my life, and you're going to pay for it in ways you never imagined."

"Apparently, I didn't ruin it enough," I replied casually. "I imagined you rotting in a despicable Chinese prison, but instead, your superiors sent you here to the Cook Islands to infiltrate from the inside, using police assistance as a front to launch a coup and install a puppet government answerable only to Beijing. Busy boy. What other grunt work are you involved in these days? It's been such a long fall from the golden keyboard, hasn't it, Shi?"

Shi scoffed. "You know nothing. My life is more complicated than you can imagine. Yes, you cost me my status in China and my position in the ministry. They downgraded my clearance, banned me from cutting-edge projects, and kicked me over here to oversee the political and economic capture of several of these miserable island countries. We're just a little farther along here than in others, but despite the lack of faith in my abilities back in

China, I'm now calling the shots behind the scenes in four countries now. These countries think they're independent, but I'm their opium dealer. Except instead of drugs, I offer money and resources. They're all addicted. All I ask for is support from them at the appropriate times. Soon, the South Pacific will be a Chinese protectorate. I intend to make my way back to the top once they see my success." He tapped his temple with his finger. "And now, thanks to the kindness of fate, my life has gotten *so* much sweeter."

Shi stepped closer to me, his voice dropping to a conspiratorial whisper. "I'm going to find her, you know. And trust me, your worst torture will not be physical."

It took every ounce of my considerable training and mental fortitude to keep my expression and body relaxed. I imagined every scenario where I jumped out of this chair and snapped his neck, but the bindings around my arms held tight, and rage wouldn't get me what I wanted.

Shi laughed, not fooled by my calm demeanor. The metal coin spun in the air once more, a flicker of silver passing between his knuckles. He caught the coin between his index and middle fingers with a flourish. "You know, I do this to remind myself that life is just like this coin. It spins, it shifts, and you never know which side will show up. Today, I'm in the Cook Islands. Tomorrow evening, I'll be back in Beijing, a hero leading you in chains. Oh, fate is a such sweet and fickle woman. And today, she absolutely favors me."

When I didn't respond, Shi called out and the guards reentered the office. I didn't know what he said to them in Chinese, but they eyed me warily and their hands rested on their weapons.

One of the Chinese guys grabbed my arm roughly. I

didn't resist. I let myself be turned around, sparing a fleeting, final glance at the statue with the recorder on the desk.

I hope you're listening.

If the phone connection was still live, *if* Manny had escaped, and *if* Lexi was listening, there was enough evidence to blow this whole operation wide-open. But I couldn't depend on that. I needed to get out of the compound and find a way to escape. But how? Armed guards, a locked combination door, and the entire compound on high alert. All created a formidable barrier, and my time was running out.

Back in the cramped closet, the stale, humid air weighed on my lungs. This time, they didn't untie me, and the tight bonds were making my hands numb from the lack of circulation, so I sank back against the wall. I could not be on that plane tomorrow. I had to come up with something. Whether that involved covert cunning or a risky confrontation, I didn't know. I just knew under no circumstances could I board that plane.

I took a few measured breaths, trying to center myself. I imagined the world outside—the real prime minister in hiding, waiting for a miracle; the puppet government tightening its grip on power day by day; the Cook Islands' future held hostage by China's ambition. And somewhere out there, Lexi was in extreme danger.

If the US wouldn't interfere without proof, and if Lexi had been listening and was able to get the transmission out to the US government, I had just delivered a treasure trove of evidence, straight from Jiang Shi's mouth. Still, there were a lot of ifs, and I didn't like depending on others to get me out of tough situations.

In less than twenty-four hours, noon would come, and with it, the plane. I made a silent vow. No matter what, I would stop Shi. Because if fate had, indeed, brought us together again, Shi had it wrong. It was for a greater, more noble purpose.

To right a wrong.

Jiang Shi had to lose everything, for good, and I would do whatever it took to ensure that coin landed on the side of justice.

THIRTY-TWO

Lexi

We listened and heard people speaking softly in Chinese. There was some shuffling noise, the swish of the door, and then a voice in English. I quickly hit the record button again.

"Slash? Am I dreaming? What are you doing here? You're the last person I expected to see in this godforsaken place."

Multiple emotions swamped me at the same time. Relief, first and foremost, because Slash was in that room, talking, and he was alive. That was followed by gut-punching fear because who would recognize Slash all the way out here in the Cook Islands? Whoever it was, it couldn't be good.

Then I heard Slash say, "Jiang Shi."

I gasped aloud, slapping a hand over my mouth. Manny and the prime minister looked at me in alarm. "Who is Jiang Shi?" she whispered.

I shook my head, putting a finger to my lips, needing to

hear the conversation. As the conversation continued, I became more and more horrified.

What crazy twist of fate had brought Slash and Shi back together again? The situation had become far more dire than I had ever imagined. Shi was supposed to be in some Chinese prison after Slash and I destroyed his plans to start an international cyberwar, but here he was, moving pieces around the board of China's chess game in the South Pacific.

What in the world happened?

We listened as Slash manipulated Shi into bragging about his role in the area, my jaw tightening with disgust as Shi denigrated the Cook Islands, calling them and other nearby island countries pathetic and fourth-rate.

Petra's expression got angrier the more Shi revealed about his actions here on the island. Her hands tightened into fists; her eyes narrowed into furious slits. I would have put my money on her if she and Shi ever got into a fight.

At some point Maivia strolled in, interrupting the interrogation, not even realizing what was going on. He started whining and complaining about not being able to find the prime minister. I hadn't been sure I could dislike him more, but I found that I actually could. The guy was a pathetic piece of work.

I wanted to leap through the phone line and strangle Shi as he threatened Slash, promised to hurt me as part of his sick torture, and called us both terrorists while promising to plaster our photos across the islands as Most Wanted fugitives. Now I imagined fighting Shi, too, and I knew the first place I'd kick him. Really, really hard.

But what Shi said next chilled me to the bone.

"I intend to extract him from the Cook Islands tomorrow," Shi said to Maivia. "I'll take him to China—to an undisclosed location. One of our more discreet facilities. He'll be...cooperative, given enough time. I'd like to have the woman, too, but—"

There was sudden silence.

For a second, we all just stared at each other around the table.

"What happened?" Petra finally exclaimed, leaping to her feet.

"I don't know," I said, panic setting in. "The audio just cut off." I grabbed my phone and then Manny's. A quick glance confirmed that neither of them was connected to Slash's phone anymore. I hit the stop record button and began to immediately download the audio file.

"Damn," Manny said, slamming a fist on the table. "We lost the connection."

"Did they find Slash's phone?" Petra asked in alarm.

I shook my head. "I don't think so. I think his phone probably just ran out of battery."

"It lasted a lot longer than mine did, that's certain," Manny said.

"Slash has a special phone, and it has a larger battery, so it was able to keep the call going a lot longer."

"Who is this Jiang Shi guy, Lexi?" Manny asked. "Why does he have it in so bad for you and Slash?"

"It's a long story, but basically, he was a hacker who faced off with Slash and me over a year ago and lost. He nearly created an electronic world catastrophe with a virus that would have created international chaos. We presumed he was rotting away in a Chinese prison, but apparently, he was exiled to the South Pacific instead. It's a very bad situation."

"What are we going to do?" Henry asked. "They're

lunatics and murderers—the lot of them. How do we stop them?"

Petra's eyes hardened. "I don't know how we'll do it, but, by God, Maivia will be tried for sedition. I guarantee you that. And this Jiang Shi, he's not going to get away with this. He'll not hurt Slash, and he will not leave this island. He's a monster who needs to pay for his crimes, starting with the assault on our country."

"Shi is worse than a monster," I said quietly. "I mean it. Under no circumstances can we let him take Slash to China. We must get him out of the compound immediately."

"I agree," Manny said. "That Shi guy is a bloody psychopath, with Maivia, the pompous idiot, not far behind. Look, I spoke with Ari, and he's in for our plan to go with him into the compound in the morning. And I have our weapons." He held up the Tasers.

"Good." I glanced at my watch. It was already early afternoon, and I was mentally, emotionally, and physically exhausted. We had less than twenty-four hours to rescue Slash.

"How do we get to Ari's store?" I asked. "I presume there will be heightened roadblocks—and now that my face will be plastered all over the island as a terrorist and enemy number one, it will be even more dangerous."

"I wouldn't worry about that too much," Manny said. "There's only one printing shop on the island that could produce that many posters, and they close at three. Maivia won't be able to get them the pictures and the money to print the posters by then."

"What if he asks them to reopen to print the pictures?"

"Oh, I'm sure he won't find them as they will be conspicuously absent from work. Plus, they are going to be very slow about opening tomorrow morning for a similar reason. It would be late tomorrow before anyone would see your picture."

"How can you be so sure?" I asked worriedly.

"Well, it's Ari's son and his wife who run the print shop. I believe if I let them know to expect some government customers late this afternoon or tomorrow morning, they'll take their sweet time getting around to it."

"Is everybody related to everybody on the island?" I asked incredulously. "And you're from New Zealand, right?"

Manny laughed. "I am, and it only seems like everyone is related because it's a small island. Technically, there are five times as many Cook Islands descendants living in New Zealand than are here on the islands. But anyway, back to the plan. We'll get to Ari's in the dark and be there by dawn. Their place is down Ara Tapu, just past the compound. It is about an hour and a half walk in the daylight. It will be longer at night. Ari says they usually head to the compound about seven in the morning so they can deliver the fresh food and supplies before the kitchen staff starts making breakfast. We'd need to get to Ari's place well before that. The safest way to travel, given the heightened security, will be on foot. We'll leave the yacht, get off the beach, and cross the Ara Tapu. From there we can take the few side roads and back trails to get to Ari's warehouse. I know this part of the island like the back of my hand, and I can get us there safely. I have a small flashlight we can use."

That was good enough for me. I grabbed a piece of paper and a pen from my bag. "Okay, let's plot every detail of this extraction down to the tiniest one. The margin for error must be as near to zero as possible."

Henry put a hand on my arm. "Lexi, are you sure going

into the compound is a smart thing for you to do? If Shi captures you, you'll be giving him exactly what he wants."

"I'm not sitting on the sidelines, Henry. No one knows Slash like I do. I have the best chance of getting him out."

Henry didn't look convinced, but he didn't protest further. Petra and Manny also remained silent. They wisely realized I wasn't going to back down on this.

Manny met my gaze for a long moment and finally nodded. "Okay, listen carefully. This is the plan I have in mind."

THIRTY-THREE

Lexi

After we went over the details of the plan at least three times and had something to eat, I took a long-overdue shower and passed out in one of the yacht bedrooms until Manny woke me at about four o'clock in the morning.

"Time to go," he said softly.

The two of us gently climbed down into the skiff that was waiting for us. The policeman and Manny rowed the boat to shore, avoiding the possible attention a small motor running might attract. Fortunately, the tide was with us and the trip was quick. Manny led the way, and I walked behind and slightly to the side so that I could see the path ahead illuminated with his flashlight. He used the red-light mode to limit the range it could be seen and to help us retain our night vision. Nevertheless, I stepped in enough muddy, sandy spots that new shoes were going to be at the top of my shopping list when Slash and I got back from our honeymoon.

That line of thinking almost caused me to trip. I'd been so focused on watching my step, I'd temporarily forgotten Slash was in real peril and we might not make it home. Fear started to bubble up from my subconscious, so I suppressed it the best way I knew how—by reciting the digits of pi.

Manny stopped suddenly, and I bumped into the back of his shoulder. "Are you okay?" he asked. I heard the concern in his voice. "You were counting, or at least that's what it sounded like."

"I'm fine. I was just reciting the digits of pi. It helps calm me when I'm nervous."

"Sure. Okay. That's a totally normal thing for a CIA agent to do. Just let me know if you start composing a symphony so I can be prepared."

I had no idea why Manny thought I was a CIA agent and what that had to do with reciting pi, but now wasn't the time to discuss it.

We plodded along until we arrived at the shop. Manny's plan had us enter from the back, so we crept down a dark alley until he stopped at a door with a lockbox. It was after six by the time Manny keyed in the code and the back door popped open. He slipped inside, and I followed.

"Let me do the talking," he advised, and I nodded.

We walked through a kitchen that, despite the early hour already had workers washing and cutting vegetables. A couple of them eyed us curiously but said nothing. Manny spotted a dark-haired man with a beard holding a clipboard and motioned for me to wait while he walked over to him. After a short hug, Manny pulled him aside and the two began talking.

Eventually, Manny waved me over. "Lexi, I'd like you to meet my cousin Ari."

"Nice to meet you," I said, holding out a hand. "Although I wish it were under better circumstances."

"Likewise," Ari said, shaking my hand. "I can't pretend I know what the bloody hell is going on, but I know Manny. One of the best men I've ever known. If he says you need to get into that compound, then we'll get you in."

"Thank you," I said, my throat tightening.

"That said, if they catch you, I'm not sure what they'd do." His expression hardened. "But this is our island, and we're not about to give it up to some foreign-backed coup, especially not one sponsored by the Chinese. Oh, and by the way, my son dropped this off last night." He handed me a piece of paper.

I turned the paper over to see a Wanted poster warning the populace about me and Slash. We were labeled as terrorists and enemies of the people, and it sent a jolt of adrenaline spiking through me.

"Holy crap," I said.

"He told me someone left a note in an envelope at his business's door while he and his family were at the beach," Ari continued. "The note promised him a lucrative payment if he printed five hundred copies immediately. My son gave it to me, saying I might know what to do with it, since he doesn't print anything without payment up front."

"Please thank him for me," I said, ripping the poster into tiny shreds while Manny and Ari chuckled. "I never thought I'd be featured on a Wanted poster...and certainly not on my honeymoon." I scowled. "And did they *really* have to use my passport photo? That's just diabolical."

Manny put a hand on his cousin's shoulder. "The delivery truck leaves soon. We need to quickly disguise ourselves the best we can."

"We have extra white jackets and hats in the back," Ari

said. "The good news is we're virtually invisible to the Chinese. They'll likely not give either of you a second glance."

"The workers that usually make this delivery—do you trust them with us?" I asked. "We need them on our side."

"Sefina and Amiri have been with me the longest and are loyal to me," Manny assured me. "They will do as I ask, so they will do what you need them to do. They are also loyal to the prime minister, because they know she aims to protect the islands."

"Do they know that she hasn't resigned and is just in hiding?"

"They do, I've told them. They understand what's at stake."

"Thanks, mate," Manny said to his cousin, and they quickly embraced again. "And don't forget to tie yourselves up and rehearse the story of how your truck was hijacked," Manny reminded him. "This is for your protection and the protection of your staff in case they come looking for you."

"I understand the mission, and I've got this," Ari said. "*Kia manuia.*"

He walked away, and I looked at Manny. "What did he say?"

"He wished us good luck. We're going to need it."

Manny and I made our way to the back of the store. White jackets were hanging neatly on hooks, and nearby were some white caps. Manny handed me the largest women's jacket he could find, and I slipped it on, buttoning it up. It was snug, but it gave me the opportunity to slip another man's jacket on over the top of it, roll up the sleeves a bit, and still give me room to move. I tucked my hair up inside the cap and stuffed another cap in my inside pocket. I was as ready as I was going to get.

Manny pulled on his jacket and cap, and we stood there looking at each other.

"Want to revisit the plan for once we get inside the compound?" I asked quietly.

"It's not complicated, and we've been over it at least four times," he replied.

"Another time wouldn't hurt," I said.

He sighed. "Okay. We carry the food into the kitchen, and at some point, we slip away to find Slash. We do what we need to do to get him back to the truck and out safely."

I shook my head. "Manny, I've been thinking it over, and we need to revise the plan. I'm the only one who is going to slip away from the kitchen to find Slash. Two of us together is too noticeable, and I'm more likely to be able to talk my way out of a situation if I get caught. I'm less threatening than you and less threatening than both of us together."

"I don't like that plan. What if you're recognized?" Manny asked.

"What if I'm not? No one is going to be looking that closely at me. I'm a lowly kitchen worker who will have her hair tucked up under her hat. And even if I'm unsuccessful, you can go back with the truck and figure out something else with the prime minister."

"There's no time for anything else," Manny said.

"For Slash and me, no. But for the Cook Islands, yes. We've given our government enough fuel to come take a closer look at things. They've also passed the information on to the proper authorities in New Zealand and the UK. Shi's plans are not as foolproof as he thinks."

"Forget Shi for the moment," Manny said. "I think we have a better chance together."

"We don't." I put a hand on Manny's arm. "Look, I'm

going to get Slash out. I'm resourceful, you know that. You have to trust me. Okay?"

He scowled. "You waited until the last minute to spring this on me because you knew I wouldn't like it."

"Maybe," I admitted. "But Slash and I have done this before. We've been in dangerous situations, and we've always been able to find a way to get through it. We're good at that. We'll do it again this time, but I need you to let me do it alone."

He exhaled, clearly conflicted. But finally, he spoke. "Obviously, I'm out of my depth here. I won't overrule you, Lexi. We'll go with your plan if you insist. As long as you let Sefina disguise you a bit more and you answer a question for me...honestly."

At this point, I would tell Manny almost anything he wanted to get his cooperation. "Sure," I answered, looking him straight in the eye so he knew I was being honest.

"People with your level of experience in 'dangerous situations' don't just magically appear in a crisis except in a thriller novel. Are you really on your honeymoon, or is it a cover?"

I hadn't expected that question, but I answered it. "We're *really* on our honeymoon. Trouble just seems to follow me like a shadow. Sometimes I look and it isn't there, but it seems to dog my every footstep. We came here—the remotest island we could think of—for our honeymoon, and look what happened. I don't know if I brought the coup or the coup brought me. But here we are. And thank you, Manny, for letting me do this on my own. I'm going to save Slash."

"Don't make me regret my decision," he said gruffly.

"I won't," I promised. "I have too much at stake."

We went out to the truck and Ari introduced us to

Sefina and Amiri. Both were in their mid-forties and reserved. Amiri stood over six feet with dark hair shaved close to his scalp and strong arms. Sefina was tiny—at least compared to me—at maybe five feet one inches, with silky black hair that fell to her waist. They were willing to assist us, even if they weren't exactly sure what they were doing. According to Ari, they only needed to know they were helping the prime minister against the coup, and they were fully in.

I'd never appreciated two strangers more.

"Just remember, do everything like you always do, but in slow motion today," Ari instructed them. "That's it."

While Manny, Amiri, and some other workers began loading the truck with sacks of flour, cartons of canned goods, and fresh produce, Sefina led me into the back room to help me look more like an islander and less like a so-called American terrorist. She pulled a chair between a couple of crates and a tower of canned goods and made me sit down. Then she turned a wooden crate on its side and perched on it so we were face-to-face.

She pulled off my hat and then removed my ponytail scrunchie so my hair tumbled down past my shoulders. For a long moment, she studied me. "You're going to need lotion and bronzer," she said and hopped off the crate. "A lot of it."

She came back a minute later with a small bottle of what looked like oil, a compact, and a large makeup brush. She first opened the small bottle and poured something into her hand. She then rubbed both hands together and slathered it onto my cheeks, chin, and forehead. It was cool and slippery.

"What is that?" I asked.

"It's tamanu oil," she replied. "It's a nut oil made by pressing the seeds of the tamanu tree. It's primarily used by

Polynesian women as an antiaging strategy, but it also helps to moisturize the skin so the makeup I'm about to put on your face will stay put for longer. Especially since you have such dry skin."

When she finished, I reached up and touched my cheeks. "Wow, it feels really soft, not greasy like I expected."

"Your skin has already absorbed it," she said, examining her work. "It's soothing."

She was right. I made a mental note to buy a bottle or two before we left the island...*if* we were able to leave the island alive.

Next, Sefina flipped open the compact and began deftly applying the bronzer to my cheeks and forehead in wide strokes.

"Easy with the brush." I winced.

"Sorry, but you're so pale. Do you even know what sunlight looks like?" Her accent lilted with amusement.

I shrugged and then gasped as Sefina's makeup brush came perilously close to my eye. "Hold still," she warned, and I complied as she resumed her strokes.

"I work with computers, which means I spend my days under fluorescent lights," I explained, trying not to move my mouth too much. "I get a tan from my computer monitor."

Sefina lifted the brush from my face and burst into laughter. "A monitor tan? Oh, that's a new one, love. Well, today we're turning you into a food warehouse worker, not a techie."

She told me to close my eyes and then dusted my eyelids with a bit more bronzer. "Done with the face," she said, snapping the compact closed. "Now it's time for the hair."

Reaching into her pocket, she pulled out a hairnet. She

quickly pinned up my hair into a neat bun, tucking it under the net and then put my hat back on.

"Stand up and let me look at you."

I stood and adjusted the oversized men's jacket. "Are you sure this is going to work? It feels like I'm wearing a sail, and I'm already so hot, I'm afraid the makeup will melt."

"Be confident in yourself," she said. "We'll make it work."

She gazed up at me, her brow wrinkling. Next to her I felt like a giant. "How tall are you?" she asked. "You look like you might be near two meters."

"I'm 1.8034 meters, to be exact," I replied. "Not quite six feet."

"Well, I can't fix your height, but most of the time the Chinese don't notice us anyway. I have a spare pair of glasses that might help."

"Thank you, Sefina," I said, putting a hand on her arm. "I really appreciate your help."

She nodded. "You're welcome. I'm no friend of the Chinese. They treat us like we are nothing, but we're not as stupid as they think we are."

We headed back to the truck to help finish loading. As they were done, Manny scrutinized me. "Sefina did a good job with the makeup. I hardly recognize you. Can you see out of those glasses?"

"Sort of. But if I have to wear them for a long time, I might get a headache."

Once the last crate was secured, Sefina and Amiri climbed into the front, and Manny and I got into the back. They had a space for us to slide in behind some crates. A worker then strategically placed a large sack so that we were obscured from all but a thorough search. We would stay out of sight until we passed the compound's gate.

Manny reached into his pocket and passed me a Taser. "Hopefully, we won't be in there long. Be careful with this. This is a Chinese model they provide our police. It smaller than the typical Tasers sold in the States, but it really packs a kick. It activates with a single button and the tasing lasts as long as you hold the button, up to five minutes."

I examined the settings and made sure I understood how to use it properly.

"Lexi, if you intend to use it, there should be no hesitation," he warned me. "Use the highest setting."

"No hesitation and highest setting," I agreed.

"And no taking a stance like a television cop." He snickered.

"Ha-ha." I rolled my eyes. "Very funny."

Chuckling, Manny rustled around in his pocket. "One last thing. Hold out your hand."

Puzzled, I held out my hand. He dropped two large green peapods into my palm. I looked at him, confused. "What's this for?"

"Slash must retrieve the recording device from the office and possibly his phone. You'd better give this to the parrot while he does that. It should shut him up long enough for you two to get in and out."

I nodded. "Good thinking, Manny. You're brilliant."

"Bloody right. I have my moments," he said with a smile and clapped me on the shoulder.

My heart raced as the engine rumbled to life and the truck pulled out. I took a deep breath and reminded myself Slash was counting on me.

Game time.

THIRTY-FOUR

Lexi

The ride to the compound was bumpy in the back of the truck crouched behind the crates, but uneventful. We passed a roadblock, where they briefly opened the door, but no one checked the cargo. I guess they figured it would be unlikely for the prime minister to be hiding in a truck of produce headed for the Chinese compound.

There were no windows in the back of the truck, so we had no idea where we were. When the truck stopped again, I heard voices talking, and we didn't move right away.

"I think we're at the compound gate," Manny mouthed.

I shrugged. A minute later, the back door of the truck rolled up. I froze, not moving a muscle. I heard Sefina saying something, and another clipped voice replied, probably a Chinese guard. The guard seemed to be poking at some of the nearer crates, and one of them suddenly tumbled over, spilling the produce.

A couple of hot green peppers rolled near my feet and

came to a stop. My nose started to twitch, so I pinched my nostrils together. I could feel a sneeze coming, so I held my breath and squeezed my eyes shut, holding it back the best I could. Tears started to leak from the corners of my eyes.

Sefina cursed and ordered the guard to climb inside and clean up his mess. Laughing, he rolled the door down, slamming it shut, just as a half-muted sneeze escaped my lips. Manny and I looked each other with wide eyes until I heard a door slam and the truck lurched forward.

We were in!

I kicked the pepper away and let out a deep breath as Manny gave me a thumbs-up sign.

I put my glasses on as the truck rounded a bend before coming to a stop again. After a minute, the door rolled up again. Sefina stepped inside and nodded to us.

"All clear," she said in a low voice.

We were out of sight from the gate and the dormitory building, behind the main compound building. There was a rear entrance to the kitchen area, and they had backed the truck up close to the door to make the unloading go quickly. It would also make it easy to get an extra person into the truck when we left. Manny and I hopped down from the truck's deck. I glanced around. If Manny was right, once we were in the kitchen, Slash would be just down the nearest hallway.

So close.

A gated swimming pool and bathhouse were located behind the kitchen. There was no one out this morning, despite it being a lovely sunny day. Of course, it was 0700, so that might have something to do with it. More likely, most of the available guards were already out looking for terrorist me and the prime minister. Little did they know I was right beneath their noses.

We started to slowly unload the truck, carrying the crates and boxes into the kitchen, moving with the pace of a snail. We still didn't see a soul. The cooks hadn't arrived yet. They were probably waiting for us to finish our delivery. Ari had been right; there were no guards to supervise us, and the kitchen manager whose office abutted the kitchen didn't even come out to greet us. We were invisible to them.

Which worked *really* well for our plan.

I put a crate onto the counter and looked around. No one was in the kitchen but me. It was time to put things into motion.

I walked over to the coffee maker and turned it on. I found some filters and coffee and began brewing a pot. Manny walked in carrying a large box and saw me getting ready.

"Now?" he asked.

"Now," I confirmed, and he kept watch while I finished my task and poured the coffee into a cup, putting it on a saucer. I took the Taser from my pocket and slipped the strap around my right wrist. I checked the intensity setting, making sure it was at its highest.

"Be careful," Manny murmured. "Stick to the plan."

"Like that ever works for me," I whispered, but I nodded anyway. "I will."

"Oh, I have one more thing for you that you'll need, and I almost forgot." He reached into a pocket and pulled out a set of lockpicks. "I gave Slash my best set earlier, but these should work if you need them. You do know how to use them, right?"

I looked at Manny in surprise. "Why would I know how to use a lockpick?"

Manny sighed. "Because you're CIA, of course. Oh, never mind. I can't figure you guys out. Take them anyway.

Maybe you can slip them under the door and Slash can free himself."

I stuck them in a pocket and left the kitchen, carrying the coffee in my left hand. I carefully slipped past the manager's office. She was sitting at her desk, focused on her computer, and never looked up.

I entered the long, shadowy, and carpeted hallway. The layout Manny had drawn indicated the office where Slash had planted the bug was at the end of the hallway on the left. Catty-corner on the right side would be the locked storage room where Slash might be imprisoned.

My heart drumming in my ears, I flattened myself against the wall and peered into the shadows at the end of the hall. I heard a scraping sound and a slight noise and realized there was someone standing at the end of the hallway. I saw a quick flash of light and realized someone had lit a cigarette.

A guard. That was good news, because a guard standing in the hall in the general area of the locked storage room made me feel more confident that Slash was there. At least I hoped so, because in a minute or so, I was about to find out one way or the other. Thankfully, it looked like just one person. That was a good sign, since I was certain one guy would be all I could handle.

I suddenly heard shuffling and footsteps behind me. I slid into the small indentation of the closed door to the room next to me. I sucked in my breath, pressing myself as tightly as I could against the door, the coffee cup digging into my stomach. The kitchen manager left her office and strode left into the kitchen without even glancing my way. Maybe she smelled the coffee.

"Crap," I whispered. I waited another two full minutes,

frozen in the doorway, until the manager strode back into the office. Indeed, she was carrying a mug of coffee.

I exhaled softly. That was way too close. I couldn't wait any longer. The plan needed to go into action now.

I summoned my courage and then walked out into the open and down the hall toward the guard. I was carrying the cup and saucer in one hand, and the other was slightly behind my back. Luckily, the darkened hallway helped with my deception.

"Excuse me?" I called out softly as I got closer. I tried using the best imitation of a New Zealand accent I could manage. It sounded horrible to my ears, but I hoped the Chinese guard wouldn't be able to tell. "The woman there" —I pointed back to the kitchen manager's office—"said I should bring you coffee."

The guard turned toward me, a cigarette dangling from his mouth. I noticed the gun in his holster. At least he hadn't drawn it.

He grunted and reached out to take the coffee. As his hands touched the saucer, I pushed the Taser forward and got him right in the gut. I held it firm as he dropped to the floor, shaking and grunting. The cup and saucer fell to the carpet and broke, but the carpet masked the sound.

I kept my finger on the Taser button and reached down and removed the gun from his holster. He was twitching on the ground, but not making any vocalizations. I stomped on the cigarette that had fallen and turned to face the door he was guarding. It was a heavy steel door with an electronic keypad.

I tried the handle, but it was locked. "Slash," I whispered as loudly as I dared, leaning close to the door. "Slash, are you in there? Slash?"

For several agonizing seconds, I heard nothing. Then, faintly, I heard a voice on the other side. "Lexi? Is that you?"

Relief flooded me. "Yes, it's me. I'm trying to get you out of here. I don't have the code, though. What do I do?"

Slash spoke again, low and urgent. "Do you see a small sensor panel near the top of the door?"

I looked up. "Yes, I see it."

"I watched them punch in the code—once. I couldn't see the last number, but the first ones are three, three, seven, four, and I don't know the final one. You'll have to try them all."

"Got it." My hands shook as I tapped the keypad with the first code, adding a one at the end. My breath hitched when the red light blinked. I tried again and again until I reached the number six. Suddenly the keypad chirped, and the door clicked open.

Slash flung it open with his shoulder and stepped into me. I threw my arms around him, realizing he wore no shirt and his hands were tied behind his back. It didn't matter, because I was so relieved to see him, I couldn't breathe.

"You came," he murmured.

"Of course I came," I whispered heatedly. "But I freaking told you so. You got caught."

"At no fault of my own," he whispered back. "I never expected there to be a deranged bird planted in the office as some kind of biological alarm."

"I'm still right."

"You are," he murmured, but he didn't sound upset, only relieved. "Come on, we have to move now, *cara*."

He glanced at the guard on the ground and then the Taser in my hand. "Good thinking, but you better activate it again," he said.

The guard had started to sit up. I'd taken my finger off

the button in my excitement at seeing Slash. He was opening his mouth to holler when I zapped him again. He went down like he'd been shot.

"Get his knife and free my hands." Slash motioned toward a knife resting in a sheath on the guard's left hip. I grabbed it and quickly sawed through the plastic ties.

Once I freed him, he flexed his arms for a second before grabbing the guard's gun and then my Taser. The five-minute duration on the Taser was ending, and we were going to have to do something with the guard. Slash turned off the Taser, but before the guard could recover, he reversed the gun and delivered a hard blow to the guard's head. The crack was audible down the hall, and I worried the kitchen manager might check. I watched for her as Slash dragged the guard into the cell, but she never appeared. Slash closed the door and locked him in.

I stripped off my top white jacket and handed it to him.

"You're wearing two jackets," he said, observing me. "Smart."

"I thought that's why you love me," I whispered.

"It's a definitely a turn-on."

I didn't have to explain the plan to him. He slipped on the jacket, hiding the gun and knife beneath the jacket and handing me back the Taser. I gave him the extra hat and he pulled the brim low over his head.

"I need to get the recording device and my phone," he said. "They're in there." He pointed to the office at the end of the hall.

"I thought you said you planted two recorders."

"I did, but the one in that office is the only one I need. I don't know if anyone is in there right now, but if there is, I've got a gun to deal with it. However, I *do* know there's a loud and annoying parrot there that'll surely give us away. I'll have to wring its neck before it squawks."

I looked at him in horror. "What? You'd kill a poor, defenseless parrot?"

Slash raised an eyebrow. "That parrot doesn't like me. If it wasn't for that parrot, we wouldn't be in this predicament in the first place."

"Ha! Now you know how it feels." I reached into my pocket and pulled out the peapods. "I'll give him these instead."

Slash's eyebrow lifted even higher. "Do my ears deceive me? Lexi Carmichael, protecting an animal?"

"Just this once," I muttered, but he had already started moving toward the office. I followed, practically standing on his heels as he turned the knob.

It was locked. Slash cursed under his breath and turned around.

I held Manny's lockpicks by two fingers. "Need these?" I asked.

"Damn, I love you," he whispered, taking the lockpicks.

"I know," I whispered back.

He picked the lock with scary efficiency, pushing me behind him as he entered the room, holding the gun out.

The room was empty except for the parrot. I immediately tossed a peapod toward the bird, and it landed on the windowsill nearby. The pod distracted the bird long enough for it to recognize the treat, hop down, and begin munching.

I glanced over my shoulder as Slash grabbed something from inside a statue on the desk, stuck it in his pocket, and then crawled under the desk.

"Hurry," I urged him. "I don't know how long the peapods will distract him."

"Good, because we're done here," he said.

I tossed the remaining peapod at the parrot as we headed toward the door. Just as we reached it, Slash put his hand on the small of my back. "You go first," he said. "If something happens, you don't stop. Get out of here any way you can, understood?"

I nodded and stepped out into the hallway, followed closely by Slash. My heart thundered so loudly I was sure it could be heard throughout the entire compound. I crept down the hallway, past the locked storage room with the guard inside, and past the kitchen manager's office. The manager was on the phone with her back facing me. Still, every word she said was magnified in my ears one hundred times over as I slipped past.

I tried not to shake, but my teeth were chattering, so I had to clamp them shut. Thank God, no one was in the kitchen, so I picked up an empty crate and started heading for the exit when Slash entered the kitchen behind me.

I tensed in case the kitchen manager came running out, but she didn't. Breathing a sigh of relief, I continued to the door with my crate. I could hear Slash's footsteps behind me. The air felt thick with tension, but only a few more feet and we'd be in the delivery truck.

I reached for the door, but it opened first. Standing in front of me were three people in white uniforms I had never seen, and they were Chinese.

I was so startled, I froze. Before I could respond, the first person, a woman, pushed past me into the kitchen without a word. Two men followed her, paying no attention to either me or Slash. It suddenly occurred to me they were the kitchen staff arriving to start breakfast.

Ari had told us we would be invisible to them, and thankfully, he was right. I slipped out behind them, followed closely by Slash, and we headed directly to the delivery truck, where Manny and the others were slowly loading the empty crates and boxes to buy us time.

Manny caught sight of us, and the look of relief on his face said it all. He signaled to the others to get into the cab. I reached the truck and loaded my crate in the back. Manny extended a hand and pulled me up into the truck.

Slash dumped his crates in the back and hopped up. Together he and Manny rolled down the back of the truck from the inside. The engine fired up and lurched once before the truck pulled away.

We hid behind the empty crates, Slash sitting next to me, putting an arm around my shoulder. I leaned my head on his shoulder and held my breath as we paused at the gate.

I could hear Amiri call out to the guard, "We're all set. See you Friday."

There was a pause, and then the truck started rolling again. I closed my eyes for a moment, grateful we'd made it this far.

I turned to face Slash. His face looked bruised and swollen. I touched his cheek gently. "Are you okay?"

"I'm fine. These are all surface wounds. Nothing time, and you being alive, won't heal." He pressed a kiss against my forehead. "Thanks for coming for me," he said. "Both of you. I presume you heard the conversation I had with Jiang Shi."

"Partly," Manny confirmed. "Your phone cut out in the middle of the conversation. We assumed it died. But we heard he intended to take you to China this afternoon."

"That was his plan."

"It's crazy that Shi is here," I said. "How is that possible?"

"Fate," Slash replied. "But no worries, he's not getting away this time."

"Do you have the recording device?" Manny asked.

Slash reached into his pocket and held it up between his fingers. "Right here."

"Excellent," Manny said. "But we're not out of the woods yet. I told Amiri to stop a mile ahead near a scenic overlook so we can get out. Motorbikes have been left in the woods for us so we can finalize our escape. It won't take the Chinese long before they find you're gone and put the pieces together."

"No, it won't," Slash said. "But we've got the evidence we need to blow this coup wide-open."

"That we do," Manny agreed.

The truck rumbled over the road, every bump jarring my knees painfully against the crates. Shortly, the truck rolled to a stop at the side of the road. Manny and Slash pulled open the back, and we hopped out. I took off my white jacket and hat, laying them in the back of the truck before I handed Sefina back her glasses. Since Slash didn't have a shirt beneath his jacket, he kept his on.

Sefina tucked the glasses in an inside pocket. "Now what?" she asked.

Manny held up some rope. "We tie you up, so you have plausible deniability in this situation. Your story is that you heard banging coming from the back, so you stopped the truck to check it out. Two men jumped out and ambushed you. They tied you up, left you here, and ran into the woods going in that direction." He pointed north toward the city, the opposite direction we were really heading.

Slash walked over to them. "Thank you both for helping us."

"If you're friends with Ari, Manny, and the true prime minister, then you are friends of ours," Amiri said.

"Absolutely," Sefina agreed. "We're not fans of what the Chinese are doing to our country, so, all the power to you. If you can help us against the Chinese, then do it."

"We will," Slash said. "But right now, I need you two to sit back to back over there, away from the road, and we'll tie you up. The bonds will be loose enough so if there's any real reason you need to get away, you should be able to slip free without much of a problem."

"Just stick to your story, no matter what, okay?" Manny said. "Ari will back you up. They should release you right away. You won't be of interest to them."

They nodded and sat without protest. Slash and Manny tied them up and we said a quick goodbye before plunging into the woods. I felt worried about leaving them there, but I also knew that it wouldn't be long before the Chinese found them.

After a minute, Manny whistled. "Over here. We got a couple of bikes waiting for us. Yours is right there."

Manny had already pulled his bike upright and sat on it. A moment later, he started up the engine.

Slash pulled ours up and climbed on. I got on behind him, wrapping my arms tightly around his waist. Slash started our bike, and Manny gave us a thumbs-up.

"Follow me," he said. "Time is ticking." He drove off and Slash followed.

"What the heck do you think Jiang Shi is really doing in the Cook Islands?" I said to Slash as we drove cautiously through the jungle.

"Skimming, cheating, laundering money, and trafficking," Slash responded. "Along with orchestrating the

Chinese geopolitical strategy in the area. But he's also giving me a chance to finish him once and for all. And trust me, I'm about to do just that."

THIRTY-FIVE

Slash

Manny pulled over and motioned for us to get off the bikes when we were close to the path leading to the beach and the yacht. We left the bikes and walked the rest of the way until we could look out across the main road and see the water. The skiff was moored to the near side of the yacht. I couldn't see anyone on the deck. We paused at the edge of the tree line and watched for any unusual activity.

It was quiet. The midmorning sun was still casting long shadows while starting to bake the dunes. The water sparkled and the waves were low. The yacht rocked gently in the water, seeming to be deserted, but we knew better. Still, it offered a sort of beacon of safety—or as close to safety as we could get right now.

A lone fisherman occupied the beach between us and the boat. When I pointed him out, Manny said he was one of the prime minister's security detail guarding the boat.

"Stay here and take this," Manny said, handing me his

phone. "Lexi doesn't have hers and yours is presumably dead. Instead of risking us all, I'll head to the boat alone to brief the prime minister. I'll call you from one of the phones on the boat. We can discuss the next plan of action then."

I took his phone and watched as Manny strolled out of the jungle, down the road, and wandered along the beach by the fisherman. He waved and made a casual greeting and then kept walking. The fisherman stopped soon thereafter and pulled out his phone. Within minutes the skiff left the yacht and headed for shore, clearly being directed to come pick up Manny. As soon as the skiff arrived, Manny hopped in, and they headed back to the yacht.

While Manny was in the skiff, I pulled my phone out of my pocket. "You were right. My phone is completely drained. Hope you got something from it."

"Oh, we did," Lexi said. "Most important was hearing Shi's plan to send you to China. I knew we had to get you out right away. Beyond that, I've sent that audio and everything else we've gathered to Elvis and Xavier. Frankie has been translating the Chinese sections for me. She and Elvis have also been feeding Candace everything we've gotten to this point. I think we're close to having enough. That recording in your pocket should seal the deal."

"Agreed. Are the twins making any progress?"

"Well, I haven't spoken to them in over twelve hours, but the last I heard, Elvis and Xavier had still not been able to connect any payments from Signet Investments to Maivia. I tracked down Maivia's official email address, and we sent him an email baited with Chinese characters and a malicious link. If he fell for it, we should own his official account by now. If we're really lucky, it will have led the kids and Elvis to his private email as well."

"That's excellent news." I smiled. "It gives us a lot of options."

"It does. Add to that, the kids are already in the system and poised to take back control of the Cook Islands' official media accounts, as well as the prime minister's personal account, upon our command."

"You *have* been busy."

Lexi kissed my cheek. "Worrying about you, yes. Slash, when I heard you say Shi's name, I thought it had to be a mistake. I couldn't breathe."

"It was a surprise to say the least."

"You sounded so calm," she said. "Whereas I wanted to jump through the phone lines and kick Shi where the sun doesn't shine."

I chuckled. "So vicious, my sweet wife, and yet, I wouldn't have stopped you. I stayed calm because I wanted him to believe I knew he was here and was in the Cook Islands to bring him down. I knew that would worry him greatly. That's when he makes mistakes."

"So, what's next?" she asked. "You had plenty of time relaxing in that closet. How do we take down Shi and Maivia?"

We discussed some possibilities, bouncing ideas off each other before the phone in my hand rang. I answered it. "Yes?"

"It's me," Manny said. "I'm here with the prime minister. Let's talk."

I put the phone on speaker so Lexi could hear. "Okay. Go."

"First of all, I want to say I'm grateful you're okay, Slash," Petra said. "I had no idea about this Shi character, and I'm so sorry you were put in harm's way."

"All is well," I said. "How are you doing?"

"We're holding up the best we can under the circumstances," she replied. "But I'm sorry to say your escape has already been discovered."

"That didn't take long," Lexi said.

"It didn't. From what we've heard on the police radio, the Chinese and Maivia are ramping up the search for you two. Listen to this."

I heard a click, and the static-filled voice of an officer crackled. "Repeat: All units be advised—the foreign nationals, both Americans, have been identified as armed terrorists, wanted for the attempted assassination of Acting Prime Minister Liko Maivia. Lethal force is authorized to eliminate the threat."

Lexi pinched the bridge of her nose. "Lethal force. It's the honeymoon every girl dreams of."

I let out a dry laugh, then winced. I was still slightly favoring my jaw—evidence of the not-so-gentle hospitality I'd received at the compound. "Shi is pissed."

"Like a rattlesnake," Manny said. "This isn't just damage control anymore. They're tightening the net. Your escape from the compound has really stirred up a *wētā* nest."

"I assume a *wētā* is the Cook Islands version of a hornet," Lexi said.

"New Zealand's version," Manny corrected her. "They're large, native insects known for their aggressive, and sometimes intimidating, presence. But you could say they're a good stand-in for a hornet."

"I'm glad he's pissed," Lexi said and then smiled. "You know, despite everything, that makes me feel pretty good."

"Regardless, we don't have much time," Petra said urgently. "We don't know how many Chinese reinforcements—police, military, who knows what else—are on the way. We can't let them tighten their grip on the Cook Islands any more than they already have, or worse, capture us."

"Then we go on the offensive," I said.

That got a reaction—meaning dead silence. I figured they were shocked by my bold suggestion. Lexi, however, looked at me like she was thinking it was about time.

"We're done hiding," I continued. "We flip this back on them. They're controlling the narrative—painting us as terrorists. We take that away from them."

"And how do we do that?" Manny asked.

"Electronically. I need my computer, and Lexi needs hers. ASAP."

Manny sounded skeptical. "What are you going to do? Post an angry Yelp review of the coup?"

I grinned at the thought of it. "Something like that. First, we contact the US government. I need to get this full recording from the compound to them right away. Second, we turn their own game against them. We now have the power to control their communications and leak the information *we* want to shift public opinion. If you're right, Petra, the people here don't want to be under China's thumb. Economic support is one thing, but what we'll expose is something entirely different. We just need to show the people the truth."

"But we have a problem," Lexi chimed in. "We're uncomfortable about using the yacht as our center of operations to strike back. It's too exposed, and it is probably just a matter of time until someone notices the unusual increase in activity here. Plus, to wage our campaign, we'll need a better internet and Wi-Fi connection, at least as good as we had back at the farmhouse. Unless you have another safe location where we could operate."

"I'll have to check with the security guys to see if there is another safe spot," Manny said. "They were supposed to be working on that. Wait a minute..." He stopped and must have turned away from his phone.

Finally, he returned. "Petra suggests returning to the farmhouse. She has reports that the police haven't returned since we left. After considering the alternatives, we agree it's probably as safe as any other location right now. Additionally, we can easily get there from here without using the roads."

"That would be great if it's safe," Lexi said. "What do you think, Slash?"

"I doubt any place is truly safe, but I think we should trust the prime minister," I said. "We can check it out first before anyone gets there."

"I'll lead you there," Manny said. "If it's clear, we can presume they think we wouldn't be dumb enough to go back. Plus, in retrospect, I'm not even sure they can link us to the farmhouse. All they know is there were two people on a motorcycle who fled the house. They never saw the prime minister or her family."

Petra's voice came through the phone clearly. "I don't know how you're going to do any of what you're planning, but I'm convinced the premise is the right one. We're running out of options and time."

"Manny, Lexi, and I will investigate the farmhouse," I said. "If it's clear, you can relocate with us. We'll send Manny back for you while we start making Shi and Maivia very uncomfortable. Pack up and be ready to move, Petra. Manny will coordinate with your security. Manny, when you return to shore, please bring Lexi's phone, our bags, laptops, and any cords or other peripherals that go with them. And, sorry to ask, is there any way you can find me a shirt? I'm doing a slow roast in this white food jacket and might as well have a bull's-eye on the back of it."

Manny chuckled. "Will do. Give me ten."

I hung up, and Lexi and I exchanged a silent glance. Shi had taken on the wrong people...again. We weren't going to go quietly, this time or ever. We'd stopped Shi and his brother before. He'd had his turn at bat, and now it was ours. All we needed was a little help from our friends.

He'd messed with the wrong honeymooners.

THIRTY-SIX

Slash

"It's time to call Candace," I said, holding up Manny's phone.

"Will she answer if it's not your phone?" Lexi asked.

I nodded. "She will. There are just a few of us who have this number."

Sweat trickled down the side of my face as I punched in the numbers and waited while the connection was made. I was hot and dehydrated, not a good mix when I needed to keep my head clear. I hoped Manny brought some water with him. Even though we were protected from the sun by the thick canopy of jungle leaves and branches, the tropical heat beat down through the leaves, making the air feel even hotter and thicker.

The phone rang at least five times before she answered. "Hello?"

"It's me," I said. "I'm free from the compound and I

have the full recording of Jiang Shi's plans. It not only links China to the coup, but it also shows Maivia, the acting prime minister, as complicit. It will blow this thing wide-open."

On the other end, Candace's brisk voice sounded concerned. "Thank goodness you're safe. You'll have to provide details of your escape later. Is your wife okay?"

"She is." I glanced at Lexi, who was kneeling beside me, scanning the shoreline with a focused ferocity. Shi had made this intensely personal to both of us. We didn't just want to push Shi off a cliff. We wanted him to hit every boulder and branch on the way down.

Candance exhaled a breath. "That's good news. Whose phone is this?"

"An ally. It's a long story."

"I bet it is. I'll say it was quite disturbing to discover Jiang Shi is alive, free, and operating in the South Pacific."

"My feelings exactly."

"You'll provide a full debrief upon your return," she said.

"I will," I replied, my voice steady despite the tension in my chest. "And maybe even do one better. I'm not planning to make this easy for them. Still, the situation remains a bit... fluid."

"Understood," she said. "When are you sending the recording?"

"As soon we get to a secure location with a decent connection. When we get there, I'll drop it in the usual spot for you."

"Good. I'm standing by. The president has alerted the Indo-Pacific Command, and they're preparing an aircraft and an away team at Hickam if we need to evacuate you or the prime minister."

"Please thank the president on our behalf. We may find good use for that airplane. Right now, though, the Chinese control the airfield here. We're working on a plan to change that."

"Don't expose yourselves unnecessarily. Shi is going to be very unhappy you've slipped through his fingers."

I clenched my jaw. "He already is. He's issued a shoot-to-kill order on us for allegedly trying to assassinate Maivia. Shi has seemingly abandoned his plan to take me to China and figures he's better off just killing me when he can. I bet he now regrets not doing that sooner."

"Damn it, listen to me. You do whatever you need to do to protect yourself. You have my full backing. Is that clear?"

"Yes." I patted my pocket, where I still had the gun I'd taken from the Chinese guard. "I understand completely."

"Good." She paused for a moment and then continued. "I've distributed all you've sent so far within the NSA, the CIA, the State Department, and our regional allies in that area, including the UK, Australia, and New Zealand." She tried to keep her tone businesslike despite the gravity of the conversation. "Do you know what you're going to do next?"

"I've got a plan. I'll outline it for you once we're clear."

"Make sure it's a damn good plan," Candace said. "And no heroics. You may be skilled at getting out of tight spots, but you're a married man now. You have to think of your wife. So, be careful. The president is watching this situation closely, and I do *not* want to be the one to tell him something happened to you two."

I smiled a bit at that. "I'm working on it. With a little luck, we should wrap this up in twenty-four hours—if we're not shot first, of course."

"Just keep me posted, funny guy," Candace said firmly. "Get it done and stay safe."

"Trust me," I said with feeling. "It's at the very top of my agenda."

THIRTY-SEVEN

Lexi

The sun was still more than an hour from being overhead, but we were clammy with sweat as we prepared to head to the farmhouse with Manny. Using the Ara Tapu wasn't a viable option, obviously, so we took the two motorbikes most of the way to the farmhouse, following the escape route Paul and I had taken in reverse.

When we passed by the boulder where our pursuer had crashed, the bike was gone, but we could still see shards of broken glass and part of a light. I told Slash about the crash, and he got a grim expression on his face. Since we weren't being pursued, he was able to drive carefully on the paths and deftly avoided the muddy spots.

Slash didn't let his guard down for a second, continually scanning the jungle for any unusual movement or a possible attack. It was his normal modus operandi, but I also felt an itch between my shoulder blades—like someone was watching us—so it was kind of weird.

We finally stopped at the edge of the pineapple field behind the house and could see the structure in the distance. We crouched down behind some bushes and surveyed the farmhouse.

Manny pulled out a pair of binoculars from his pack and went about checking out the house. I could smell a fresh piece of the mint gum he'd been stress-chewing since sunrise, and that was somehow comforting. From my vantage spot, the farmhouse looked just as we'd left it: weathered shutters, one of them hanging crooked, and a tin roof reflecting the late-morning sun. No movement. No vehicles. No ambush, unless someone had mastered the art of invisibility, which—given the week we were having—felt entirely plausible.

"Looks safe so far," Manny said. "How about I go ahead and check it out? After all, I'm just an ordinary guy on a motorbike, not a shoot-on-sight international terrorist."

I rolled my eyes as Slash nodded. Manny climbed on his bike and headed off down the path around the field. The house remained quiet as he approached. Manny got off his bike and began exploring the backyard before circling the house to the front.

Fifteen minutes elapsed before my phone rang. "Hello?" I answered, punching it on speaker so Slash could hear.

"The place looks clear," Manny said. "I checked inside, and everything seems to be as we left it. There are no signs of a struggle or fight."

"Are we clear to approach?" Slash asked.

"Yes. But stay alert."

We climbed back on the bike and Slash cautiously approached the house. I could feel his tension with my arms wrapped around him. He was on high operational alert.

Manny had gone back in the house when we first got back on the bike but had now come out and was waiting for us at the edge of the yard.

He handed us cold water bottles and protein bars. We immediately dug in, both of us starving.

"Maivia's forces clearly didn't spend any time here," Manny said, taking a sip from his water bottle. "The fridge is full of food, the electricity is still on, and the house wasn't visibly ransacked. I suspect they weren't sure this was where the prime minister was hiding."

We mumbled incoherent responses around the chewing of the protein bars.

While we ate and drank, Manny took our bike and pushed it out of sight behind the nearby shed. When he returned, something rustled in the underbrush at the edge of the yard to our right. There was nothing professional about our response. We must have looked like a dysfunctional gymnastics team. Slash and Manny went for their weapons, while I jerked and tossed a water bottle in the air that nearly clipped Slash.

The rustling abruptly stopped. A second later, a coconut rolled into the yard, bumping and bouncing along like it had somewhere to be.

I let out a breath I didn't know I'd been holding. "Wow. An assassin dressed as a coconut. Bold strategy."

Manny didn't laugh. Neither did Slash.

I sighed. "Come on, guys. I'm trying to lighten the mood. I thought we decided no one would figure us for being dumb enough to come back to the farmhouse. Are we not going with that anymore?"

"We're being prudent," Slash said shortly. "I'm going to do one more sweep of the perimeter and house just to be extra safe. Manny, you wait here with Lexi and take cover in those bushes over there until I give the final all clear." He jogged off across the field and disappeared.

"Your man is in a good mood," Manny quipped.

I sighed. He was cranky, not that I blamed him. Just hours before he'd been beaten up, tied up, threatened, and locked in a closet. He'd earned that crankiness fair and square.

We waited for ten minutes, then twenty. Finally, Slash came back, sweat dripping from his temples and beading on his neck.

"I've checked the entire perimeter, and it's quiet," he said. "No one is here, and the house looks clear. Inside, everything seems to be as we left it. You're right, Manny. No signs of a struggle or fight, so I wonder what happened to Rangi and the security guys we left behind."

No one had the answer.

"Can we go inside?" I finally asked. I was hot, sweaty, and needed to go to the bathroom.

"Yes," Slash said. "It's safe to go in."

I went to the bathroom and then joined the men in the kitchen. Slash handed me another water bottle from the fridge, and I drank it almost as quickly as the first.

I checked my phone to see if the Wi-Fi was still operational, and indeed, it had connected. I headed directly to the office to begin setting up our equipment while Slash and Manny did a more thorough room-by-room check looking for bugs, cameras, or any surprise parting gifts that might have been left by the police.

They found nothing.

"I guess they really didn't think the prime minister was here, or that, if she was, we'd come back," Manny commented. "Or maybe they just want us to get comfortable."

"Too late for that," I said. "I haven't been comfortable on the island since my last glass of banana-infused wine. One of the best parts of the honeymoon to this point."

"I didn't see any alcohol in the house," Manny said. "But seriously, a glass of wine right now sounds pretty good to me."

"We have to keep our wits sharp," Slash said. "And let's keep the house dark—except for a little light in this room or the kitchen—so it appears uninhabited. The curtains will remain tightly closed and all doors locked."

"Party pooper," I quipped, and that at least elicited a small smile from him. "Guess we should call and let the prime minister know our situation here."

Manny pulled out his phone and called her, putting her on speaker so we could all hear. "Petra, we've made it and did a thorough check of the farmhouse and immediate area. It's empty. It looks like Maivia's forces left in a hurry—the place is mostly untouched. If your security agrees, I feel like it's safe for you to return."

"Okay," she replied. "Let me talk to Henry and security, and we'll call you back."

Manny hung up and slid the phone in his pocket.

"Do you think she'll come?" I asked him.

"I do. They're getting tired and cramped on the boat, and you're right, it's too exposed. Her security team saw it as a place to escape to, not a place to hide for long."

Slash headed off to the kitchen to brew some coffee. While he was gone, Manny's phone rang. I overheard Manny say he'd return to coordinate the move with her security team.

After he hung up, he turned to me. "That was Petra. They're planning to move her now. Her security wanted to wait until dark, but she overrode them. My instructions are to assist with the transition. Will you two be okay here by yourselves?"

"Sure, as long as we have Wi-Fi and some quiet time.

"Computers are set up," I said just as Slash walked into the room carrying two mugs of coffee. He handed one to me and another to Manny, who declined. I noticed immediately that Slash had added my usual half cup of milk, and I appreciated him for that.

"Would love to have a cup, mate, but off I go to get the minister," he said.

Slash drank the coffee instead. "Get her here safely, Manny."

"You've got my word on that," Manny said, heading for the door. "See you soon."

After he left, the first thing we did was plug in Slash's phone to charge. Slash surveyed the arrangement of the laptops and cables and nodded. It wasn't exactly a state-of-the-art field setup, but it would get the job done as long as nobody shot us or blew up the farmhouse. Two distinct possibilities.

Slash started by downloading the audio file from the recorder we'd risked our necks to get. Once the file was on Slash's computer, he hit send. While the file started crawling its way to Candace, I sent an email to Elvis to update them on what was happening on our end and get them on board for our plan this evening. Elvis answered within two minutes. They were on high alert.

"Please tell me Slash is alive. And that you guys are safe."

"Slash is alive, thank God," I responded. *"We'll have a*

story to tell you about how that happened. But for now, at least, we're safe. Unfortunately, we've graduated to the police's 'shoot-to-kill list' and are being identified as dangerous American terrorists. It's making things a bit dicey here. However, the good news is—even after all that—Slash and I are still married."

There was a long pause before a response came back, and this time Elvis added an emoji with its mouth wide-open.

"Wow, that IS shocking. Not the terrorist thing, the still married thing. It must be true love."

I laughed, feeling the tension ease a bit. They were reacting with humor, which was just what I needed.

"So, what's next?" he typed. *"What do you need us to do?"*

I quickly relayed our initial plan, with Slash occasionally chiming in. We carefully refined and outlined everyone's exact role in it. After answering several questions and engaging in a bit more discussion to fine-tune the details and ensure everyone was on the same page, we wrapped it up. Elvis confirmed they were ready.

"It's a good plan, so good luck, you two," he said. *"I mean it."*

"Thanks, Elvis and team," I replied. *"As always, we appreciate your support and assistance."*

"Hey, we're always in to save the day. Now, let's get this done."

Slash and I logged out, leaned back in our chairs, and looked at each other. We were spent, exhausted, hungry, and extremely close to the end of our ropes.

"Has the file made it to Candace yet?" I asked, sipping my coffee.

"It just finished," he said. "Took forever. But now, it's

time to get something to eat other than protein bars. I'm famished."

"I could use some real food." I stretched my arms over my head. "Like, seriously, could life get any crazier?"

He started to answer when we heard a man's voice speak from the doorway to the office. "Well, look who we have here."

THIRTY-EIGHT

Lexi

I glanced up in alarm before I realized who it was. Slash had already whipped his gun out and aimed at the person in the doorway.

"Rangi!" I leaped from my chair in surprise. "You're okay."

"Yes, and so are you, two, thank goodness. Um...can you lower the gun, please?" he asked Slash.

When Slash lowered the gun, Rangi breathed a sigh of relief. "What are you two doing here?"

"We could ask the same of you," I countered. "We thought you were captured by the police and hauled away."

"No, we faded back into woods after the cyclist took off after you," he explained. "We didn't resist, just watched them go through the house. They barely had time to confirm the place was empty before they suddenly ran out of the house, jumped in their cars, and drove away. We weren't sure what had happened, but we were afraid they'd caught the prime minister. Thankfully, that isn't what happened."

"They were probably contacted by the thug on the bike who was chasing us," I said. "He was definitely in need of a little rescuing."

Rangi shrugged. "Whatever the case, we waited to see if they would come back. But they never did. So, I sent the security guys home to get some rest and look after their families. I stayed here watching the farmhouse, hanging out in the outbuildings, and taking food from the fridge and pantry. I couldn't go home, as I was sure they'd be looking for me by that point, so this was as safe a spot as any."

"Why didn't you let the prime minister know you were okay?" I asked.

"I no longer had any way to reach her," Rangi said, spreading out his hands. "She changed up phones, using borrowed and burner ones to protect her and her family's location. I asked my team to see if they could track her down from their colleagues. I finally reached her about an hour and a half ago and updated her on my situation. To my surprise, she called me back about thirty minutes ago and told me you were on the way back here to the farmhouse. I remained hidden until you arrived and had an opportunity to look around. I just wanted to make sure no one had followed you."

"I knew it!" I exclaimed. "I felt like I was being watched."

"Sorry about that," Rangi said. "I didn't mean to spook you. After I was convinced you'd arrived here unaccompanied by any unwelcome parties, I called Petra back to tell her you'd made it safely. She informed me she is on her way here, too. Apparently, a lot has happened that I don't know about."

"A lot," I confirmed.

"How did you get into the house?" Slash asked. "I locked all the doors and windows."

Rangi reached into his pocket and held up the key. "The old-fashioned way. The prime minister gave me the key before she left."

"How many of the security team are with you?" Slash asked.

"Four, including me," Rangi replied. "None of us were apprehended."

"Well, that's good news for a change," Slash said. "We'll need all the people we can get."

"For what?" Rangi asked. "Look, you've got to catch me up. Why are you coming back here? Why is the prime minister coming back here? What's going on?"

"We're implementing a plan to help the prime minister," I said. "We needed a stable and decent Wi-Fi and internet connection, so we came back. We figured no one would expect us to return to a place they'd already raided. But before we go any farther, we're absolutely starving. Want to join us in the kitchen for something to eat?"

"I'd be delighted," Rangi said.

We moved from the office to the kitchen. I heated up a couple cans of soup while Rangi laid out some crackers and cheese, and Slash topped off our coffees.

Once the food and drink were on the table, we quickly brought Rangi up to speed on what had happened since the escape from the farmhouse. Rangi was shocked to hear Slash had been taken prisoner by Jiang Shi and what had transpired within the compound.

"So, Liko Maivia has been in on this from the beginning," Rangi fumed, his expression darkening. "I knew it. He sold out the Cook Islands for money and power."

"A tale as old as time," I said, biting into a cracker. "Though given his character, I'm almost convinced it was as much for recognition as power. There's nothing about him that asserts power or control. I think he's comfortable being told what to do. It means he has to think less."

"He has no moral compass, no loyalty," Rangi said. "I will ensure he is prosecuted to the full extent of the law."

"As long as you leave Jiang Shi to me." Slash finished his soup and pushed the bowl aside. "If you can, Rangi, recall your security team. We're going to need them to help with our plan, which we'll explain to you in detail once the prime minister gets here. In the meantime, can you keep an eye on the perimeter and let Petra and the others in when she arrives? Lexi and I have work to do in the office."

Rangi stood, pulling out his phone. "Will do." He stepped out of the room to make the calls and head outside.

Slash and I cleaned up the kitchen and returned to the office to work. We'd been at it for about forty-five minutes when we heard a noise at the back door. Slash went out to see who it was while I continued to work.

"It's Petra and the others," Slash said, coming back a few minutes later. "They made it here safely. The kids are headed upstairs to watch television, and Petra, Henry, Manny, and Rangi are waiting for us in the kitchen to strategize."

"Give me a minute and I'll be there," I said.

I set a few routines in motion and left the laptops running, returning with Slash to the kitchen. A couple more chairs had been added to the table and someone had started brewing more coffee and heating up water for tea. To my surprise, Petra gave Slash and me big hugs as soon as she saw us.

"Thank God you're safe," she said. "I don't think I could have forgiven myself if anything had happened to you."

"None of this is on your shoulders, Prime Minister," Slash said. "We know exactly who's responsible, and we're about to bring them down."

On that somber note, Slash and I squeezed into the empty chairs. Manny poured more coffee and made tea for the others before we began to discuss the final details of the plan.

Rangi spoke first. "Lexi and Slash have updated me on the latest developments. Maivia is a lying, conniving piece of rubbish. And the Chinese...don't even get me started."

"Liko Maivia will be tried for his part in this deception," Petra said, her eyes steely. "We're in full agreement on that."

"The coup has to end first," Slash said in a quiet tone that grabbed everyone's attention. "We've assembled the mechanisms to reduce their advantage, but we can't change people's minds. Only you can do that, Petra."

She nodded. "I'm ready. What do you want me to do?"

"The populace needs to hear from you," Slash continued. "Directly from you. They need to know you have not resigned and you're fighting back against this illegal seizure of power."

"I agree," Rangi said. "But how is she going to that? She can't just show up in a parking lot or in front of a government building. She'll be dragged away, arrested, or even shot, and there's no guarantee anyone would even see her or hear what she has to say."

Slash leaned forward on the table. "Lexi and I have created a plan to get the prime minister's message out across the islands. Petra, you'll be happy to know we now have control of your social media, the government website, and both your official and personal accounts. We intend to use them to blast out a video of you speaking the truth about what's happening and who's responsible for the coup. Lexi has also identified the internet feed that sends the television signal here to the other islands, and we can interrupt that and replace it with your video, too."

"You hacked all that...already?" Petra asked, stunned.

"Us and some friends," I said. "Close friends, who are really, really good at what they do."

"Apparently, so," she replied, clearly astonished. "I don't know how to thank you for all you've done. But what video of me are you talking about?"

I held up my phone. "The video we're about to record."

Petra took a moment to take it all in. "Ah, okay. While I'm fully appreciative and ready to record that video, I'm still in shock about how quickly you managed to wrest control of my online accounts from the plotters. Do you think the video will be enough?"

"What do you mean?" Slash asked.

"My biggest concern is, not everyone will see my social media accounts or the government webpages. And even if you now control my official email, how many people will really see it or believe it's actually from me?"

"All valid points," Slash admitted. "We certainly can't reach everyone, but if we reach a critical mass, hopefully the word will spread."

Rangi rubbed his temples, clearly trying to think it through. "I have a question. What's stopping Maivia and his team from taking down the internet altogether once they realize they can't control her accounts anymore? If they shut down the internet, they could twist the narrative somehow. Say her video is fake or AI-generated or something like that."

"That's certainly a risk." I noted, "But the word will have gotten out, and they'll no longer have the sole narrative. If they take the internet down after that, it will only look worse for them."

Petra stood. "I think we're underestimating the Chinese and this Jiang Shi person. Slash's escape and my video will push them to extremes. They're not going to care what people *might* think. They'll blame the internet outage on sabotage by the American terrorists and simply leave the internet down until they can find us and regain control. Plus, what would prevent them from importing hundreds of additional Chinese police at the request of the acting prime minister to help them restore order? We can't give them that time or opportunity."

"Then what do you suggest, Prime Minister?" Slash asked.

She began to pace the kitchen, thinking. "My initial video will set the stage and confirm, for some at least, I haven't resigned and am still fighting. However, a video made in a secret location doesn't present the image of a courageous leader who fully intends to rouse the people to oust Maivia and the Chinese. They need to see me live on television. That's where I'll have the greatest reach here and throughout the other islands."

"Live television?" Rangi gasped, astonished. "That's suicide, Petra. Not to mention, the television station is tightly guarded for exactly that reason. It's the one place they'll have guarded the most except for the airport. Even if we got in, the police and the Chinese will know exactly where you are. And, in case you forgot, the television station is on the opposite side of the island. Just getting there would be dangerous."

"It's all dangerous, Rangi," I said. "But no more

dangerous than continuing to stay on the run from Maivia and Shi's goons. It's not ideal, but at least it forces a public showdown—a showdown where we control the narrative."

Petra patted his hand. "Rangi, I know and appreciate your concern. But Lexi is right. There is danger all around us. I need to speak directly to the people—live—so they know I'm here to defend them and our country. It shows them that if I'm willing to resist, they can, too."

Henry considered and then rubbed the back of his neck. "I don't typically interfere with my wife's work, but I stand by her on this. Live television is a risky move, but I agree the payoff could be high. To overturn this injustice, our citizens need clear, succinct communications and leadership." He turned to his wife. "That leadership must come from you if you're to succeed. You're the glue that holds us together."

Petra gave her husband a grateful look before her gaze fell on Manny. "Manny, what do you think?"

Manny set his coffee mug on the table with a thump and sighed. "Storming a guarded television station isn't my idea of a good time whatsoever. It's risky, dangerous, and bloody mental from an operational perspective, if I'm being honest. I'd offer a saner alternative, if only I had one."

Rangi pointed at Manny. "Finally, the voice of reason."

"However," Manny continued, drawing out the word slowly, "I think the kids and Henry are right. You're the best weapon we have, Petra, which is why Maivia is desperate to find you. He's scared. But the longer you're on the run, the harder it will be to unseat them."

Rangi deflated, his mouth turning into a frown.

"I believe we have to look at it this way," Henry interjected. "Right now, we are caught between Scylla and Charybdis. Petra, you pose an extreme threat to them when you are free. But the longer you remain in hiding, the more your power will diminish, and you'll lose the influence needed to oust them. Jiang Shi knew that when he told Maivia to ignore you, but Maivia is a fearful and weak man, short on patience. We can take advantage of this if we take matters into our own hands. And if we are to do that, let us do it at the time of *our* choosing, not theirs."

I wrinkled my brow, trying to follow. "You lost me at Scylla and Charybdis, Henry. Are they Māoris or Polynesian gods? What was their deal?"

Henry pressed his hand to his heart. "My apologies, Lexi. As Petra will attest, I occasionally go all professor on everyone. I'm referring to Greek mythology. Scylla was a sea monster who lived at one side of the Strait of Messina, opposite the inescapable whirlpool called Charybdis. Ancient mariners had to very carefully navigate between the two of them since the smallest mistake could lead to their death."

Manny chuckled. "Well, I for one am glad Lexi asked. You don't want to know how badly I fared in my literature classes."

Everyone laughed, breaking the tension a little.

Rangi crossed his arms against his chest. "Okay, back to reality...even if we somehow get the prime minister into the news station, how are we going to prevent Maivia from cutting power to the station once she goes live?"

"I sincerely doubt Shi or Maivia have the team or equipment in place to do that on short notice," Slash replied. "If anything, after the first video blast across the prime minister's social media and the government websites, he'll have his technical team busy trying to retake those accounts or taking down the internet. He doesn't have the bandwidth or the talent to do both."

"Then it's settled," Petra said, looking around the room.

Rangi reluctantly nodded. "Fine. I'm still on the fence with this, but if everyone else agrees, I do, too. It looks like the goal now is to pick a time when most people are already watching television. To me, that would be seven o'clock in the evening—the time when the local and national news comes on."

"Agreed," Petra said, and we all nodded.

"So, we figure out a plan to get you into the television station by seven o'clock this evening," I said. I glanced at my watch and then angled it so Slash could see the time. It was five minutes after one.

"Prime Minister, we can be ready on our end by seven tonight, but how will we get there in time?" I asked. "Rangi said it's on the other side of the island in Avarua. A car is out of the question. Motorbikes, perhaps?"

"I wouldn't recommend that," Rangi said. "Ever since your escape from the farmhouse, there have been a lot more patrols on bikes. They may be safer to use out here, but closer to the city, discovery would be far more likely."

"How about the Cross-Island Track?" Manny suggested. When he saw Slash's and my blank stare, he explained. "It's a trail that runs up over the mountains through the middle of the island. From here to the capital, it would only take us about three hours to hike. We could easily move under the radar, especially in a small group."

"Not a bad idea," Rangi said, "but it would be tight to get there, check out the station, and get the prime minister inside before seven. We'd have to leave here shortly."

"Then we leave here shortly." Petra exchanged a glance with Henry. "What about my family?"

"We can leave them here with some of the security staff," Slash said. "In a few hours, when we release the video of you on the social media accounts, the island will be in chaos trying to figure out what's going on. I assure you, no stray police officers will be wandering here in the dark looking for your family when all the action will be at the television station."

She nodded, a relieved expression on her face. "Okay, let's do this. What's next?"

I held up my phone. "You and I do the recording and then I send it off to my friends and let them take care of things from their end. Are you ready?"

"Just give me a couple of minutes to compose myself and comb my hair so I look presentable and figure out what to say."

"No more than five," Manny warned. "We need to get moving."

"All you have to do is be yourself, Petra," Rangi counseled. "Be honest, and authentic. Make your concern for them and the country come through. Keep it short, too. That's always good advice for a politician."

She smiled. "It's good advice for anyone. What's after that?"

"We start the hike to the television station," Slash said. "Manny is right—we need to move fast. We'll release your video an hour prior to your television debut. That will give us an hour for the word to spread and get people riled up. Perhaps some will even take to the streets to figure out what's going on. That tight timeline is hard on us, but it'll be harder on the coup leaders. That's part of our strategy. It doesn't give them time to plan for what's coming. Petra, just make sure to say at the end of your video that you'll have a special announcement to make at seven p.m. Don't say where the announcement will be coming from, just that an announcement is coming."

"Will that be enough?" she asked.

"Hopefully. But just in case, Lexi and I have a few other aces up our sleeves to keep Shi focused elsewhere. It will also keep Maivia busy."

With that, Petra, Henry, and Rangi headed upstairs to get her ready while we headed back to the office to set up for the video.

"Are we really going to take a three-hour hike?" I asked Slash. Even though it made sense, I totally wasn't feeling it. Not that I *ever* felt like a hike was a good option unless it involved an air-conditioned vehicle.

Slash lifted his hands. "Looks like it."

Manny walked behind us and overheard my comment. "It's a solid option from an operational point of view, Lexi. I'm sure you had physical drills as part of your training."

"I'm a geek," I said, holding up my hands. "What physical training am I supposed to have had?"

"I thought all CIA operatives had to go through some kind of physical operations training," Manny said.

I stared between him and Slash. "Why are we talking about the CIA?"

"Never mind," Slash said, patting my arm. "You'll do fine on the hike."

"But why can't we just take the motorbikes at least part of the way?" I knew I was whining, but I felt tired, grumpy, and wanted nothing more than to sink into a hot tub for the next forty-eight hours.

"Sorry, Lexi," Manny said, giving me a sympathetic look. "The Cross-Island Track is specifically designed for hiking—no vehicles of any kind are allowed on the trail, not even bicycles."

"What if Maivia's forces are guarding the trail?" I asked.

"No one will be guarding the Cross-Island Track," Manny said. "Trust me, no one *ever* guards the Track. If there's a problem on the trail—say, someone twists their ankle or runs out of water—help is called up. There isn't anybody whose only job it is to monitor the trail. And even if by some chance Maivia has arranged someone to watch it, there would be no more than one person near the exit into the city. I think between us, we'd be able to handle one person."

"Manny is right," Slash said, pulling apart two cords. "The police are focusing on the main roads and government buildings. The Track will be the safest option for us."

I was not thrilled with the idea, but it was clear I was outvoted. "Fine, hike it is. I'm just warning you—this is not the type of hike I agreed to for our honeymoon. I just want it on the record I'm doing this under duress."

"Duly noted," Manny said. "Take it up with your man later." He winked at Slash, who shook his head.

We were ready with our setup when Rangi, Henry, and Petra returned. She had combed her hair, put on lipstick, and wore a blazer over a black T-shirt. "I found these in Victoria's closet," she said. "I hope she doesn't mind I'm borrowing them. I'll let her know it was all in the name of national security. But you're going to have to film me from the waist up. None of the pants or skirts fit."

"No problem," I said, showing her where to sit and adjusting the view on my camera.

Petra was as good as her word. The video lasted one minute and seventeen seconds, and we only had to retake one section.

"That was amazing," I said when she finished. "I got chills. You are really good at your job, Prime Minister. Clear message, positive energy, proof of wrongdoing, and to the point. Way to go." I plugged my phone into my laptop and began downloading it.

Slash paced back and forth in the room, his brow furrowed, clearly thinking. "Is there a house or a place in the capital where we could safely hide out and create a command center of sorts?" he asked Petra as she shrugged out of the blazer.

She thought for a moment. "Doesn't Paul's sister live near the television station?" Petra asked Rangi.

"Who's Paul?" Slash asked.

"The guy who brought your wife safely from the farmhouse to the yacht on the motorbike without getting shot," Rangi answered. "Big blond guy. He just took Lani and Noa upstairs to watch television. Let me check with him. I do think he has a sister who lives not too far from the television station, which would be ideal."

When Rangi returned, Noa came with him, running to his mother, who gathered him in her arms and hugged him tightly. I felt my heart twist in my chest. The stress on this family was palpable, as it was on all of us. Standing up for what was right—even when it seemed like everything and everyone were against you—was a true badge of courage.

"Are you leaving again, Mum?" he asked.

She ruffled her son's hair. "For a little bit. But your dad will be here. I'll come up and see you all before I go. Okay? So run up and watch the telly with your sister. I'll be up shortly." She gave him one more hug before he darted up the stairs.

When he was out of earshot, Rangi spoke. "You were right, Petra. Paul's sister lives relatively near the station, and she has agreed to help us. We can set up at her house, but we'll have to leave in the next twenty minutes to stay on the timeline and give us an opportunity to surveil the station."

Petra nodded. "I'll change quickly."

"What are you going to do about the police at the television station?" Henry asked Slash after Petra left. "How do you intend to get past them?"

"I don't know yet," Slash replied. "Once we figure out what we're up against, we'll determine the best way to get in. We have to be both flexible and adaptable. I have some ideas I want to run past Manny, but the prime minister doesn't have to worry about that part now. She can leave that to us. We'll make sure it's as safe as it can be before we insert her."

"You take care of my wife," he said, looking somberly at each of us.

"We will, Henry," Manny said, putting a gentle hand on his shoulder. "I promise you—we'll protect her with our lives."

I swallowed hard, imagining how he was feeling, the mood in the room suddenly turning grim.

Petra called out to her husband from the stairs. "Henry, I need to say goodbye. Can you come up here, please?"

"Yes, dear," he responded, giving us one more long look before he headed back upstairs.

For a moment, we just stood there before taking a collective breath. The gravity of what we were about to do weighed on us all.

Manny cleared his throat. "Um...I'll get the packs ready. We need to go."

Slash looked at me and nodded. "We do. It's time for the offensive team to take the field."

THIRTY-NINE

Slash

Lexi stayed in the office to ensure the prime minister's video had been successfully sent to Elvis and Xavier before she started packing up our equipment...again. The rest of us helped Manny throw together some makeshift backpacks stuffed with water, food, and essentials.

I made a point to find Paul and thank him for getting Lexi safely from the farmhouse to the yacht.

"Considering we almost died several times, Lexi did great," Paul said affably. "Rode the bike like an expert with minimal screaming. Good on ya, mate, for finding such a plucky woman. She held her own."

I didn't want to hear about the almost dying part, but I grinned at the plucky part and thanked him once again.

A few minutes later, we gathered in the farmhouse kitchen one last time.

We were a group of eight—Lexi, me, the prime minister,

Rangi, Manny, Paul, and two of the loyal police officers. That left Henry, the kids, and four security guys behind at the farmhouse to protect them. I personally didn't think the family needed more than two of the police for protection, but I read the expression on Petra's face and immediately agreed to the split. It was far more important to have her focused on the matter at hand than to be worried about what might be happening to her family. No one else objected, either, so it was settled.

The prime minister adjusted her backpack before nodding resolutely. "Let's go," she said.

We filed out of the farmhouse, blinking in the bright afternoon light. The humidity hung heavy in the air, and the sound of our shoes crunching against the crushed shell road was the only noise we heard until we moved into the jungle and toward the trail.

Manny and Paul scouted ahead at some distance, scanning the area to ensure there were no immediate threats. Behind them walked another loyal policeman, followed by Petra, Rangi, Lexi, and me. The last police officer brought up the rear.

The heat was oppressive, the air thick with the smell of earth and vegetation. I stayed close to Lexi, partially to make sure she didn't trip over anything, but also to make sure she stayed safe. The weight of the gun against the small of my back was reassuring.

As we walked, we fell into a comfortable rhythm. My mind raced through the upcoming plan, looking for any weaknesses or shortcomings I might have missed. Unfortunately, there were a lot more shortcomings than I would have liked, but it was what it was. I was used to missions that required precision and stealth, but a hike across the island with seven other people—most of whom were untrained for the type of mission we were about to launch—felt different.

The operation, at this point, wasn't fully in my control anymore, and that concerned me. Our friends back home would take care of their part, so I wasn't worried about that. The truth was the success or failure of this operation would come down to the strength and fortitude of the prime minister and her desire to save her country. I'd seen the fire in her eyes and believed she could do it, but we couldn't afford mistakes and timing was everything. It was very uncomfortable risking everything, including our lives, on someone else.

We had to be precise. All of us.

Once we reached the start of the Cross-Island Track, it was a relatively easy incline for the first twenty minutes. Manny and the guard were vigilant, keeping an eye on the path ahead. But soon the path narrowed, and the ground underfoot became more heavily crisscrossed with thick tree roots and jagged rocks. I kept a hand under Lexi's elbow to make sure she didn't twist her ankle as we began to climb in earnest.

The air cooled as we entered a section where the jungle canopy thickened, blocking out the sun. It was a welcome relief from the heat, but it also became harder to see the ground beneath our feet. The trail became even steeper as we climbed toward the higher reaches of the island, the sounds of the jungle swirling around us.

At some point we came to a section where a rope had been fastened to the rocks, allowing hikers to pull themselves up the slippery terrain. We stopped briefly to catch our breath, have a water break, and admire the beautiful waterfall nearby.

"This is the Papua Vai Marere, better known as

Wigmore's Waterfall," Petra said, scanning the view. "It's about fifteen meters high and has about two thousand cubic meters of water cascade over its crestline each day."

"It's stunning," I said.

"It is," Petra said, smiling. "A lot of young couples come to this spot. This is where I had my first kiss with Kodi Turua when I was fourteen years old."

I glanced over at Lexi, who was not looking at the gorgeous waterfall, but instead eyeing the rope leading up the slope with a mistrustful expression. "I'm not sure kissing would be on my mind knowing I have to pull myself up that incredibly steep slope with nothing but a rope," she said.

"Oh, it's not so bad, you'll see." Petra smiled, reaching for Lexi's phone. "Come on. Let me take your picture in front of the waterfall. It will be a lovely honeymoon memento for you and Slash."

Lexi hesitated, glanced over her shoulder at the waterfall, and then reluctantly handed over her phone. "I guess one photo won't hurt." As she stepped backward, she stumbled. Her balance faltered, and she teetered dangerously.

"Whoa—!" I lunged forward, catching her arm just before she fell. I pulled her into my arms, steadying her. After a moment, I planted a big kiss on her lips while the others laughed, clapped, and whistled softly.

"See, it's the perfect spot for kissing," I murmured against her lips.

Petra tapped away on the phone, taking multiple shots. After a moment, she encouraged us to face her. "Come on, one more nice photo with the two of you facing me with the waterfall cascading in the background."

We both faced the camera and smiled as she snapped a few more photos. Finally, she handed Lexi back her phone.

"Here you go. I got some great honeymoon shots—I promise."

Lexi grinned sheepishly as she took her phone back and pocketed it. The tension lifted—the levity sorely needed.

I finally convinced Lexi to let me carry her laptop bag, and one by one, we used the rope to climb the slick slope. To my surprise, Lexi moved more adeptly than I'd expected, even though I climbed close behind to stop any potential backward slide. We were at a distinct disadvantage compared to the others, who had shoes and boots better suited to hiking than we did. But we worked with what we had and trudged onward.

The trail only grew more treacherous. More steep inclines and thick tree roots made the trek extremely difficult. We had to ford a couple of brooks and streams, wetting our shoes even more. Without the provided ropes, I wasn't sure how most people would be able to get up the slopes.

"I thought you said this was a trail," Lexi complained to Rangi at one point, bent over and gasping for breath. "We're supposed to be hiking, not rock climbing."

"Well, I may have hyped the trail a bit," Rangi explained, his cheeks tingeing pink. "It can be a tricky climb and a little more slippery and sharply uphill than one might envision when they first think of the word *hike*."

"A *bit*?" Lexi repeated in disbelief and shook her head. "But at least I understand why we couldn't take the motorbikes, and probably why this trail is not regularly guarded by anyone."

Manny, whose face was also red with exertion, patted her on the shoulder. "I'm sorry, Lexi. I did downplay the Track because we need you and I didn't want to scare you off. But you're doing an amazing job, and the good news is, we're almost at the Needle. It's the second highest point on the island. After that, everything is downhill. No worries."

Lexi looked doubtful, and even I wasn't so certain of those assurances, either, but I kept my mouth shut. Shortly thereafter, we reached the Needle. Somehow, I had envisioned a rest area with a bench or an observation lookout, but no. Nothing. The Needle was simply where the slope jutted to a sharp point to the right of the trail, and that was it. We took a few seconds to admire the spectacular view of the island, but we didn't linger. We didn't have the luxury of time.

Going down the back side of the Needle didn't initially seem like it would be easier. We had to use the ropes to slide down the slope. After another half hour, my adrenaline had completely worn off. The hike was starting to feel like a strain even to me. I was hungry, hot, exhausted, and my shoes were muddy and uncomfortable. I imagined Lexi was feeling worse. But to her credit, she didn't complain or let it slow her down. She stayed focused on the mission, as did I.

We pushed on, crossing a few streams that made it futile to even try and keep our feet dry. Lexi waded through the water without even trying to balance on rocks. Her shoes were already wet and, apparently, the least of her concerns.

As we got closer to the end of the trail, hand signals came back from the policeman in the lead. We were directed to get off the trail, scatter and hide. Someone was coming up the trail toward us.

The vegetation was heavy, so moving quietly was difficult. Fortunately, we didn't have to go far to be fully hidden. I crouched down next to Lexi behind some bushes and kept my other hand near my gun. We tried to stay as still as possible, although the insects buzzing around her were proving to be a nuisance.

"Why don't the bugs bother you?" Lexi hissed, slapping at a mosquito near her neck. She was sweating, moisture trickling down her temples. "There's not one bug on your person or around your head."

"They know better," I said, shrugging.

We quieted as the sound of people talking got closer. From my vantage point, I could see a middle-aged couple walking along. The woman had a walking stick, and the man had a backpack and a set of binoculars hanging around his neck. We didn't have to worry about making too much noise while hiding. They were easily drowning out any sounds we might have made.

Tourists.

"I thought you said we were going on a hike," the woman said. "This isn't a hike. This is mountaineering."

Lexi wagged a finger at me and mouthed the word *mountaineering*, clearly in agreement with the woman's assessment of the trail.

"Yes, it's a bit steep, Elizabeth," the man agreed. "But not all bad. At the hotel, they said the views from the top are spectacular."

"If we ever get up there, given the shape of our knees."

"Oh, what's a vacation without a little adventure?" he said, leaning over and giving her a kiss on the cheek.

"I guess that's true," she responded, and they continued along the trail.

Once the couple passed, we got back on the Track going the opposite direction of them and toward the city.

"I told you this wasn't a hike," Lexi said, shaking a finger at me. "And my assessment was just supported by that random tourist."

I slung an arm around her shoulders. "True, but what's

a honeymoon without a little adventure?" I kissed her on the cheek, and she swatted me.

"You're lucky I'm not punching you right now," she grouched, and I chuckled, taking her hand...just in case.

"You're doing great, *cara*. We're almost there."

Our pace picked up slightly until we reached the end of the trail.

"Thank God that's over," Lexi said when we saw the trailhead sign. "I don't want to do that ever again." Her shoes squished water with every step. "How far to the safe house?"

"About half a mile," Rangi replied, handing Lexi, Petra, and me ball caps, which offered a bit of disguise. Lexi quickly tucked her hair beneath it.

"We need to break into smaller groups to move through the city," Rangi continued. "Paul, you and your men take the prime minister and Manny to your sister's house first. Lexi, Slash, and I will follow a few minutes later."

Our instructions clear, we watched as Paul, Manny, and Petra headed off. We followed a few minutes later, with Rangi taking us along back alleys and less-trafficked streets.

At last, we reached our safe house—a small, inconspicuous cottage—and Paul quickly ushered us inside. The furniture looked both functional and comfortable while giving off a beachy island theme, which felt wholly appropriate.

"Where's your sister?" I asked Paul, looking around.

"She went to stay with our mum and won't return until tomorrow," he said. "That's for her protection."

"Smart," I said. It was a good move in the event anything went sideways.

I glanced at my phone—it was 4:42 in the afternoon. Not quite an hour and a half before game time. We had made great time crossing the island. Lexi immediately sat on the floor near the door and removed her shoes and socks, laying them out to dry. Paul tossed her a towel to dry her feet, and she gave him a grateful look as she wiped them down. I kicked off my shoes and did the same, as did several others of the group.

As soon everyone was present, we assembled barefoot in the small living room. It was time to put this plan into action.

"Manny, you need to go now to surveil the television station," I said. "Prime Minister, you and Rangi monitor the television and social media. Paul, does your sister have internet access? Lexi and I have some work to do on our laptops, and we need the Wi-Fi password. The rest of you, stay vigilant for any unanticipated visitors."

Paul stepped into the kitchen to call his sister as Manny headed out the door to surveil the station. I placed our laptop bags on the table so Lexi and I could set up.

"Are you ready for the final stretch?" I asked her, plugging in our laptops.

"As ready as I'll ever be," she replied. "How about you?"

"I'm ready," I said. "Let's just hope Elvis, Xavier, and the others are at the top of their game."

"They're *always* at the top of their game," she said with a slight smile, but I saw the fierce determination in her eyes. "And so are we. Together, we're unstoppable. So, let's get this done."

"Absolutely," I agreed. "Time is ticking."

FORTY

Lexi

Slash and I set up our laptops and easily connected them to Paul's sister's Wi-Fi, thankful she was willing to share the password. Her Wi-Fi was a little better and faster than the farmhouse connection, perhaps because we were closer to the capital.

Once online, we checked in with Elvis and Xavier. Elvis confirmed everyone was ready and standing by, so Slash and I did a final check on our end. Paul rustled up some food, and we ate while keeping an eye on things.

I glanced at my watch. Five thirty. Thirty minutes until the plan launch.

A few minutes later, Manny returned from his surveillance trip. We gathered in the small living room, ready for his assessment of the security at the television station.

"Here's the situation," Manny began, his voice serious. "Two cops outside, no backup. According to my source inside the station, there are no extra police inside right now.

Apparently, Slash's escape from the compound forced them to pull extra security from the station. That means we have two men on the outside and no one inside guarding the station. The purpose of the two policemen outside seems primarily to let in authorized staff only. I recognized a few familiar news anchors going in, probably getting ready for the evening show. There's nothing physical blocking the entrance, and no apparent backup close by. The station is calm inside, but the mood is mutinous. Staff feel as if Maivia and his team are muzzling them. Given this information, I believe we should be able to get into the station with minimal effort and expect to be supported by the news staff inside."

The prime minister appeared relieved to hear that, and she clasped her hands together. "Excellent. Rangi and I know some of the news staff personally, so that should help. What's next, then?"

Manny slid his phone out of his pocket, swiping it on and pulling up some photos. We crowded around him. From what I could see from my vantage point, the first photo showed the station entrance with the two policemen standing in front of the door, one of them examining a badge that hung around a young woman's neck.

"As you can see, these two officers are just standing there and checking staff credentials while keeping everyone else out," Manny said.

The prime minister studied the images. "How do we get in without causing a scene, raising an alarm, or hurting anyone?"

"We don't need a full-on confrontation," Slash warned. "Hopefully, we'll be able to use the crowd outside as our cover."

"What crowd?" Paul asked.

"A crowd we anticipate forming in public spots, including the television station, in the next hour or so," I explained. "We don't need a lot of people, although that would be nice. Just enough to make the police uneasy."

"The social media blast," Petra said, quickly grasping where we were going with this. "You're counting on a protest, a crowd, or a distraction of some kind after my video is broadcast."

"Yes," Slash confirmed. "But not only. We can't rely on a crowd to perform on our timeline. We need to create our own diversion as well. No one knows where your seven o'clock announcement will be coming from. I believe Maivia and the Chinese will be expecting another social media video. They won't have a big presence at the station until after you start broadcasting live. That's when they'll rush to intercept you."

"Good," she said resolutely. "I'm counting on it."

Paul stood behind Manny, staring at Manny's phone. "You know, there's something about that policeman on the left that seems familiar. Manny, zoom in on him, would you, mate?"

Manny did as he was asked, then handed Paul his phone.

"That policeman on the left, I know him," Paul said. "He's just a kid—Aolani Kekola. He went to school with my daughter. He's barely eighteen. I didn't know he joined the police force."

Manny passed around his phone as we all studied the photo. "His posture speaks volumes," Slash said. "He clearly hasn't been a police officer for long. He probably doesn't know much beyond his orders to stand there and only allow authorized news staff inside the building."

"Well, no matter what we do, we're not going to hurt

anyone," the prime minister said firmly. "Certainly not a teenager. In whatever manner we carry this out, we do it peacefully."

We all nodded in agreement, and Manny got his phone back and pocketed it.

"The idea here is simple—as agreed, we don't charge in guns out or blazing," Manny said. "If the crowd isn't large enough, we create just enough of a distraction to break up the police's focus. That gives us a window for us to slip in behind them unnoticed."

"Are there any other doors we can go in if one of the staff from inside opened it for us?" I asked.

Manny shook his head. "No. There are only two other doors, one on the side of the building and one in the back. Both have been chained shut. You might be able to open them far enough to hand something out, but a person wouldn't fit."

"Has it always been like that?" I asked. "That's seems like a fire hazard to me."

"Nope, you can thank Maivia and the Chinese for that one," Manny said.

Rangi blew out a breath. "So, once we're inside, we're trapped?"

"I'm afraid so unless you have some bolt cutters," Manny said.

Slash spoke, his voice measured. "We'll have to go in through the front. It's like Manny said, we don't need mass chaos, but we need that distraction, whether it's organic from the crowd or instigated by us. But we won't have to time to waste, so the distraction must happen almost immediately after our arrival."

There was a brief silence, the weight of our deadline hanging over us.

"What do you have in mind for a distraction?" I asked Slash.

"Something subtle," Slash replied. "Perhaps a fight—verbal. Something heated but not dangerous."

Paul gave a crooked smile. "That's easy enough to do. We just trash talk a rugby team and be obnoxious enough about it to make it look like we're about to tear into each other. A few shouted insults and a little shoving should pull the police's attention and bring them over to us."

"But don't let it get out of hand," Manny warned. "We don't want a full-on riot."

"Be cognizant of that," Rangi agreed. "We just need to get the police to do their job—break up the fight. And while they're focused on that, the rest of us will slip inside."

"No worries, mates," Paul said. "We've got this."

The prime minister looked at each of us in turn, assessing our expressions, her mind already working ahead. "Okay, what happens once we're inside?"

"We have to move fast," Slash explained. "We don't linger. Once the police are distracted, we secure the station from the inside."

"The prime minister will be immediately recognized by the television staff," Rangi protested.

"I'm counting on it," Slash said. "She'll have a chance to speak to them personally before the broadcast, explaining what has happened. We need the staff to be on her side, to support her and give her the space and platform she needs to tell the population what's really happening."

"I know what I need to say." Petra's jaw was set in firm determination. "To both the news staff and the people. I'm ready."

So were we.

The room fell quiet for a moment before I spoke up.

"We only have a few minutes until the social media blast goes out. Once it becomes known we've taken back control of the prime minister's official and personal media accounts, it will cause chaos within Maivia's and Shi's camps. While they're busy sorting that out, we'll make our move on the television station. For us, that means we need to be inside the station no later than 6:40."

"That's in less than an hour," Paul said. "And it's a twenty-minute walk to the station."

"Sixteen minutes, if we walk briskly," Manny corrected him.

My feet hurt just thinking of it. Another hike ahead, but at least this was on mostly straight ground with no slippery ropes, cold streams, or muddy slopes.

"I suggest everyone gets their shoes on, because we're leaving in staggered groups shortly," Manny said. "Petra, Slash, and Lexi, you will need to keep the caps on and keep your gazes down the best you can for the walk to the station. Paul, once we're all there, you and your men start the distraction outside. The rest of us will slip in. Once inside, we'll lock it up from the inside to stop or slow down any police who may try to follow or enter before or after seven p.m."

"Don't forget to lock the other doors to the station," Slash said. "The police might have the keys to unlock the chains. Manny, you stand guard inside the second door. If they try and enter, an alert will give us a few extra minutes."

Manny nodded. "Copy that."

"The rest of you will have to talk to the news staff and get Petra in front of the camera by seven," Slash said. "Lexi and I have another card to play once we're inside."

To my surprise, no one challenged him or asked for

details. At this point, they just accepted we knew what we were doing and went with it.

"Okay, everyone knows their roles," Manny said one last time as we finished putting on our shoes and socks. Both of mine were somewhat dry, having baked in the patch of hot sun beneath the window. "From this point on, there's no turning back."

"No turning back," Petra repeated firmly, pulling the cap's brim low on her face.

I put on my cap as well and stood by the door, tightening my laptop bag securely across my body. The tension in the room was palpable.

Just then my watch beeped six o'clock, and the plan went into motion.

"It's time," I said, opening the door. "Let's go change history."

FORTY-ONE

Jiang Shi

Jiang Shi sat in the office, his posture rigid, eyes fixed on the chair where Slash had sat just hours previously, tied up and at his complete mercy. Now he was in the wind, freed by a woman who had waltzed into a secure compound and tased a guard.

Lexi Carmichael. He knew it had been her. She'd slipped in with delivery personnel and gotten Slash out with ease. It infuriated him so much he could hear the blood rush in his ears.

He'd been so enraged when he'd heard Slash had escaped that he had personally disciplined the guard who'd been on duty. He glanced down at his bruised knuckles and felt a flicker of satisfaction. Tased by a woman. Who trained these imbeciles, anyway?

He inhaled slowly, tried to temper his anger, but it didn't work. He should have tortured Slash on the spot, found his woman, and made him confess what he was really doing here. Only, he'd thought he had time—glorious time—

to do whatever he wanted once Slash was in China. But the American had slipped through his fingers once again, leaving him with nothing.

It infuriated him even more.

His anger still boiling, he glared at his laptop screen. The Cook Islands were small, the airport remained closed, and he'd tightened the ports. Slash and Lexi would not get off this island alive. It was only a matter of time before he found them and the prime minister. Still, he had to be cautious, calculate every mood, and anticipate every challenge. His opponents were good, but he was better.

The door to the office suddenly flew open with such force and surprise, it sent the parrot flapping and screeching about. Chen, his chief of staff in the Cook Islands, and in whose office he now sat, stood in the doorway, holding a printed email with a look of alarm in his eyes.

"Sir, you need to see this," Chen said, voice strained with urgency. "Immediately."

Shi's gaze narrowed. "I'm busy. What is it?"

Chen crossed the room and put the paper on the desk in front of him. "It's from Maivia. It just came through. He... I don't know how else to say it. He's resigning."

Shi's mouth dropped open. "He's *what?*"

"Resigning, sir," Chen repeated.

"What do you mean, he's resigning?" Shi snatched the printout, his eyes scanning the contents. He had to read it twice.

Maivia, the idiot, had emailed a public resignation letter. A letter that explained the coup wasn't his idea, but was, in fact, orchestrated by China. Maivia's apology was as profuse as it was pitiful, but it was the closing statement that sent a shock wave through Shi's body.

Maivia named the mastermind behind the upheaval—a Chinese national named Jiang Shi.

Shi felt the blood drain from his face. The stupid idiot had mentioned him by name. Worse, the email apparently contained an audio file, too.

"Where's the audio file?" Shi demanded.

"You'll have to pull it up on your laptop, sir," Chen explained and then walked Shi through it. "I already sent it to you."

Once it was pulled up, Chen told him to hit play. Shi instantly recognized his own voice. He heard himself speaking openly to Slash about the Chinese government's true intentions—how they were quietly infiltrating and taking control of small, insignificant Pacific nations to expand China's geopolitical influence in the region and build support in the UN.

It was damning. It was true. It was everything Shi had worked so hard to keep hidden.

"Get Maivia on the phone. Now!" Shi shouted at Chen, slamming the printout down on the desk, his knuckles turning white as he gripped the edge.

Chen moved quickly, dialing the number. The line connected in an instant. Shi grabbed the phone once Maivia answered, his voice barely restrained.

"Maivia," Shi said, seething with anger. "What the hell is this resignation email? And what's with the audio? Where did it come from? To whom did you send this email?"

On the other end, Maivia's voice was full of confusion. "I...I don't understand, Shi. What resignation? What are you talking about?"

Shi's mind was already racing and came to a quick to a conclusion. *Slash.* Slash had done this. The person who had ruined his life, tormented him, and constantly interfered in his operations. Always one step ahead. Shi had underestimated him, and now he'd flipped the narrative in a way Shi had never imagined.

Next time he had Slash in his grasp, there would be no flying to China, no prolonged torture, just instant, immediate death.

"Take down the internet now," he shouted at Maivia. "Government websites, social media accounts, everything. They've been compromised. Get a team working on reclaiming those pages this very minute, or I swear to God, your head will be on a platter. Get to the bottom of this immediately."

Maivia's voice wavered. "I don't know what's going on! What are you talking ab—"

Shi slammed the phone down.

"Sir," Chen said hesitantly. "It looks like this email also went out to every member of Parliament in the Cook Islands, neighboring islands, and several news outlets here, and in New Zealand and Australia."

Before Shi could respond to that devastating revelation, the phone rang. Shi snapped it up as Chen quietly slipped out of the room.

"Who is it?" he growled.

"This is Lin Wu," a man's voice said. Wu was Shi's chief of staff in Kiribati, a nearby island country in the Micronesia subregion of Oceania. "Sir, what's happening in the Cook Islands? A recording of you has just been released to the government in the capital city of Tarawa. You're calling them fools, saying how easy it was to buy them and the island, and how much more China would've paid for their loyalty, if they hadn't been so desperate for scraps. They're calling me, right now, as the Chinese representative on their island. They want answers and they're not happy. What am I supposed to tell them?"

Shi felt a wave of nausea, but he could still spin this. "Tell them it's all lies," Shi snarled. "Artificial intelligence, fake news, propaganda, whatever. All fomented by the Americans. Get them to calm down and tell them we're handling it." But even as he said it, he knew it would ring hollow. People would now be looking closely into his personal actions and behaviors, exactly the things he did not want his bosses in China poking around. They were not going to be pleased. Not at all.

His mind spun, each new revelation worse than the last. He had to act fast and gain control or everything would come crashing down.

Shi hung up while Wu was still talking. When Chen returned, his face pale.

"What now?" Shi asked.

"The email, the information, it's all over the Cook Islands' websites and social media. But worse, the prime minister is alive and talking. She made a video and is telling everyone she's been in hiding, but she's back now and ready to fight for the country. She's saying the Chinese engineered the coup. She's calling out our involvement—your involvement specifically."

Shi's vision blurred with rage. "What is she saying?"

"She's saying Maivia is a puppet leader put in place by China and asking people to tune in to an important announcement tonight at seven o'clock. She's promising more details then."

Shi slammed his fist down on the desk. "Get Maivia back on the line."

Chen called, but Maivia still had no idea what was going on. "I don't know what's happening," he moaned. "It looks like someone hacked into my email. I'm trying to deal with that now. I told you we needed to focus on finding the prime minister, and now I have no idea where she is or what announcement she will make."

Shi's head throbbed; his fingers clamped tightly on the phone. He glanced at the clock. Fifteen minutes until seven o'clock. "Whatever it is, Maivia—stop it! Get the internet down and send reinforcements about town. Who knows where she intends to make her announcement? I don't care what you do, just don't let her talk to the people. Take her into custody immediately."

He slammed down the phone again before Maivia could answer. He had no idea what the prime minister would say, but he knew it would only make things worse. He had to shut her up.

Shi rose from the desk. "Chen, start destroying anything that might be incriminating. You know what I mean. And get my plane ready to go. If we must leave the island, we leave nothing behind. Understood?"

"Understood, sir." Chen started moving while Shi churned over what was coming next. He couldn't afford to lose his grip on this operation. If the Cook Islands and Kiribati slipped through his fingers, it would be the beginning of the end. But perhaps there was a way he could still survive this.

It was all Slash's fault. His career had started and ended with Slash once before. Not again. He wouldn't allow it.

A storm was coming, and Jiang Shi was determined to survive it.

FORTY-TWO

Slash

The trip to the television station was easy in comparison to the arduous hike across the island. Thankfully, no one paid attention to us as people began spilling onto the sidewalks, talking anxiously with their neighbors and clustering in groups. Their voices rose in confusion and anger. Anti-Chinese sentiment could be heard at every turn. By the time we reached the television station, at just after six thirty, a decent crowd had already formed.

I was in full operational mode, scanning the crowd and environment for any unanticipated variables or unexpected visitors. The scene remained stable. The two lone policemen still stood guard by the door. There was a glass outer door and a metal door a couple of steps inside. It was an odd arrangement, but I surmised it was due to the cyclones. The young kid Paul had identified was already on his radio, looking scared and certainly calling for backup. They had their hands full with the growing commotion.

A quick scan of the faces in the crowd indicated distrust, concern and confusion. People were mostly calm—a few shouted—but I feared that could change at a moment's notice, especially when reinforcements arrived. We had to act fast. The social media blast and video had bought us the crowd we needed, but the anger and discontent were palpable and growing.

"At least we're blending in," Lexi said in a low voice. "No problem there. The crowd gathered faster than we anticipated."

"I was just thinking that," I said. "People have been wondering what's been going on for days. Maivia has no idea what he's doing as a leader."

"Because he's not a leader," Lexi responded. "He's doing whatever the Chinese tell him to do. The people want the truth."

"Are *demanding* the truth," I corrected. "As they should."

"Hey, where's the real prime minister?" a man shouted at the policemen, drawing a chorus of nods and anxious murmurs from the crowd. "Where is she? Is she in there?"

I resisted the urge to look over my shoulder at the prime minister and instead followed Manny around the left side of the building, near the side where the young policeman stood. They weren't letting anyone in or out at the moment. We gathered loosely, the prime minister carefully keeping her head down and cap pulled low so she would not be recognized. Yet.

Unfortunately, the crowd had backed the two policemen closer to the doors, and we needed to remedy that. I motioned to Paul to start the scuffle on the other side of the door so we could get in from the left. He nodded, and he and his guys moved through the crowd into position.

A minute later, we heard some shouting and yelling that a fight had broken out. Like clockwork, the two policemen jumped in to break it up. This was something they were trained to do, not guard doors against a hostile crowd.

I was the last of the five of us to slip into the station. Just as I reached for the door, I could see the older guard turn toward me. He must have been apprehensive about leaving his post unguarded. Before he could complete his turn, Paul hit him from behind, and he went down. I slipped in, and we immediately locked the first door behind us. It didn't take long for others to start banging on the door, wanting to get let in, too.

It took mere moments to secure both doors. Manny volunteered to keep an eye on them. Once inside, Petra quickly shed her disguise and faced the news crew. Several stared open-mouthed at her and Rangi, who stood beside her in support.

We stood to the side and watched. Several of the television and technical crew scrambled around, still oblivious to the prime minister standing in their midst. The team at the production desk were frantically typing on their computers —probably trying to figure out what was going on with the release of the prime minister's video. Their fingers flew over the keyboards as the room buzzed with panic, and people called out questions and shouted answers.

Suddenly, a large, commanding man with brown skin, graying stubble, and a badge hanging around his neck stepped forward. His eyes were sharp and intelligent, and his sheer presence commanded authority. I presumed he was the station manager or news director. Definitely someone in charge.

"All, cease!" he shouted. The power in his voice quieted the newsroom instantly, save for some automatic clicking noises in the background. "Petra," the man said, clearly surprised to see her. "You're alive and well."

"Hello, Tane." The prime minister walked forward to greet him, and he gently took both of her hands in his considerable ones. "I'm sorry to appear here unannounced, but desperate times require desperate measures."

"Completely understandable," Tane replied. "I want to say I'm surprised, but with what's been going on, I'm not. Desperate times, indeed. I assume you have a purpose coming here. How can we help you?"

Petra addressed Tane and the news team with a calm that seemed to steady the room. "I need to speak to the people of the Cook Islands at exactly seven o'clock tonight. That's in eleven minutes."

She spoke quietly but with authority, her voice carrying. "I do not condone or support the actions of Liko Maivia, who acted under the direction and orchestration of the Chinese to seize my position without authority, my consent, or due process. I have proof of Chinese involvement. I've been in hiding since their takeover, gathering evidence and opposing them at every step. Several police officers on the force have hunted me and my family and endangered people who have stood for our islands, me, and the truth. Some have been arrested, threatened, and even harmed. I want to make sure you and the world know I'm alive and resisting this foreign-sponsored coup."

"Whoa, Prime Minister, are you sure you want to broadcast that?" a young man asked. Concern and fear were etched on his face. "Once we put you on the air, live, the Chinese will know you're here."

Petra's gaze never wavered. "I'm aware of that. But to back down now will be even more dangerous for the Cook Islands. It's time for the truth to be told. I'm not afraid to speak so the lies are exposed. The people deserve to know what has happened and what China really thinks of us. They are using us as pawns in their own geostrategic game."

There was a murmur in the newsroom as the crew and staff looked at each other uneasily, their hesitation and anxiety palpable.

Tane's expression stayed calm and thoughtful. After a moment, he finally spoke. "If anyone wants out of this, go to my office right now and lock yourselves in. No repercussions, no judgment. If need be, I'll say you resisted and I locked you in my office for not cooperating. Many of you are young and have families. There's no shame in stepping aside if you want no part of this. But go now, because I'm putting the real prime minister on the air in a few minutes."

There were a few gasps, murmurs, and whispers before a hush fell over the newsroom. No one moved—not a single person. Even the heavily pregnant woman with long, dark hair who stood leaning against a desk stayed put, her chin lifted and her eyes on fire.

"I said, go *now*," Tane snapped. "We don't have time for a discussion. I don't know how this is going to turn out, and you have every right to disagree with what I'm going to do."

Still, not a soul in the room moved. It was an astonishing show of bravery, and I'd seen plenty such moments.

Petra closed her eyes, and I could see the show of loyalty had touched her. "Thank you for your support," she said, her voice thick with emotion. "Our country, as small as we may be, appreciates you deeply."

Tane shook his head as if he couldn't believe it. "All right, team, the die is cast. Let's get to work. We have about five minutes until airtime. You know what to do. Go!"

As if someone had flipped a switch, the newsroom suddenly turned into a hive of activity. People started yelling orders, running around, and typing frantically on their computers.

Tane put a hand on the prime minister's arm. "We've got your back, Petra. You go up there and do what you need to do, and so will we."

"Thank you, Tane," Petra said, giving him a handshake and then a hug. "This means a lot."

A woman with a set of earphones around her neck abruptly approached them and hustled Petra and Rangi toward the cameras, just as Manny tapped me on the shoulder from behind.

"We've got company," he said in a low voice. "I've blockaded the second main entry door with file cabinets and furniture, but they may be able to blast through in a few minutes. They've already got through the first door by breaking the glass. They're discussing what to do about the second since it's made of metal. I can hear the knuckleheads talking through the door. Their actions are drawing quite a crowd. That's good for us."

"It is," I agreed. "But before they take major measures to break in, they'll need to get permission," I said. "They don't know what they're up against. It'll take them a bit of time to sort it out. We've also occupied their leadership with other issues to make them hard to reach and every second counts. I'm surprised they haven't thought to cut the power. Not a sophisticated lot. Let me help Lexi for a minute, and then I'll come help you."

Manny returned to his post while Lexi and I quickly set up our equipment. With help from the news crew, we got connected. A quick glance indicated the internet was still up and the social media accounts remained secure and continued to broadcast the prime minister's video. No one had been able to bring down the government website yet.

I walked over to Tane, who was speaking with a woman who was madly typing something on her iPad. "Can I speak to you for a moment?" I asked him.

Tane nodded and stepped away, taking careful measure of me. He didn't know me, but I'd come with the prime minister's inner circle, and that meant something.

"What would happen if the electricity to the studio was cut?" I asked. "Do you have a generator?"

"We do. It's back behind the studio about thirty feet and surrounded by a concrete wall. We get a lot of cyclones here. The generator automatically pops on when the electricity goes down."

"Thanks," I said, and he nodded, walking over to the stage to say something to Petra. I glanced at my watch. Three minutes until she went live.

I checked on Lexi one more time. She had everything ready, including her phone. She would record the prime minister live so we could make sure the broadcast reached more than just the local area.

I kissed her on the forehead. "Stay safe," I murmured.

"Likewise," she said as Rangi exited the stage, leaving on the prime minister standing alone, ready for her countdown.

I joined Manny. "Any new developments?" I asked in a low voice.

"Nah. The reinforcements have arrived, though," he replied. "They've pushed on the door a couple of times but are unsure what to do next. They've been calling for instructions, but it seems like it's hard to reach the Chinese at the moment."

I lifted an eyebrow, amused. "Imagine that." I maneuvered him away from the door. Hey, do you have Paul's number?" When Manny nodded, I continued. "Good. I want you to call him and have his team do what they can to discreetly protect the station's generator, which is about thirty feet behind the building and surrounded by a small concrete wall. Just in case Shi or Maivia think to cut the electricity, the generator automatically comes on, so we'd be okay for a bit."

"Good thinking," Manny said and whipped out his phone out of his pocket, moving away from the doors to speak softly into the phone.

I stepped back in view of the stage just as Petra turned to face the cameras with the calm poise of a leader who had been preparing for this moment her entire life.

"Good evening, fellow islanders," she said.

FORTY-THREE

Lexi

The walk to the television station had been nerve-racking, but that was tempered by the ease of our entrance into the building. Our plan was proceeding on schedule, but there was always time for everything to go sideways.

I happened to know a lot more about that than most people.

Now was the moment of truth. Petra stood in front of the cameras as a woman with headphones on held up her hand and silently counted down from five on her fingers. I readied my phone, tapping the record button as Petra started talking.

"Good evening, fellow islanders," she began, her voice strong but measured. "Today, our country stands at a crossroads. Forces outside our borders wish to see us become pawns in a game we did not choose. While we are a small nation, we will not be used or silenced."

She succinctly explained what had happened, giving a

brief summary of the proof she had gathered regarding Chinese involvement and Maivia's complicity. Her calm words rang out, filling the studio. Despite the tension, there was a riveting power in her delivery. She was fighting for more than just her own survival. She was battling for the soul of the nation, and that came through loud and clear.

"The time has come to ask for your support," the prime minister continued. "We must resist these forces and keep our ties strong with our historic partners in New Zealand, and with all nations that stand for democracy. We may be small, but our voice is not insignificant. Together, we fight oppression, we fight corruption, and we fight for the future of our children."

A security guard appeared at Tane's side, leaning close to him and whispering urgently. Tane waited for a natural break in Petra's speech and took a moment to speak from off camera. "Prime Minister," he called out. "Liko Maivia and some police are gathering outside the station. They're coming for you."

Petra's face tightened, but she didn't flinch. Instead, she kept her expression defiant. "They may take me away, but to stop the free spirit of the Cook Islands, they will have to remove every single one of us. The truth will be known."

She stepped away from the camera as the crew moved quickly to cut the feed. I immediately stopped the video on my phone and dashed to my laptop to download and send it to Elvis and Xavier.

"Protect yourselves," Petra said to the news staff. "Please. I intend to go out and face them. Just tell them you were coerced."

"Petra, no, I will not let you do that," Rangi protested hotly. "They might kill you on the spot. It's lunacy."

"He's making sense, Prime Minister," Tane said. "Listen to him. Think about what you're doing."

"I will not go into hiding again, and I'll not stand down," Petra said firmly. "The truth is out there now. What is done with it, my friends, is now up to you. But thank you, Tane and Rangi. You are both true friends, and I'm honored to know you." She turned and faced an eerily quiet newsroom. "In fact, my gratitude extends to all of you for your courageous stand. I'm proud to represent you."

I lifted my eyes from my laptop and saw Slash step away from the door, where the banging and shouting was even louder now. They would be here soon anyway.

Slash had picked up the filming from his phone now, and others in the newsroom had started doing it, too.

Our eyes met across the room, and I immediately knew what he was thinking, because I was thinking the same thing. The risks were high, but this was her show now. It was up to Petra to save her country. Slash and I had done what we could. Anything from here on out was up to the people of the Cook Islands.

Rangi finally fell silent, realizing nothing he could say would persuade the prime minister to change her mind. Petra walked past Slash, put a hand on his shoulder, and then came face-to-face with Manny.

"Open the door," she instructed him.

"Petra, I—" he started, but she shook her head.

"Don't argue. Just do it, Manny. Please."

He stared at her for a long moment and then with a sigh began moving the furniture. Rangi went to help him while Slash came to stand next to me.

"I want everything on camera from this moment on," Tane ordered his staff. "Multiple views and sound. We're going live right now. Let's show the people what's really happening."

The team behind the cameras scrambled as they yanked the equipment off the tripods and hoisted the cameras onto their shoulders. They moved into awkward positions around Rangi and Manny, filming between the prime minister and the door that was slowly opening.

"Let's go," Slash said to me, cutting off his video and sticking his phone in his pocket.

We grabbed our laptops—my video had downloaded and was now sending to Elvis and Xavier—and headed deeper into the station with several other members of the news crew.

I glanced over my shoulder as Manny moved the last piece of furniture and the police spilled into the room, shouting and grabbing the prime minister by the arms. The last thing I saw was Petra being escorted out of the station with Manny and Rangi right behind, shouting at the police. The news crew continued filming as they followed her out.

We ducked into a room along with the pregnant woman and the woman wearing the headphones. She locked the door behind us.

"Can you pull up the live feed?" Slash asked her.

"I can," she replied and went to a laptop on a nearby desk. She typed several commands, and suddenly the feed was projected onto a wide screen attached to the wall.

The police had Petra outside in front of the station, held on either side by officers. Manny and Rangi were also being held—and Manny was already cuffed. The crowd had grown to twice the size it had been when we had arrived. Voices were rising in a swelling tide of anger and support. I couldn't make out what they were saying, but Petra's stance was impressive and unshakable.

Then, the moment came. The crowd parted as Liko Maivia, with the pin containing the image of the jeweled coat of arms of the Cook Islands on his lapel, marched into sight with several police officers accompanying him, including some Chinese ones. One of the cameramen zoomed in on the pin, and there were some audible gasps from the crowd.

"Prime Minister, you are under arrest," Maivia declared.

Petra, who was still being held by police on each side of her, cocked her head at Maivia, looking puzzled. "For what, exactly, am I under arrest?" she asked.

"For..." Maivia started, suddenly realizing he hadn't thought this through. "For resisting arrest. For spreading propaganda."

"For telling the truth, you mean," Petra said. "For exposing your Chinese-backed takeover. I did not resign, nor did I agree to relinquish my position as prime minister to you. You forcefully took it, with the assistance of the Chinese, and when I escaped your arrest, you had to make up fabrications to account for my disappearance. You are a traitor and a disgrace to the Cook Islands by falsely wearing that pin, which has been peacefully passed down for generations. I neither presented it to you nor believe you are worthy to wear it. But now the truth is out there, Liko. What are you going to do about it?"

His face flushed with anger. "I'm going to put you where you belong. In jail."

He turned sharply on his heel, and the police officers started to follow with Petra in tow. But members of the crowd suddenly moved to form a protective barrier between her and Maivia.

"Do not let them take your spirit or your independence," Petra cried. "Stand up for the truth."

The crowd began to shout and protest.

"Stand up for the truth!" one of the protesters cried, and the others began to echo her, their voices blending and rising to a roar. "You won't take our spirit or our island!

Suddenly, the mood and energy began to shift. The crowd began to shout in a frenzy, and they closed in tight around the police officers. Someone threw something, a piece of food, perhaps, that knocked off the cap of one of the police officers. It was quickly clear they were going to have an impossible time taking the prime minister anywhere.

We were seconds from an ugly explosion of mob violence when I noticed the kid who had stood guard outside the television station had stepped away from the rest of the police officers.

"Slash, what is that kid is doing?" I asked, pointing him out on the television. "That's the kid Paul recognized. I think he said his name was Aolani."

"I remember," Slash said.

"What's he doing?" I asked in a hushed voice.

Aolani had been positioned behind the prime minister, but now he came around to the front and wiggled his way in front of Petra. His hand hovered at his side, and then, to the shock of everyone, me included, he unclipped his gun belt and placed it on the ground in front of her feet.

"Release the real prime minister," he shouted, lifting a fist in defiance.

"Holy crap," I said. "This is getting real."

We were riveted to the screen. The two women in the room gave audible gasps. Slash put his arm around me, pulling me in close. For a few heartbeats, I held my breath.

Then, one by one, the other Cook Islands police officers

began to follow suit. Their weapons clattered to the ground, each one laying down their weapons and gun belts. When the police officers holding Petra let go of her and did the same, Maivia realized he was left with just the few Chinese cops. When those Chinese police officers turned and pushed their way free of the crowd, Maivia stood alone.

The chanting grew and the crowd tightened until Maivia was forced to turn and face Petra. After a long moment, he unfastened the pin on his lapel and gave it to Petra without a word.

Petra shot her hand in the air, holding the pin, and the crowd erupted in cheers. In our room, everyone let out huge sighs of relief. I was in awe at what I'd just witnessed.

The power of the people.

"Wow," I said. "I don't even know what to say. That was really scary and beyond cool at the same time. We saw a revolution unfold right before our eyes."

"We did, indeed," Slash said and smiled.

We all started cheering and hugging each other in our little room, including the two women we didn't even know. Familiarity didn't seem all that important at this historic moment in time. We had all just shared something exceedingly special, and that created a bond that made hugging and familiarity appropriate. The roars of the crowd from outside, and the cheers coming from inside the station, shook the very foundation of the building.

I planted a big kiss on Slash's mouth, laughing and cheering on my own. Because, right now, in our world, all was finally right.

FORTY-FOUR

Jiang Shi

Jiang Shi's eyes were fixed on the television screen in the office, his fists clenched at his sides. His forces were inept. Maivia's idiots hadn't brought the internet down or broken into the station to grab the prime minister yet. Supposedly, some of his own police officers were getting the electricity shut down to the building, but it hadn't happened and now it was too late. Incompetent work from the lot of them.

Instead, the prime minister spoke live and every word that came from her mouth made his blood boil. She poised in front of the cameras, acting like some kind of hero, talking about how China had "engineered" the coup, as if they were the villains in this entire mess. It wasn't his fault the islanders had been willing to sell their souls for some equipment and an actual, functioning police force. Or maybe they were just too stupid to see the writing on the wall. Led by China, they could have become part of the greatest empire in the world, but in the end, the Cook Islands had proved themselves not worthy of that honor.

Finally, the prime minister stopped her pathetic drivel, and the camera feed went down. A glance at the clock indicated she had spoken for a mere four minutes. It didn't really matter what she said or how she presented herself, because no one outside this wretched island would see it anyway.

But finally, she shut up, because every word had grated on his nerves.

A minute later, a shaky camera feed showed her being arrested—at last—and led outside where a large crowd had gathered. Shi leaned forward in his chair. Time for the showdown with the real leader.

Maivia walked into the frame, calm and poised. Shi smiled. Time for Maivia to flex his authority in real time.

"Prime Minister, you are under arrest," he declared, pointing at her dramatically.

The prime minister remained calm and unflappable. "For what, exactly, am I under arrest?" she asked.

Maivia faltered, stumbled. "Uh, ah…"

Shi closed his eyes. This couldn't be happening, and yet, somehow it was.

"For resisting arrest," Maivia blustered. "For spreading propaganda."

Shi smacked his head with the palm of his hand. Maivia was a complete fool. "Say something useful," he shouted at the television.

Instead, Maivia faltered, which gave the real prime minister the opening she needed to plead her case further. A minute later, the crowd started shouting in support of her, and a young policeman disarmed himself and put down his weapon, followed by the rest of the force. The few Chinese police that accompanied Maivia turned tail and fled. They were smart enough to see what was coming.

Then Maivia, the idiot himself, surrendered to the prime minister without a fight. The cowardice was too much for Shi to bear.

"Imbecile," Shi muttered, his voice low and dangerously calm. He'd never seen such weakness, such cowardice.

It was time to exit this disgrace of a country.

He grabbed his phone, dialing Chen's number.

"I want my car and driver ready to go in twenty minutes," he barked. "Make sure the plane is ready. And recall everyone to the compound. I want all staff here immediately. We'll need to make sure that whatever's left of our diplomatic immunity is preserved. But for now, I trust the integrity of the compound and our people to manage any hostile crowd."

He threw the phone down on the desk and glanced at the clock. Fifteen minutes, maybe twenty, and he'd be out of here. He had the money to go where he wanted. He had many passports and people who owed him. He'd pack a bag, get on the plane, and head somewhere—anywhere—far from this miserable island. But he couldn't go home to China, and he knew it.

He would not be forgiven this time.

His car and driver were ready when he went to the front. They headed for the airport and encountered remarkably little traffic, although people seemed to be out all over. Shi's eyes narrowed. He wondered where Slash was at this very moment.

"The next time I see him, it will be his last," Shi muttered to himself. His grip tightened around the armrest as the car glided through the streets.

His driver drove around the back of the airport, was

waved through a gate by Chinese police who obviously hadn't received the recall alert, and pulled up to the tarmac. Shi stepped out of the car, waiting for his driver to retrieve his bag. Once the bag was in hand, he marched toward his private business jet, a sleek black aircraft. The head pilot and the flight attendant bowed to him on the steps, but Shi ignored them, pushing past, his mind focused on leaving this nightmare behind as quickly as possible. The attendant took his bag from the driver and stowed it.

"Take off immediately," he ordered the pilot, his voice harsh. "I'll tell you where to go once we're airborne."

The pilot hesitated and exchanged a nervous glance with his copilot. "Sir, we'll need a destination for the flight plan."

Shi barely looked at him. "You need what I *tell* you I need. I don't care where we go, so long as it's away from this worthless island. Get us in the air, now, and I'll decide where we're going as soon as we're in the air."

The pilot hesitated again but finally nodded, inputting commands on the flight deck. Shi settled into his seat, his gaze darting to the window, his fingers tapping on the armrest impatiently. He really couldn't leave this hellhole fast enough.

Suddenly, two black police SUVs drove up. They swerved and parked in front of the plane, effectively blocking its path.

"What the hell?" Shi breathed.

The pilot called back to Shi. "We have a problem, sir."

"I don't care. Take off now," he ordered.

"We...we can't take off," the pilot protested. "Those cars are blocking our path. They're signaling for us to open the door."

"No. Don't open it."

"Sir, we can't leave, and we can't stay in here. They're showing me a badge and insisting I open the door. We are required to follow the instructions of law enforcement. I'm doing it."

Shi peered through the window and noticed that the SUVs were ones that had been provided to the local police by China. The ungrateful peasants!

Shi's jaw clenched. "Fine. Open the damn door," he spat. "Just make sure they know this is a diplomatic Chinese aircraft and they may not board without my permission."

"Yes, sir."

The door opened slowly and, as if summoned by a cruel twist of fate, Slash stepped onto the plane. His eyes were hidden behind a pair of dark sunglasses, but his cool demeanor was a stark contrast to the anger that burned in Shi's chest. Out the door, Shi could see three local police officers with hands on their pistols. The pilot backed into the cockpit without a word and closed the curtain.

Shi rose slowly from his seat. "You have no right to board this plane. I'm protected by diplomatic immunity. I demand you get off at once."

A slow smile spread across Slash's face. "You and your bluster. Do you even understand the scope of the situation you're in, Shi?"

"I'm warning you, get off this plane now or you'll cause an international incident."

Slash shrugged and took a step forward and another, casually resting his forearm on the seatback. "I guess it'll have to be the incident. Your little coup failed miserably, and your words regarding the Cook Islands, and other islands in the region, have spread. I know you're familiar with Kiribati. Well, just a few minutes ago, the president of Kiribati, Karu Ata, called the *real* prime minister of the

Cook Islands, telling her his Parliament has now officially severed all formal relations with China. They're expelling all Chinese officials and forbidding their return. And guess what, Shi? Your name is on that list. And, because of your massive failure, now New Zealand and Australia will be discussing new security measures with several other island countries in the region to see if they would like to 'reconsider' or 'review' any arrangements they may currently have with China. Oh, I assure you, China's arrangements throughout the entire region are now being carefully reviewed in those countries in which you've established similar programs. I'm sure your description of the integrity and independence of those countries, and how cheaply they have allowed China to manipulate them, will certainly inform that review."

Shi's hands fisted in anger. He wanted more than anything to hit Slash directly in the face. But it was three against one, and he didn't think the pilots would step in to help him.

Slash looked at Shi with something close to pity. "Do you think Mother China will be conducting a similar review of *your* efforts? If so, I'm afraid you're not going to be popular."

Shi felt his stomach turn. "You can't touch me," he repeated. "I have immunity."

Slash shrugged. "Maybe you do, but maybe you won't. We'll have to see, won't we? You have immunity unless China withdraws it. Now, why might China withdraw that? Perhaps if their esteemed diplomatic representative in this region was found skimming millions for himself—funneling money from hardworking Chinese nationals and businesses on this island—they might not be so tempted to protect him. Let someone else make him pay for his crimes."

Shi pressed his lips together but said nothing.

"On the other hand, maybe they won't withdraw immunity," Slash continued. "After all, isn't your president leading a highly public anticorruption campaign? And sadly, you can't get more corrupt than this affair right now. It's already all over the news in multiple countries. But of course, China wouldn't just torture and throw you in jail because the Cook Islands told them to do it. No, they'd need some hard evidence of misdoing, or perhaps a confession? Oh wait, maybe they accidentally received an audio file of you describing all your entrepreneurial activities in the region. So, maybe they won't waive the immunity. Perhaps they'll use the same interview chair that you had prearranged for me."

Shi was so angry he shook, but that seemed only to amuse, not intimidate, Slash. Instead, the hateful American stepped forward, lowering his voice so Shi had to lean forward to hear it.

"I'm sure your bosses will be disappointed to find out just how much you've been stealing from them. You see, Jiang Shi, the crude phrases you used to describe your bosses and the people with whom you're working won't endear you to them. So, while I'm happy to escort you onto a plane with the rest of your staff that will take you straight back to China and into those welcoming arms, it won't be this one."

Shi seethed with anger. But he could say nothing. The noose was tightening.

"Oh, there's a funny thing about diplomatic immunity that even a professional like you may have forgotten," Slash continued. His voice was so calm, so self-assured, Shi wanted to throw up. "It just prevents you from being prosecuted for a crime. It doesn't guarantee you free access to move around, or even luxuries. Furthermore, it doesn't proscribe how long someone may be detained or under what conditions while the investigations into a crime are undertaken. All these points are being made with Mr. Chen right now, so, unless I'm mistaken, he'll soon be offered a swift and safe return to China in exchange for his knowledge of the accounts where you've been depositing your gains. I'm confident he realizes you're a loser and a liability and there is no benefit to him in protecting your personal accounts. Agree?"

"You're bluffing," Shi growled, but even to himself, the words sounded hollow. He felt as if he were suffocating.

Slash shook his head and gave Shi a pitying look. Shi had to resist the urge to leap forward and claw the sunglasses off Slash's face. "I'm not bluffing, and you know it. I don't have to. You're not leaving on this plane, Shi. The prime minister of the Cook Islands has already made arrangements for you. She's not releasing you—or your staff—until you've handed over all the accounts where you've stashed your illegally gained money. It's a small price to pay for the trouble you've caused. I have no doubt they'll see this as a nice compensation for China's so-called investment in their islands. Oh, and in case you think you did a good job hiding those accounts, Shi, you didn't. You and I both know you really didn't."

Shi couldn't be sure Slash knew where his all accounts were hidden. But even if they didn't know, he doubted his bankers would stay bought when they felt the heat from the prime minister and potentially New Zealand officials. The walls were closing in, his options narrowing with every passing second. Slash was already steps ahead of him, and his toes were sinking farther into the sand with each passing wave of revelation.

"So, then, and only then, will the prime minister allow you and your staff to return to China—without your money and as a political embarrassment." Slash's expression softened, but only slightly. "However, I'm offering you a deal. How would you like to go somewhere other than China? This location would protect you from the people in China who may not be pleased with your actions, but only if you cooperate. Since you personally cannot waive diplomatic immunity—only your country can—you'd have to defect. And if you defected, you'd still be subject to prosecution for any crimes you may have committed against the US. If convicted, the accommodations may not be quite as luxurious as those to which you are accustomed, but you can weigh it against what you might imagine your government in China has planned for you, considering you've set them back at least a decade or more in the Pacific region. The choice is entirely yours."

Shi didn't want to hear it or even entertain it, but he knew what awaited him in China if he went back. Execution would be too easy after what he had done. He would suffer. A lot. And he and Slash both knew it.

"What choice?" Shi asked between clenched teeth.

"A one-way ticket to the US and perhaps a reunion with your brother."

"My brother is a traitor."

"And so are you, Shi." Slash stuck the final knife in and twisted. "You aren't going to get a third chance in China, and we both know it."

Shi's mind raced. He needed an out—there *had* to be an out—but he could think of none. Shi wavered. *Better the US than China*, he thought. *At least I'll have a second chance there.* With a final, bitter breath, Shi's shoulders slumped in defeat.

"Wise decision." Slash rapped on the bulkhead next to the pilot's curtain. "Does anyone in the cockpit speak English?"

"I do," said one of the pilots cautiously.

"Please come out here and witness a statement by Mr. Shi." When the pilot emerged, Slash asked him to take a seat near Shi. "Please note that Mr. Shi is making this statement of his own free will. I'm not holding him under duress, and I'm not carrying a weapon to threaten him. Now, Mr. Shi, do you wish to relinquish your Chinese citizenship and defect to the US? Do you do so knowing you are not promised favorable conditions or immunity from prosecution for any crimes that you may have committed against the United States? I need two yeses from you. One for defecting and the other that we have not promised you any favorable treatment or immunity. Understand?"

The humiliation was overwhelming. He couldn't even look at the pilot or Slash. The honorable thing to do would be to commit suicide, but he didn't have any means and he wasn't sure he could do it even if he had. This was his point of no return. He wanted to plead with Slash for some other option. What could he trade? He stole a quick look at the American. He couldn't see his eyes, but he knew Slash would not negotiate any more than he would have if the situation had been reversed.

"Yes, and yes," he said quietly.

"I need you to say it louder. I want to make sure we know that you want to do this of your own accord."

"Yes, damn you," he shouted, his anger and frustrations breaking lose. "Yes, yes, yes, yes, whatever."

Slash turned to the pilot. "You may report this conversation to whoever in China needs to hear it."

Slash leaned forward and grabbed Shi's arm, yanking

him into the aisle and frisking him like he was a common criminal. Slash took his wallet, phone, passport, and everything he had on him. Slash then pulled him none too gently off the plane and down the steps. When they reached the tarmac, Shi was cuffed, and Slash faced him one last time.

"These officers will hold you until a plane arrives in a few hours to transport you to the US. Do not attempt to bribe them. They were not fooled by you and Maivia. They faithfully protected the prime minister from your attempts to harm her and her family. Also, they do not have to put you on the airplane in pristine condition, so I wouldn't irritate them."

Slash started to walk away, then turned back to face Shi. "You were right about one thing though," he said, a smile crossing his face. "Fate is fickle and fair. But she was never working for you, Shi. She worked for me."

Shi glared as he was dragged away and shoved into the waiting police car. He watched from a distance as Slash pulled out his phone and spoke into it. He was pretty good at reading lips, so he narrowed his eyes to make out what Slash was saying.

"Did you get all that, Candace?" Slash asked. "Looks like we're going to need that plane after all."

Shi wasn't sure what his future held. It wouldn't be good, but at least it was a future.

FORTY-FIVE

Lexi

I awoke to the soft breaking of waves on the beach and the rustling of palm trees coming from the open French doors at the back of the bungalow. I stirred, stretching luxuriously as the warm sunlight streamed in, casting patterns across the floor. I stretched and sat up, the view of the ocean beyond the veranda immediately bringing a sense of calm. A light breeze danced through the room, and with it the salty scent of the sea.

Slash slept beside me, one muscular arm resting against the pillow, breathing deeply. He'd arisen while it was still dark out to go to the airport and meet the Americans and the plane that had arrived to pick up Shi. Apparently, all had gone well, because when he returned and snuggled in, he'd whispered it had all been taken care of, and he'd sounded happy.

Now, he looked peaceful and at rest. As I watched, his dark lashes fluttered open. When he saw me sitting there with the sheet pressed to my chest, he smiled.

"Good morning, *cara*." His voice was still husky with sleep.

"Good morning, Slash."

He snaked his arm across my waist, pulling me toward him until I lay next to him, my cheek resting against his warm chest. I snuggled in closer, feeling the steady rhythm of his heart beneath my fingers. His hand slid down my back, resting comfortably on my hip.

"I can't believe we're here, alive, and still married after everything that happened on our honeymoon," I murmured.

"Why still married?" he repeated, sounding amused. "You think I'd leave you because of a coup?"

"No. I think you'd leave me because of a black cloud, even if it's ours now."

Slash pressed a kiss to the top of my head. "It may not have been the honeymoon I imagined, but it's ours. And *cara*...you know I will never leave you. Ever."

"I hope you mean that, because I don't think that little black cloud is ever going to leave us alone. You know, Slash, this time I really believed we were going to lie on the beach all day, drink cocktails, and complain about sand in weird places."

"And as usual, we got more than we bargained for." Slash cupped my cheek, and I leaned into his warm hand. "But we made it. Against all odds, we're still standing...or lying down, in our present case."

I lifted my head to look at him, and he gently brushed a strand of hair from my face. "I'm just glad we got out of that mess, the prime minister is okay, and Shi will be locked away forever. I came a lot closer to losing you than I care to admit, and it scared me."

"It scared me, too." He took my hand, running his thumb across my engagement and wedding rings. "You know, sometimes the bad guys win. But not this time. You were amazing and patient with me even as we navigated the bumps on our honeymoon, the evolving marriage code, and facing Shi once again. We make a good team."

"The best team." I sat up again, wrapping my arms around my legs and resting my head on my knees. Slash propped himself up on one arm, the gold cross that had belonged to his father sliding down his chest. He looked at me for a long moment before his gaze drifted to the open doors and the sea beyond.

"Candace is over the moon we're bringing Shi home," he said. "We gave them a coup of their own—an intelligence one. Shi will spill immediately, and he'll have a lot of valuable information we can use."

"It's nice that Candace sent a plane so fast," I said.

"Apparently, we had one in Australia we were able to divert. I gave her a brief rundown of the outcome of the plan this morning, and she was pleased. She's sitting on a wealth of evidence if the Chinese ever protest, but I don't think they will. It's in their best interest to cut their losses with Shi and the islands in this region for now. Candace did say the president, the CIA, and the State Department are looking forward to my full debrief."

"That makes for a busy Monday for you when we get home."

A smile played at his lips as he tugged me back toward him. I fell to the sheets, and he rolled over me, his dark hair falling forward from his face. "Let's not talk any more about going home and focus on what we're doing right now. We deserve several more days of peace and quiet on our honeymoon."

"We do," I agreed. "I think we've earned it."

"We have," he murmured, nuzzling my neck.

"As far as I'm concerned, the only real adventure we need now is time alone on the beach to drink another bottle or two of that banana wine," I added.

"Agreed," Slash said, his tone light, but there was a flicker of something deeper in his eyes. He adjusted down to his elbows, using his hands to cup my face. "I just want you to know I love you with every fiber of my being, *cara*. You've changed my life forever."

"I feel the same," I said. "Without you, I'd still be eating Cheerios and trying to battle orcs on my weekends."

"It would have been a lot safer."

"No way. Have you seen how vicious those orcs can be?"

He laughed, we kissed, and for a gloriously long moment, we lay in silence listening to our heartbeats. The pressure and danger of the previous days were finally behind us. I sighed, savoring the safety and intimacy of his arms. No matter what came next, we'd face it together...as husband and wife.

And we always would.

FORTY-SIX

Lexi

After we got dressed, we stepped out onto the bungalow's veranda to enjoy the morning breeze and the spectacular view of the ocean. It seemed like weeks instead of days since we were last here. The water sparkled under the gentle rays of the sun, promising a beautiful day and giving me a sense of peace and gratitude. Slash stood behind me, his arms wrapped around my waist, his chin resting on my shoulder. For a few glorious minutes, we said nothing, just took in the gorgeous scene in contented silence. Unfortunately, we couldn't linger, as we'd been summoned to the prime minister's house.

But first, we had friends to thank.

Slash and I settled into the living room with our laptops open and I connected the video call. It rang twice before Elvis's face appeared on the screen, grinning from ear to ear.

"Well, look who finally found the time to check in," Elvis said, and I saw everyone behind him jostling each other to see us. "What's up, lovebirds? You guys just get up?"

"Hey, we had a tough day yesterday," I said, twisting my hair up into a ponytail and then leaning back on the couch. "We almost died a couple of times, but we're still alive, thanks to you guys."

There were sounds of whooping and hollering, and I exchanged a smiling glance with Slash.

Xavier muscled in next to his twin on the screen, his face practically touching Elvis's. "We got your message late last night with word the plan was successful. You also promised us a debrief, so, of course, we called the entire gang in to hear it."

There were more shrieking and excited whooping. I saw glimpses of Angel, Frankie, Wally, Basia, Brandon, and others as they fist pumped and gave each other high fives.

"So, what happened?" Elvis asked, raising his voice to be heard over the others. "Did everything work as planned? Any glitches?"

"You're not going to be disappointed," Slash said, leaning back and stretching his legs out. "Everything went off without a hitch. Sheer perfection, down to the second."

Angel stuck her head in between Xavier and Elvis. Her red hair fell like a curtain over Elvis's shoulder. "The social media blast. Was it effective? Did the audio work properly?"

"It was perfect," I said. "You and Wally did a fantastic job on that front. The blast did exactly what it needed to. Riled up the people and got them marching to the television station. And, Frankie, we would have been lost without you. The translations were critical, and your work was flawless. You guys were absolutely amazing."

We filled them in on the details of the past days in

greater detail. We didn't speak much about Shi—we'd fill them in on that in more detail later. We did, however, answer as many questions as we could and clarify issues.

"I bet no one expected Maivia to fold that easily," Elvis said at one point.

"I don't think even Maivia expected Maivia to fold that easily," I said. "He was so sure of himself. But once his email went out and the crowds and Parliament read his confession that the Chinese were backing him, he had no choice but to concede. I've never seen anyone so easily defeated, especially after that live television moment. Watching him surrender to the real prime minister made for riveting television."

Xavier nodded. "Definitely a showstopper. You guys are lucky the police didn't storm the station while all that was happening."

"We barricaded the doors and held out long enough to make sure the prime minister's message went through," Slash explained. "Maivia is finished and so are the Chinese."

Basia leaned in, a grin on her face. "Well, for a couple who is supposed to be on their honeymoon, it looks like you've had very little time off."

"Well, we were just getting started when everything went south," I said. "But now, we're going to kick back and enjoy the last week of our honeymoon. I promise."

"You'd better," she said, shaking a finger at us.

Slash leaned forward, resting his arms on his thighs. "All kidding aside, we really appreciate you guys. We couldn't have done it without you. Your hacking, the translations, the intel—none of it would've come together without your help. You kept it together when everything could've fallen apart. Lexi and I might have been hurt or worse, and the Cook

Islands might have fallen to the Chinese. This operation succeeded because of you. So, you have our sincere thanks, gratitude, and love."

"Hey, we're always game to save the world," Wally shouted from the back of the room. "But I wouldn't turn down some tropical-flavored liquor as a thank-you."

"Forget it, Wally," I said. "You're not twenty-one yet."

"Darn," he said, and everyone laughed.

"Now, stop saving the world and go enjoy what's left of your time off while you can," Elvis said. "We're signing off."

With one last round of good-natured banter, I ended the call and shut our laptops.

Slash ran his fingers through his hair, his relief visible. "You ready to go talk to the prime minister?"

"Not really," I said. "But I *am* ready to restart our honeymoon. And, at the moment, talking to the prime minister is the only thing standing in my way."

FORTY-SEVEN

Slash

When Lexi and I arrived at the prime minister's residence, we were immediately escorted into the large, elegant library. The scent of fresh coffee filled the air. The prime minister sat at one end of the room looking calm and composed. The coat of arms pin was once again fastened to her lapel, and she smiled when she caught me looking at it. Rangi and Manny were also there, waiting with mugs of coffee on the table in front of them.

It would have been an idyllic scene except for the surprise of finding a green, yellow, and red bird sitting on a window perch. The very parrot that had delivered me into the clutches of Jiang Shi. It squawked excitedly when it saw me and flew in my direction, just high enough so I couldn't reach it.

I pointed at the bird in surprise as it squawked and screeched, flying loose around the room. "What's *that* doing here?"

"Oh, it's the bird that was cooped up in the Chinese

compound," Petra explained. "We had to do something with it, and the kids have been begging me for a pet, so I decided to bring it home. It wasn't his fault he was stuck with the Chinese. He's kind of cute. But for some reason, he really doesn't like you."

There were chuckles around the room. I made eye contact with it, making sure it knew not to get close too close to me. The parrot, however, must have remembered Lexi giving him the peapods, because he landed on the back of a nearby chair and eyed her with interest.

"Please, help yourself to some coffee and have a seat," Petra said. "I hope you're both well rested."

"Considering the circumstances, we slept really well," Lexi replied, pouring coffee into a mug and adding at least a half cup of cream. I poured myself some coffee, black, and settled in beside Lexi on the couch, keeping a wary eye on the bird.

"I'm sorry to jump right to it, but we have much to discuss," Petra began. "I trust you've been updated on the immediate aftermath of the coup, but I wanted to fill you in on everything we know up to this point. I'm sure you have questions, as do I."

I took a sip of coffee and leaned forward. "I've been wondering about the king's representative. Is she okay? Was she released?"

"Yes," Petra responded. "Iona has been released and is home safely. Maivia tried everything he could to force her to sign documents claiming she supported him, but she held firm and refused. She wouldn't let herself be used, even with the pressure from the Chinese."

"Good for her," I said.

"Yes," Petra said. "She stood by me—by what was right—and refused to betray her country."

"So, what's going to happen to Maivia and the police officers who sided with him?" Lexi asked. "There's bound to be a public backlash against them."

Petra sighed, her expression betraying the burden she carried as a leader. "There's a lot of anger in the country right now. People want them to pay for what they've done. The three of us and my family included. But, as you might imagine, there are still some who sympathize with their position. There are even some in Parliament who believe their actions were justified. There is no easy solution."

"And yet, you can't just let them off the hook, can you?" I asked, balancing the coffee mug on my knee.

Petra shook her head. "No, I can't. But I also don't want to create martyrs for the opposition. That's why I've made arrangements with the New Zealand government. We're sending Maivia and a few of his deputies there. They'll be 'hosted,' as it were. A house arrest of sorts." She raised her hand slightly. "As part of the deal, they've agreed to surrender their passports and not leave New Zealand. It keeps them out of the political spotlight here, and they'll be monitored closely."

"That's one way to handle it," Lexi said, but I heard the reservation in her voice. I felt it myself.

"What about the rest of the police?" I asked. "Those who participated but aren't seen as a threat?"

"They'll be monitored," Petra confirmed. "I'm leaving it to loyal officers to keep an eye on them. The last thing we need is another uprising. But we're not letting those thugs who supported Maivia get off without penalty. We've arrested all but a few of those who have been identified as supporting the coup, including my attempted assassin. We are printing posters and looking for the rest. We intend to send them to prison for a long time."

"Good," Lexi said, and I was in full agreement with her.

"You'll handle this, Petra," Rangi said. "The people believe in you."

"Thank you for your confidence, Rangi," Petra said, her voice softening. "But I can't do it alone. We'll need everyone's help and cooperation to heal from this."

"Well, don't count on me," Manny interjected good-naturedly. "I'm *not* coming out of retirement again."

We all laughed for a moment until Lexi spoke up. "I have a question. How are Ari, Sefina, and Amiri doing? Are they okay?"

"They're fine," Manny replied. "Amiri and Sefina were found by the Chinese, still tied up near the truck shortly after we escaped. They were questioned, but the Chinese cut them loose and left. So, Amiri and Sefina simply drove the truck back to the store, cut Ari free, and that was it."

I shook my head in disbelief. "What did Ari have to say about it?"

Manny chuckled. "Well, Ari was happy to hear you got away safely, and Shi got what he deserved, but he's disappointed the Chinese left, because he'd charged them twice the going rate and they never complained."

There were more chuckles and Petra said she had already assured Ari she'd order produce from his store for the next state function.

Petra then leveled her gaze at me. "I'd ask about Jiang Shi, but my people tell me he was whisked away this morning by American officials."

"He was," I confirmed.

"Then I consider the matter closed—he's all yours."

"We appreciate that, Prime Minister," I said, dipping my head.

Petra hesitated for a moment before continuing.

"There's one more thing. Chen, Shi's chief of staff here at the compound, supposedly handed over all of Shi's illegal accounts this morning. But we noticed something suspicious. There were some transfers just before the accounts were turned over."

I raised an eyebrow. "Well, that's something we can investigate. You're sure all the accounts were transferred?"

"No, I'm not sure," Petra said, frustration edging her words. "That's why I need you to verify it. I want to ensure that all the illegal accounts are shut down."

"Leave it to me," I replied. "I'll confirm everything and get back to you."

Petra's gaze softened, and she sighed, a weight seemingly lifted from her shoulders. "Thank you, Slash."

The prime minister set her coffee mug on the table and pressed her hands together in her lap. "I want you all to know, I will be awarding medals and commendations to certain individuals who have helped preserve the integrity of our country. Iona, the king's representative, and the young policeman in front of the television station who laid down his weapon first will receive special commendations. Tane, his news crew, Ari, Sefina, Amiri, and those police officers who stayed loyal to me will also be commended. And, of course, Manny and Rangi, I will be recognizing you both for your personal courage and resourcefulness in defense of our island and me."

Lexi and I smiled and clapped as Manny and Rangi tried to convince Petra the recognition wasn't warranted.

"I insist," Petra said. "Now, both of you be quiet, because I won't change my mind. Besides, awarding medals and commendations is one of the perks of my job."

Then Petra turned to us. "You two will be presented with the Queen's Medal for Courage for helping in the defense of the Cook Islands. It's an honor we bestow on foreigners who come to our aid and defense in time of great need."

"Wow, Petra, I don't think that's necessary," Lexi protested, holding up a hand. "It's okay to just say thank you."

"Oh, it's more than necessary," Petra said. "I'll also send an official letter of thanks to your president to express our grateful appreciation for your bravery and courage in face of great danger. And there will be a fancy ceremony in a couple of months."

"A...ceremony?" Lexi repeated, a horrified expression on her face. The parrot squawked as if upset by her reaction.

Petra smiled, and I could see she was teasing. "Although I figure you'll be back home by then and won't be able to attend. So, unless you tell me otherwise, we'll have the medals sent to you, along with a couple of cases of our famous banana wine from the Koteka Winery." She smiled knowingly at Manny. "I heard from a little birdie that you quite enjoyed it."

Lexi's eyes lit up. "Are you serious? That was the best wine I've ever tasted."

"It's a personal favorite of mine, too," Petra assured her. She lifted her mug and took a sip of coffee. "So, what's next for you two?"

"Well," I replied, "we intended to spend the second week of our honeymoon on your remote island of Aitutaki, but we're not sure if we've still got a reservation there after the delay or even if flights are operating again."

Rangi grinned. "No need to worry about that. I'll take care of all the arrangements. Furthermore, your new flight, your villa, food, and any outings—it's all on the house."

They wouldn't listen to our protests, so we accepted with the caveat that no parrots would be present to welcome us. Everyone grinned—and that seemed to conclude the meeting—so we stood and chatted a bit while waiting for our driver.

At some point, Lexi and I pulled Manny aside, thanking him for his help. Manny deflected the praise, modestly attributing it to our own resourcefulness and skill.

"We'd love for you to visit us in the States sometime," I offered. "We'll take you around and show you the sights."

"I've never been, so I might just take you up on that as long as I can get a tour of the CIA. You can arrange that, right, mate?" He gave me a wink, his smile genuine.

I smiled back. "I'll see what I can do."

Just then, the prime minister's daughter, Lani, walked into the room, holding her phone. "Can I take a picture of you two with my mom?" she asked us shyly. "I want to add it to my collection of photos of famous people."

Lexi glanced over at me. When I shrugged, she said, "Well, we're hardly famous, but we're happy to take a picture with your mom. She's the real hero here. Would you mind sending me a copy? I'd like it as a honeymoon memento."

"Sure," Lani said. "I'll send you the photos."

Lexi gave Lani her phone number so she could text it to her. We posed for a couple of snaps, and Lani immediately sent the photos, blushing and thanking us profusely before dashing out of the room.

"I think she has a crush on you," Lexi said, pulling the photos up on her phone.

I rolled my eyes but glanced over her shoulder at the photos. While we all looked exceptionally tired, we also looked...content.

As we said our final goodbyes, Petra clasped my hands in hers. "Remember, you've not only earned our gratitude, but you've also earned our respect. Enjoy the rest of your honeymoon. And remember, the Cook Islands will always welcome you back."

With that, we left the prime minister's residence, knowing we'd helped a country find its footing again. It was a good feeling—a momentous one.

But all I could think about as we drove away were the quiet days ahead with Lexi and the gentle, unhurried pace of a quiet, remote island.

FORTY-EIGHT

Mick Watson

Mick sat in his car with his camera propped loosely against the open windowsill and pointed toward a luxury brownstone condo in an exclusive neighborhood in Bethesda. He was about to take a picture he could sell for a tidy sum to the highest bidder.

Tom Senstrom, the young billionaire biotech CEO, had it all. Good looks, acclaim, a trophy wife, two kids, and lots and lots of money. He also had a company that hadn't turned a profit in three years. None of it made sense to Mick, but he hoped a little of that money might rub off on him this afternoon.

Senstrom also had a date tonight with a certain Olivia Messandaro, a rising young supermodel who was in Washington, DC, to promote a new European fashion line with a photo shoot at the Lincoln Memorial. How they had hooked up, he didn't know. But his source was impeccably accurate, and he had been well positioned for a few nice covert dinner shots.

He already had all the photos he really needed, but he'd learned that getting the perfect exposé photo with a shocked expression could triple the value versus an ordinary one. Scandal paid well in his line of work. Senstrom and the model had entered the condo building almost two hours ago. He knew Senstrom had about three hours until his planned departure on a private flight out of Dulles back to the West Coast. So, he would be exiting the condo soon.

The waiting was the worst part of his job. He loved the planning and the chase, but those minutes of excitement barely punctuated the boredom of hours of waiting. Still, it paid the bills, and these photos could bring him a tidy little sum. Scandal paid well. Almost as much as mystery, which was why bad Bigfoot images still had a market.

He sighed. Still no sight of either one of them. His camera was ready, but he hoped they hurried it up. He had hockey playoff tickets tonight and wanted the luxury of getting to the arena early enough to watch the teams warm up. At least he had his favorite tabloids to pass the time. He never read any of the articles. They were as believable as an IRS auditor saying he was there to help you.

Instead, he flipped through the tabloids looking at the pictures. What were the hot topics? Who was in the news? What made the first page? He thought of it as business intelligence. He might be old-school, but he knew that tastes and interests moved quickly these days, and he needed to keep up. After flipping through several of the lesser rags, he picked up the *Global Enquirer*, one of the heavy hitters in terms of paying for photos.

The headline articles included blurry pictures of UFOs and an "expert" discussing the presence of aliens among us. He was certain the UFO pictures were recycled. There were also the latest pictures of movie celebrities who were in the middle of their third cycle of an on-again, off-again relationship, and reports of a drug overdose for yet another rocker under twenty-five years of age.

Suddenly, something caught his eye. In the middle of the tabloid was a dark picture of three people. The headline under the picture read, Honeymooning Couple Helps Foil Cook Islands Coup.

What?

He looked closer at the grainy photo. The photo was backlit, clearly taken by an amateur. But, what the heck? Two of those people looked familiar. He tapped his finger on the young woman until it came to him.

That mystery power couple who'd evaded him on the way to the airport.

He squinted more at the photo. That's who they looked like, but he couldn't be certain because of the poor quality of the photo. The size and staging, including some emojis in the corner, looked like something a kid might post on their social media feed, and some opportunistic photographer had picked it up for a resell.

He quickly read the short article, noting unnamed sources saying the couple had stopped an assassination attempt on the prime minister and prevented a foreign-backed coup from taking over the country. The names of the couple were not mentioned, but that woman in the middle was clearly identified as Ms. Petra Askari, the official prime minister.

Mick sat back in his car seat, his mouth falling open. He had his answer. They had to be US agents sent abroad to stop threats around the world. A real-life Mr. and Mrs. James Bond.

Damn. Now it all began to make sense. No wonder the

president had showed up at their wedding. He wasn't sure how the pope played into that, but hey, no matter how you looked at it—this couple was one hell of a story.

He stroked his chin, thinking. He didn't need to rush. They'd be coming back at some point, and he'd be ready for them. He knew where they lived; he knew what they looked like. They would be the biggest story he ever broke. He just needed to be patient.

Mick was still dreaming of how he would spend the ginormous amounts of money he would make covering this enigmatic couple when the young billionaire emerged arm in arm with his tryst partner. They paused exactly where he'd expected.

Swearing, Mitch fumbled for his camera, but it was too late. He'd missed a perfect shot.

Sighing, he watched Senstrom drive off and the model disappear back into the condo. That elusive, mysterious couple had bested him once again, and now, they owed him another one.

FORTY-NINE

Lexi

I sank deeper into the hot tub, enjoying the view from our secluded bungalow on Aitutaki. The gorgeous sparkle of the sun on the ocean provided a soothing and relaxing view. The thatched roof above me offered a bit of shade and a tropical, rustic charm.

I glanced over at Slash. His eyes were closed, and he had a contented look on his face. His head rested against the ledge of the hot tub, his dark hair slicked back from several ocean swims. We'd been here on the small island for three glorious, peaceful days, basking in its blissful and remote tranquility.

"This is what I imagined our honeymoon would be like," I said with a relaxed sigh, my fingers idly tracing patterns in the water.

Slash shifted slightly, the water sloshing a bit. "I agree. No television, no deadlines, no crowds, and no crises."

He exhaled a slow deep breath, and for a few minutes we watched some fluffy, gauzy clouds sail past.

"Given everything that happened with the coup and Shi, do you ever wish we'd picked Patagonia instead?" he finally asked.

I watched a cloud that looked curiously like a gaming controller drift by while considering his question. "It's hard to argue with what we're experiencing right now, but after you stopped the assassination attempt, we went on the run with the prime minister, and then Shi kidnapped you...well, I did have my doubts. And yet, I can't help but be grateful we were in the right place at the right time to help Petra and the Cook Islands. This place is growing on me, and so are the people."

"Me, too. You know, I spent a lot of time in that closet cursing myself for thinking I could find a place remote enough, where nothing ever happens to us."

We shared a laugh.

"Navigating the marriage code under extreme duress wasn't exactly on my bucket list, either," I admitted. "Especially since I'm not even finished defining the requirements yet, and you haven't had a chance to add your input. But it was kind of cool to say 'I told you so' in the midst of chaos and uncertainty. There's power in that."

"Which number is that in the marriage code?" he asked with a smile.

"It's number five, but I'm considering moving it up to number three because of its importance. What do you think?"

"You only like it because you got to use it." He chuckled. "Wait until it's my turn."

I pursed my lips at him. "That reminds me, you told everyone I was a klutz and they had to be careful around me. What's with that?"

He cracked open an eye and looked at me. "I don't think

I specifically said you were a klutz. I may have mentioned that everyone should take steps to protect themselves against a variety of random, peculiar things that tend to happen when you're around. I also asked them to look after your safety. Is that not a husband's prerogative?"

I narrowed my eyes. "Did you have a disaster management plan for our honeymoon? Answer me honestly."

"I'm always honest with you, *cara*. And there's nothing wrong with being prepared. But I assure you, none of my plans remotely involved what actually happened to us. So, the jury is out on whether those kinds of plans remain useful or not."

I sighed and sank deeper into the hot water, so it came up to my chin. The bubbles massaged my upper back and shoulders. It felt heavenly. "What do *you* think the marriage code should contain, Slash?"

He picked up his wineglass from the edge of the tub, swirled it, then took a sip. "Honestly, I'm not sure what rules, particular methods of communications, or long-term plans anyone needs to have for a successful marriage, let alone us. I'm figuring it out along with you. However, I do have an interesting story. During my very first trip to the United States, I heard a country song on the radio that claimed to know the secret to a good marriage. The lyrics went something like this, 'A good woman stands by her man's side during bad times, and that leads to lasting love.' At the time, I wondered if Americans really believed that was necessary for a lasting relationship. Can you enlighten me?"

I saw the twitch of his lips and knew he was teasing me. Still, I played along. "Oh, I'm happy to enlighten you, Slash. First, it's clear a man wrote those lyrics because a woman would have written, 'A good woman stands by her man's side during bad times to tell him none of it would have happened if he'd just listened to her.' And *that's* what leads to lasting love. It's the I Told You So rule. That makes a lot more sense."

Slash laughed so hard he nearly choked on his wine. "Touché. I guess we'll have to research this marriage code together to make sure we get the programming just right. Luckily, we're both excellent programmers, so I anticipate a first-rate platform and one that is uniquely ours."

I smiled. "I like that plan, and I also anticipate a superior outcome. But we're not at the point yet to initiate subroutines, as we can't program those until we have the overarching structure firmly laid out."

"Fair enough," he agreed. "We have time after all. A lifetime."

We lapsed into comfortable silence before Slash spoke again. "Do you remember the Italian phrase *'Non tutte le ciambelle riescono col buco?'* Nonna said it at our wedding."

A smile tugged at my lips at the memory. "Oh, I remember. It means not all doughnuts have a hole. I had no idea what that meant until you explained that in Italy, it means that sometimes things don't turn out the way we plan them, but it doesn't necessarily mean that's a bad thing. Is that right?"

"That's right," he confirmed. "Sometimes it could be destiny correcting its course. Other times, it's fate. In our case, I think fate was on our side for our honeymoon. It favored us."

"It did more than that—it *saved* us," I corrected.

"Which is an odd thing to say when we just barely survived a coup and an encounter with one of our worst nemeses," he pointed out.

"It certainly is. But it is what it is."

I scooted closer to him in the tub, still holding my glass. He put his arm around me as we sat in quiet contemplation, sipping wine and watching the sky and the ocean.

My phone suddenly dinged from the picnic table. "You got a text," Slash said.

"Who'd be sending me a text now?" I wondered aloud.

I climbed out of the tub, grabbed a beach towel, and wrapped it around my waist. I dried my hands before I picked up my phone, which sat next to my prized bottle of Cook Islands tamanu skin oil, courtesy of Sefina.

I swiped open my phone. "It's from Basia." My eyes scanned the message before I gasped.

"What's wrong?" Slash asked in alarm, standing up in the hot tub. "What happened?"

"There's been an earthquake. A devastating, 8.1-magnitude earthquake. It hit southern Chile and Argentina about an hour ago. The deaths are likely in the thousands. There are currently two million without power in Patagonia, and all major routes in and out are closed. It's a catastrophe. I...I told Basia we'd considered Patagonia for our honeymoon."

We stared at each other in stunned silence, absorbing the enormity of the information.

"We chose the Cook Islands for our honeymoon," I finally said in a hushed voice. "We could have chosen Patagonia. That was my idea. We could have died in that earthquake, Slash."

He shook his head, his expression somber. "No. We didn't choose the Cook Islands. Remember? We left it up to numbers, to chance, to...fate."

He climbed out of the hot tub, wrapped a towel around his waist, and came to stand beside me, gazing out at the ocean.

"Cosa ci riserva il destino?" he murmured.

"What does that mean?" I asked, still stricken.

"I asked, 'What does fate have in store for us?'" His hand touched the cross on his bare chest. "Sometimes I wonder."

I slipped my hand into his. "Whatever comes next, we'll handle it together as husband and wife. I'm just glad I'm with you, Slash."

"I feel the same way, *cara*. You are my soulmate."

Later that evening, we sat on the veranda again, letting the warm breeze nourish us and carry the worries of the world away, at least for a time. Hand in hand, we watched the sky turn a soft pink, yellow, and orange before melting into a picturesque sunset.

We were smart, but there were a lot of things in life we didn't know or understand. We weren't even sure how to properly proceed as man and wife.

But we knew this time, for once in our lives, fate had led us to exactly where we needed to be.

THANK you for taking the time to read **No Time Off**. If you enjoyed this story, the greatest way to say thank you to an author and encourage them to write more in the series is to tell your friends and consider writing a review at any one of the major retailers. It's greatly appreciated!

∼ turn the page for more from Julie Moffett ∼

LEXI CARMICHAEL MYSTERY SERIES

"The Lexi Carmichael mystery series runs a riveting gamut from hilarious to deadly, and the perfectly paced action in between will have you having onto Lexi's every word and breathless for her next geeked out adventure." ~**USA TODAY**

THE WHITE KNIGHT SERIES
by Julie Moffett

Geeks, Spies, and Teenagers! What an awesome combination. Check out the White Knights Mystery/Spy series for tweens, teens and the young at heart. Check Julie's website at www.juliemoffett.com for more information. You can find details and links on the website as to where to purchase the series.

JULIE'S BIO

Julie Moffett is the best-selling author of the long-running Lexi Carmichael Mystery Series and the young adult, spy/mystery, spin-off series, White Knights, featuring really cool geek girls. She's been publishing books for 30 years, but writing for a lot longer. She's published in the genres of mystery, young adult, historical romance and paranormal romance.

She's won numerous awards, including the Mystery & Mayhem Award for Best YA/New Adult Mystery, the HOLT Award for Best Novel with Romantic Elements, a HOLT Merit Award for Best Novel by a Virginia Author (twice!), and many others.

Julie is a military brat (Air Force) and has traveled extensively. Her more exciting exploits include attending high school in Okinawa, Japan; backpacking around Europe and Scandinavia for several months; a year-long college graduate study in Warsaw, Poland; and a wonderful trip to Scotland and Ireland where she fell in love with castles, kilts and brogues. She almost joined the CIA, but decided on a career in international journalism instead.

Julie has a B.A. in Political Science and Russian Language from Colorado College, a M.A. in International Affairs from The George Washington University in Washington, D.C. and an M.Ed from Liberty University. She has worked as a proposal writer, journalist, teacher, librarian and researcher. Julie has two amazing sons and two adorable guinea pigs.

GET THE LATEST NEWS ABOUT JULIE
Sign up at www.juliemoffett.com for Julie's occasional newsletter (if you haven't done it already) and automatically be entered to win prizes like kindles, free books, and geeky swag.

FIND JULIE ALL OVER SOCIAL MEDIA
Julie Moffett Fan Group:
facebook.com/groups/vanessa88/
Exchanges, giveaways, and active friendly rapport.

- facebook.com/JulieMoffettAuthor
- x.com/@JMoffettAuthor
- instagram.com/julie_moffett
- bookbub.com/authors/julie-moffett
- amazon.com/stores/Julie-Moffett/author/B001H-MQMHU

Made in United States
Troutdale, OR
05/08/2025